COMING HOME

COMING HOME

by father & daughter

BRUCE & VERNAE
EWING

HIGH BRIDGE BOOKS
HOUSTON

Coming Home
by Bruce Ewing and Vernae Ewing

Printed in the United States of America
ISBN (Paperback): 978-1-946615-65-7

High Bridge Books titles may be purchased in bulk for educational, business, fundraising, or sales promotional use. For information, please contact High Bridge Books via www.HighBridgeBooks.com/contact.

Published in Houston, Texas by High Bridge Books

Contents

To God Be The Glory

This book is dedicated to
our family and friends who serve
the kingdom of God with steadfast love.

Blessings on you!

Stolen treasures are of no value, but
righteousness delivers from death.
—Proverbs 10:2

Unless the Lord builds the house,
those who build it labor in vain.
—Psalms 127:1

Prologue

"Matt, Matt … where are you?" A strange, small voice echoed, sending a gnawing, tingling sensation down matt's back as he slept. As he tossed and turned, sweat beads dripped from his brows. The voice continued reverberating in his ears, and painfully familiar sounds seemed to linger.

"Who are you?" Matt tried to mouth, but to no avail. Trying to open his eyes, he felt a piercing pain tighten around his heart. Gasping for air, his body felt the sting of pain and torment while the soft voice cried out in desperation. An evil presence was heavy, trying to choke out the pleas for a liberator. As Matt seemed to sink more into unconsciousness, the last sounds emanating through his mind were the pleading words, "Matt … come home…" The voice dissipated, leaving Matt with a deep emptiness.

1

The Wedding Chamber

A GENTLE, COOL BREEZE FLOWED THROUGH A PARTIALLY opened window in the wedding chamber. The wind lightly moved strands of Patience's beautiful, dark brown, curly tresses. Shifting her body closer to Matt for warmth, she was suddenly awakened by his heavy breathing. She felt his warm breath on her neck.

"Matt, are you awake?" she said, giggling, assuming he was awake. A smile overtook her full lips, as another soft giggle escaped and echoed through the large wedding chamber. Smiling and slightly turning, she found him still asleep. Her dark brown eyes scanned Matt's well-formed frame as he rested. Afraid she would disturb him, she laid still, pretending to be asleep in hopes that Matt would continue to rest.

Having heard the sound of her voice, he groggily turned and opened his eyes; observing her beautiful face, he touched her lips with his fingertips. With a wide smile, Patience opened her eyes as Matt's gaze poured over her. She scooted closer to him, expecting a gentle embrace but found resistance instead. Alarmed by the unexpected response, she took notice of his countenance and sensed his thoughts were elsewhere. He had never been unresponsive to her. She knew that he was troubled and wanted to find out what disturbed him.

"What's wrong, Matt?" Patience said, pushing back a strand of hair from his face.

"Not sure. A bad dream, I guess," he said, rubbing the back of his neck.

Grabbing Matt's cheeks into her hands, Patience lifted his face to look into his piercing green eyes. "What was the dream about?"

Matt's eyes softened as he looked at the innocent face staring back at him. "I can't remember ... only bits and pieces. But I feel uneasy."

Nodding at his response, Patience wanted only to comfort him. She wanted to push past her own worries and do something to put his mind at ease. She filled her hands with his hair and pulled his face close to hers until their lips touched.

"Wonderful. Now we can start our day," she said teasingly, knowing very well that Matt wasn't going anywhere. She kissed him again, then pretended to get out of bed.

"Is that it?" His words engaged her playful spirit. She scooted to the opposite side of the bed, teasing Matt. In one easy attempt, he caught and pulled Patience back to him and held her close. His senses took in every part of her. She giggled, excited by Matt's pursuit.

Suddenly, a knock on the door interrupted and startled the honeymooners. Patience looked at Matt, then gazed at the door, surprised at the intrusion. Somewhat uncomfortable at the interruption, she whispered to Matt, "Who do you suppose that could be?"

"Your guess is as good as mine," he said curiously. He called out, "Yes, can we help you?" They heard a rustling noise coming from under the door. Turning his head to one side, Matt pushed himself up to survey the bottom of the door. Glancing down, he saw a sealed envelope with the royal seal of King Jedidiah Devoble.

Overcome by curiosity, Matt emerged from the goose down covers and moved toward the door. He whispered to Patience, "I'll get it."

"Get what?" she whispered back.

"The envelope on the floor."

Patience peaked over the bedsheets. "Please bring that olive oil back with you," she said with a teasing giggle.

"For what?"

"To soften your rough hands," she laughed.

Shaking his head, he grinned and picked up the envelope. "It's an invitation to brunch. Your dad and Poppy would like to speak with us, and it has Poppy's seal."

The puzzled look on Patience's face stirred Matt's curiosity. "Why is there a royal seal, and it's Poppy's?" she asked.

"I don't know, but it must be important,"

"Why are we still whispering?" Patience chuckled.

Shrugging his shoulders, Matt said, "I don't know..." while still whispering.

"Then stop it." She laughed and threw a pillow, hitting him in the face.

"Did you know about..." Before Matt could finish his sentence, she threw another pillow.

"No, I didn't know anything about a brunch meeting, but I'm excited to find out what it's about," Patience said, laughing at Matt's sheepish expression. She threw another pillow, and Matt caught it in midair. He lunged toward her and grabbed her arms, pinning them to the bed. She struggled to loosen his grip on her, but it was too late. Matt began to tickle her until she could hardly catch her breath. "Stop, Matt, stop. I give up. Put some oil on those cacti hands of yours…" she said through uncontrollable laughter. "Whatever you have in mind will have to wait until we return from brunch," Patience laughed, still struggling to slip out of his grasp.

"I don't know what those two could be thinking about," Matt said, affectionately kissing her shoulder. "We are on our honeymoon."

"You better stop right now," she protested, "or we are not going to make brunch." Matt rose and swept her up into his arms and pecked her on the cheek as he reluctantly sat her back on her feet.

"I guess you're right," he said as he let her go. Gathering his robe, he followed her into the bath chamber, and light laughter could be heard echoing throughout the wedding chamber.

****

The touch of Patience's hand on the marbleized, crystal wall activated separate, flowing streams of hot, warm, and cool water, all in perfect sync. From the floor came a fragrant mist for cleansing and refreshing the body. Sunshine poured in through the crystal ceiling, providing warmth to the newlyweds, and an array of multiple colors filled the room.

Many thoughts ran through Patience's mind as she took a quick rinse and then a dip in the cleansing pool. Most of her thoughts were questions about why her father and Poppy would ask to meet for brunch on their honeymoon.

As the fresh water surrounded Patience, she relaxed and sunk deeper into the warm mineral waters. Matt dove into the pool, splashing fresh water in every direction. When he came up for air, water flowed down his handsome face and body. Patience swam toward him, and they both were rejuvenated by the rare minerals in the water, one of the many gifts from the Treasure Tree. Instantly, they were refreshed and renewed with energy.

"Unbelievable! What's in this water? It's a new experience every day! I could stay in here all day," exclaimed Matt.

"No, you can't," said Patience, shaking her head. She reminded her husband, "We are expected elsewhere, remember?"

Matt came after her, and she splashed water on his face, then turned quickly to escape. She swam to the steps leading up out of the water. Matt raced to capture her but was unable to reach her before she ascended out of the pool. Teasing him with a smirk, she wrapped herself in her robe and stood at the edge of the water. She laughed and kicked water into his face and raced into the foyer across from the bedchamber with Matt close behind her. Hearing Matt's footsteps, she turned to face him and stared deep into his eyes.

"You know, Matt, emerald isn't a bad color, especially when I look deep into your eyes." Raising an eyebrow at her sneaky jest to deter him from throwing her back into the water, Matt was amused. He had no objections playing along.

"I like yours better," he said, brushing her wet hair back to get a better look.

"Why? They are only brown."

"I know, but there is something else."

Curving her lips in amusement, she asked, "What?"

"Well, when I look in your eyes, I see light."

"Light?"

"Yes, light."

"What kind of light?" Patience asked, tilting her head to the side.

"It's not always there, but it's there enough for me to notice it."

"Does that make you uneasy?" she asked, a little concerned.

"No, not at all. I told you that I love your brown eyes…" Matt stared into her eyes for a closer look.

Patience looked back at him, widening her eyes for amusement. "What are you doing…?"

He laughed. "I'm wondering!"

"Wondering what?"

"Who gave you those precious eyes?"

What an odd question, Patience thought. "They came from my parents."

"I know that, but I was wondering if there was some other connection."

"I don't think so, other than God," she said with a tone of mystery. The way she interacted with him pleased him greatly.

"You know, love, we haven't really had a chance to talk in-depth about your family," Matt said.

She looked at him, placed her hand in his hair, and played with the natural strands that fell over his eyebrow.

"Matt, we are going to be late for brunch." Silently, he still waited. She let her hands slide down his face. "Okay, you're not going to let me out of telling my family's life story, are you?"

"Right," he said.

"Fine, but I want to hear about your family first."

The tone in her voice took him by surprise. He knew she was serious. After all, he had lived with her family for several years. She hadn't even met his.

Matt paused a moment, whispering under his breath, "Home…" Tears filled his eyes as thoughts of home came to his mind. "I think about them every day." Looking at Patience, he forced a slight smile. Their talk only reminded him of the deep desire in his heart to see them again.

Patience could tell from his expression that she had stirred feelings in him that he may not have wanted to visit. "Matt, are you all right?" she asked, grabbing his shoulder with a gentle squeeze.

For a few seconds, there was no response, then Matt took a deep breath. "Ever since I had that weird dream this morning, home has been on my mind. I just feel that it's time for me to go home."

She nodded with a smile. "I think so too. As soon as we meet with Father and Poppy, we should request time to visit your family."

Matt was delighted and once more pulled her into his arms and kissed her. As she melted into his warm embrace, she noticed the invitation on the bedroom bench.

"Okay, time is slipping away. We should get ready for brunch." Smiling, she slid from his arms and headed for the changing room.

Matt stood a moment, staring out the window, lost in deep thought. Patience assumed that he was following behind her, but she didn't hear his steps. "Matt, aren't you coming to change?" There was no answer. "...Oh, and when do you want to leave for your home?" Still no answer. After she put on a simple but beautiful royal blue dress, she stuck her head around the corner.

"Matt, did you hear me? What's taking you so long? When do you want...?" Patience paused. She didn't see him anywhere. "Matt, Matt, where are you?" she said, giggling. "Stop playing around. We have to go."

She peeked around corners, looked in the spacious bedchamber, and then the bath chamber but didn't find him. Across the room, the curtain moved as if someone was behind it. Smiling, she expected him to jump out and grab her.

"Matt, come on out. You're so funny." Laughing, she pushed back the curtain, but to her dismay, he wasn't there. It was only a breeze from the window that moved the curtain.

Matt was nowhere to be found. It wasn't like him to just leave her without an explanation. Pausing for a moment, she closed her eyes, and to her amazement, she no longer felt his presence. Patience needed answers, and she knew exactly where to go and find them.

2

Matt's Disappearance

Patience opened the door from their wedding chamber, and her concern grew as she walked down the hall. *Maybe he decided to go ahead since we are running a little late,* Patience thought to herself, trying to shake the uneasiness that something was terribly wrong. As she walked towards the kitchen, a wonderful aroma filled her nostrils. She heard soft chatter coming from the dining area. Hoping to see Matt, she rushed in, nearly knocking over freshly-made bread sitting on the side counter. Briefly scanning the room showed no sign of Matt. Her mind and heart started to race.

"Where could that husband of mine be? He knew we had this brunch..." she mumbled, biting her lip. "Wait until I see him!" she said out loud, as her thoughts trailed off. Then she heard a delightful familiar voice.

"Excuse me...?" an older woman said, interrupting Patience's thoughts. Surprised, Patience looked up and saw a delightful smile on the face of a beautiful woman sitting at the table. Some said that God touched her with the beauty of Abraham's wife, Sarah. Pricilla sat, watching her granddaughter's mood change back and forth as she pondered on disturbing thoughts. Pricilla's eighty-plus years showed very little signs of aging. Only her wisdom and the streaks of gray in her waist-length auburn hair told of her years of life. Her smooth olive skin and sparkling, deep hazel eyes portrayed that she still had many years ahead of her—a gift that seemed to have been passed down to the women in her family.

With concern in her eyes, Patience asked, "Moa, have you seen Ma—" Before Patience could finish her sentence, she was interrupted by another woman pushing her way through the pantry door with a tea tray of honey and mint. Entering the room, Heather almost crashed into Patience.

"Oh, excuse me, darling," said Heather, smiling as she set the tray down on the table. Heather was the spitting image of Pricilla, except that her eyes were light blue, and her hair was dark brown with streaks of auburn and tints of golden highlights from working in her garden. Heather saw worry in her daughter's eyes and knew that Patience was in deep thought.

"And how are you this morning?" Heather asked, waiting for a reaction from Patience. Looking up, Patience noticed beaming smiles from two women who had been watching her the entire time.

Walking towards them, she asked without pausing, "Mom, have you seen Matt? We were supposed to meet Poppy and dad for brunch." The two women remained silent. When Patience finally took a breath, she noticed a surprised look on both her mother and grandmother's face. It finally dawned on her the lack of etiquette and manners she had shown. Without so much as a good morning to her mother and grandmother, she had overlooked their presence. Glancing over the two beautiful faces staring at her, she pushed down her frustration and forced a small smile.

"My apologies, Mom, Moa. I can't find Matt, and I've looked everywhere for him."

3

Patience's Concern

Heather and Pricilla never stopped observing Patience's bewildered face. Heather walked closer to Patience and directed her to the nearest chair. The last thing on Patience's mind was sitting down. However, she remembered that she had shown very poor manners and decided that sitting might be a good idea. Biting her lip, she sat, waiting for one of them to explain or say something regarding the whereabouts of her husband.

"Good morning, Patience," said Moa, while pouring a glass of goat's milk and placing it in front of her as if she was still five years old. "I know that you are anxious about Matt and his sudden disappearance. Drink your milk, dear, while your mother gets your meal."

"No, thank you, Moa. I'm not really thirsty. I just want to know where Matt is, and—"

"In due time, dear. Now finish your milk," Pricilla interrupted and nodded with encouragement. Patience put the glass to her mouth as Heather sat a plate of eggs in front of her with thin slices of veal, shredded potatoes, and a bowl of fruit. Pricilla motioned for Heather to sit on one side of Patience while she took the opposite chair. Patience looked at her mother, then to her grandmother, suspecting that what they had to say was not what she wanted to hear. Patience was not happy. She sat, waiting for the two women who had reared her to say something.

"I really appreciate the breakfast and intriguing conversation, but I need to know where Matt is," insisted Patience. Both mother and grandmother listened as Patience poured out her concerns about Matt.

"Matt is fine. You need to calm down, dear," said Heather.

"Fine? Mom, is that all you're going to say? I need to know where he is. Now, please."

"He is in a place where young men of his anointing must go," said Pricilla with a smile.

"What do you mean?" Patience asked.

"All the times, even when you were small, you visited your grandfather to be trained in wisdom and faith. Spiritual training is what your grandfather called it," said Pricilla.

"What kind of training is Matt doing? And how can he be at training now when we both were invited to have brunch with Dad and Poppy only an hour ago?" Patience said.

"That's a question you'll have to ask your grandfather," stated Pricilla.

4

Encounter with Pia Warriors

After a rough landing, dressed in his undergarments, Matt found himself standing in the middle of unfamiliar territory. Things happened so fast that it took him a few minutes to focus. One moment he was thinking of home, and in the next, he found himself looking at a forest terrain half-dressed.

"Here we go again," Matt said to himself, wondering what kind of test Jedidiah had in store for him and what kind of explanation he was going to give Patience for disappearing. Looking down, he saw a midsize, closed bag next to his feet. Opening the bag, he saw clothing and shoes. Exhaling with relief, he quickly changed while observing his surroundings. Matt's stomach churned for throughout the area there was an unpleasant smell of rotting animal flesh.

As Matt continued to scan the surroundings, he observed that he was in the middle of a thick forest with very little sunlight streaming through. Adjusting his eyes in the hazy fog proved to be difficult. He was, however, able to see an opening leading out of the forest. As he walked closer to the opening, he could hear a waterfall in the distance. Matt felt relieved, having only a few steps to go from escaping the forest.

Suddenly he heard footsteps crackling on fallen leaves. Slightly turning to the side, he saw a glimpse of a human figure approaching. Uneasy, Matt picked up his pace, barely reaching the opening when an arrow brushed passed his face hitting a nearby tree. Alarmed, Matt quickly turned to locate the source of the arrow, and suddenly three men emerged from the trees, covered in warrior garb of water buffalo. Strength and confidence emanated from the tall aggressors. Startled by the abrupt intrusion, Matt thought it would be wise to run away.

Is this another one of Jedidiah's fantastic escapades? he asked himself. Or was it by some random chance that he found himself in the middle of nowhere with aggressive men trying to kill him? *Who are these men, and what do they want?* A hundred unanswered questions filled his mind.

Aware of his attackers' position, Matt determined that if he retreated, there wouldn't be enough time to escape. If he could possibly befriend these strangers, maybe they would cease the attack. Cautiously, Matt moved toward the men, hoping to make friendly contact to find out where he was and who they were. His first step almost became his last.

One of the three warriors moved swiftly towards him, carrying in his hand a long spear. With precision, he leaped high in the air, attempting to distract Matt while releasing the deadly weapon. The release was executed so well, if not for Matt's own agility, the spear would have sunk dead center into his chest instead of the tree behind him. Matt showed no signs of fear but perceived that what he was facing were warriors who intended to eliminate him. He was irritated but had no malice towards the warriors. However, he had no intention of being impaled by a spear or used as a target.

"I don't know who you are," he shouted, hoping to avoid another near-death experience, "but I suggest that we talk before another spear is thrown."

The warrior eyed Matt intently, wondering why his spear hadn't hit its mark. His comrades spoke to him in their native language, warning the young warrior to be cautious. To Matt's surprise, he understood their native tongue.

"How is that even possible? Thank you, Jesus," Matt said under his breath. As Matt heard them call the young warrior's name, he sought to address him.

"Lire, is that your name? I don't mean to intrude. I don't know how I got here, but I mean no harm. Can you tell me where I am?"

They were astonished that Matt could understand and speak their language. "Bruk, Caleb ... you hear that? He says he doesn't mean to intrude," Lire shouted loud enough for Matt to hear. His mocking response regarding Matt caused the other warriors to laugh.

Matt looked at the men before him and knew that they were formidable warriors. Matt assessed the mouthy one called Lire to be the youngest. He was quick and light on his feet. His handsome features were set off by his dark, ruddy complexion and short, loose auburn curls that covered his eyebrows. He had courage, but Matt concluded that his lighthearted humor was used to compensate anxiety. However, the display of his strength and agility had convinced Matt that he was indeed a warrior.

Matt took a long look at Bruk and concluded that he had to be the oldest of the three. His disciplined demeanor displayed courage, strength, and experience. He had light brown eyes with smooth, dark skin. His strong chin portrayed a handsome, rugged appearance. His hair was cut short, revealing a tattoo on the back of his neck. Then there was Caleb, the tallest of the warriors, with a strong muscular frame; his eyes were a dark brown set off by a small scar over his right brow. His features were different from the others, but there was no doubt that the warrior spirit in him surpassed his comrades.

They moved swiftly, surrounding him, watching every move he made. Matt stood his ground, amazed at how sharp his senses had become. He heard every step they made and knew every man's position. Matt decided to reason one last time.

"What is it that you want? I'm sure that we can sort out…" Another arrow flew towards him, barely missing his face. As the warriors continued to approach, extreme tension filled the air.

Waiting for the next move, Matt saw a new figure emerge from the shadows of the trees. He carefully watched him as he moved closer. He seemed to be the oldest, maybe wiser than the others. His features were strong and regal. His skin was darker than midnight, and his age was only revealed by the grey in his hair. As the man continued to walk, Matt examined his demeanor.

"Abdi, do you want us to move in on him?" Caleb shouted, keeping his eyes on Matt. Matt sensed tension in the air. He wasn't sure which warrior called out to the older man, but he knew that all of their efforts were focused on him.

"Abdi…" Matt repeated the name under his breath. He knew he had to tread lightly, so he simply waited for the man's next move.

"You have violated this sacred forest, and for that, you have forfeited your life."

Matt heard strong emotion in the older man's voice but could not tell what his next move would be. "Sir … wait a minute. It wasn't my idea to be here. I apologize for violating your sacred place." Matt's voice filled the air with genuine concern, not for himself but for the warriors. Sucking in cool air to calm his heart, Matt thanked God under his breath for that few hours training with Jedidiah and Steven.

He had often pondered on how Poppy could turn a few hours into three months of training and why they chose the second day of his honeymoon—it was still incomprehensible. One moment he was asleep, and the next he felt only wet, cold marble underneath his fingertips. Startled, he sat up to see four piercing eyes staring at him. At that time, no explanations were given. "Time to train for your future, son," was Jedidiah's and Steven's only saying throughout the training. When the training ended, he found himself transported back to his bedroom, standing in the middle of the room. Patience was resting peacefully while sunrays lightly touched her hair. Shaking his head, he thought that only inside the Treasure Tree could something like this happen.

His eyes searched the perimeter for a convenient way out. Twenty meters away, he spotted the remaining warriors stealthily moving through the woods towards him.

Matt was doing his best to avoid a fight, but all attempts to negotiate had failed.

A look of disdain crossed Abdi's face. He observed Matt's physique; he looked like a warrior. However, in Abdi's eyes, the begging and pleading depicted a coward. Abdi thought to himself, *Is he a warrior or a coward? We will see what he's made of.*

"Cut off his head and put it on a stick. You can leave the body for the dogs," shouted Abdi. Raising his left hand, he signaled the three men to attack. Matt was jolted back to reality when a two-edged spear sought to tear apart his flesh. He shifted his body weight away from the weapon and effortlessly used his left hand to push aside the spear's blade from his torso, which caused it to sink into the ground inches from his feet.

As Matt evaded the second attack, he watched with keen eyes, noting the direction from where the spear originated. Smirking, Lire stood, getting ready to throw another spear, while the others looked astonished by Matt's strength and agility. Seldom had they seen a warrior evade Lire's spear. *Okay, Lord, help me out here. What do I do next?*

A familiar voice rang in his ears. "Use your mind, son."

The unexpected response caught Matt off guard. He quickly looked around for the owner of the voice.

Again, the voice spoke. "Remember, Matt, when you walk by the Spirit, He will show you a way to survive without killing." Matt continued to listen, but there was only silence. Seeing the warriors approaching, he anxiously waited for further insights from the voice, but nothing came.

Frustrated, Matt only had seconds before his attackers were upon him. He remembered Jedidiah saying, "Take heed to the path of your feet, then all your ways will be sure."

Abdi had no time to warn his men; even as he raised his voice for them to attack, it was too late. With great speed, Matt ran toward Lire, snatched the spear from his hand, and snapped it in half. Before Lire could react, Matt grabbed him by the neck, causing him to gasp for air. Lire grabbed Matt's right hand, trying to pry Matt's hand from around his neck, but the grip only became tighter. Matt's arm muscles contracted as Lire's feet lifted off the ground. The young warrior's eyes grew wide as he felt Matt's powerful hand raise him off the ground. Sweat beads trickled down his face, Lire knew that it was only a matter of seconds before he died.

Trying to anticipate Matt's next move, Lire quickly raised his knee, ramming it hard into Matt's ribcage. Flinching from the pain, Matt pushed Lire's leg down while still holding him with a single hand in midair. The fight seemed like an eternity to Lire. Matt saw the other warriors rapidly approaching. With them only seconds away, Matt knew that he couldn't escape. He pulled Lire closer and looked into his eyes.

"I'm not trying to harm you. I just need to protect myself. Tell them to stand down." As Matt made his demand, he carefully squeezed Lire's neck while eyeing the approaching warriors. Lire, gasping for more air, held up his hand to signal the approaching warriors to stop. Lire's warning instantly caused the men to pause. Seeing a chance to escape, Matt slowly backed away, keeping his eyes glued to every opponent. He knew he had minimal time to escape before his opportunity disappeared.

In Matt's attempt to move away, Lire eyed his comrades, indicating that he understood their next move. Lire closed his eyes and yelled a war cry; he then lifted his body, locking his legs around Matt's arm to loosen the grip around his neck. Matt knew he had to switch his method of engagement to an offense tactic if he was going to make it out alive. He forcibly slammed Lire to the ground, knocking the wind out of him. Matt quickly used his agility to run further into the forest, hoping to avoid conflict.

"Caleb, kill him!" screamed Abdi. With skill and precision, Caleb landed a heavy blow to Matt's right jaw, followed by a kick to the abdomen. Satisfaction shown in Caleb's eyes.

He will not survive, Caleb thought to himself as he raised his hand, confirming Abdi's command.

Matt, staggering back, regained his senses. Wiping the blood from his mouth, Matt stared firmly into Caleb's eyes. Caleb was taken completely by surprise at Matt's unwavering stamina as he lifted himself up.

"I don't know how you are still conscious, but you won't be for long," Caleb said.

"It's going to take more than that to get rid of me," Matt said, taking a deep breath. In a split second, Matt grabbed Caleb and tossed him in the air, landing him several meters away from Lire's broken double-edged spear. Matt saw Caleb's intent, and they both took off running towards the spear.

Heavy breathing could be heard from the two men rushing toward the spear. Matt got ahead with ease, but Caleb's determination caused him to leap forward. With only seconds remaining, Caleb grabbed the broken spear just before Matt's fingers could seize it. Quickly turning,

Caleb shoved the spear toward Matt's throat, but the attempt was futile. Matt moved swiftly to his right and brought up his left fist with a powerful cross to the warrior's jaw, causing Caleb to stumble back. In the stumble, Matt quickly grabbed the spear from Caleb's hand. The force sent Caleb flying back several meters, landing him hard against a tree, leaving him unconscious.

Furious war cries could be heard from Abdi and Bruk.

Without warning, Matt took off running, leaving the warriors astonished.

"Coward! Such a coward. You will not escape today," Abdi shouted bitterly. Both warriors found themselves being challenged by his speed and agility. Matt moved through the forest like a gazelle. Looking over his shoulder, he saw his opponents gaining speed. "Bruk, take him from the right," Abdi said while he moved toward the left side of Matt.

Matt was surprised at how fast the warriors were gaining speed. Looking down, he saw the double-edge spear still in his hand. Matt turned and threw the spear at Abdi. Abdi sidestepped the oncoming spear.

"We can't let him get into the thicket," exclaimed Bruk.

"I know. Throw your bolas and bring him down," shouted Abdi. Bruk took a strong leather cord out of a bag around his waist. On each end of the cord were two round balls of iron with tiny, sharp spikes protruding out covered with thick layers of leather. Bruk whirled the bolas above his head at high speed, then with great precision, hurled it towards Matt.

Just as Matt reached the edge of the deep woods, the bolas wrapped around his legs, causing him to fall onto the hard surface. The enemy was approaching fast. Trying to untie his feet, he flinched at the spikes in the leather around his ankles. "Think, Matt…" he said, trying not to panic. He could hear their footsteps inching closer. With every attempt to be set free, bloody gashes formed around his hands and ankles. *Stop wasting time, and get it done.* With one powerful jerk, the leather broke. Jumping to his feet, Matt saw a large ravine in the distance. *If I get enough speed, I can jump over the ravine.* As Matt gained momentum, he reached the edge and leaped with all his strength.

With a hard landing, half of Matt's torso hung off the ravine. Pulling himself up, he suddenly felt his body sinking. "Oh, no!" exclaimed Matt. The war cries in the distance proved that another set of bolas successfully wrapped around his legs. Matt continued to climb the ravine, but the rocks under his feet suddenly gave way. Quickly eyeing the sides of the ravine, he tried to grab hold of anything within reach. Matt's strong hands caught hold of a thick vine.

As he hung from the vine, excruciating pain shot through his fingers. In spite of the pain, he continued to climb. His weight became too much for the vine, and it snapped, sending it downward. With wide eyes, Matt thought, *This can't be the end, Lord. Are you taking me home already?*

Inhaling for what he assumed would be his last breath, Matt closed his eyes and thought of Patience. Suddenly, he felt his body become immobile and sticky. Matt opened his eyes and saw that he landed on a large web.

"This is just not my day!" Matt yelled loudly as his frustration echoed through the ravine. Realizing he was still tied-up, he reached down and ripped the bolas off his legs. Turning from side to side, he saw that the web seemed to stretch for miles. "Lord of Mercy, this is all I need. Taken from my bride twice during our honeymoon, chased by crazy warriors, and now I'm stuck in a blasted web. Come on, Lord!" he bellowed.

****

"Look, Father. He's stuck in that large web. Do we retrieve him?" asked Bruk.

"No," replied Abdi. "Let him stay right where he is. Whatever made that web will be coming soon to check on it. Besides, did you see how he tore loose from your bolas? He has more strength than I thought."

Seconds later, Lire and Caleb appeared after shaking off the effects of their encounter with Matt. "How'd he get down there?" asked Lire, looking over the edge to get a better view.

"Your brother used bolas on him just as he leaped to cross over the ravine," explained Abdi.

"You mean he was attempting to jump over the ravine? That's more than 60 feet across," Lire stated in shock.

"I know?" Caleb smirked.

"I don't know what he was thinking," said Bruk.

"He was thinking about saving his life," explained Abdi.

"With the way he was running, he may have made it if my bolas hadn't stopped him," said Bruk.

Matt struggled to get out of the web. The web cords were stronger than he thought. Observing his surroundings, he couldn't help noticing a large hole a few feet away. Pulling his right arm hard, he was able to free one side of his body from the web, giving him leverage to do the same for his other side.

****

Suddenly a rope was dropped from the top of the ravine. Matt's brow raised as he studied the rope and the men looking down at him. "If you're dropping that rope down to help me, you have lost your minds! Do you think I'm going to trust you?" yelled Matt. As soon as the words left Matt's lips, he heard eerie growls coming from below. Alarmed by the sounds, he weighed his options. In the time it took him to make up his mind to take a chance with the warriors, a massive claw tore into the large web, tearing the web and also leaving a gash in Matt's side.

"Lord Almighty," came a scream to the ears of the warriors.

"What's going on down there?" Abdi said under his breath.

Squinting with pain, Matt quickly moved away from the torn web. The beast below tried again to get Matt, however, this time, it was met with a hard, solid foot. The creature's guttural roar echoed through the ravine. As Matt continued to escape suddenly, the web completely broke loose sending Matt to the bottom of the ravine. The hairs on Matt's neck raised, sensing his life was about to end. As he fell, he saw the faces of the warriors looking down at him.

Finding a firm grip on the web, he swung toward the wall of the ravine and grabbed vines to slow his pace. Matt was only a meter from the ground when he saw a large creature running toward him. With precision, just before the beast attacked, he pulled the web back and released it, causing it to strike the beast on the head. The web stuck firmly to its face as Matt landed on the floor of the ravine.

Moving swiftly, he wrapped the creature in the web. Desperately the beast tried to claw its way out of the web but found itself completely wrapped and immobile.

Matt knew that it would eventually free itself, and when that happened, there was only one choice—*kill the beast or be killed*. Quickly, Matt found a large stone and hurled it at the beast and struck it in the head. The beast gave a loud cry and fell dead to the floor of the pit.

Wincing in pain, Matt suddenly remembered the beast left a deep gash in his side. Matt was losing too much blood, and he knew if it wasn't bandaged quickly, he'd bleed to death. Looking down at his wound, he noticed his hands were still sticky from the residue of the web. *Okay, this might just work*. Hurriedly walking toward the dead creature, Matt pulled off just enough web to bandage his wound. To his surprise and satisfaction, his idea worked. The web closed the wound, and the bleeding stopped.

Matt looked around for an escape, but the pit was quickly becoming darker. However, a few rays from the sun still lit parts of the ravine. Matt realized that in a few minutes the ravine would be completely dark. Suddenly, an alarming stench engulfed the area. Scanning the ravine, Matt spotted another creature slowly approaching through a narrow opening.

****

"Hey, are you alive down there?" came a voice.

"Yes, no thanks to you!" Matt annoyingly retorted. Eyeing the new creature, he moved towards the walls and discovered they were slick and hard to grasp. Matt estimated that he was approximately 40 meters from the top of the ravine. A hissing sound he had never heard before came from the approaching beast. *Lord, being down here is not my idea of a honeymoon,* he thought.

The eerie sounds came again with more intensity. Matt focused his eyes on the thick darkness in the back of the ravine and saw several large glowing eyes looking back at him.

"Always expect the unexpected," Jedidiah had warned him. There was always something below the natural surface of things.

The ruckus below got the attention of the warriors above. "Sounds like huge lions fighting down there," said Caleb to his comrades.

"No, those are bostis," said Abdi.

A large bosti began to approach Matt. As the darkness finally engulfed the entire ravine, Matt, squinting, could only see the outline of one beast that hid in the shadows, but instinctively he knew that there were more. The beasts stealthily moved towards Matt; he knew that it was going to take a miracle for him to escape. Being saved by the tribesmen above the ravine sounded more appealing every second Matt stayed in the pit.

"Should we lower the rope further down, Father?" asked Bruk, knowing that without their help, the man would die.

"Not unless you want to be a meal. We must not forget the reason why we are here. Let's see what he does with the beasts," said Abdi.

"They will kill him if we don't do something," said Bruk.

"I know," retorted Abdi.

"Then we are to leave him to the beasts?" asked Lire.

"Be silent, and let us see what he does," said their father, seemingly without pity. Then, to the young warriors' surprise, their father threw a torch into the pit; all watched as it hit the bottom.

The fire from the torch gave off very little light. Matt could barely see, but his senses told him the monsters were there. He also knew that he was being watched from above. The three men stood watching as their father threw another torch down into the pit. It hit the bottom of the pit, sending sparks in every direction. The torch continued to burn even in the three-inch puddle of water. When three more torches landed on the ground, Matt didn't know if he was being helped or attacked. The flames startled the beasts long enough for Matt to pick up a torch and wedge it between rocks.

"What's he doing? Why doesn't he use the torch to ward them off or climb the rope?" asked Bruk.

"He's foolish, that's what," answered Caleb.

"No, I don't think so," exclaimed Abdi.

"Then what?" retorted Bruk, bothered by the fact they did nothing to help the man in the pit.

"Excuse me, but what do you all see? It's so dark in the ravine that I can barely see the fire. How is it that you all can see everything?" exclaimed Lire.

"You need more training, Lire. Let's just watch and see what happens. The bostis are not easy to overcome," said Abdi.

The ravine was now dimly lit, just enough for Matt to see the beast. Cautiously stepping forward, he saw four creatures pacing back and forth, looking for an angle to attack. Then, the beasts began to roar. It was like thunder pounding Matt's ears until he had to cover them with his hands.

"What's going on?" asked Lire.

"Evidently, it's the way bostis frighten and subdue their prey for the kill," said Abdi.

"Those bostis are so loud that the roar is causing the rocks to fall from the walls!" yelled Bruk. The warriors felt the ground under them shaking. They quickly backed away from the edge of the ravine to keep from falling in.

The sound of the bostis was deafening. Matt had never heard anything so shrill. *Lord, I've had enough of this,* he thought, removing his hands from his ears. With one quick move, he swung another large bolder around and threw it in the direction of the roaring beasts. There was a sudden impact, and Matt could hear the sound of rock smashing against flesh. The roaring ceased, and the sound of rushing feet headed his way.

As the beasts came into view, Matt saw their astounding size. Chills ran up his back as he readied himself. Without warning, the smallest of the four creatures lunged forward, attempting to bite off the nearest part of Matt's body. The beast was met with the force of a powerful fist under its jaw.

Matt rushed toward the other beasts with fiery ferocity. Before the monster could engage his fangs and claws, it was met with a powerful kick to the head. Matt wrapped his powerful arms around its neck and threw it to the ground. He kicked and stomped on its head, leaving it motionless. No sooner had he finished one, then another came. The men above were watching the whole scene.

"Did you see that? I don't believe it. Nobody can do that! He fights like the devil," said Caleb.

"Or like an angel of the Lord," retorted Bruk.

"What? I still can't see anything," complained Lire.

Abdi was silent, watching every move the young intruder made; his raised eyebrow indicated approval.

Another huge rock struck the head of the oncoming bosti. It laid immobile in the dust of the pit, stunned but not dead. Matt wrapped his arms around the neck of the beast, lifting it from the ground, then with one powerful jolt, flipped the beast over and sent its head into the floor, breaking its neck on impact.

"I don't believe it," said Caleb, laughing and holding onto Lire. The men watched in wonder as two more beasts charged. Rage possessed them as they rushed forward to tear Matt apart. Matt ran toward the other side of the ravine wall. Grabbing a torch from the floor, he raised it at the oncoming beasts. His attempt to stop the beast was futile; the monster quickly turned its head and sunk its teeth into Matt's arm, causing him to drop the torch. Wincing in pain, he felt his flesh tearing, and with quick reflex, he punched the creature hard enough to knock out several of its teeth and send it to its knees. When the other beast joined in, they both shook with rage and circled Matt for the kill.

"Oh no, you're not going to trap me like that," he said. Suddenly he ran toward the approaching bostis and dove between them. With lightning speed, he grabbed one by the tail, swung it around, and let go. The flying bosti hit the other, sending them both into the side of the ravine. The impact brought down rocks and debris. With the Lord's help, the overhanging stones fell straight down on top of the beasts, instantly killing them. "Thank you, Lord," was all Matt could say.

Breathing heavily, Matt noticed only one beast remained. Standing on its hind legs, it towered over Matt by five feet and was larger than any of the other bostis. Matt had never faced anything so ominous in all his life. He could clearly see every part of the beast and sensed a deep evil in it.

"Now, Lord, if you would just take care of this one, I would be eternally grateful," he said, taking in another deep breath.

Saliva drooled from the large fangs hanging from the beast's mouth. The malevolent creature's urgent desire was to kill. With growing rage, it stared at Matt. Matt observed with caution as he prayed for help. Without warning, the beast lunged forward. With both hands, Matt caught the paws coming down, simultaneously kicking the beast in the belly and sending it back against the wall. It roared so loud that its echo vibrated throughout the ravine. More rocks fell around Matt, but he did not move.

The beast was enraged. It stood on all four of its legs, kicking up loose gravel, water, and dirt. Charging again, the bosti stopped in its tracks, sensing the presence of something wild and fearless emerging from the place where the two beasts had been thrown earlier. An awesome power filled the pit. Matt felt the presence of his companions, and so could the bosti. Nevertheless, the wicked beast's mind was fixated on Matt, desiring to devour him.

Then, as if by magic, from the mouth of the bosti came words that sounded human but were eerily not. "Human beings are usually weak and easily captured because they have no claws or talons to defend themselves. They grow tired quickly and often faint when confronted by my kind, but you are different. You have won this small conflict, human, but you are destined to die. There is a war coming, the magnitude of which you can't imagine. On that day, you, along with all your kind, will be meat for us," said the bosti. Matt stood with his mouth opened astonished to hear articulate words come from the beast. Backing slowly into the dark opening of the cave, the monster saw no need to collect its dead companions. *It is better to leave and return with reinforcements than take the chance of being killed,* reasoned the bosti to himself. Snarling, he disappeared into the darkness of the ravine.

Matt breathed in slowly and released the tension from his muscles. It seemed, for the moment, fighting beasts was over. His immediate concern turned to getting out of the ravine. Looking around, Matt didn't see any way out, except the rope left by the warriors. Still, it was too high to reach. Although his wound was rapidly healing, it still caused him pain. Pondering how to get out, Matt heard a voice.

Use your running skills, said the voice in his head.

And just how am I supposed to do that? he questioned. The rope hung just a few meters lower than the web but was still unreachable.

"Use your skills, Matt," came the voice again, only this time it was audible.

What's going on? I'm finally losing my mind.

"You are not losing your mind, Matt, only your doubts. Now start running, and run with all your strength," prodded the voice.

Come on, Matt. Where is your faith? It can't hurt. With one quick step, Matt started running full force around the walls of the ravine. The faster he ran, the better his side felt. He could feel his body healing; on the third lap, he pushed off the wall into midair, catching the rope and swinging himself upward. He knew that there was no way he was going to clear the top without help. And so, he asked for it. *Help, Lord…*

The answer came back in the form of a gust of wind beneath him. As he neared the top, he let go of the rope and bolted above the heads of the onlooking warriors. Glancing down, Matt saw their astonished faces. Knowing he only had seconds to spare before they pursued him, upon landing, he hit the ground running. Abdi signaled for his men to get him, but they were too late. He was out of sight before they took a step.

"I can't believe someone can run that fast," said Caleb.

"It's a good thing that you are a good tracker," said Lire.

"Yeah, so let's get after him," said Bruk.

Smiling, Abdi was pleased with his boys. He never had to say a word. They did what trained Pia Warriors naturally do; they pursue.

Aware that the warriors were too far behind to catch up, Matt slowed his pace. His body was almost completely healed, but he winced as he felt a sharp pain shoot through his side. *Well, Lord, at least my bleeding has stopped.* He looked at the wound and discovered that the web had dissolved. He moved quickly toward a thickly wooded area. Once there, he could conceal himself from his pursuers and rest. Scanning the surrounding area, he spotted an open grassy field. Just beyond it, he could see a cluster of large rocks and behind them more woods. It looked like the best place for concealment for a hunted man and looked easy enough to reach without too much effort. He ran toward his destination. Wincing in pain, Matt grabbed his side and saw blood dripping from the wound.

"How could this be? I thought I was over this! If I could just make it a little further..." he said, grabbing his waist. Matt regained momentum with every step. The grass in the field suddenly grew higher. "Lord, this is weird," he said.

Unaware of the danger before him, he entered a field that was filled with live parasitical particles. These parasites attached themselves to anything that passed through the field. Matt had no idea how deadly the voyage through the field was. Glancing down, Matt discovered he was running on top of the remains of dead animals. He was disturbed by the eerie scenery, and even more so when he felt the grass reaching for his waistline. Trying to keep his pace, he focused on the boulders in front of him, where he planned to rest.

Nearly out of the grassland, he noticed visible particles started to attach themselves to his wound. The seeping blood drew more of the particles with every step he took. By the time he reached the cluster of rocks, fatigue and dizziness had overtaken him, and his side throbbed. Approaching the boulders, he noticed a crevice in the rocks that was covered in green moss.

"Well, Lord, this should keep me safe from my trackers, at least for a while." He leaned against the cool stone and rested his head against it. Drifting in and out of consciousness, he thought of his beloved Patience, and to his surprise, he heard her call, beckoning him home. "It seems so real," Matt said dismayed.

His parched throat ached. Matt needed water badly, and leaning against the dampened stone didn't help his thirst. Unexpectedly, he heard footsteps coming in his direction.

Hearing the rustle of grass as the footsteps grew louder, he pressed his hand against his waist, attempting to stop the bleeding. He braced himself for the attack, but it never came. Matt knew he wasn't in any shape to fight back, so he began to sink further into the crevice.

5

THE HELPER

THE STRONG FIGURE STANDING IN FRONT OF MATT TOOK A quick survey of his condition. In his delirium, Matt resisted the intruder as best he could but to no avail.

"Patience ... Patience. Oh God, help me, Lord..." he exclaimed in exhaustion. The stranger reached out and firmly grabbed him. One hand covered his mouth, and the other held him still. Matt struggled, trying to free himself from the stranger, but only caused his wound to widen.

The strong figure holding him said with a deep tone, "Quiet. If you keep moving, you'll make it come closer." Matt had two thoughts in his mind. The man was either talking about the warriors or more of the creatures from the ravine, which one he didn't know. "The more you struggle, the wider your wound will be."

Despite the voice in his ear, Matt could not see anything but blurry darkness. Groans from Matt increased as the throbbing pain continued, but no sound was heard, for the man still had a tight grip on his mouth.

"This is going to hurt, but it will save your life..." In disbelief and shock, Matt felt the man's hand reach into his wounded side. In the anguish of his pain, all he could think of was Patience. The pain was excruciating, sending him into unconsciousness.

****

After his wound was cleaned and bandaged, his senses immediately returned. It was like breathing in fresh air. He found himself looking through hazy eyes into the face of the stranger, an older man, who pointed toward the field. Matt could barely see, lying in the field, the outline of a beast like the ones he had fought in the ravine. Only it was lying at the edge of the field dead. It had been consumed by the parasites in the grass.

"You are blessed to be alive young man. Most people would have died coming through that field," said the old man attending to his wound.

Matt asked, "What happened to me?"

"You went through that field," said the old man, nodding his head towards it. "People from around here know not to go through that field unless you are looking to end your life." Matt listened with interest to what the old man said, staying conscious of his surroundings. He watched as the mysterious old man held out his hand, showing him several metal beads. Still blurry-eyed, Matt wasn't able to make out what laid in the hand of his provider.

"What is that?"

"These parasitical beads are the cause of your illness. If they had stayed in your wound any longer, you wouldn't be in the land of the living. Thank God that you have an amazing constitution for resisting this kind of stuff. See that dead bosti out there?" asked the old man as he pointed to the beast. "The parasites in the field did that to it. The beast knows better than to come through that field, but I suppose that its craving and taste for human blood overrode its sense of survival."

Matt was silent, trying to see and listen to every word. Was the old man helping him out of kindness, or was it to get an advantage by gaining his trust? Regardless of what he thought, Matt could not discount that his wound was dressed and bandaged. Overtaken by fatigue, Matt laid his head back to rest and fell into a deep sleep.

****

The next morning, he awakened and found himself lying on a cot in a small candlelit room. He quickly surveyed the room and noticed a pair of eyes staring back at him from behind a midsize lattice. He instantly sensed that it was one of the men who had chased him. Matt heard other voices coming from the adjacent room and attempted to sit up in protest but was easily subdued by the man behind the lattice.

"Rest, my son. You have had a mighty battle with both beast and sickness. I am astounded that you conquered them both." The man before him did not appear to be the same one who had dressed his wound. This man he recognized as one of the warriors in the woods. Matt struggled to raise himself up; however, dizziness overcame him, and he laid back down. "Take it easy, my friend," said his captor. "You are feeling the side effects of the medicine the old seer gave you. I was instructed to tend your wound until you could stand on your own. You will not be harmed, so rest."

Matt didn't believe the man's words. How could he? After all, wasn't he one of the warriors trying to kill him?

Smiling and amused at how persistent Matt was in trying to stand, the older man said, "You are extremely strong. Most would have died before they made it out of the grasslands."

"Who are you, and why am I here?" asked Matt.

Ignoring his questions, the man rose and mashed what looked like different herbs in a wooden bowl. Coming closer, he sat on the chair next to Matt. Matt felt uneasy about this mysterious warrior and was trying to decide if he was more dangerous than he appeared. In case the others showed up, he wanted to be alert. Without warning, Abdi lifted Matt's bloodstain garment. Still a little lightheaded, his reflexes were not as quick as usual. He shifted his left arm to block the man, but to no avail. To Matt's surprise, the senior warrior evaded his move and continued applying the salve. It was evident that Matt was coming out of his cloudiness as his speech was more coherent, his vision clearing.

"You healed on your own very well," commented Abdi as he applied the last bit of salve the old seer left behind. Matt glanced down at his wounded side. To both of their amazement, the wound had closed, and his body was rapidly repairing itself. The only scars left were those from the field. The older warrior smiled and waited for Matt's questions.

"How long have I been here?"

"Not long, only a day."

"A day, and my wound is completely healed?"

Ever since Matt worked in the fields of plenty with Jedidiah, he gained a deeper appreciation for the Lord's creation. The fields of plenty had given him tremendous health and strength. It had also transformed him in ways he couldn't explain. He had gained vitality that not only affected his body but also his spirit and soul. When he thought about it, he hadn't been ill since the day he arrived at The Treasure Tree. He had also noticed that none of those who lived in the Treasure Tree and ate of its provision experienced illness.

"It seems that your body heals very well," said Abdi.

Matt was thankful for the help, even if it did come from a man with unknown intentions. He wanted to ask more questions, but his mind was preoccupied with Patience. *She must be frantic over my absence. I must get back to her as soon as possible,* he told himself. Now that he was healed and seemingly at peace with these crazy warriors, he saw no reason for delaying his return to Patience. The only problem was how. He was in the middle of nowhere and stuck in a place filled with unknown dangers that offered him the constant, horrible expectation of being tracked by madmen and chased by wild beasts. However, just when it seemed that hope was gone, an old man with a staff and lines of time in his face entered Matt's room.

"You must be wondering about this place and why you have been brought here," the old man said with a hint of cheer in his voice. Just from appearance, Matt could tell that he was in the presence of a man of wisdom. The old man looked so familiar to him.

"Yes, sir, I am," said Matt, waiting for an explanation.

"Your questions will be answered soon, my son, but for now, get a little more rest. You'll need it for your journey ahead of you." Before Matt could speak, the old man turned and was gone. Matt laid back, amazed and full of questions. He closed his eyes and slipped into a deep sleep. Just before sleep took him, he thought he heard the old man talking to other people in the next room. He tried to listen, but the instructions to sleep from the old seer took effect. He peacefully dreamed of his beloved Patience.

Morning came quickly, and the sun blazed its way through the open window, its rays striking Matt in the face. The warmth awakened him. He still felt a little lightheaded, but it didn't stop him from sitting up. Looking around, he noticed that he had been moved. This was not the same room. This room was well lit, with a different view. Outside the window, mountains could be seen, and there was a large tree packed with critters. There were also five other beds in the room. *I wonder who sleeps there,* he thought to himself.

The smell of bandages and salve were gone. The aroma of bacon, eggs, and freshly baked biscuits filled the air. Matt heard noise from the dining area and felt strong enough to walk over and satisfy his curiosity. A marvelous breakfast was displayed on a large table. Abdi appeared in the doorway and motioned for Matt to come. Still cautious, Matt made his way toward him.

"We have the master chef this morning, and he has made a sumptuous meal for us all. Come on in, and I'll introduce you to my sons," said Abdi. Matt stood in the doorway, and his eyes immediately perused the room for exits. Two men were in line getting the rest of the food to set on the table, while another stood with his back to the wall, watching every movement Matt made.

"This is Matt, and he will be joining us for breakfast," Abdi announced with a slight smile. The warriors stood, facing Abdi and Matt, then moved forward. As they approached, Matt became uneasy. He placed his right hand on one of the logs attached to the doorway just to his right. Looking them over as they approached, he recognized them all.

"Hey, boys, the mighty intruder is looking us over," exclaimed Lire, pointing his finger at Matt.

"It's you!" Matt said, readying himself for another fight. To his surprise, Lire didn't move, only stood, staring and grinning. "Evidently, I amuse you in some way. Mind telling me how?" Matt said suspiciously.

Bruk smiled, shifting his weight from one foot to another while observing the foreigner. Matt switched his gaze from Lire to Bruk. He noticed the markings on both men. There was no mistaking—these were the same men who tried to kill him. One with an arrow and spear, the other with bolas that almost got him killed in the ravine. *Lord, you want to tell me what this is about?*

Abdi placed his hand on Matt's shoulder. Surprisingly, comfortable with Abdi, Matt never moved. "So, if these are your sons, why do they disrespect you by calling you by your first name instead of father?" Laughter suddenly erupted in the room.

"It is not permitted to use familiar titles during dangerous conflicts because enemies will hear and use that weakness to destroy us. The boisterous one is my youngest, Lire," Abdi said proudly. "Next to him is Caleb, not my blood son, but just as much my son as any of my children." Caleb stared at Matt with cautious eyes. He did not trust Matt and didn't bother to hide it. "Next to him is Bruk, my number one, and he keeps the others in line," Abdi laughed. "We are Pia Warriors from the land where humanity began," he said proudly. "And we have been summoned here to train you."

Matt was not sure what to say. He certainly didn't want to offend the warriors, but he had other things in mind than being a Pia Warrior. "I am honored to be in the presence of Pia Warriors. I have heard of the courage and integrity of the Pia Warrior from Jedidiah and my father-in-law. It is an honor to be considered, but my heart is the heart of a Grower. I tend the lands and grow things. I provide for the people of Truevine and for those who are far away. It is the gift from God to all faithful Growers," he said with conviction. The warriors looked at each other and then at Matt.

"You are not serious, are you?" asked Lire.

"I'm afraid so," responded Matt.

"This is an outrage," said Caleb.

"No, it's an insult," retorted Bruk.

"You dare choose growing beans over being a warrior?" protested Lire.

"It is those beans, my friend, that provide the energy for your bodies to function, which in turn makes you the warriors you are," Matt explained with his arms folded.

"Father, let me cut off his head and be done with this idiotic baboon," said Caleb.

Abdi stood, watching the dynamics between the warriors and the grower. Tempers were rising, and Matt could tell that in a moment or two, he would be in the heat of a battle with three hotheaded Pia Warriors.

You know, Lord, I believe I can take this bunch … with your help, of course. However, I'd rather be back home with Patience, taking care of my fields, than standing here arguing with these unreasonable, thick-headed warriors. If this must be, then let it come. Although if the battle takes place here, this cabin is not going to be standing.

Before Bruk and the others could approach him, an older man in an apron stepped out of the kitchen and came forward. The atmosphere completely changed; a calmness filled the room. It was the same man who had saved his life in the field, and Matt knew that in the presence of this man, he wouldn't have to fight the warriors. The old man brought with him peace and respect.

Maybe this is the right time to leave. Maybe I can find my way back to Patience, with the Lord's help. Matt thought to himself. Without warning, he dove through the window and took off like a gazelle towards the forest.

"Did you just see that? He's a coward all the way," Caleb said bitterly.

"We have to get him back. We've been tasked to train him," Bruk said. The warriors started after him but were stopped by their father. Abdi knew that somehow the old seer would intervene.

After hearing a familiar voice ringing in his ears, Matt immediately came to a halt. He looked around, expecting to see his old mentor jump out from behind a bush at any time.

"Here I am, Poppy. Where are you?" he asked, still looking for his mentor.

The voice said, "The Lord is always with you, son, and whenever he allows, I will guide you. Abdi can be trusted. He is a dear friend and the best trainer of Pia Warriors. Return to the cabin, and you will be instructed on what to do."

Matt thought hard on the words spinning around in his mind. Was it Poppy telling him to return to the men who tried to kill him, or had he completely lost his mind? If not for the peace that came over him while he pondered the matter, he would have ignored the voice and fled into the woods. Matt returned as instructed to the cabin.

"I see you've changed your mind, my young friend," Abdi said, walking slowly toward Matt.

"Yes sir, but it wasn't my idea," Matt said, watching him carefully.

"Of course not. That old seer Jedidiah has a way of influencing the most stubborn of us to obey his commands," said Abdi with a chuckle. "How about it? Did he convince you that we mean you no harm?"

"Ah ... yes, for now, but I'm not completely convinced," Matt said, watching the older warrior as he leaned against a humongous sequoia. Abdi laughed at the expression on Matt's face.

"Well, I'm glad that you are certain enough to stop running. The day before yesterday was a long day. I don't think my boys and I have ever run so much in our entire lives. Thank God for rest," laughed Abdi. Matt smiled and walked next to Abdi as they started back towards the cabin.

"Sleeping in peace will be nice for a change," Matt said in relief.

6

SEARCHING FOR MATT

PATIENCE BEGAN TO PONDER MOA'S WORDS REGARDING Matt's disappearance. "I'm not really sure how to react to all of this. I want to know what's going on, but feel that I'm not getting any help," said Patience, placing her cup of tea on the table.

"My dear, it is the will of God that the two of you be trained in both spiritual and physical warfare. You have a great advantage over many of our people because you have the privilege of being trained by both your father and grandfather. Every time you came to visit us, you were being trained. As a child, you came to the Treasure Tree because you loved your Poppy. And the times your grandfather sent for you were not only because he loved you but because it was the Lord's will," said Moa.

"And now, you and Matt are almost ready for your life's purpose. Of course, Matt must go through more rigorous training than most because of his position in life. And you must keep in mind that he hasn't lived among us as you have." Pricilla paused a moment, watching her granddaughter's reaction. "By the look in your eyes, I can see that you have questions, child. Let me assure you, my dear, that most of your questions will all be answered in due time,"

Pricilla said, as she poured more hot tea for the three of them.

"Where are they training Matt, Moa?" Patience asked.

"He is at the Great Falls and is quite safe. He has concluded that he is no longer in Truevine," continued Moa. "He really is very astute for a young man his age. Your grandfather taught him well."

Patience was speechless; she couldn't believe the conversation she was having with them. *They talk like everything is normal. My husband is missing, and everything is normal?* "Hey! Am I the only one here noticing a missing husband?" she said sarcastically.

To settle her emotions down, Moa suggested that they move to the sitting room where they could be more comfortable. "I see that you haven't done your hair yet. Come and sit so that I can weave diamond tips into your hair," said Heather. Patience took the suggested seat and waited to hear Moa's explanation regarding Matt's location.

"He is actually near the Great Falls, dear. Poppy sent Matt there to place him in the care of Pia Warriors. I spent a great deal of time there and found it to be very exhilarating, though it is inhabited by extremely savage beasts that actually hunt humans," said Heather. Patience was taken aback by her mother's odd explanation of the Falls.

"I thought you said that Matt is safe."

"He is safe, but the land of the Great Falls is not. The woods are full of killer beasts," explained Heather.

"Killer what?" asked Patience. If Patience hadn't been worried before, she was now. "He's not prepared for that. Pia Warrior training is brutal," she said with great concern.

"He is not only being trained, my dear. He's also being tracked by the warriors," said her grandmother without concern.

"They are Pia Warriors, and they are very aggressive, Moa. Matt is a grower, not an aggressor. He won't be prepared for them," Patience said, rising out of her chair.

Heather gently pushed her back down, allowing Pricilla to continue explaining, "Of course, he will not be prepared, not for the four of them, but Matt has been trained by your father and Poppy. He will adjust to whatever they have in mind."

"I need to let Matt know what he's up against," Patience insisted.

"No, you do not," said Heather, still working diamond tips into her daughter's hair. "You need to rely on the Lord and let Him guide your husband without you interfering."

"Mother, I don't want to interfere, I just want to make sure that he's all right," insisted Patience.

"He is, sweetheart, and I can assure you that your father and grandfather will watch over him. They love him just as we love you," explained Heather. Their words calmed her down, even if only for a brief moment.

"There. You're done," said Heather, weaving in the last piece of thin, flat leather. Patience's beautiful, dark hair sparkled with diamonds that laid against the thin leather strips laced throughout her hair.

"What are the diamonds for?" Patience asked.

"They are for the next stage of your training. You must learn to use every part of your being, which includes body, soul, spirit, and mind, to accomplish your life's purpose," said Pricilla with a little chuckle. "You will discover that the particles of the Sun Stone inside of you, combined with your faith, will prove to be more than enough to meet the challenges ahead." The words of her elders were endearing, and she welcomed them. However, Patience's heart gave her no rest. Until she could find Matt and make sure he was safe, it was going to be hard for her to quit holding her breath.

Patience spent the rest of the day meditating on verses from the Holy Book.

"The teaching of the wise is a fountain of life that a man may avoid the snares of death."

The verse in proverbs went through her mind as she walked through the flower garden across from the wedding chamber. She visited many of the gardens in Truevine as a child. It was one of her favorite things to do. She and Matt talked for hours, walking through them. The fragrance filled her senses with bittersweet delight, as she thought about Matt. Delight because of the laughter and love she and Matt enjoyed; bitter because Matt wasn't there.

Patience prayed, "Abba, I miss him so much. Please take care of him. You know how much we love each other. I miss him so, Lord, and there is fear in my heart, even though I know that you are with him as you have been with me all my life. I don't know why I'm so worried, but I am. I want to find him, to see him, to put my arms around him, and then I think I'll be fine." For the next hour, she poured out her heart to the Lord.

"Patience, there is no need to fear. I have given you my peace, not what the world has to offer, but my peace. My grace is sufficient for you. Rest in me," said a consoling voice.

****

Morning came quickly, and Matt was up and dressed before dawn. He needed time with the Lord to get confirmation of all he was told. Jedidiah had been correct about Abdi and the young warriors—there was no reason to mistrust them. When he entered the cabin, the others were dressed and sitting at a table eating breakfast, which had been prepared by none other than the old man who had dressed his wound and saved his life.

"Come on in, Matt, and join us," said Abdi. Bruk and the others made room for the young Grower. As soon as he sat down, a stack of hotcakes was placed in front of him along with eggs, bacon, sausage, goat's milk, and juice. Matt looked up at the face of the man who was serving him. It was not Jedidiah, though the resemblance was remarkable. To Matt, this man was a healer and a friend.

"A hearty breakfast for warriors with a long day before them," said Trobus, the old seer. Matt smiled and dug into the delightful breakfast. It didn't take long before every single morsel was gone. The old seer tapped Matt on the head with his spoon. Matt looked up. "You want seconds?" He smiled. Matt patted his stomach, shaking his head no.

Lire wasn't the only one surprised at how the old man treated the young Grower. There was true affection between them. Matt could feel it as well. He wasn't sure why, but he knew that the healer was special.

As breakfast came to an end, the old man addressed the men, saying, "I will soon take my leave of you and head back to my home in the lower Falls. Matt, you have already encountered much, but you are to continue your training just as Jedidiah told you. However, in the land of the Great

Falls, you will encounter much opposition from both worlds, seen and unseen. So be aware of your surroundings. You will also have to use your strength wisely. This is not just any training—you can die if you do not pay attention to Abdi and the others' instructions. You are not in the great Treasure Tree. This land is large, wild, and wonderful but must be brought under the authority of the Lord King. The evil in it must be vanquished. You have learned many things from everyone around you, but you have not achieved perfection. Your interaction with Abdi and his warriors will increase your skills expeditiously."

"Excuse me, my lord, but do you think that this Grower will match our level of warriors in such a short time?" asked Caleb.

"He will, my son, and you will do well not to take offense at those chosen by the Lord. Remember, discipline and obedience are key to our success."

It was obvious that Caleb had some dislike for Matt. He could not explain why. He found him to be honorable and easy to get along with, yet offense nagged at his heart. Maybe it was jealousy or pride. He wasn't sure which. What the old man said left a bitter taste in his mouth. Caleb knew immediately that it would be a matter of prayer to rid himself of it.

"Your wife expects you back, and I'll never hear the last of it if you fail to return," said the old man. The healer's words brought a smile to Matt's face, but a scowl to Caleb's.

Could that be it? Caleb thought to himself. *Am I jealous of his marriage to Patience*? Caleb knew that for years, he had feelings for Patience, but she had only shown deep brotherly love towards him. Hearing the words of the old man brought it to light. Abdi caught the expression on Caleb's face and knew that it had to be addressed. Patience was married to Matt. She made her choice and a good one at that. He would speak with his son later. The code of Pia Warriors was strict obedience to God and His authority. Matt was married to the daughter of their king. There could be no hint of sin or disloyalty in the heart of Christ-followers.

Standing next to Caleb, the old seer abruptly threw his kitchen knife at the floor near the front door. A poisonous viper had crawled through the cracked door in search of food and warmth; in an instant, it found a knife in its head as it squirmed on the floor.

"Whoa! That's a big snake," exclaimed Lire.

"That is how offense, mistrust, and sin find their way into our hearts. All they need is a small window or door of opportunity called pride, lust, and vengeance to let them in." The old seer smiled and told Caleb to retrieve his knife. The warriors knew that the message to Matt from the old man was for them as well. They had never known the old man to speak with such emphasis.

"Now gather around and bid me farewell as I bless you in the Lord's name," said Trobus. Men of this kind rarely embraced, but since the old man initiated it, every man took his turn. Matt was the last.

"When will I see you again?" he asked.

"You mean, when will you see Patience again?"

Matt laughed as a blush filled his face and wondered how the old seer knew his thoughts. The seer patted his shoulder and stated, "After you're done here, son."

"Then I'd better get done soon," Matt answered with intent.

"I believe he will, my lord," said Abdi, wrapping his arm around Matt's shoulder.

The old man did something very familiar as he departed—he tapped Matt on the head with his staff. "Farewell, son," said the old seer.

Matt smiled in response and said, "Farewell Popp..." He paused in thought, then lightly laughed at almost calling the old seer by his mentor's name. The healer took ten paces, looked back, and vanished before their eyes.

"That old man really likes you, Matt," said Lire.

"I kind of like him, too," responded Matt.

"What's not to like? He tells us stories, fixes us breakfast, binds up our wounds ... shall I go on?" asked Bruk, smiling at his brothers. It was a harmless tease but held much truth.

Caleb noted the admiration given to Matt and tried not to envy. *Lord, deal with my heart on this matter,* was Caleb's prayer. It was evident that there was much love for Matt. They all heard what the seer said regarding the door of temptation that leads to sin. *The Grower is Patience's husband,* Caleb kept reminding himself through clenched teeth. He viewed her as more than a sister and had hopes that she would marry him or one of their own. *She should have chosen a Pia Warrior from the land of Ethiopia, her father's kingdom, and not some village pauper*. Caleb thought, desperately trying to subdue the envy rising in his heart.

Matt lingered a moment longer against the door, surprised by Trobus' abrupt disappearance, "Well, you don't see that every day," he said to himself.

"Hey, Matt, come join us," called Abdi.

Matt then turned to join his new companions, but there were still many unanswered questions stirring around in his mind. In due time, he felt all his questions would be answered. However, what nagged him most was the why. *For what purpose am I being trained*?

Bruk and Lire observed Matt. Like him, they had questions of their own. It was understood that Pia Warriors never meddle into another warrior's personal matters without invitation. Nevertheless, it was easy to see that this young Grower had great favor and affection with King Jedidiah, Steven, and the old seer.

"Let's go!" came the command from Abdi, bringing wandering minds back to focus.

As they journeyed towards the training encampment, Lire's curiosity got the better of him. "Matt, how did you overcome the bostis in the ravine? That was no small task you had on your hands down there."

Matt continued to walk ahead without looking back. "Bostis … so that's what they're called," Matt said under his breath, remembering the near-death experience. Sighing with relief, Matt answered Lire's question. "It was the Lord."

Lire slightly nodded but was still curious. "Ah … okay. I'm sure that you are right, but I would like to know more detail if you don't mind," Lire eagerly inquired, catching up and placing his hand on Matt's shoulder.

Matt didn't take offense at the young warrior's curiosity, and he didn't mind sharing as long as he didn't let pride get in the way of giving God the credit. Lire was taller and younger than Matt but seemed to be well beyond his years as a seasoned warrior. "I'll tell you, Lire, that I didn't know what I was doing. The Lord just helped me. One minute, I was standing there staring into the eyes of death, and the next minute, I was fighting for my life."

"From what I heard from the top," said Lire with a curious grin, "it sounded like 'big teeth' was going to win. We were all surprised when you came out on top. There is definitely more to you than meets the eye. Man, you have some serious skills."

A clearing of the throat from Abdi got the warriors' attention. "Okay, I need you boys to focus on the task at hand. We will be entering the dark part of the forest within the hour." Looking at Lire, he chuckled. "Big teeth, huh?" Lire grinned sheepishly at Abdi's response.

Abdi stopped and paused with his nose in the air. "Do you smell that?" asked Abdi.

"Smell what?" asked Caleb.

"That horrific stench in the air. What's wrong with your nose, boy?" asked Abdi.

"Nothing. I just figured a smell that bad had to be coming from one place," Caleb said, nodding his head towards Bruk, who, of course, paid no attention to him.

"If Bruk stops eating those hot peppers and beans, we could all breathe again," said Lire, laughing and elbowing Matt in the side. Everyone laughed, including Bruk.

"That's enough. Let's move out," commanded Abdi shaking his head. "Lord, if we make it through this training, it will certainly be by your hand," Abdi said under his breath.

****

By the time they reached the training ground, half the day had worn away. Night came quickly in the forest. A fifty-mile hike was child's play for a Pia Warrior. Abdi was pleased that Matt showed no signs of fatigue. "You may be a grower son, but you have more endurance than a lion. Then again, running is one of your rare gifts," he said as Matt dropped his pack on the ground.

"I suppose so, sir," he said, studying his surroundings. The others did likewise and proceeded to mark off a circle around the ground for a campsite.

"Make sure that you secure this entire area. I have a strange feeling about this place," said Abdi.

Caleb started a fire while Bruk and Lire dressed down the wild boar they killed on the way to the campsite. Matt unpacked cooking utensils. He found a large pot, filled it with water, and placed it on the fire. The pot heated quickly. Bruk and Lire each took a leg of the boar and dragged it to the hot pot and stretched it out on the ground. Matt poured the hot water over the hog while the two warriors scraped hair from the body of the wild boar with their hunting knives. Bruk drove a stake through its ankle tendons, attached a rope, and hoisted it up over a tree limb. They stretched the hog out over a hole. In a matter of minutes, the dressing was done, and the meat was thrown on a heated rack. Herbs and spices were added, and the aroma of roasting meat filled the air, a sure invitation to any carnivore in the area.

While the meat cooked, the men continued clearing out a place for training. Abdi wanted it done before nightfall. "Hey, Lire, I can use a hand over here," yelled Bruk.

"I only have two hands. Get Caleb—he's got four," smarted Lire. Matt laughed as he jumped across Lire's back to give Bruk a hand with the gear tent.

"Watch it, man. You just don't jump over a man's back without warning. I have quick reflexes. You could have died," said Lire, eyeing Matt with a joking expression.

"I don't know how that boy became a Pia Warrior. I don't think there's a serious bone in his body," said Bruk.

"Actually, I'm glad he's that way; he takes the edge off things," said Matt.

Bruk nodded. "I guess every team needs a jester."

"I guess you're right. If not for him, Caleb would be a regular grump," said Abdi causing the entire camp to laugh.

"Thanks for the help, Matt," Bruk said.

"Don't mention it. I'm glad to serve," smiled Matt.

There was movement in the nearby bushes. "Hey! Did you hear that?" Bruk whispered to Matt.

"Yes, I did, and it's coming from the thicket on the other side of the fire," Matt said, never taking his eyes off the bushes.

"Let's check it out," suggested Bruk.

"Way ahead of you," said Matt. The continuing rustling of bushes and breaking of sticks gave Bruk and Matt reason to pause. Caleb, Abdi, and Lire had also taken notice and drew weapons. All eyes watched with anticipation to see what was emerging from the bushes.

Abdi was surprised but relieved to see what appeared to be Pia Warriors coming out into their camp. Two of them matched Matt's stature; however, the last man was a head taller than Bruk and large enough to eat the wild boar by himself. The men approached, dressed in Pia Warrior attire.

"Greetings, my brothers," said one of the warriors, as they slowly approached. After receiving a hearty welcome and paying proper homage to Abdi, all were invited to a meal of meat, bread, and cool spring water.

"Come and sit. Tell us why you are here. Is all well in our homeland?" asked Abdi. The men settled themselves around the campfire, a good distance from the roasting meal. All hunters and warriors knew that the smell of food could be fatal where predators roamed, especially if the smell of smoke from the meat lingered on their clothes.

"I am Elias, and my brothers are Ezera and Gedeyon. Our journey was long, and our homeland is in trouble," explained Elias.

"What do you mean trouble?" asked Abdi. The warriors took meat and bread as they told their stories of strange animals and beings of massive size that looked human but were not.

"They are moving into our lands. There are many unexplained deaths, and our people have grown very frightened. From what we have seen, even lions are no match for these beasts. For this reason, we have come for you. It is time for King Marwari to return with us, to rid us of this evil," said Elias.

"Have you seen these beasts or human-like beings?" asked Bruk.

"I saw the beings but not the animals," said Elias.

"And I saw the animals but not the beings," Gedeyon chimed in.

"It seems that they can hide themselves at will," said Ezera.

"We have told you what we know. We do not know more, except..." Elias paused to take a deep breath.

"Except what?" asked Caleb.

Elias continued, "I think one of them followed us."

"What makes you think that?" queried Lire.

"Because I could feel something watching, following, tracking us the moment we entered this land. I felt it once or twice in our country, but more so when we entered this land of the Great Falls," explained Elias.

"What do you suppose it wants?" asked Bruk.

"I do not know," said Elias.

"It is as Jedidiah has spoken. There are demonic forces in this land, and they control these beasts. I believe they catch the scent of the first human they encounter and pursue it until they capture it. Much like a cheetah that picks out its prey and runs it down," said Abdi. "Jedidiah also said that there are many different kinds of beasts in this land that are more dangerous than bostis." The words from Abdi unsettled the men.

"Are you telling us that other beasts besides this one could be after us?" inquired Gedeyon.

"Yes, my son."

"Like what?" asked Lire, staring at his father.

"There are at least three that I know. The Trianthropos, which many call human-like beings, can control all evil beast and birds. Then there is the Deathmus, which is an uncontrollable creature that creates chaos wherever it goes. The only thing that can control a Deathmus is the Trianthropos. And of course, you know about the bosti, which are pure evil and speak in human tongue.

The warriors took hold of their weapons. "It's like the beasts in the cave. They see us like meat," exclaimed Caleb.

"Yes, and they are looking forward to the appointed time, the beast called it a day of war—when beasts think like men and usher in a time of horrific, destructive conflicts," said Matt, running his fingers through his hair.

"If that is the case, we had better watch and pray that we stay alert so that no harm happens here tonight," said Bruk. The men looked at each other. It was not the first time they faced war, but to face beasts that could think like men and strange creatures appearing as humans was a bit much, even for experienced Pia Warriors.

"I think it is time for us to get rest. Enough of this talk. You will need your strength for tomorrow's journey," Abdi reminded them. The warriors agreed and sought a place of rest. "Make sure that you sleep with your weapons in your hand and stay close to the fire. I prefer seeing you all alive in the morning." Abdi meant it as a witticism, but no one laughed. Each man took his place and did as Abdi told them.

Elias pulled Abdi aside. "My lord, your presence is needed at home. The king has been away too long, and now you are here as well. Our people need you both, especially with this new threat that seems to be invading our land."

"Your concern is noted, Elias. I will inform the king. Meanwhile, you and your brothers will go back and prepare our people for this evil force that seems to be everywhere. I will give you a sealed order tomorrow for the governor. You will inform him to carry out these orders immediately. Now you take the first watch, and in the morning, you and your brothers will be on your way."

"Yes, my lord."

So, Elias stood watch as the others slept. He kept a sharp eye, looking back and forth, listening for the slightest movement and hoping for an early sunrise. Within the hour, his body grew tired, and sleep began to overtake him. Resting against a stone, his head dropped in slumber, and the fire died down to sparks and smoke.

It was only for a moment that he dozed, but it was long enough for a creature in the shadows to come out. Stealthily, it moved towards the dozing warrior. By the time the warrior snapped out of his doze, it was too late. The beast snatched him up in its mouth. Cries from Elias awakened the others. They ran towards the horror of a comrade being eaten by a beast twice the size of a bosti. It stood up on two of its four huge legs and roared with an indescribable sound.

"What is that?" shouted Lire, grabbing his bow.

"I don't know, but it's got Elias," screamed Bruk.

Elias was brave to the end. Even while in the mouth of the creature, the warrior fought the beast, stabbing it with a short dagger that finally pierced its hide.

"Hang on, Elias," yelled Abdi, hurling his spear towards the heart of the beast. As Abdi's spear sank into the heart of the beast, it raised its head and dropped Elias to the ground. The spear was deep in the beast's body, but it was far from dead. It reached down to grab the body of the dying warrior with what looked like iron claws, but before it could grasp Elias, Gedeyon rammed his massive body into the beast, pushing Abdi's spear deeper into its flesh. The beast stumbled back, then tried to escape.

Matt jumped on the back of the beast and tried to wrap his arms around its neck, but it was too massive. With powerful hands, he took hold of the beast's protruding horns and gave an abrupt yank. The beast released a loud blast from its middle horn, startling Matt. Continuing to hold on to the horns, he broke its neck with one powerful twist. The deathmus dropped to the ground, next to the warrior's body.

"Where did that thing come from?" asked Caleb, holding his sword tightly.

"It is as we feared. The beast has been following us since we entered the Falls," said Gedeyon, looking at his brother lying beside the dead beast. A low moan came from Elias.

"He's alive, he's alive!" shouted Ezera.

"Help him! Somebody, help my brother," bellowed Gedeyon, barely holding back tears. Abdi grabbed his bag and took a vial of ointment he had gotten from the old seer and began to apply it to the wounded warrior's body.

"I pray that this will help. There is little else we can do. It is up to the Lord to intervene," said. Abdi. "But if there is one of these things out there, you can be certain there are others."

"I think they travel in packs, and this one seems to be a scout," interrupted Bruk.

"I believe that it is a scout, but I don't think they run in packs," responded Caleb.

"Is this the animal you were speaking of?" Abdi asked.

"It resembles the animal, except for the horns. I don't know what the devil that thing is ... maybe some of them do have horns," said Ezera.

"How is Elias doing?" asked Gedeyon, deeply concerned for his brother.

"I don't know, son. By the grace of God, I think he'll make it."

"Do you really think they travel in packs, these creatures?" asked Lire.

Before Abdi could answer, each warrior could feel a malevolent presence surrounding them.

"They are here. Take your positions and stand your ground. If it's a fight they want, they have come to the right place," Abdi said, clenching the sword in his hand. "We are Pia Warriors. Make sure you fight like one or be meat for these beasts."

7

THE FIGHT

IN THE DISTANCE, THE MEN COULD HEAR THE SOUNDS OF creatures quickly approaching. Concern was on every man's face.

"Does anyone have an idea how many are coming?" asked Caleb.

Glancing in Caleb's direction, Abdi said, "Just be alert, boy. You won't die today."

"What do you think they are?" asked Lire, taking his position.

Sighing with impatience, Abdi answered, "I'm not sure. We will know when they get here."

"I hope to God they're not those deathmus things," said Caleb.

"Be quiet, you two, and focus," Abdi sternly warned. It didn't matter to Abdi what they were fighting. He had given the order, and every warrior was ready to do battle.

To the horror of all, emerging from the woods came a pack of bostis. They came in all sizes—some twice the size of lions with piercing eyes. Others were the size of long-forgotten, savage sabretooth tigers. A familiar voice spoke from the dark woods.

"I have returned to kill you, human, and the puny lot you call warriors. I will avenge the blood of my brothers whom you have slain. We heard the sound of our leader's great horn that called us to this place. After you are destroyed, the name of Abrus will be feared among humans," said the large bosti.

"I can't believe that thing is actually talking, and I can actually understand it," exclaimed Lire.

Matt remembered those words from the creature in the ravine. "You should have escaped while you had the chance," said Matt, kicking aside the carcass of the dead deathmus and stepping forward.

"Taunt us as you will, but in a moment, you will feel my fangs crushing your throat."

No man answered or moved from his position. Abdi had given the command to stand firm in faith, and so they did. When the beast understood that his words had little to no effect on the warriors, Abrus roared, inciting all the bostis to attack. The men could feel the vibration of the roar all around them. The bostis started moving in, each roaring in sync with Abrus, creating instability in the rocks and underground sinkholes. Such roaring became more and more intolerable as the beasts moved in from every side. The men still stood their ground and readied themselves for the battle of their lives.

Precipitously, Abrus jumped from the shadows and landed a few feet from Matt. Clutching his spear, Matt hurled it at the head of the beast but missed as the bosti moved its head with snakelike quickness. Abrus came close enough to Matt's face that he could smell its foul breath. He jumped back to regain his focus, but the beast quickly reached him. Matt had never encountered such tenacity from an animal.

"Look out, Matt," yelled Bruk.

"Doesn't he know that those things are possessed and trained by demons?" shouted Caleb.

"He will if Big Teeth takes a bite out of him," Lire said facetiously.

Matt stood, watching for the bosti's next move.

"Don't just stand there, Bruk," yelled Abdi. "Throw that thing!"

Bruk threw his spear with precision, striking Abrus in the neck. Letting out a loud, painful roar, the bosti used its claws to tear the spear from its neck and broke it in half. Seconds later, it was pursuing Matt once again. The eyes of the warriors perused the beasts around them. Matt was fighting hard, when abruptly from the woods emerged another vast influx of raging beasts.

"My God, help us. Here come more big teeth!" cried Lire.

"The Lord helps those who help themselves, boy. I suggest you fight while you pray," shouted Abdi.

Lire aimed his bow, and with perfect precision, he shot multiple arrows, hitting every mark—the heart, the eye, the throat, and the head. Lire was sure of his hits, but to his dismay, the creatures kept coming. Something was wrong. Every warrior engaged in the vicious battle; the beasts charged in, overtaking the campsite. It looked hopeless. Caleb's arms were tiring, and two bostis had him trapped in a corner against a huge stone.

Suddenly, they all realized that fighting these creatures called for a different strategy. If the demons were sustaining the beasts, then the Lord was going to have to intervene. Abdi observing the entire scene, prayed, as did they all.

"Father, help us. Lend us your strength and skill to fight this diabolical foe." Even as he prayed, he never gave up. Abdi, his sons, and the other two Pia Warriors fought valiantly until their bodies were exhausted.

"Matt!" A familiar voice came to Matt's mind.

"Yes, Lord, here I am," he said.

"Be courageous and let your faith guide you. Remember that you are not alone."

Matt stood before the large bosti from the ravine, ready to fight, but he had no weapon in hand. "Come on. I'll give your carcass to the buzzards," he shouted.

The beast leaped forward and lowered its head to devour Matt, but it was met with a powerful fist to the head, sending it staggering back. Confused by the powerful blow that it received from the puny human, Abrus became more enraged with blood lust. The beast was not giving up its prey. Studying Matt, it slowly circled him.

"Feeble human, you will only serve as a morsel to the pack," said Abrus.

"Feeble? I'll have you know that my wife considers me a fine specimen of a man," Matt said, running his fingers through his hair.

"You mock me now, human, but your next breath will be your last," grunted the beast.

Abrus pursued Matt, attempting to satisfy its fury and insatiable craving for human blood. Matt tore a limb from a nearby tree and stood, waiting for the attack. Within seconds, Abrus was inches from Matt's face, sinking its teeth into the tree limb, trying to rip it from Matt's hands. Matt saw deep hollow darkness in the black eyes of the beast. Eerie chills ran down his back.

What are we dealing with? he asked himself.

The limb began to break under the pressure of the beast's teeth. Matt, knowing he had limited time to act, pulled the beast in close, grabbing its neck tightly. Abrus let go of the limb and went for Matt's head. Teeth inches away from his face, Matt kneed the creature hard under its jaw. The beast screamed in pain, dazed by the blow. Matt immediately grabbed Abrus' front left leg and ripped it off. He then jumped on the bosti and drove his fist into the back of its head. The sound of cracking bones could be heard. Abrus laid motionless. Matt exhausted, took a deep breath, and turned his attention to the other warriors.

The Pia Warriors were beyond exhaustion. They had been fighting for over two hours, but it felt much longer.

"Stop playing around with those things and kill them," came the stern voice of Abdi to Lire and Caleb as he pulled his spear from a beast. All the men heeded the command and focused on finishing off the diabolical creatures. Caleb thrust his sword through the neck of the beast he was fighting, while Lire brought down his blade on the back of another, cutting through muscle and spine. The other two warriors, Gedeyon and Ezera, had just killed bostis that left them with deep claw marks and bruised bones.

"Do you see how large these beasts are?" exclaimed Bruk.

"Yes," replied both Gedeyon and Ezera.

Matt could hear the trembling sounds from Abrus as the beast exhaled its last breath.

Abdi, scanning the campsite, said, "It looks like we killed all the beasts." Everyone took a deep breath, assuming the battle was over. The death of Abrus brought relief to Matt's exhausted body. He was glad they won the fight.

However, the moment of victory soon vanished. An uneasy feeling churned in Matt's stomach as he sensed an ominous presence. In the distance, he heard a loud shrilling sound, indicating more bostis were coming. Out of his peripheral vision, Matt saw two small bostis coming towards him. Gedeyon ran towards Matt, intercepting one of the bostis, slammed it to the ground, and ran his sword through its chest. Matt threw the other beast down, pinning its body to the ground while Gedeyon kicked it in the head, breaking its neck.

"Thanks, Gedeyon," Matt said, getting up from the beast. Smiling, Gedeyon nodded.

Surveying the destroyed area, Matt noticed a sapphire jewel behind the right ear of the deathmus. "What is that?" Matt asked curiously. His words caught everyone's attention; they moved closer for a better look at the deathmus. However, just before Matt grabbed for the jewel, a shrieking sound was heard in the distance.

"Sounds like more bostis are on their way here," said Caleb.

"What do we do?" Lire asked, troubled by the thought of facing more bostis.

Matt seemed unfazed by the commotion of the warriors. Studying the jewel, Matt reached down for it, but it suddenly vanished, as did the shrieks.

"What happened? I don't hear any shrieking noises anymore," Caleb said.

"Yes, you're right." Relief filled Lire's face.

Abdi, still on guard, studied Matt and the spot where the jewel abruptly vanished. "I'm guessing that's how the Trianthropos control the deathmus and the bostis," Abdi said.

"What?" everyone asked simultaneously.

"That jewel was inserted into the deathmus' ear as a control element. I'm certain that's how we were bombarded with an overwhelming amount of bostis. But then the bosti suddenly vanished when Matt almost touched that jewel," Abdi said. Silence ensued; everyone was thinking about the horrors to come. Breaking the silence, Abdi said, "No need for concern. Those bostis won't be back tonight. You boys clean this place up, and I'll check on Elias."

"Let's just pray we don't see any more of those things for a while," Matt said to Lire while they cleaned the campsite.

"I sure hope Father is right because I could use the rest," sighed Lire, only half joking.

8

Visit to the Great Falls

Patience was anxious to find Matt. Even though her mom and grandmother had explained that Matt was with the Pia Warriors, she decided to have Girma, one of three large catlians, take her to him. Girma had knowledge of almost everything within the earthly realm.

Walking down the Great Hall, she came to the rug in the middle of the hallway and called to him in her mind. Girma immediately emerged from the large rug. He was one of the largest beasts within the walls of the Treasure Tree and looked even larger than she remembered.

"Oh, my word, look at you," she said, wrapping her arms around his neck, as far as they would reach. "Where are the others?"

"They are on assignments for the Creator," explained Girma.

"When you see them, tell them I miss our times together," she stated, reminiscing on the years she spent with them as she grew up.

"It has been a while since you and I last engaged in conversation," said Girma.

"I know. It's my fault, and I must apologize. I have been so busy and taken with my husband that everything else has been neglected. Please forgive me."

"There is no need to forgive or apologize, little one," he said.

"Tell me how things have been with you. I have missed you."

"You have conveyed that sentiment, Princess."

"Yes, I have, and I must remember that you are one of few words," she laughed. "I am looking for Matt, my husband. Can you help me find him?"

"He is not lost, little one. He is engaged in a most important undertaking for the kings, your father, and grandfather and shouldn't be disturbed."

"Yes, I know, but I want to find him to settle things in my own mind regarding his safety. Will you help me?" she pleaded.

"It has been well established, little one, from past experiences, that if I do not help you, you will take it upon yourself to accomplish the task alone. And since I am your guardian and cannot allow harm to come to you, it is in the best interest of all that I escort you," Girma proudly stated.

"I'll take that as a yes," she smiled with relief.

"Of course, you know that if I am asked by the kings where you are, I will answer them accordingly."

Patience nodded. "I understand, but I hope to be back in one day, two at the most. I will leave a message for Mom and Moa," she said.

"They will know, little one, without a message. Discernment is part of a faith walker's gifts. They are blessed of God."

"Thank you for reminding me," she giggled.

"Are you ready, Princess?" he asked. Without delay, Patience prepared herself as Girma wrapped his appendages around her waist and lifted her up and placed her on his back.

"I am so glad that you are my protector. Of course, you know that Matt is also my protector," she said teasingly.

"He is a delightful young man, one well suited for you, Princess. Between the two of us, we should be able to keep you safe and out of trouble."

"If I didn't know better, I would suspect teasing in your voice, Girma." She laid her head facedown and hugged the large animal with affection.

"It is the will of the Creator that all of His children are protected. As careless as your species is, I am amazed that humans ever reach adulthood." Patience laughed. She knew that he was right. "You and your family are my charges. All humans need guardians, and those who ask God for help, find us near them. It has always been my honor to serve the Creator. King Jedidiah decreed by the word of the Lord that you and your husband would be caretakers of the Great Tree."

"What does that mean?" asked Patience.

"That you both are part of His commission to take care of Truevine and its people. You and Matt will bring the Lord great honor by showing others how to serve. Now shall we go, Princess?"

Patience couldn't help smiling, pondering on all that Girma said. "Yes, indeed, you are my brave protector," she giggled. And together, they took off, diving straight into the rug. In a matter of seconds, she was standing in the forest of the Great Falls.

"Well, Girma, where do you think he is?" she said with excitement in her voice.

"He is with seven Pia Warriors."

"Yes, I know. Mom and Moa told me. They are from the land of my father, and Matt is training with them. Is Matt well?" she asked, concerned.

"He is well, Princess. Would you like to see him?"

"Yes, of course, but I don't want anyone to see us." Girma acknowledged that with a nod, then with lightning speed, Patience found herself hovering above Matt and the seven warriors. Girma's ability to camouflage kept Patience and himself from being seen. "I haven't been away from him a whole day, and I miss him terribly!"

"I believe that is called love, Princess," Girma snorted.

"So, you find my inability to stay away from him amusing, do you?"

"Not at all, Princess. It just reminded me of your mother and father and those before them. All humans who find love seem to react the same way."

"You mean, senseless?" Girma remained silent and allowed Patience to ponder on her own assessment. "Ok, I get it," she said, smiling. "Put me down over there to the right of that clearing. It looks like their campsite." Girma landed away from the campsite in a place where Patience could not be seen. "Girma, stay here while I go in closer to hear what's going on."

"Why don't you use your spiritual discernment? You can quickly ascertain their intentions by reading their thoughts," he said.

"I think Matt may take that as an invasion of privacy. Besides, I still need practice," she conveyed, sliding down from his back. "I don't want Matt to know that I'm here. He is in training, and I don't want to interfere." She looked at Girma and knew she was contradicting herself. "But I'm here, right?" She paused. "Because I really want to see him. I didn't get a chance to say good-bye before he was taken away," she voiced justifiably.

"Go find your young man, and I will wait for you here. However, you should know that time shifts with Matt's training. He has been away from you far longer than a day," Girma said.

"How long?" she asked.

"About two weeks," he answered. Patience grimaced. "Remember, little one, time is of very little importance to your grandfather." Patience wasted no time in moving through the brush leading to the camp. As she halted at the edge of the site, Matt and the other seven men entered the camp area.

It was midday, and Abdi and his warriors were still tired from the previous night of fighting the beasts. "I know you boys are still recovering, but we need to evaluate our situation and prepare for training. You have fought well, Matt," stated Abdi with a slight curve to his mouth. "From the first encounter with us, you have shown great courage and strength of character. When arrows and spears attempted to kill you, you did not seek to kill but instead sought to explain. Even when you fell into the ravine and fought the beast, you did not panic or complain about your predicament. You have shown yourself to be a formidable opponent, and it is evident that you have been trained by a master warrior."

"I was not alone in the fight, sir," Matt interrupted, meaning no disrespect. Embarrassed, he fell silent while

Abdi continued to address him. The other warriors remained silent as well, watching and listening to the words transpiring between their father and Matt. Abdi motioned for them to sit on the ground while he continued.

Matt's suspicion of the warriors waned in the aftermath of the battle. Though still cautious, he called the men who fought beside him brothers. From Jedidiah, he had learned to read people and knew much of what was in their hearts. Without question, they were loyal; however, he could sense conflicting emotions among them. He also had conflicting questions and needed answers.

Lord, is it the life of a warrior you want for me or that of a grower? I love my new home and tending Truevine's land. How am I to have a warrior's life and still work in the fields? Nevertheless, I belong to you, Lord, and in whatever direction you send me, I will be content, he prayed as he continued listening to Abdi.

Abdi, observing the weariness of the warriors, cleared his throat and addressed them with encouragement. "Let me say that I am proud to be your father and leader. All of you boys were amazing. I pray that we never encounter that kind of attack again; however, in this place, we probably will. I must say I've never seen Caleb and Lire move that quickly." They all laughed.

"Yes, I was surprised to see how well we all came through that crazy battle," expressed Bruk.

"I have to agree with Father. Our grower warrior handled himself very well," chimed in Lire.

"I didn't realize how strong you were until you jumped on that thing's neck and started wrestling it," said Bruk, laughing.

"God has given you strength and endurance that warriors only dream about," reflected Lire.

"I, for one, am glad you were there; otherwise, I'd be in the belly of that beast," said Elias, still in pain from the deep wounds inflicted by the deathmus.

Matt was embarrassed to hear words of gratitude pouring out of the mouths of his new brothers. "We were all in this together. It was the Lord and teamwork that saved us," Matt conveyed sincerely.

"I know that it was the Lord who fought for us, but He used you to inspire us," voiced Abdi. All but Caleb stood and gave accolades to Matt with raised wooden mugs and pats on the back.

"To our great grower Pia Warrior," said Lire, laughing and slapping Matt hard on the back again. In agreement, everyone raised their mugs again.

Matt noticed Caleb's reclusive demeanor and started towards him but stopped when he saw Bruk approaching Caleb. Bruk, like Matt, also had noticed a change in Caleb's behavior.

"What's going on, Caleb?" Bruk asked.

"What do you mean?"

"You know what I mean. Everybody's celebrating, except you. We have just won a great victory. You ought to be thanking God for the victory and for sending Matt as a new brother."

"I know," responded Caleb.

"Then why are you dragging around like you've been kicked in the gut?"

"Sorry, Bruk. Guess I have a lot on my mind."

"Does it have to do with Matt?"

"Yes, it does," Caleb admitted.

"Then why don't you talk to him about it?"

"I think it's best if I leave it between the Lord and me," said Caleb, rubbing the back of his neck. "That's fine, but don't let it sit in your mind too long. What you ponder about has a way of controlling your actions," voiced Bruk.

"You're right. Even though I can't talk about it now, I would appreciate your prayers on the matter."

"You know I'll be praying. What say we join the others?" Bruk didn't wait for an answer. He wrapped his arm around Caleb's neck and dragged him into the circle of warriors.

****

The day wore on, and the men regained much of their energy and readied themselves for what laid ahead. "Come and gather around, I have something to say that will impact our people," Abdi told the men. Bruk led the way and took a seat on a nearby log, joined by Caleb. Matt and the others stood near while Elias continued to rest. Abdi turned to address Ezera and Gedeyon about their departure. "In a few days, you are to return to our homeland and carry out my orders. It will give the kings time to arrive and Elias the time needed to recover. King Jedidiah is a great seer. He will have great insight. I have a feeling that these beasts are spreading like a plague throughout the lands."

****

From her hiding place, Patience scanned the campsite and saw the damage as well as an injured Pia Warrior. It appeared no one else was severely injured, for which she was thankful. Abdi's words of a coming war gave her great concern. She wanted to rush out and greet them all. It had been such a long time since she had last seen her kinsmen. However, she restrained her emotions and watched them continue cleaning the camp. She then returned to where Girma was waiting.

"So, did you see your husband?" he asked, knowing by her emotions that she had.

"I did, I did. It was also delightful seeing Uncle Abdi and the boys. I have missed them so," she said excitedly. "Please leave me and come back tomorrow to pick me up."

"Are you sure that you want to go gallivanting through these woods unprotected?" he asked, concerned.

"I'm sure. I have my weapons with me, and it's only for a day. What can happen in a day?"

Girma noticed Patience's eagerness and knew it was futile to argue with her. After all, she had free will. "I shall be back before the sun rises," he said reluctantly. She kissed him on the head as he departed. Like lightning flashing in the sky, he was gone.

"Well, girl, you best be getting to it," she told herself. Patience planned to signal Matt by using the mocking bird call she had learned from the happy little mocking bird, Bree, who sat on the perch of her window each morning. She had perfected many bird calls, but this one between her and Matt was special. Only he would know it was her.

The camp was clean, and evening was approaching quickly. Suddenly Matt heard the sweet sound of a bird call in the night air. "Patience?" A smile crossed his face.

Abdi started walking toward Matt to discuss tomorrow's training but noticed the change in his demeanor and decided it could wait till morning.

Matt saw him approaching and wondered why he decided to turn around. He heard the senior warrior say loudly enough for all to hear, "I think it is time for us to retire to our tents, boys. We have a lot of training in the morning, and we will need our rest to accomplish the task before us. Goodnight."

Within twenty minutes, every man was tucked away in their tents, and Matt found it hard to sleep. His hometown, Columbidae, was on his mind again, and so was Patience. Just as he turned his thoughts to prayer, he heard the sweet sound of a bird call again. He sat up and waited. There it was again.

Without so much as stirring a leaf, Matt got out of his tent and moved towards the sound of the call. Two hundred yards away from camp, he walked softly towards the beautiful sound. Then he stopped. He closed his eyes and breathed deeply. There it was—he caught the scent of her through the gentle breeze that came his way. Looking up, he spotted her seated on a tree limb. With one jump, he sprung up towards her and landed next to her. She was amazed at his agility. Without a word, he took her hand and then gathered her into his arms and kissed her, as if he had been away from her for a thousand years.

"Wow. I like the way you kiss me," she said affectionately.

"I have missed you, my love, but you know that it was not my idea to leave," Matt quickly explained.

"I know, my husband. Let's not talk about nonessentials right now. Just kiss me again like—" Before she could get the words out, Matt pressed his lips to hers.

The two of them enjoyed their time together immensely. By the time it was almost daybreak, Matt knew that he had to return and get rest, or he would not be ready for training.

"Sorry, my darling. I must return, as do you. I'm sure that by now your mother is looking for you," Matt said, kissing Patience's hands.

"Yes, I suppose you're right. Both of them are probably looking for me. Most likely, they know where I am," Patience said, blushing.

"I'll see you when I get back, Lord willing," he said as he hugged and kissed her again. Then with a powerful jump, he landed softly on the ground. In a blink of an eye, Matt was back in camp. As he laid his head down on his sleeping gear, he suddenly heard a loud familiar roar.

"What the heck was that?" asked Lire.

"It sounds like a bosti to me," shouted Bruk.

"Smells like one too," chimed in Lire.

The sound had come from the direction where Matt left Patience. The terrifying scream of a woman sent Matt running back as fast as he could to his beloved. When he arrived, Patience was nowhere to be found. He yelled her name loud enough for the entire forest to hear, but there was no sound or sight of her. Matt looked in the tree where they had met and saw signs of a struggle. Blood dripped down the large tree.

He was so distraught over her that he thought he would lose his mind. Then, he heard the sound of a bird call in the distance. Unmistakably, it was her, singing to let him know that she was safe. "Thank God," said Matt, relieved.

The others arrived with torches, looking for signs of the kill. They knew that the beast had seized some poor woman and had torn her apart. When Matt search around the tree, he was surprised to see the remains of a bosti shredded to pieces. Portions of it hung from the tree, and other parts were scattered on the ground.

"What could have done such a thing to a bosti of this size?' asked Bruk.

"I don't know, but it had to be more powerful than 20 of those things," said Caleb.

"I have heard of such a beast. They walk in both worlds," Abdi said, keeping his eyes open in all directions.

"Really? Another beast? What do you mean they walk in both worlds?" Matt asked.

"It is said that neither angels nor demons have the power to subdue them when they are called out to do God's bidding."

"Do you believe that such creatures exist?" asked Matt, still concerned about Patience.

"Whatever did this to that bosti is a friend of mine," said Lire, breaking the mood with levity.

"Let's return to camp. We still have a full day's training ahead of us," Abdi reminded the men as he led the way back to the camp.

Matt couldn't stop thinking about Patience and the blood-curdling scream. The last sounds of Patience's sweet bird call gave hope and assurance to his heart. As they were walking back, Caleb asked Matt who he was calling when they heard the scream. Of course, Matt played it off with silence, hoping no one else would ask questions regarding his sudden outburst.

****

"Thank you, Girma! That bosti caught me completely off guard." Patience sat snuggly on Girma's back, secured by his appendages to prevent her from falling. They flew over the campsite to capture one last glimpse of her beloved before heading home. "I hadn't seen one of those things since I was a girl. I don't think I've ever seen one that large before. It was frightening then, and even more so now." She thought for a moment. "No, I don't remember them being that huge. If you had not been here, I fear to think of what would have happened," Patience said, patting Girma's head.

"I heard your heart before you screamed," replied Girma.

"I'm so thankful that you did. You put yourself between me and that beast. I saw it strike you several times before you destroyed it. It was trying to get to me, wasn't it?"

"Yes, Princess."

"But why?'

"Because you are human and of the royal family. The bostis are evil animals, and some are controlled by demon spirits. That one had a legion in it. It was bent on destroying you and any other human it encountered. They have been here since Nimrod, son of Cush, invaded King Bosti's domain and slaughtered his people. As you know, Nimrod was a mighty warrior like your father, only he did evil to a people that meant him no harm. Before King Bosti breathed his last breath, he put a curse on Nimrod's descendant by calling on demons from the darkest place in hell to avenge him. However, he did not count on demons invading wild beasts and turning them into savage human hunters. The animals craved human blood. Not just Nimrod's descendants, but all humans—even the ones who serve the evil prince of this world. Thus, the animals were named after

King Bosti for the curse he placed on the people of Nimrod."

Patience was shocked by Girma's explanation. "And so, they are still killing humans because of a generational curse?" Patience inquired.

"It would seem so," Girma replied.

"That is not possible, according to the Holy Book. It is my understanding that our Lord paid the price for all humans when He went to the cross."

"That is correct, Princess, and all authority has been given to Him, but not all demonic activity has been brought under control," said Girma.

"That is true," she said sadly.

"Be of good cheer, Patience. The Lord has overcome all evil and will soon subdue even the devil," Girma said with a voice of confidence. "But until it happens, we must stay our course and do our part in this fallen world. Presently, my first duty is to make sure that you are safe. You and your family are a priority. It is a command that I have been given."

"I was terrified at the thought of you being harmed," she stated. Below, Girma spotted the perfect clearing, where they could catch a few hours of sleep before morning. "Why are we stopping, Girma?" Patience asked, confused.

"To allow you time to rest before your mother and grandmother interrogate you," Girma said, amused.

"Girma!" Patience exclaimed. Girma heard surprise in her voice and decided to explain.

"You have experienced much in the Great Falls, and you need time to rest." After landing, he laid down to give Patience a place to rest. She crawled next to his large body and rested her head against him. "Princess, there is never a reason for you to worry about me. Have you ever known me to be harmed by any creature?" he asked.

"No, I can't say that I have."

"The Creator has made my kind in a way that no living creatures can harm us. Everything that exists belongs to God. He decides our destiny. That is His right as the Creator and our privilege as guardians." Patience listened with great care, enjoying the words of an old friend who had proven to be faithful to her family for many years. She settled herself, and sleep swept over her the moment she closed her eyes.

****

Morning came, and standing in front of Patience's wedding chamber were three women—her mother, grandmother, and one woman she hadn't seen for almost five years.

"Shall I knock, or will you?" Heather asked Moa.

"We all know that she isn't in there, so why bother?" retorted the beautiful young woman.

"Layla, my dear, things are not always as they appear. For instance, your aunt Heather and I are aware that Patience isn't in her room," said Pricilla.

"You are? Then why come here to look for her?" asked the young woman.

"We came here for your benefit, dear," stated Heather.

"I'm sorry, but I don't understand. What do you mean for my benefit?"

"Please come in, and we will talk with you," explained Pricilla. Halfheartedly and with an inkling of what was about to happen, Layla entered the wedding chamber. Before she could speak, Heather started.

"My dear, it has been nearly ten years since your mother went into the arms of our Lord. I miss her very much, and I know the void in your heart is still empty. Moa and I have great concern for our family, particularly when one of them is troubled." Layla said nothing but continued to listen to Heather with interest.

"You are the only girl among four men just as Patience has three brothers, but she is eldest among them. You, my dear, have brothers older than you and not just any brothers, but Pia Warriors. Much of your last ten years were spent with Steven and me because we loved you like a daughter, and we thought it best that you had access to your cousin Patience. The two of you are like sisters and have always been inseparable. So, when your mother passed, we decided, with Abdi's approval, to have you to spend more time with us." Heather studied Layla, unsure if the young woman was comprehending her words. The look on her face seemed odd, but she seemed to understand.

With a somber smile, Layla said, "I remember crying out to God, who my father said would hear my prayers. He said that God understood how much I loved and needed my mother. Well, it may have turned out best for some of you, but it was the worst day of my life. I trusted God, and He let me down. I love and respect you all, but I'll never trust God again," she said with tears, and the anger in her eyes told them that she was ready to explode.

Layla sat quietly, consumed by all she had heard. Pondering and sifting through a maze of feelings and emotions she thought had long subsided surprised her. She thought that she had dealt with those issues, but talking with her aunt and Moa proved her wrong. Everyone wanted her to believe in God, and she knew that she should, but her bitter, unforgiving heart prevented her from doing so.

Aware of Layla's strong will, Heather sighed and thought, *It definitely runs on Steven's side of the family.* Smiling, Heather continued to comfort Layla while praying that God would soften her heart.

Taking a deep breath, Layla spoke softly, "I know that you are trying to explain why God took my mother, and I appreciate your kindness, but whatever you say won't bring her back."

Heather grabbed Layla's hands and gave a gentle squeeze. "Honey, I know that you have been hurting for a long time. Please forgive me for not spending more time helping you work through this." Fighting back tears, Layla nodded but still refused to be pushed towards God.

Seeing Layla's turmoil brought even more compassion from Moa. Her gentle voice and loving hands easily disarmed Layla. "Dear, Susanna was a wonderful witness for Christ—for your father, for your brothers, and for you, if you want it." Layla remained silent. "Susanna knew true love, and you, my dear, whether you want to embrace it or not, are part of your mother's love tapestry."

Somberly, Layla spoke. "Even if I am part of her tapestry, I'd much rather have her here, with me, than have her gone and miss her so much. Tapestries can't talk to you or hold you."

"I know this, dear. God is aware of our sorrows. Yes, He allows them to come; yes, He understands the pain and anguish we endure. He experienced them all when Jesus died," explained Moa.

"Yes, but He is God. He can handle that kind of tragedy," retorted Layla.

With one gentle pat on Layla's head, Moa sat next to her and, with her delicate hands of wisdom, gently took Layla's hand into her own. Moa remained silent, waiting for Layla's response. Taking a deep breath to calm her anger, Layla decided to speak.

"I was a child. He knew how much I needed my mother—to see her, hear her, and embrace her. I needed her to hold me and love me," she sobbed. Layla saw her tears fall to her lap. Surprisingly, there were already other tears she hadn't noticed. Tears from the eyes of two women who surrounded her and deeply loved her. "I don't understand how you could love a God who deliberately kills those who love Him," she continued sobbing. "I want no part of a god that, that..." The tears choked the words in her throat.

Heartbroken, the two women embraced her from both sides and quietly held her. Moa whispered in Layla's ear, "The Lord will call to you, my dear, and when He does, you must listen to Him." Moa kissed her head and became silent. Layla surprised herself by allowing them to hold her. "I think we all need a respite. How about a piece of my famous apple pie with buttery cinnamon sauce? If I recall correctly, it was one of your favorites," offered Moa with a smile.

Layla could never resist Moa's charm or apple pies even when she was in the worst of moods. Heather placed her hand on Layla's head and gently ran her hand down her curly black mane and bent over to kiss her on the head. Layla took hold of her arm and laid her head on it and allowed the atmosphere to clear.

"I'm going to slip down to the kitchen. You two, freshen up, and join me in a few minutes," voiced Moa, making her way towards the kitchen. After reaching the kitchen, Moa took from a beautiful handwoven basket a freshly baked pie. In a moment, she had placed three pieces of pie on fine royal decorated plates. Heather entered the kitchen with Layla still attached to her arm. The two of them sat while Moa served, and then Moa took her place next to Layla. The atmosphere became calm and lighthearted as the three of them sat quietly, sipping tea and eating pieces of Moa's delicious apple pie.

After a while, the three of them took a long walk through the Great Hall silently. Layla walked between them. High above them came a beautiful sound—it was Bree singing her heart out, sitting on top of one of the larger chandeliers in the hall.

"It's Patience's little mockingbird," said Heather.

"She sings beautifully," remarked Layla.

"Where do you suppose Patience is?" asked Layla, grabbing the last piece of pie from the basket Moa held.

"I know exactly where she is. She did the very same thing I would have done if I had been in her place," said Heather.

"And what might that be Aunt Heather?" questioned Layla.

"She went to find the love of her life."

"Does she know where he is?" probed Layla.

"No, but Girma does, and if I'm guessing right, she talked him into taking her."

Layla was not sure who Girma was, but she figured that if her aunt wanted her to know, she would tell her. "So, what do we do? Wait until she returns?" asked Layla.

"No, dear, you are going after her," said Moa. "She doesn't know it, but part of her training will take place right where she is."

Layla was excited about the prospect of seeing her cousin again.

9

When Cousins Meet

"Wake up, Princess. We are here." Girma hovered over a small hill of lush high grass.

"Girma, where are we?" inquired Patience. "This doesn't look like the way back to the Great Tree."

Within moments, she heard light laughter below. Looking down, she saw a beautiful, dark-haired woman observing two squirrels fighting over an acorn. Eyes widening, Patience recognized the woman as her longtime friend and cousin, Layla. Patience yelled out to her, and she looked up, surprised to see her best friend gliding down what appeared to be an invisible hill. Layla was awestruck.

"What in the world? Patience, is that you?" Layla asked, full of emotion. The two young women stopped within ten feet and began to intently eye each other. With each step, their demeanor became warlike though calm. Neither smiled but kept intense eyes on each other with every step. Suddenly, they both let out a war cry, and then a joyful scream followed as the women embraced. They stood, embracing each other, laughing, crying, and screaming before finally letting go. It was the way female Pia Warriors greeted each other. Patience and Layla learned the greeting exhibition from their mothers. It was the way their mothers greeted each other, and now the ritual belonged to the young women facing each other.

"When did you get here, and how long are you staying?" asked the young princess.

"I arrived just yesterday, and I will be staying for two weeks. Moa and Aunt Heather sent for me," she explained while hanging on to the young princess.

"Only two weeks? Surely you can stay longer than that?" protested Patience.

"After two weeks, you will pray that I leave, my sister."

"Whatever do you mean? I want you to stay for six months or a year," exclaimed Patience.

"Oh, no, you don't, not after what I have to tell you," emphasized Layla.

"And what's so terrible that I wouldn't want to have the pleasure of your company?" Patience asked, smiling.

"Training!" bellowed Layla.

"Training! That's all I've been hearing since Matt and I have been together. Just how much training is going on around here?" Patience sighed.

"More than you think. Right now, my father and brothers are training with your husband, whom I have yet to meet," Layla teased. "I am to assist Aunt Heather and Moa in preparing you for your next stage. But for now, it's just you and me."

"So, when is this training supposed to start?" asked Patience.

"How about now?" answered Layla.

"Now? Wouldn't you like to have a day or two to talk about old times?" voiced Patience.

"We'll have plenty of time to do that when we return to the Great Tree," Layla explained, taking Patience's arm.

"This is all moving too fast. Can we slow down a minute?"

"Oh, you are still so funny, Patience. How I missed our times together."

"That's what I'm talking about. We need time to unwind."

"Well, the way I see it, it is best to get it done!" insisted Layla.

"I suppose you're right, but shouldn't we pray about this?"

"You're stalling. What's wrong with you, and why the sad face?"

"I guess Matt is still on my mind," lamented Patience.

"I see. As soon as we get started, you won't have time to think about anything but completing your training." Layla gently pushed Patience toward the training ground. "By the way, do you mind telling me about how you got here? I did see you descending from the sky, didn't I?"

"Whatever do you mean?" Patience said, teasing her cousin. Layla just kept in step, looking puzzled for a moment, and then Patience burst into laughter. "Girma brought me," she said, watching her cousin's reaction. Layla looked in all directions trying to see what Patience was talking about. "You won't be able to see him, but trust me, he is real and huge. He has been my friend since childhood." Layla looked around again and saw nothing. Patience laughed again. "Why are you still looking? When he wants you to see him, you will."

"Why haven't I known about him before? We lived together for years and told each other everything."

"It was a command from Poppy. When I was five, he introduced me to Girma and told me that I was not to ever tell anyone about him—that is, until now."

"Why now?"

"I don't really know. I just know that it is alright to do so."

Layla shook her head and looped her arm around Patience's and walked forward towards the specified training area drawn on a map by Moa. Patience tightened her grip on Layla's arm, delighted that they were together. Memories of childhood flooded their minds. What thrilled Layla the most was that she never knew what Patience was going to do next. She was unpredictable, and following her usually ended up in an adventure. It was one of the great qualities Layla loved about her cousin.

"Are we almost there, Layla?" asked Patience, observing Layla's inattentiveness. Chuckling, Layla realized she had been consumed with her thoughts.

"Yes, we are here. It's just over that hill," Layla said, pointing to the nearby location. Patience smiled and quickly walked over. When she reached the designated area, she was surprised to see a few trees and a large semicircle of strange-looking rock formations protruding out of the ground. Layla said, "This is the appointed place. Moa told me that you were to put your hand on that rock in the middle, the one that has a strange color."

They both move towards the rocks as instructed. When Patience placed her hand on the multicolored rock, they suddenly found themselves in the middle of a forest.

"What is this place?" asked Layla.

"If I'm not mistaken, we're on the backside of the Great Falls," answered Patience.

"The Great Falls? What is that?" Layla asked in awe of the scenery.

Patience's demeanor became serious. She looked around, scanning the area for movement of any kind.

"What's wrong with you, girl? You're giving me the creeps," uttered Layla.

"That same smell is in the air," said Patience.

"What smell?"

"You don't smell that stench in the air?"

"Of course, I smell it, but what does that have to do with us?"

"It means that we are in a dangerous place. Bostis are in this region. That's why the stench is so heavy. They kill everything they see. They have this insatiable appetite for human flesh, especially for female Pia Warriors," Patience said, half-joking but with a serious tone. Layla poked her with the blunt end of her spear. "What's that for?"

"You know what it's for," Layla said, giggling. "The stench in the air is good."

"What's good about it?" inquired Patience.

"It will keep us alert while we train."

Patience couldn't help but laugh, "I see you haven't lost that strange sense of humor."

"Let me remind you, my inexperienced trainee, that you don't become a warrior by running from danger. As a matter of fact, real warriors run to danger," retorted Layla. Patience admired the courage her cousin displayed.

After setting up a small camp, the young women started their Pia Warrior training. The training was fast and rigorous. Layla insisted that they continue until Patience had perfected each technique of Pia warfare. Each day, Patience mastered more of Layla's training tasks, and she did them well. Layla was surprised how quickly the princess caught on and was even more surprised at how strong she had become. It was amazing how much endurance she had gained.

"Patience, what have you been eating? You've grown in strength, even though I can't see bulging muscles on those skinny bones." Patience laughed. "I think that we are ready to join the others for the final training," Layla said with a smile.

"You mean it?" said Patience, smiling and laughing as one thought entered her mind. *I get to see Matt.*

"Let's pack up and go," said Layla.

"You don't have to tell me twice," answered Patience. "By the way, how long have we been training?"

"Oh, I'd say about three months."

"Three months! There's no way. It feels like, at most, a week," Patience said, amazed by the swiftness of time.

Layla placed a hand on Patience's shoulder. "Yes, but we are in the realm of the seers, and you know how time fluctuates with them."

"You're right. Matt and I both have been experiencing such fluctuations since our honeymoon. Still, it only feels like a few days," replied Patience.

Within the hour, they were on their way back to the appointed place. Upon reaching their destination, relief and laughter flooded Patience. She stood in front of a different rock formation similar to the one they saw before. This time there were black stones, and in the middle was another multicolored stone.

"What's so funny?" Layla asked.

"I was just thinking about all the times Poppy told me not to venture into the forest alone and to stay out of the small woods, but I was very curious."

Layla nodded at her cousin's response. "Evidently, he thinks you've grown enough to venture out."

"I suppose so," Patience giggled.

"Patience, I am so proud of you. You have mastered your bow and spear and hand-to-hand combat, including Moa's diamond technic with those long braids of yours. Your knowledge of finding your way in the woods is superb, I must say. Throughout our time in training, you never complained, not even once. I guess you've grown into that name of yours," she said teasingly.

Patience playfully pushed her. "Thank you, Layla. I have an excellent teacher, and I appreciate your fortitude and diligent spirit. I guess it's time to get back..." As Patience reached out to touch the colorful stone, they both heard a loud rumble coming through the forest. Patience knew that sound all too well. Girma had saved her from such a beast. She immediately touched the stone, and in seconds, they found themselves in the presence of Pricilla and Heather.

"What a joy to see you both," shouted Heather.

"Would you look at them? I think that training has transformed our little duckling into a warrior," said Moa.

"An excellent one at that Moa," confirmed Layla.

The women hugged and greeted each other with much affection. However, the reunion was short-lived due to the plans and tasks Moa and Heather had for the young women.

"Come with us, my daughters," said Heather.

"Where are we going?" asked Patience.

"You will see," remarked Moa.

"But I was hoping to see Matt, if only for a little while," pleaded Patience.

"You will, my dear, but first, there are other pressing matters we must address," Moa stated, watching her granddaughter's reaction.

"How many more matters will we have to address before I see Matt?" she asked curtly. Immediately, her heart convicted her of her impatience. "I'm sorry Moa, I just..."

"I know, dear. It is hard to control desire, especially when it's the right kind. But endure a little while longer, and you will see your desired outcome."

"Come with us," instructed Heather as she and Pricilla walked with the young women between them. In a moment, they came to a clearing. There stood Girma, waiting.

Suddenly, Patience heard Moa talking to Girma, but her lips weren't moving. Patience became alarmed until she realized she was hearing the conversation between them in her mind. Immediately, she understood how important this kind of communication would be in times of trouble or distance.

I wonder how far or close I would have to be to communicate with them, she thought to herself.

Distance makes no difference, dear. Faith is the key to this kind of communication. It is a higher degree of discernment, her mother mentally communicated.

Yes, you will be able to talk with many others as you train your mind to focus, interjected Moa.

More training? Patience mumbled to herself.

I heard that dear, giggled Heather as Patience laughed out loud.

Layla could tell something was going on between Patience, Moa, and her aunt. She said nothing but watched intently.

"Girma is waiting, girls," said Moa.

"Girma is here?" asked Layla.

"Of course, dear. Stand next to Patience, and you'll see him."

With reluctance, Layla did so. As Girma showed himself, Layla took a warrior's stance. "Whoa! What is that?" she asked, petrified at the sight.

"That is my friend Girma. Remember? I told you about him."

"Yeah, but you didn't say that he looked like that."

"I did too. I told you that he was huge."

"Yeah, but ... you didn't say that he was that big and ferocious-looking."

Girma was golden in color, the size of a mastodon. His eyes were silver with black oval pupils. His full black mane alone made his appearance frightening. His teeth were made for gripping and tearing flesh, fangs hung from his jaws, and his claws were long and curved. The fire he spewed from his mouth could not be extinguished until the object of destruction was gone.

"Come on, girl. Put your weapon away. Besides, weapons can't harm him."

Reluctantly, Layla put her weapon away but stayed close to Patience.

"We are ready, Girma," said Moa. Leather-like appendages from Girma reached out and gently wrapped around each woman and placed them on his back. As they sat, his appendages secured their legs and hips to keep them from falling during flight. Girma took to the air with ease, carrying the four travelers to their next destination.

10

Training Reunion

Landing just outside Abdi's camp, four beautifully-clad women approached. Joy filled Matt's and the Marwari men's hearts as they stood watching with delight.

"Well, hello! Welcome, welcome," came the strong voice of Abdi, smiling as they all came together. Suddenly, there was a rush of wind behind them. They turned and saw Jedidiah and Steven walking into the camp.

"Well, you two have impeccable timing," said Heather, smiling as she stood between Layla and Patience.

"I see that everyone is here." Jedidiah laughed and held his staff up, pointing it at his family. Patience ran toward Matt but was caught by her uncle Abdi. He swung her around and tossed her into the waiting arms of her cousins. The boys passed her around like she was a fresh melon.

"What a beauty you've turned out to be," said her Uncle Abdi.

"Yeah, look at her. She's grown into those arms and legs," said Bruk.

"I guess that's what married life will do to you!" yelled Lire, dodging her playful swing at his head.

Regaining her composure, Patience felt strong hands wrap around her waist. Immediately blushing, she teasingly withdrew, but Matt pulled her closer, whispering in her ear, "I missed you..." He gently kissed her earlobe, causing instant chills down Patience back. Embarrassed by the forwardness of a loving husband, she protested, "Matt! Then, relenting, she said, "I missed you too, my love. They are watching us, aren't they?" She continued to blush.

"You can say that," Matt voiced, holding Patience up and swinging her around for all to see. "I love this woman, I love this woman," he shouted, unashamedly with a teasing smile.

"Yeah, we can tell," chimed Lire, unable to hold in his laughter.

"I think you should put me down, Matt," she said, laughing. As her feet touched the ground, she heard a familiar voice.

"It looks like you two are enjoying your training," came the voice. Turning her head, she let go of Matt and ran towards two men waiting with open arms to receive her.

"Daddy, Poppy," she called, flinging herself into her father's arms. "I've missed you both so much."

"We've missed you too," said Steven as he wrapped his arms around his child.

Jedidiah tapped them both on the shoulder. "I expect the same attention young lady,"

"But of course, Poppy," she giggled. In one motion, she was in the old man's arms, receiving hugs and affection from the king himself. Matt, laughing at the joyous occasion, approached his new family.

Layla stood, watching the lively interaction between the people she loved. Without warning, Patience took her hand and dragged her over to Matt.

"Matt, this is Layla, my best friend and cousin. We grew up together. Our fathers are brothers, and our mothers are…" her sentence broke off.

Smiling, Layla finished the words Patience hesitated to say. "We are cousins, but we consider ourselves sisters—same as our mothers did," she said with a tone of sadness in her voice.

"Layla, I am delighted to meet you, and I am privileged to have a sister. I have heard so much about you and feel that I've known you forever," Matt said enthusiastically. Layla stood dumbfounded in front of the man addressing her. "Are you all right?" he asked. For a moment, nothing came out of her mouth. She just stood gawking at the man, evidently taken aback by his demeanor and handsome features.

"Wow, you got the whole treasure chest in this one," Layla whispered to Patience.

"I completely agree. I am a blessed woman; he is the love of my life," said Patience.

"As you are mine, my love," Matt said, unabashedly drawing her closer. The three of them decided to join the others. As they were walking, Layla grabbed Patience, locking arms with her. At that moment, she felt peace and wanted it to last forever.

The family reunion was amazing, and conversations of past and present echoed throughout the group.

"So, now that we are all here and seem to be finished with training, when do we leave to go home?" asked the excited Lire, thinking about laying his body in his own bed for a change. A still quietness filled the air as eyes focused on the youngest brother. Lire looked puzzled. "Did I say something wrong, forget to bathe, or do I just look funny?" Lire said, eyeing the group.

"No, little brother, you just forgot where you are and who you are with," said Caleb, giving a brief smile to ease Lire's tension.

"Think, Lire. Why would all of us come here if training was over? We would all be, as you say, going home if it was over," retorted Bruk.

"Well, hit me in the head with a rock. I don't plan these things," said Lire, making faces at Bruk.

"I understand, Lire," said Jedidiah, stepping forward. "Let me have everyone's attention. Lire is right. We should be heading home for rest and a good night's sleep. However, we have this last training task to perform because of the added danger we have encountered. Hopefully, this training will be brief since we are already skillfully gifted in warfare. This is the first real training that will engage both men and women. There are new enemies that we will be facing that are unfamiliar. At the end of this venture, you all will thank God you had this additional training. Immediately after this training, Elias, Gedeyon, and Ezera will travel back to their homeland and implement all they have learned. We need every realm to be ready for the war ahead. Any questions?" asked Jedidiah in a solemn voice.

There was a mixture of feelings among them. Jedidiah could tell that every warrior was ready to engage. He took a deep breath and continued his address. "After two days of intense instruction on the rules of engagement together, it is necessary for Pricilla and her daughters to separate in order to learn secret war strategies that belong only to women. In three days, we will rejoin and finish group training."

****

Moa and Heather took the women with them, while Poppy and Steven headed out in the opposite direction with the male warriors. All minds were clear and ready for training. Each warrior was alert to the myriad of possible dangers. The 12-hour days of non-stop training were grueling, but worth the outcome. Everyone engaged in every manner of conventional weaponry.

Heather and Pricilla had long mastered the training they were now teaching Patience, but they needed the Pia Warrior experience to perfect Patience's skills. Since Layla had trained with her father and brothers from childhood, she proved to be everything Heather and Pricilla anticipated in training Patience. What none of them expected was the short span of time it took Patience to learn and master her instructions. Patience even surprised herself at how quickly she comprehended her new skills.

"It has taken her only a day to learn all the techniques. Tomorrow, God willing, she will master them," acknowledged Heather.

"Yes, such a feat had never been done before. I think she'll do just fine," Moa said, smiling.

****

The second day of training with Layla helped Patience tremendously. Everyone perceived that it was the Lord's wisdom that enhanced Patience's comprehension. Layla was astonished at how Patience had become so aggressive in her fighting skills and intellectually astute in warfare tactics, yet gentle in her demeanor and in caring for people. It was unheard of—no one could accomplish what she did without great assistance.

"It is the Spirit who intercedes for you, my child. His anointing in this area has fallen on you," recognized Moa. Layla was not surprised by the explanation, but she dismissed it as she had done with everything else pertaining to God. However, it was the only reasonable conclusion.

The three women looked at Patience and smiled. Moa whispered again, "It is the presence of the Lord King who works in her as He pleases."

Heather squeezed Moa's hand in agreement. "Yes, I feel His presence, too," Heather said. She noticed Layla's reaction to their conversation. She was aware of Layla's confused heart and wanted to share with her but knew that now was not the time.

Layla had been watching the three women during the entire training period. There was a kind, gentle spirit about them, even during the most rigorous part of the training. Several times during Pia Warrior training, she caught herself yelling at Patience for some small infraction that didn't really matter, and Patience did exactly what her name stood for—she patiently took no offense. No matter how loud or obnoxious Layla became, Patience willingly listened and obeyed every command. Suddenly, hearing laughter brought Layla back to reality.

****

"Well, ladies, this ends our physical training for today. Heather and I will share with you impartations of wisdom." Pricilla directed her daughters to sit. She smiled, took a deep breath, and began to speak. "Listen to what I have to say to you, my daughters. Think about all that you have been taught and embrace it through the love and Spirit of God. You will need everything you have learned to defeat the devil and the forces that follow him. I have imparted to you what was given to me from the Lord. Ponder the matters in your heart, and embrace wisdom and my lessons, with faith and understanding."

Eyeing Patience, Moa walked over and held out her hands. "Patience, my dear, I have given you a bow made from acacia wood. I have tempered it with spices and prayed over it with words from the Holy Book. The bow is precious and should only be used to serve the cause of our Lord. Only your faith will make it work properly."

Patience eyed the bow with delight. "It's so beautiful. Are we training in the art of archery today?" she asked excitedly.

"Yes, my dear, but in a different way than you have learned in the past. It's a matter of using your mind rather than your physical skills. What you think in your mind will determine the course of the bow. Patience, you have demonstrated during your training that you are very effective in hand-to-hand combat. And you may be able to defeat your foe with your skills. Nevertheless, mastering the bow will exponentially increase your chance for survival. You must practice your gifts and skills daily to maintain proficiency. If your bow should fall into the hands of your enemy, it cannot be used against you. You simply hold out your hand and speak her name in your mind, and the bow will appear in your hand, no matter where you are. Also, your quiver will always be full of arrows," explained Moa.

Walking closer, Layla noticed something peculiar about the bow. "The bow looks like a simple walking cane," said Layla.

"Yes, it does, but it's quite the contrary, my dear. The moment Patience takes it into her hand and reaches back for an arrow, the walking cane, as you say, will become a bow, and an arrow will appear in her hand."

Layla and Patience laughed. "Patience, can you imagine walking around with an old walking stick? That doesn't match you at all," Layla laughed loudly. Heather, pressing her lips together, gave Layla a stern look, which caused her to immediately stop laughing.

Moa, shaking her head, continued. "There are a few other things that the bow will perform."

"Yes, like fetch you a bowl of soup," Layla jested.

"It may well fetch a bowl of soup, but that is between Patience and the Spirit. The bow will become a part of you and will change its shape to fit your needs. In due time, you'll see it grow in power as you grow in faith," explained Moa. "Do you understand what I am saying, dear?"

Patience nodded, ignoring Layla's funny comments. She looked around, taking in the sight of the three adoring women, and she knew that what these three women had done for her was priceless. They had imparted gifts of love with great affection, and they were cherished and appreciated. "Yes, Moa, I understand, and thank you all for helping me. Oh, one other thing, Moa."

"What is it, dear?" Moa asked.

"Does my bow have a name?

Heather and Moa looked at each other and smiled. "It's a name you'll never forget, my dear. It is your mother's honor to tell you," voiced Moa.

Patience turned to Heather, smiling, waiting, listening for the name. Then in silence, Heather spoke the name of the bow in her mind.

"How appropriate," said Patience, extremely pleased. Silence ensued for what seemed like an eternity.

"Well, what is the name…?" Layla asked emphatically. No one responded to Layla's curiosity.

"By the way, dear, I'm sure that you will admire the decorative carvings on the bow. However, as Layla pointed out, you may not want a walking stick. You may want something less old-fashioned," she chuckled. "Just think about what you want the bow to look like, and it will come true."

Patience expressed her grateful heart by kneeling face down to the ground before the Lord and the three women in front of her. Layla looked on as Heather and Moa knelt beside her in worship and grateful gratitude to God for the training of their daughters. A solemn peace fell over the area. Layla had an urge to join them, but something inside her refused to surrender. After the prayer, the three women rose, and Layla walked over and embraced Patience.

"Congratulations, my sister. I'm so proud of you."

Patience embraced her back, with a teary-eyed smile and a giggle. "Thank you for helping me, and I'm glad that we are sisters."

Layla's heart was touched by Patience's words. She had always known Patience to be gracious, regardless of circumstances. "By the way, you mind telling me the name of the bow?" Layla asked persistently. Feeling a slight tug on the arm, Layla turned and found Moa standing in front of her.

"My child, the matter of the bow is between the Lord and Patience. You need to know that the Lord loves you and has a similar plan for your life if you are willing to surrender to Him." Layla stood silent as a thousand thoughts flooded her mind. Moa embraced her lovingly. "Layla, I can assure you that the Lord has not forsaken you. He loved your mother more than you will ever know."

Layla started to protest, but the words never left her lips. She suddenly heard the whispers again. *I have a gift for you, my love, but it will only work when you learn the lessons of love, repentance, and forgiveness.* Nervous tension overpowered Layla—it was the same voice that plagued her mind during her sleep. Now it seemed to be infiltrating her mind during her waking hours. Shaking her head, Layla mentally blocked the invitation.

****

As the hour became late, everyone retired to their tents for the evening. Smiling at the exhausted two young women, Moa and Heather watched Patience and Layla enter their tents. Layla fell asleep as soon as her head hit her makeshift pillow. However, Patience peaked out of her tent to observe if anyone was awake. Relieved that everyone was sleeping, she made her way through the woods for a rendezvous. However, just before she started for Matt's camp, she suddenly heard a soft voice call out to her.

"And just where do you think you're going, young lady?"

A slight chill ran down Patience back. Turning around, she saw her mother only a few feet away. "Oh, Mother … what are you doing up?" Patience asked sheepishly.

"I was just about to ask you that…?" Heather said, folding her arms while chuckling at Patience's innocent expression. "I'm assuming you are going to see Matt?" A huge grin on Patience's face answered the question. "We have lots of work tomorrow, you may want to think about getting some rest. Give Matt my greetings and make sure you are back before midnight."

As Heather turned to leave, Patience became curious and asked, "Mother, what brought you out here?"

"Discernment, my dear." She smiled. "You weren't the first one to think of doing such a thing."

"Would that be you, Mom?" Patience teased.

"Never mind me," her mother said with a blush.

"Does Moa know I snuck away to visit Matt?"

"Of course, she knows. You can't hide things from her. She knows everything," Heather laughed. She kissed her little duckling's forehead and warned her again to be careful.

"Mother, you know Girma will be near. I'll be safe," she said with a kiss and then headed for Matt's camp.

****

As Layla slept, a gentle voice whispered in her ears. "Layla, you are loved and adored; you are called to be so much more. It is not good for you to resist Me. You must submit to My will and become all that I created you to be…"

Startled by the voice, Layla sat up. The voice confirmed Moa's words that "the Lord will call to you, my dear, and when He does, you must listen to Him." Those same words from Moa came full force into her mind. Sweat beads trickling down her forehead, and she curled her legs and arms into a ball. The rest of the night, she was afraid to sleep, afraid to listen, and unwilling to obey. She locked the encounter into a secret place in her mind, reluctant to share her vulnerability with others.

11

Men's Training Time

Jedidiah and Steven watched closely as Abdi and his warriors trained Matt in ways that exceeded the skills of the most experienced Pia Warrior. There were times Jedidiah and Steven were pleased with the training and times they held their breath. On the first day of training, everyone's prayer life took a giant leap. Through it all, God received the glory, and Matt, with his new companions, received the development.

"Matt, I never thought that I would say it, but you are better than any of us. It took years of training before we could do half the things you do," acknowledged Lire.

"I agree," concurred Caleb with a smile. Bruk whipped his head around, surprised at Caleb's kind statement. Seeing Bruk's obvious surprise, Caleb simply nodded.

"The kings have taught you well, which did not leave much for us to do," voiced Abdi with a teasing smile.

"We have ended today's land training. At dawn, we will venture into the waters," Jedidiah explained.

"The waters? What waters?" asked Matt a little apprehensive.

"The dark waters of the lake in these woods. You must learn how to handle yourself in water just as you do on land, young prince," answered Abdi.

"I hope you can swim," said Bruk.

"Or we're going to dunk you," laughed Lire, slapping Matt on the back.

"I wouldn't eat too much in the morning. We wouldn't want you getting a cramp," Caleb teased.

"I suppose you guys think this is funny," Matt said, expecting them to laugh again, and they did.

"Hey, if you're going to be a Pia Warrior, you have to know how to survive in the water. No exceptions," said Bruk.

"That's right. No exceptions, but from what I have already observed, Matt would never ask for any exceptions." The conviction in Abdi's voice spoke what everyone already knew. In their eyes, Matt was already a Pia Warrior and one of unusual skill.

As the sky darkened, Matt felt his body giving way to sleep. "If you don't mind, I'm turning in for the night," Matt said with a yawn.

As Matt started for his tent, Lire grabbed his shirt by the collar. "Aw, come on, Matt. The night has just begun," said Lire, messing with Matt's hair. Matt politely removed Lire's hand from his head, unamused by Lire's good-humored attempt.

"Goodnight, Lire. Goodnight, everyone," he said as he continued towards his tent. Everybody stared with amusement at Matt's polite but abrupt response to Lire.

"I guess I should leave him alone, huh?"

Steven shook his head. "Lire, it's been a long day, and everyone is tired. I think Matt has the right idea. We should all get some rest," said Steven, messing up Lire's hair. Chuckles were heard among the men as they moved towards their tents.

Just before Caleb entered his tent, Bruk slapped him on the back. "Hey Caleb, I'm glad you've resolved whatever tension you had with Matt. It seems like that prayer time worked," said Bruk, smiling.

"Yes, I suppose you can say that. Thanks for the encouragement."

"You are welcome, my brother. Let's say we get some rest. These days are longer than I'm used to," laughed Bruk.

"Yeah, I have a feeling that Matt is going to be a handful tomorrow with that water training," voiced Caleb.

"If he's anything like he is on land, you're right," grinned Bruk as he headed for his tent. "I'm looking forward to it."

"Me too," stated Caleb.

Morning came earlier than the warriors expected. Abdi was present at the dark waters, waiting on the warriors to arrive. The training was an all-day event. Caleb, Bruk, and Lire showed Matt a myriad of water skills. By the end of the day, Matt had mastered high dives, deep submerging, and underwater fighting techniques. During submerging training, Matt was instructed to hold his breath for as long as he could. On average, most Pia warriors could hold their breath five to six minutes.

"Bruk, don't you think Matt has been underwater too long?" Lire asked.

"I guess you're right. It seems that he's been underwater for almost 10 minutes," Bruk said. With concern permeating through the group, Bruk began to run toward the water when suddenly Matt emerged from the water, relaxed and in control.

"Whoa, Matt! We thought you were dead," Lire said, wiping sweat from his face.

"Yeah, you could have told us ahead of time that you can hold your breath as long as a dolphin," said Caleb.

Abdi commented that he had never seen anyone master land and water skills with such ease. "Your water training was superb, and after such an ordeal, everyone deserves a break," said Abdi, guiding everyone toward the campfire. Abdi prepared a meal of fish, bread, and an assortment of vegetables with fresh spring water. After an enjoyable meal, everyone seemed satisfied.

"I think I'll go for a walk to clear my head," Matt said, getting up from the fire.

"Not too long, my young friend. Dawn will be here before you know it, and working in water takes a lot of energy. You'll need your rest."

Matt nodded to Abdi respectfully and disappeared into the woods. As he walked, an eerie feeling invaded his mind, then a soft voice called to him. *Matt, Matt, come home…* The voice was disturbing but dissipated as quickly as it came. Matt realized that it was the same voice from his dream. He stood, wondering why the urge to go home became even stronger.

****

In less than five hours, the dawn will be here. I have just enough time to see Matt and grab a little rest, Patience thought. Climbing up a tree, she found a thick limb on which to rest. This time Girma never left her side. She gave her familiar night call and waited, hoping that Matt would hear and come. From her view, she could see the men as they threw logs on the fire. However, she didn't see Matt among the others as they laid down for the night. Moa, Heather, and Layla were resting on the outskirts of the men's camp. The women likewise had raised their tents. As part of training, each had to put up their own tent and prepare their own meals.

Patience's limb on which she sat had a mossy, soft curve. *This was made for me,* she thought. *Now, Lord, it would be an answer to prayer if Matt was up here with me.* No sooner had the words formed in her thoughts than a majestic figure stood on the limb next to her. It startled her so badly that she began to fall from the tree. A strong hand caught her by the arm and lifted her back onto the limb.

"My love, what are you doing here?"

His words melted her heart as she embraced his strong body. "Looking for you, my darling. My heart could not take the separation any longer. I'm sorry I came, but I had to." She dropped her head thinking that he was displeased by her coming.

Matt lifted her head with a gentle hand and looked into her eyes. "Don't be sorry, my darling, I long for you more than the air I breathe," he said, embracing her. When she was able to draw a breath, she sighed with relief. Matt laid down on the limb, and Patience laid against his chest. With his strong arms around her and laying against his warm body, she knew that she was safe and out of harm's way. Unknown to Matt, Girma stood guard below, his presence warded off all would-be predators.

"What will we tell them in the morning?" she asked.

"The truth, my love. Our hearts found us," he laughed and kissed her just before sleep overtook them.

****

Early the next morning, Steven, Heather, and Moa stood in the middle of the woods next to Jedidiah, watching Patience and Matt peacefully stroll towards them, while Layla and her brothers sipped on hot spiced cider.

"Are you two ready?" asked Steven, smiling.

Matt and Patience looked at each other, relieved by such a generous greeting. "We are ready," she said, giving her father a kiss while winking at Moa and her mother. "I'm glad you're not upset with me, Father."

"No, my dear, you were only doing what comes naturally to a young married woman."

"What do you mean, Father?"

Smiling, Steven briefly explained, "You were going after the man you love. As I recall, your mother did somewhat of the same thing our first few months of marriage." Patience blushed and hugged her father as he kissed her on the head.

"Hey!" came a familiar voice. Patience turned to see her grandfather smiling at her. "Your grandfather is standing here too young lady," said Jedidiah, expecting the same greeting.

"Of course, Poppy, please forgive me," she said, giving him a big kiss followed by a tight hug. Jedidiah smiled and signaled for everyone to join him.

12

TEAM TRAINING

JEDIDIAH STOOD PROUDLY AS HE OBSERVED ALL HIS SUBJECTS. "Today, you will train together for your final test. You will break into two teams. It will be Matt and Patience against the rest of you. Pia Warriors against Pia Warriors. I know that it is unusual for women to fight against men, but with the coming war, it is imperative to train in such a manner. Now let's begin," called out Jedidiah, signaling Steven to start.

"Are you ready for this? I think it's going to be interesting," said Steven to Heather.

Heather smiled and said, "Do you think they will be all right?"

"Don't worry. They'll do just fine, my love," Heather nodded and followed him towards the others. Jedidiah and Pricilla stood a short distance away. Leaning on his staff, Jedidiah allowed Steven and Abdi to work without interruption.

"You will place Matt and Patience at the north end of the camp and Bruk with the other warriors at the south end. Tell them to follow instructions and make sure you carry out what we talked about earlier and adjust as you see fit," said Steven.

"Yes, my lord," Abdi responded. Meeting in the center of camp, Abdi gave each team their instructions and sent them to their designated areas. "Ready yourselves and listen for the ram's horn that will begin and end the training." Abdi moved forward with Bruk, and the rest of the warriors, while the kings and their queens watched.

Minutes before the last training began, Abdi had second thoughts and became concerned with the uneven number in both teams. He signaled to Steven, who immediately joined him. "Sir, this is not a fair match," said Abdi with a look of deep concern on his face.

"What is your point?" asked Steven. Abdi's demeanor became very formal and serious. Protocol required honorable compliance. Steven was not only his brother but also king over his people. An important lesson Steven and Abdi had learned from their father, Peter, was to give honor to whoever it was due. Abdi had practiced this statute all his life and had also passed it on to his sons.

"Sir, I know that the young prince is amazingly gifted, but my children and I have been warriors since the day we could walk. You know this isn't a fair match for us to go against the young prince, who has only been in training less than a year. And the princess, though very capable, is still our princess," Abdi said with great concern. "May I suggest that we not engage in full contact? I would not like to see them harmed."

"I see your point, Abdi, but just bear with me for a while," said Steven with a smile. Heather heard Abdi's words and squeezed Steven's arm. Steven looked back and saw the concern on her face. "They will be fine, my love," he said, reassuring her. She sighed and waited for the training to begin.

"As you wish, my lord," said Abdi.

"And Abdi?"

"Yes, my lord?"

"If I were you, I wouldn't take those two lightly. They may surprise you," Steven said as he wrapped his arm around Heather and walked towards Jedidiah and Pricilla. It was easy to observe the whole match from where they stood.

All the warriors readied themselves for battle. Layla stood close to her father as Abdi addressed the Pia Warriors, who were to engage Matt and Patience. "You are not to harm them. They are of the royal family," Abdi instructed.

"What do you think he means?" asked Lire.

"Just what he said," responded Bruk.

"You have to be kidding me. After all, we have seen him do, he wants us to go easy on him?" complained Lire.

"That's what the man said. He's probably thinking of Patience," said Caleb.

"I don't know why! That girl can put a dent in your head just like Matt," said Lire. "You guys can take it easy, but I'm looking out for me, and if you know what's good for you, you'll do the same."

Bruk chuckled under his breath.

"You have a point there, Lire. Let's just follow Father's lead," Caleb said.

"All right, but I'm telling you that somebody is going to get hurt, and I know who that is likely to be," said Lire, watching his brothers.

The men nodded that they understood Abdi's instruction not to use deadly force. Elias, Ezera, and Gedeyon stood silent, ready to engage when and wherever they were needed. The weapons carried by the Pia Warriors were all different. The object was to test Matt and Patience's skills in warfare. It was expedient that every member of the royal family be trained in self-defense. Patience had always been excited about training. Nevertheless, this was not a game; the weapons could maim, cripple, or even kill if not used properly.

Steven blew the ram's horn, and the scrimmage began. Bruk and Caleb sprang into action by hurling spears directly at Matt and Patience. As the spears came towards them, Matt moved in front of Patience to protect her, but there were too many. Patience held up her hands, and like hitting an invisible wall, the spears dropped in front of them. Heather and Pricilla smiled.

"Did you see that?" asked Caleb.

"Yes, it looks like our little cousin has perfected her shield of faith. No time to chat. Let's put them to the test," cried Bruk.

Layla and her father came from behind with more arrows, spears, and a couple of battle axes. Matt picked up heavy tree limbs and whatever was at hand and hurled them at the warriors.

"Look out! Here comes a tree," yelled Lire.

"I see it. Get out of the way, Layla," yelled Caleb.

Patience called her bow forward and met every arrow shot by the warriors with one of her own.

"That's impossible," voiced Gedeyon.

"Forget what I said earlier about going easy on them," said Abdi. "Protect yourselves. They are more advanced in war skills than I thought."

"That's my girl," said Steven, nudging Jedidiah in the side with his elbow. The elders laughed, while Abdi and the warriors scrambled to regroup. Abdi signaled for Layla to shoot arrows while shouting at Lire to throw his battle axes. Abdi threw his spears and boomerang blade with precision. The blade was thrown with such force that it cut strands of hair from Matt's head.

"That was close. You'd better pay attention, love. They mean to win this scrimmage," said Patience.

Abdi ordered Elias and his brothers to engage from the opposite side. Bruk and Caleb shot arrows directly at Patience. Abdi knew that Matt's attention would be given to the princess instead of protecting himself. Matt had already proven that he would do anything to save Patience from harm, even letting his guard down to protect her. When the barrage of arrows fell upon Patience, Matt turned his attention to saving her just as Abdi had predicted. Matt reached Patience and effortlessly moved her from the target area.

Abdi had anticipated his move, and the battle-axes and spears would be on him before he could adjust himself. The boomerang blade was thrown last as a follow-up to ensure success. Seeing the deadly weapons about to hit Matt, Patience could not hold the scream inside. Matt turned to see the axes and spears coming towards him. Then Abdi and his sons were astonished at the sight they saw. It was like watching a pet fetching a stick. There stood, in front of Matt and Patience, Trueball and Lightening, Matt's dog-like companions, with the weapons in their mouths. They laid the weapons at Matt's feet.

Both dogs faced what they viewed as enemies and started to pursue. The animals did not make the distinction between training games and war. They only knew that a deadly assault had been made on their master and perpetrators needed to be stopped. Matt quickly called them back but not before Lightening gave a thunderous growl at them as a warning to stand down.

"What the heck is that?" cried Lire.

"I'm not sure, but it's strange, don't you think?" exclaimed Bruk.

"Your Uncle Steven didn't tell me everything about these two," mused Abdi.

Lightening and Trueball rubbed against Matt and Patience, still not allowing the attackers near them. Steven was beside himself with laughter.

"So, you think this is funny, do you?" yelled Abdi.

"I do. Never have I seen six warriors disarmed so fast and by novices. You should have seen the look on your faces when those animals appeared out of nowhere. I thought you and the boys were going to choke-out, but as Pia Warriors, you stood your ground even against the unknown," stated Steven.

"Are we done with training?" inquired Caleb. "I don't see a need to continue, not after what I just saw."

"Not just yet. There is one last area that Matt has to be tested in," said Steven.

"And what might that be, Uncle Steven?" asked Lire.

"That would be hand-to-hand combat. I know that there is no one better than you boys in hand-to-hand fighting. If you would all take your places in the circle, we will begin. Remember that if any of you are thrown out or leave the circle for any reason, you can no longer engage in combat," instructed Steven.

"Sorry I asked," Lire said under his breath.

"What about me, Father? Don't I need this training as well?" asked Patience.

"Yes, dear, but you will train with Layla now and with your husband later."

"Lord, is this training ever going to end?" muttered Layla.

"I heard that," said Moa.

"Okay, Moa," Layla sighed.

"I can do one more bout, but I'd rather do it against the boys," voiced Patience, looking at her father unapprovingly.

"I know that you feel left out, Patience, but you are no longer a child to be tussling with boys. It is not proper for a woman to engage in full-body contact with men," expressed Steven.

"But Father, you and Poppy have always trained me. I see no harm in scrapping with my cousins," she said with a chuckle.

"That may be so, but the Lord requires appropriate respect between males and females, whether it's between fathers and daughters and even grandfathers. Things are different now that you have grown up. Even though you were trained in fighting, I do not approve of women fighting against men unless it is absolutely necessary."

"But, Father, didn't I just do battle with them?" she exclaimed.

"Yes, but you were never touched, and that is why you will learn from your husband. And should the time come for you to engage in battle you will have the knowledge and training to do so. You have mastered the bow, and in war, it will be your weapon of choice. Your enemy will fall before they reach you." She took a step towards him to speak. He recognized the persistent look in her face and held up his hand. "Patience, the matter is settled," stated Steven.

She lowered her eyes resolved in her heart that her father was right.

"Yes, Father," she said, moving next to Layla.

Steven turned to Matt. "Son, I noticed that when Patience was attacked, you went to her defense, thereby leaving yourself open for an attack from other warriors. Your action could have cost you your life. Never take your eyes off your enemy. Worrying about Patience or anyone else while you are in battle can get you both killed." Matt nodded to acknowledge the seriousness of his action, then entered the circle, while Patience and Layla stood next to Steven to watch the match.

Abdi instructed his sons and the three other warriors to enter the circle with caution. It was six against Matt.

"Wait a minute, what about those wild dogs or whatever they're called? Are we going to have to fight them too?" protested Lire.

"Not at all. It will be only us in the circle," Matt laughed.

"Good! Now, my cousin, let's see what you are made of!" said Lire, relieved.

"Wait. It hardly seems appropriate for the six of you to take on poor Matt," Abdi teased.

Matt smiled and beckoned them to come forward. As they faced each other, Matt focused on the position of each man and kept in step with each of their movements. Suddenly, Bruk and Caleb ran towards Matt. Patience instinctively took hold of her father's arm as they watched. The warriors tried a surprise attack by leaping high into the air, hoping to subdue him while Lire, Elias, Ezra, and Gedeyon rushed in from the sides with the intent of using their body weight and brute force to take Matt down. To their surprise,

Matt caught Bruk and Caleb in midair and tossed them on top of the four oncoming warriors, which took them down like a ton of bricks.

Bruk took out his bolas and hurled it at Matt's feet. Matt took a fall forward. The other men were on him in a second. Matt showed no signs of fatigue. Unfortunately for Bruk, the bolas didn't hold Matt for long. With one jerk of his ankle against the other, the leather was broken. They wrestled, punched, struggled, and tried every fighting technique known to Pia Warriors.

Finally, Abdi ordered the warriors to step back. He alone stood facing Matt. Then, without warning, he threw a white powder into the air. As it came down, it took the shape of a large bear-like beast. It stood up on its hind legs like a bear and stood several feet higher than Matt. Abdi and his sons stood outside the circle while Matt remained. Matt didn't know if the beast was real or phantom. He only knew that leaving the circle would mean defeat. The claws on the beast struck Matt, breaking the skin on his left arm. The cut was deep enough to cause Matt concern.

Abdi watched as the beast closed in on Matt. His sons seemed concerned but knew that interference would not be tolerated. It was Matt's battle to fight, no matter how deadly the situation became. Patience stood by her father, worry filling her eyes. She took a step towards Matt but was stopped by Steven.

"He needs me, Father," she said through anxious tears.

"He must use his training, little one," said Heather confidently.

The beast leaped on Matt and brought him to the ground. With all of his strength, Matt held the beast at bay.

He could not understand why Lightening and Trueball didn't come to his aid.

"Lord, help me. This beast is too powerful. The more I fight it, the stronger it becomes," he prayed.

Matt, the battle is not yours; it's Mine. You must rest in Me and allow yourself to trust Me completely, said the voice in his mind.

"How am I to do that with this thing on top of me? If I let go, it will kill me," protested Matt.

It will not kill you. The beast you fight is your own fear. By trusting Me, your fear will subside, and the beast will go away. Perfect love casts out fear, continued the voice in Matt's mind.

The message was hard for Matt to obey, especially with a large beast growling above him, ready to sink its sharp fangs into his jugular. Matt held on to the beast as he came to the last of his strength and knew that giving up would end his life.

Everyone stood watching Matt struggle—seeing and not seeing, hearing his struggle but unaware of the beast he fought. Patience stood quietly by her father, praying for Matt's protection. Steven saw the tears drop from his daughter's closed eyes.

"Jesus, help me" were the last words Matt said just before he released his hands off the beast. What happened next was amazing. Matt was still alive, he was no longer tired, and the beast was nowhere to be seen. The ram's horn sounded loud and clear, ending the hand-to-hand scrimmage.

"I have seen enough. Well done, well done, warriors," shouted Steven.

"Man, I'm glad that's over," said Lire.

"We all are," chimed in Abdi, watching the warriors come together.

Jedidiah smiled, lifting his staff for everyone to gather around him. "I am so very proud of you all. This training has been grueling, and you have all proven yourselves to be exceptional leaders in warfare." Jedidiah placed his arm around Steven, saying, "I have tasked King Steven Marwari with developing warriors throughout the kingdom. You are the best-prepared warriors we have. I need your help in establishing trained warrior units throughout Truevine and the surrounding villages. You will also aid other territories outside our land if they need our help. Each unit will consist of 12 men and will be placed in every village to train their people. King Marwari and I, along with the elders from other villages, have sought the Lord and prayed much regarding this matter, even before your training began."

Jedidiah paused to make sure his words were sinking in with the Pia Warriors, then continued. "I don't have to tell you how cunning, evasive, and deadly the demonic world is. Right now, on the outer villages of Truevine, they are mobilizing the most depraved part of humanity imaginable. These people are far more wicked than the City Dwellers my father dealt with long ago. My grandmother was one of many who were killed by them. This shouldn't be a surprise to us because wherever good dwells, evil seeks to abolish it. It has been the devil's plan ever since he was expelled from Heaven to destroy everything good," exclaimed Jedidiah. "That old serpent intends to use everything in his power to destroy us all, and that includes our families and friends."

Patience put her arm around Matt's and whispered, "I've never seen Poppy like this before. He is worried, and that deeply concerns me."

Matt put his arm around her and pulled her closer, "I hear the strong warning of his words. Everyone here can feel it. He is a seer from the Lord, and the Lord will guide us in and out of whatever we face." Matt's words calmed her spirit. He felt Patience relax as they listen to the rest of the old seer's words.

"You are expected to know every move of your fellow warrior. You will not have a second chance to correct your mistakes. Any mishap can cost a life. I know that you are well equipped to do battle. However, a warrior never stops learning, training, and working toward perfection. To reach the level of oneness, you will work and train until your body, soul, and spirit are in sync with each other and the Spirit of the Lord." Jedidiah paused to give an encouraging smile, knowing that those before him were destined to carry the cause of God forward in the face of grave opposition. "God will give us the courage to accomplish His will." The old man had challenged their warrior hearts. And every warrior looked forward to doing battle. Jedidiah knew that they would stand regardless of the odds against them, but he also knew that many of his people would die.

The old seer watched Matt and Patience; they were inseparable. Jedidiah raised his staff, signaling for them to approach him. Taking her hand, Matt strode towards the old prophet with a thousand thoughts going through his mind. Jedidiah spoke softly to them. "Matt, you've been having strange dreams about your homeland, correct?" Astonished, Matt could only respond by nodding his head. "Son, it is time for you to journey home, but only for a season. Of course, Patience and your comrades will accompany you on the journey. Expect many challenges on your way home."

"What do you mean, Poppy?" asked Patience.

"I mean, my dear, that this will also be part of everyone's advanced training. The journey should prove to be very interesting."

"What do you mean by interesting?" she inquired. "I know that look on your face, and it means more than you are telling us."

"That is true, but where is the fun in telling you everything?" He chuckled.

"I know your idea of fun, sir, and it's not always fun," chimed in Matt.

"You two are so suspicious," the seer chuckled again.

"After being unexpectedly whisked away during our honeymoon, we don't know what to expect," Matt said.

"All I can say is that it will develop a strong bond between all of you. Apart from Elias, Ezera, and Gedeyon, you six will eventually be unbeatable, but you must first go through the impossible." Jedidiah abruptly ended his words and signaled for Abdi to ready the group. Everyone watched in admiration as Jedidiah wrapped his arms around Matt and Patience. Matt was in awe of how Jedidiah told him every detail of his dream. "Wisdom and foresight come from God, and He will direct you," Jedidiah told them.

The old seer approached the warriors with Matt and Patience close by his side. "Abdi, they are in your hands. Heather, Pricilla, Steven, and I will keep you before the Lord during your travel. We are going to spend time in scripture and prayer," said Jedidiah.

Abdi nodded in obedience. "We will leave for Matt's home in a few days. Gather what we need for the journey, and prepare yourselves for travel," said Abdi.

"To Matt's home!" Lire shouted.

Everyone cheered, "To Matt's home."

"What's the name of your village, Matt?" asked Lire.

"It's called Columbidae," answered Matt.

"And I know that we are just going to love it," added Patience.

"How do you know that you are going to love it, my darling?" asked Matt with a smile.

"Because you came from there, and any place you call home must be wonderful." For that answer, she received a kiss from Matt.

"I just asked for the name of the place, not a full romance story," chuckled Lire.

13

Preparing for the Journey

It was early morning, and everyone was enjoying breakfast. Heather watched Steven as he observed their daughter and son-in-law discussing preparation for the journey to Matt's home. Everyone was talking at the same time about all that happened during training. There was much laughter and teasing over the many incidents and events that had taken place among them. After breakfast, the band of warriors dispersed to gather their belongings for the journey.

"I'm going to miss our children," Steven said under his breath. Heather reached out and touched his arm.

"It's time for us to return home as well, my love. We have been away for a couple of months, and a kingdom cannot continue for long without its king," said Heather.

"Nor its queen," responded Steven, taking Heather's hand and moving outside to take in the freshness of the morning.

The three visiting warriors approached the king to receive instructions as ordered by Abdi.

"Your Majesty, we are awaiting your orders," said Elias.

"Good! You, Ezera, and Gedeyon must leave immediately and inform my parents and our people of all that you have seen and heard. Start the preparation to defend our land and ensure that leaders have the provision they need to sustain us. Queen Heather and I will follow you soon."

"Yes, my king," responded Elias.

"According to King Jedidiah, my father will be expecting you. Make sure you follow his directions and keep order among our people," said Steven.

"Yes, Your Majesty," replied the warriors.

"Take care, and God's speed."

The three warriors took off running. Steven and Heather watched the warriors as they became specks in the distance. "I'm glad your parents are there," said Heather.

"I am too. They are well respected among our people and will provide the spiritual support needed to defend against unseen forces. Elias, Ezera, and Gedeyon are great leaders. They will help Mother and Father keep order," stated Steven.

"Of course, you are right, my dear," Heather said, embracing him then smiled as she felt his arm tighten around her waist.

Steven and Heather's thoughts were bittersweet, knowing that the time had come for Matt to journey home and that their daughter was going with him.

It would be her first time away from home, away from under their care.

"Do you think they will be all right?" asked Heather with concern.

"She is with the strongest man on the planet, who also happens to have a good head on his shoulders." Steven smiled, hoping to alleviate her fears as well as his own concerns. Gently grabbing Heather's hand, Steven said, "I have something for you." Then without warning, he took her into his arms for a kiss, causing her to blush.

"You know everyone is watching, don't you?"

"Let them. Maybe they will learn a thing or two," he said jokingly.

"Steven!" she blushed again.

"Don't worry, my love. They'll do just fine. Looks like they are about ready." Still holding her hand, he led her towards Jedidiah and Pricilla.

Jedidiah, Pricilla, Steven, and Heather came forward and stood proudly in front of their warriors. The old seer stepped out to say a few words before their departure.

"Matt, it's time to go home. It's been a while since you have seen your folks. I must say, son, it's been a pleasure having you here with me. Your heart for the Lord has blessed me and my whole house. I'm glad that you are part of us. That girl standing beside you is the heart of us all. The Lord saw fit to give his best when he gave you to each other. The two of you are blessed. Remember your vows to God and to each other," said Jedidiah.

The old man stepped back, and Steven stepped forward, holding back tears at the thought of his baby girl leaving. "You know what? I think it's the perfect day for travel. How about breakfast before you go?" Steven said loudly, covering the emotion in his voice.

It was obvious to everyone that Steven was making an excuse to keep Patience and Matt longer because it had only been a couple of hours since breakfast. They all laughed, and then Jedidiah raised his staff. Suddenly a doorway appeared, and they all walked into the Treasure Tree.

"Get freshened up, and we will meet in a couple of hours for brunch," said Moa. Everyone went their way and then showed up for the farewell meal at the appointed time.

"It is wonderful that the Lord has given us favor and protection in all that we have done. Matt, you and Patience received an invitation during your honeymoon. It was to bless and equip you for life. You have fulfilled every requirement of the invitation and even more. The Lord has granted me my request by preparing you for His purpose. I'm sure that He will continue to cover you as you venture into your destiny. Let's enjoy this meal and time together as we give thanks," said Jedidiah.

What a time they had fellowshipping. When the hour of departure came, Abdi rose from his seat. Everyone knew it was time to go. Patience took extra time saying goodbye to Jedidiah and her parents, while Matt helped everyone else take care of the last details of packing the wagons with provisions.

"Make sure you two pay attention to the world around you. As you know, there have been reports of strange things happening around our land," Jedidiah said to Patience.

"You mean things like the bostis?" she asked.

"The bostis have not yet entered Truevine. I hope they never do. However, the land of the Great Falls is full of them. There have been reports of unfriendly tribesmen, like the City Dwellers. It seems that some have found their way to our shores. I have noticed their movements, and I am concerned that they may be moving closer to our territory.

It's been a few years since I last encountered them. I remember the stories of my father and grandfather. They were unfriendly then and are probably still the same. Just because we have not engaged them for a while doesn't mean that they do not pose a threat," said Jedidiah. "I have given you instructions to govern your steps on your journey. They will keep you safe wherever you go. See that you follow them." Then with great fatherly affection, Jedidiah embraced her.

"We will be careful, Poppy. I promise," said Patience.

"You make sure that you are," chimed in Steven, giving his little girl a hug and kiss before lifting her up onto the wagon.

"I'll take good care of her, Father. Don't worry," yelled Matt, packing the last crates of food.

"I know, son. Just the same, Abdi, the boys, and Layla are with you."

Abdi raised his hand, signaling the others that it was time to move out. Layla hugged and kissed the kings and queens before climbing up to where she and her father would sit. Abdi embraced and kissed his brother and sister-in-law, then eased himself upon the wagon next to Layla.

Steven slapped Matt on the back cheerfully. "Matt, you are wise beyond your years but still lack experience in many things. You have skilled warriors traveling with you. See that you use them as counselors. Your brothers and Abdi are your trainers, but you are still the leader of your unit. You have trained well together. Be alert and enjoy your time with your parents."

As Matt and Steven conversed, Heather took advantage of the few minutes left to speak to Patience.

"Prayer is your shield, honey. Use it at all times," she reminded Patience. Her mother could not hold back the tears in her eyes. Patience looked at Matt, who smiled with understanding, and then Patience jumped down from the wagon to give Heather one last hug.

"How far is your home from here, Matt?" inquired Heather.

"Due to the wagons, we have to take the long way around, so it will take at least a week," Matt replied.

"We will be fine, Mom," said Patience, trying to console her mother and hold back her own tears. "Matt and I have been well trained by you all. And look at those big guys over there on the wagons. Who in their right minds would dare attack us?" She giggled. "I don't want you to worry about us. Besides, we faith walkers walk by faith." Patience wrapped her arms once again around Heather and Moa, who had stepped up beside her.

"Be safe, my darling. We love you." Heather smiled, remembering that her words to Patience were the very words her parents said to her and Steven when they left for their journey. Moa simply smiled and hugged her granddaughter again.

When the last bags were placed on the wagon, and the young men traveling with them had double-checked the goods in the other wagons, Layla yelled, "Let's go, or we'll be here another week." There were chuckles in the background.

Patience stalled a little longer to say a last goodbye. "Poppy, take care of them for me while I'm gone," she said, sniffling. Then Heather and Steven wrapped their arms around Patience tightly and kissed her. Steven called out to his son-in-law. Matt turned, and to his surprise, Steven swung Patience up and down as if she was still a child. Matt knew what was coming next, so with open arms, he caught her like she was a feather. The joy of laughter and a tinge of regret filled them as Matt gave the word to move out.

Suddenly Moa yelled out, "Patience, aren't you forgetting something?" Patience turned and saw in Moa's hand one of the most important treasures she had acquired from training—the old wooden walking stick being held out by Moa. With a gentle smile, Moa let go of the precious item. Patience held out her hand, and the walking stick flew from Moa to Patience. It turned from a walking stick to a beautiful leather belt that wrapped around Patience's garment.

"Impressive," said Poppy, smiling.

"Thank you, Moa," Patience said, waving and throwing kisses from the wagon. Matt had been observing the old walking stick in Moa's hand and wondered how it flew into Patience's hand.

"That's some stick you got there," Matt said.

"You better believe it," she laughed.

Finally, Abdi blew the ram's horn to depart. Steven stood with his arm around Heather, looking at their little girl as she began her first journey away from home as a new bride. He couldn't stop the tears that formed in his eyes. It was every father's heartbreak and joy. He knew in his heart that she was in good hands. She had a good husband, and she had the Lord. Heather slipped her arm into his and whispered, "They'll be fine, my love."

As the group traveled towards Matt's home, wagons loaded with provisions, Patience began to sing an ancient song familiar only to her family. Singing always calmed her heart and brought her joy. Those who heard her voice appreciated the sweet sound of her precious gift. Patience's singing made the time move swiftly. Matt grinned from ear to ear.

"Wow, I didn't know that you could sing like that. You are so full of surprises," he said, throwing one arm around her and holding the reins with his other hand.

"Thank you, Matt. You get a double kiss for that," she said, kissing him on the cheek. She pushed back the strand of hair in his face and smiled. "I attribute a lot of my singing abilities to my mother and, of course, Bree."

"Bree? Who is that?" Matt asked curiously, trying to remember if Bree was at the wedding.

Patience laughed. "Honey, Bree is a mocking bird. She visits every morning and sings melodies by my bedroom window."

"Really? That is amazing," Matt said. Patience squeezed Matt's hand and kissed his cheek again, enjoying the surrounding scenery. "You know, Patience, while we are traveling home, this would be a good time for you to tell me about your family." He smiled, knowing she had no excuse to evade his request.

"I suppose so if you insist," she responded.

"I do," said Matt, giving her a kiss on the nose.

"When I finish, I want to hear everything about you, too, and I mean everything." She paused a second, then reiterated. "You're going to tell me your story as well, agreed?" She gave him a quick wink before he could answer. Matt simply smiled. "What do you want to know about your mysterious wife?" she asked teasingly.

"I want to know everything about you."

"Matt, that could take a long time."

"That's okay. We have about a week's journey before we reach home. Just tell me what you can in the time we have. We can always pick up where you leave off."

"I suppose so," she said. "But I don't know where to begin."

"Why don't you start where you feel comfortable? Tell me about your childhood, as early as you can remember," he replied, pushing her dark brown hair from her face. Patience reached into her bag and pulled out a leather-bound book. "What's that?" Matt asked.

Patience turned to face him and replied, "A copy of my family's journal. I take it with me wherever I go."

Matt sat quietly, periodically lifting the straps attached to the horses to encourage them to keep moving. He kept his eyes on the road, but occasionally took a quick glimpse at his wife.

"I'll start with my four fathers back, Joel and his son Trobus. From the age of five, up to my adulthood, my family told me about my four fathers back and their families. They were all great men of God and possessed gifts and skills very few people had."

"Wait a minute," Matt interrupted, not wanting to be confused, "By four fathers back, you mean your great-great-grandfather, right?"

"That's correct, my love. His name was Joel, and he was the most benevolent of kings among the Growers. His love for God and people surpassed the people of his time, and he was hated for it. Poppy was 12, and my second aunt back, Beverly, his sister, was four."

"Poppy's sister, Beverly, is your great-aunt, right?" Matt asked, trying to keep things straight in his head.

"Yes, love. Why do you keep asking me the order of my family?" she asked, surprised at his reaction.

"Because I've never heard anyone speak of relatives in numbers before," Matt said, rubbing his neck.

She laughed. "Okay. I'll speak plainly. "Poppy used to sit me next to him in the love seat and tell me wonderful stories about our family. His father and mother were Trobus and Emma. Trobus was a Grower, but he had a warrior's heart. He felt duty-bound to protect the Growers and his family from all predators. He was responsible for training the growers in horticulture and the art of defense. He exceeded my great-great-grandfather in height and strength." Matt smiled at the adjustments Patience was making to accommodate him. "Is there something you wanted to say, my love?" she asked, tempted to pinch his cheek.

"No, please continue," he said, pleased with the sound of her voice.

She continued, "No one among the City Dwellers or the Growers could match Trobus in wisdom and insight. He is brilliant, but you wouldn't know it unless you spent time with him. He never talks about himself or boasts about his accomplishments. He has this quiet demeanor of grace that escapes the common mind. He is tough in making decisions and strong in character, which is why, among many people, he is called sage. Sage is short for sagacious. Father Trobus doesn't ignore evil because he knows that evil will always repeat the same deeds. Love is always present in his heart, but so is justice."

Matt's mind started to reminisce back to the old man who cared for him when he was wounded in the Great Falls.

"Am I boring you?" Patience asked, seeing Matt's eyes glazed over.

"Oh no, my love. Your description reminded me of an old man I recently met. Please continue," he said, smiling to himself. She smiled back and continued.

"My great-grandmother, Emma, says that Grandpa Trobus only has eyes for her. That he always puts her before anyone except God. I love the way she speaks of him, and I adore the way she loves him. It is the same way I feel about you, Matt," she said with a whisper.

"I feel the same," he said, feeling her emotions tug at his heart.

Smiling with satisfaction, she continued speaking. "He taught Poppy all that he knows, and when he reached the age of 200, he passed the responsibility of seer and king to Poppy, even though he is still very healthy."

"Wait a minute. You talk as though he is still alive," Matt said curiously.

"That's because he is," she said, amused with Matt's response.

"How can that be? People don't live past 100."

"Don't tell Father Trobus that. He doesn't consider age a problem. When you see him, you will get my meaning," she said, teasing Matt. Matt ran his hand through his hair, amazed at what he was hearing, wondering if his sweet bride was teasing or telling the truth. "You think I'm teasing you, don't you?" she said, staring at him.

"What else can I think? The oldest person in my village is 108, and she resembles a dried-up piece of fruit." Matt meant no disrespect; it was the only example he could think of at the time. Patience laughed at Matt's blushing face and decided to carry the teasing a step further.

"Are you calling me dried up?" she snickered.

"Of course not," Matt protested. Then he realized she was baiting him. "Wait a minute. Just how old are you?" he asked with a raised eyebrow. She jumped up and grabbed him from behind with her arm around his neck and then grabbed his left arm and twisted it behind his back. Matt held the horses with his right hand, laughing as his bride tried to subdue him. With all her strength, she tried to move him, but he didn't budge an inch.

"No fair, no fair," she protested, knowing she was no match for the amazing man she was trying to wrestle. "Matt, didn't your mother ever tell you that you don't ask a woman her age, even if she is younger than you?" She laughed, still trying to get the better of him. Matt pulled her around to him and held her tightly in his arm, laughing at her squirms as she tried to get free.

"Yes, she told me, but you're my wife, and I can ask you anything. Besides, it's too late for me to do anything about it now," he chuckled.

"Oh, you're going to regret that comment, mister," she said, struggling. Matt kissed her playfully. He was enjoying their time and the teasing between them. He realized that for the first time in his life, he had a best friend, and she was beautiful. Hearing the laughter of others in the wagons behind, he realized that they had drawn attention to themselves.

"You know, I think that I have met your great-grandfather Trobus. I didn't get a good look, but I'm certain that it was him."

"Where?" she asked.

"Oh no, you don't. We will talk about that later. Get on with the story," he insisted. "However, I am curious," Matt said, relaxing his hold on Patience.

"About what?"

"If your 200-year-old great-grandfather and your aunt Beverly are alive, why didn't I see them at the wedding?" he asked with a bit of a smirky smile on his face.

"Oh Matt, that's because he and Aunt Beverly can't leave the Great Falls right now. Father Trobus is the overseer of the entire region of the Falls, and presently he cannot leave the work unattended."

"I see," he said sardonically.

"I mean it, Matt. If he and Aunt Bev could have been at our wedding, they would have. And they would have brought with them other members of the family as well." Matt didn't say anything. He simply kissed her again and smiled. "Oh no, you're not. I know that look," she said, lightly grasping his hair in her hands. "You're not getting away with that raised eyebrow and smirky grin on your face, Matt. As soon as we get the time, we are taking a trip to the mountains to see father Trobus."

Matt was delighted at her suggestion. "That's a great idea," he agreed. Patience just laughed, knowing very well that Matt was still messing with her. "I have to say, my love, I've never seen anyone past 200 years," Matt said. He wondered how wrinkled a 200-year-old man would look. He chuckled, thinking to himself that he must have more wrinkles than a prune. However, the man he had met in the Falls couldn't be over sixty.

"He is not wrinkly," Patience laughed.

"Huh? I didn't say anything."

"No, but you thought it."

"That doesn't count. You have to hear it out loud before it counts," Matt said, leaning over to get another kiss. She looked at him with an alluring smile.

"Okay, only one kiss if we intend to get back to the journal," Patience said as Matt nodded in agreement.

"Yes, please continue, my love," he said, happy that she was sitting next to him.

"Trobus was not as easygoing as his father, founder of the Growers, King Joel. Trobus had a joyful heart, but he was very serious about the safety of our people. The journal says that he was a warrior without fear. I know this to be true because when I was 13, my brothers and I were in the meadows of the great mountains hunting for medicinal berries for Moa. Out of nowhere, a bosti charged at us to kill and eat us. It was strange because evil animals like the bosti were not supposed to venture into the land of Truevine. They are forbidden. We had heard of the bosti but had never seen one before. I thought lions were big and ferocious, but seeing such a beast as a child was more frightening than you can imagine. I put myself between my brothers and the beast, hoping that my life would satisfy its hunger if my plan of escape failed. It just so happened that Father Trobus was close by and came to our rescue. With his bare hands, he killed the beast. He pounded it with both fists. I saw its head sink into the ground like it had run into a stone wall. Then he told us to never venture into the woods again without protection. He scolded us all and told us to go home. Based on the way he shook his finger at us, I think the idea of us being hurt shook him. What he didn't know was that I had my bow, and the boys were safe behind me. However, I didn't realize bostis were evasive savages, swift of foot, and unrelenting in their craving for human flesh. I was glad that great-grandfather Trobus was there." Patience paused a second, noticing the puzzled look on Matt's face. "What's on your mind, my husband?" she asked, looking at the questions in Matt's eyes.

"I've heard you mention your brothers, but I've never met them, not even at the wedding."

"That's because they were with Aunt Beverly at the Falls."

"How old were they when you encountered the bosti?"

Raising an eyebrow, Patience studied Matt for a moment, wondering why he had so many questions. "Why? Do you think they're eighty or ninety?" She snickered, and Matt laughed loudly.

"Let's just say that I just look forward to meeting them someday. Then I'll know for myself." He grinned. "I'm not sure if I'll ever get used to this."

"Used to what, my love?"

"It amazes me how well you can read me. I guess it's true that women have that gift of intuition. You certainly seem to have it."

"The gift is discernment, Matt, and all believers have a degree of it."

"Interesting," Matt said, curious to know more. "I have been with Poppy for a while now, and my discerning gift is nothing like yours," Matt said, scratching his chin.

"But I have been with all of them my entire life. That's four generations of influence. I have been surrounded by prophets, healers, and faith walkers all my life," she said without pride or a condescending tone. It was just a matter of fact.

"What a legacy you have," declared Matt.

"Not just me, my love, but you as well. I have seen so much of the Spirit's work in you and the passion you have for seeking Him out." Matt was a little embarrassed by Patience's edifying observation but thankful that the presence of the Lord in his life was evident. "The more we listen and practice our gifts, the more they will manifest themselves," she said, excited."

"That is amazing."

"Then why the puzzled look?"

"The puzzled look is about the family I've just joined."

"What do you mean?"

"It seems that your whole family is nothing short of perfect. I see no bad habits, flaws, or even normal conflicts. And I must tell you that most families I know have them all."

Patience smiled and giggled a little. "Matt, we have all of that and more. You just haven't seen it yet. And it doesn't last very long because we practice not taking offense. The Spirit will not allow us to pout, hold grudges, or carry hurt in our hearts for very long. You know what it says in the Holy Book, don't you?"

Matt paused a second, then said, "I'm anxious to hear."

"It says that we should never let the sun go down with anger in our hearts. So, we do our very best to practice that every day." Patience pulled his face to hers and kissed him. "See what I mean?"

"Yeah, you'd rather kiss than fight," he said.

"Absolutely," she replied, ruffling his hair.

Though they had been traveling for a while and the sun was sinking low, they hadn't found a place for a campsite.

"The day is coming to a close, the horses are tired, we need water, and we need to stretch our legs and set up camp," said Matt.

"How about that clearing over there by those trees?" Patience pointed.

"Perfect, that will do just fine."

Matt gave the signal to the other wagons to follow him. Abdi proceeded, followed by Bruk and the others who set up camp while Layla, Caleb, and Lire searched for firewood and water. They returned shortly with all the firewood and water they needed.

"I don't know how, but everywhere we turned, we seemed to find what we need," said Lire.

"It's the Lord's doing," interjected Caleb.

"Can we get this done quickly so that we can get a good night's sleep?" insisted Layla.

"My thoughts exactly," uttered Lire. After setting up camp, watering and feeding the animals, they all sat down to give thanks to God and eat dinner.

"I'll see you guys in the morning. Sleep is calling me, and I'm going to accommodate it," said Layla, throwing an extra log on the fire.

"Me too," said Lire. Everyone else followed suit and headed for their tents. As the night progressed, Matt found it hard to sleep, thinking about reaching home. Patience snuggled next to him as they laid down for the night. Abdi made sure that he and the warriors secured the area. Each of them was assigned guard duty throughout the night.

"Are you tired?" Matt asked Patience.

"I'm more excited than tired. I'm so ready to meet your family."

"I know what you mean. It's been several years since I last saw them. You're going to love them, and I know that they are going to love you."

"I hope so. I would die if they didn't like me," said Patience nervously.

"Not a chance. They love the Lord, and so do we. That alone is enough to ensure harmony between us all."

"What do you suppose they are doing right now?" she asked.

"Right now?"

"Yes, right now."

"Most likely, they are snuggled together in that old love seat of theirs," Matt laughed.

"Why are you laughing?"

"Because they have had that thing for years. Every time the cushions wear out, Mom just makes new ones, and then it's another ten years before she even thinks about doing it again." He chuckled.

"I think it's wonderful. Maybe we can start that kind of tradition," Patience said with a teasing smile. Her words moved him; the notion of starting such a tradition stirred his heart. "Are you all right, Matt?"

"Oh, I just miss them and all the things we used to do together. The last thing we did before I started this journey was go fishing."

"Fishing? I love fishing," she said enthusiastically.

"You do? I would never have guessed that about you. You surprise me every day."

"That's okay. I surprise myself," she said, giggling. "I can't wait to see your town."

"There's nothing really to see. It's just the typical little village everyone lives in."

"Matthew Loman, so far, I have found nothing typical about you. When we get there, I'll let you know what I think," she said, using her elbow to jab him lightly in the stomach.

Matt wrapped his muscular arms around her. "Now, how about you tell me a bedtime story about your parents and brothers before we sleep," Matt chortled.

Patience sighed, thinking to herself, *This is going to be a long conversation*. But he wanted to know, so she settled in her mind to tell him whatever he wanted to know. She made herself comfortable against him and cleared her throat. "My mother was the apple of the eyes of my grandparents. They named her Heather because the Lord put it on their hearts. It turns out that among the Growers, she was more knowledgeable than most just as her name proclaimed. Poppy and Moa taught her everything. Her name means 'she knows,' and it also means a flowering evergreen plant that thrives on peaty-muddy barren lands."

"What?" he chuckled.

"I know it sounds funny, but it fits her well. She can plant seeds in any soil, and it will grow. By the time she was my age, she knew every plant and its use. Plants that heal, plants that kill, plants for pain, plants for sleeping, plants for herbs, spices, and seasoning for foods, for cleaning wounds or removing stains or making stains. She knows the use of every tree, from maple trees for syrup to a bilberry bush, which is what some people call huckleberry bush. It's used to increase night vision and protection for eye injuries."

"How do you know all of that?" Matt asked, surprised at how knowledgeable she was about such things.

"My family, of course, prayed over all of us to receive gifts in the Spirit. Prophecy runs deep within us."

"Prophecy...?" Matt repeated the word.

"Prophecy is passed down through our family. We are trained by the Spirit, who gives us knowledge, wisdom, and insight to hear and know people's thoughts."

"Excuse me...?" Matt suddenly sat up, trying not to laugh out loud. "How is that possible?"

"Well, we all have discernment, right?"

"I suppose, to a degree," he stated. '"Well, we just cultivate ours with the Spirit's help to use it as a tool to safeguard our families and the Lord's people."

Matt was a little surprised but knew it was true. She had already told him things that were in his mind that he never voiced. Could it be true? "So ... can you read my mind?"

Patience grinned widely. "Of course, I can, but I choose not to because it is rude and invasive. Besides, I still need training," Patience said, sighing and feeling a little sleepy.

"I'm amazed that it can even be done. And your whole family does this?"

"Yes, some more than others. My parents and the elders can, and even some of my cousins on my mother's side can."

That is so amazing," he said again. "To think that your whole family can do that."

"Not my entire family, Matt, only my immediate family, as well as my first and, occasionally, second cousins. And of course, to whomever the Spirit desires to bless."

"Astonishing ... just astonishing," chuckled the young warrior.

"If you keep saying that, your knowledge of language is going to shrink," she laughed.

"You don't understand, honey. The possibility of hearing people's thoughts is incredible."

Patience just stared at Matt, enjoying his excitement. He made her laugh by his enthusiasm.

"Is it possible for anyone to do that? I mean, besides your family?"

"Yes, my love, I told you if the Spirit wills it." Studying Matt's face, she could tell he had become serious. Patience sat up. "Let me clarify—not just anyone because the Spirit gives gifts according to His will. I think the reason you and I can link our thoughts is because we are married. We have mixed our blood," she said as he looked at her, smiling. "I'm sure since you are one of us, your ability will expand. Poppy will show you how all that works."

Matt was in another world, loving every word coming from Patience. Satisfied with her explanations, he pulled her to himself. The look on Matt's face made her smile.

"You want me to continue?"

"Of course, please."

"It is our tradition that every generation teaches the next all that they know in order to pass it on to the following generations. Otherwise, much history and life-sustaining information would be lost. If the Lord wills, I too will pass on my knowledge to our children if we are blessed to have them," she said with a blush. Matt smiled and listened as she continued.

"My father is king of the whole region of Ethiopia, but I don't really want to talk about my father because I feel that Poppy should talk to you about him."

"Any particular reason why?" Matt asked.

"I just think that a king has more perspective on another king and will be able to throw more light on who he really is," she said, reminding Matt that both her father and grandfather were kings. Matt did not take her words offensively but understood that she wanted him to have greater insight about her father than she could give.

"Okay, then tell me about your great-great-grandfather."

"How about first thing in the morning after breakfast? I'm a little sleepy," she yawned. Before Matt could object, he felt her body relax in his arms.

"I don't believe it. She's actually asleep." Her light snoring confirmed his words. He kissed her, covered her with his blanket, and slept comfortably next to her warm body.

****

Morning came quickly, and the smell of breakfast was in the air. "Do you smell that, Matt?" Patience asked, closing her eyes to take in the aroma.

"Yes, I do, and I'll beat you to it," he laughed. Matt started to rise, but Patience pushed him down and ran out of their tent. Laughing all the way to where Abdi had a plate of hot eggs, fried fish, and biscuits with honey running over it.

"Thanks, Uncle Abdi," she said, taking the enticing plate from his hand. Matt was a couple of seconds behind her.

"Man, when you say breakfast, it's best not to get in the way of that girl," he said, pointing towards Patience. Abdi laughed and handed Matt a plate.

"Good morning, everyone," said Layla, joining the breakfast group. "Whatever that is, it smells delicious." Abdi gave his baby girl a plate and kissed her on the cheek. "Thanks, Daddy. May I have another piece of fish?"

"Of course, sweetie." Abdi smiled as Layla walked to where her sister and new brother sat. One by one, they all came over to feast on the delicious meal Abdi prepared. "Make sure you eat well because we will be back on the road within the hour," he said.

"That gives us just enough time to take a swim, Matt."

"A swim?"

"Yes, I need a bath from all that dust." Matt laughed at Patience's response. "The lake is just down the hill, and it looks inviting," she said.

"Okay, but we can't stay forever. Abdi said we leave within the hour."

"I promise we'll be back before an hour," she said, and they headed for the lake. "Matt, let's try the mind link," she said before diving into clear water, splashing like a fish. Matt quickly joined her, and they both felt refreshed.

Matt paused with a smirky little grin on his face.

"What is it?" she asked. "Tell me."

"You're the one who can read minds," he teased. Not saying a word, she just looked at him, waiting. "Okay, I was wondering why you would dive into unknown water without checking for what lies below the surface?"

She held on to him as the water ripples swirled around them. "I knew the depth was fine, love."

"How could you possibly know that?"

"I don't know. I just know. I knew how deep it was." Patience drew near to Matt. Touching his shoulders lightly, she pushed her body up so her forehead could touch his.

"What are you doing?" he asked, puzzled by her action.

"Shhh ... I'm trying to link our minds, but you must clear your mind and focus on me. It should only take a few moments."

Matt focused intently, and within seconds, he heard raindrops echo in his mind.

Can you hear anything, Matt?

"Yes, I hear raindrops. Wait, your lips are not moving. Oh, my Lord, this is amazing," laughed Matt. "Thank you, Lord, what a wonderful gift. Talk to me some more."

What shall I say?

"Anything, everything, whatever comes to mind," he laughed.

Well, my love, you can only hear me for now, but after Poppy trains you, you'll be able to communicate with others. It is rare to find mind linking outside of our family. I mean, outside our bloodline.

"I know what you meant, love. Mind linking can be very useful, especially in exchanging information that could save lives. To save a life is well worth the training, don't you think?"

"I certainly do," she agreed, embracing his enthusiasm.

"It is a shield of protection. Just think—we will be able to coordinate war strategies and keep in touch even when we are out of each other's sight. Oh, by the way, how far can we be away from each other and still communicate?" he asked.

"This technique only works when we are Christ-focused. We can't turn it on and off whenever we feel like it. Holy Spirit directs us in the use of gifts. As we walk by the Spirit, we are directed. Since we are one, we are on the same wavelength, which makes mind linking easy for us."

Matt pushed his hair out of his face to get a better look at Patience. "You never cease to amaze me. Let's try it underwater," he said, then pushed her head underwater and swam off.

"I'll get you for that!" she yelled, following him.

"Will you look at that," said Lire, pointing at Matt and Patience.

"If you didn't know better, you would think they were married," laughed Bruk.

"Better call them back. It's time to go," said Abdi.

Lire nodded and turned to call them, but he didn't see them anywhere. They seemed to have disappeared. Looking closely, he found no trace of them "Hey, can any of you guys see them?"

"No, I don't see them," said Caleb.

"Can you see them, Father?" asked Lire. "No, how long have they been missing?" Abdi asked, alarmed.

"It's been about six minutes," yelled Lire.

"I saw Matt swim down into the lake, and Patience followed him," said Bruk. Everyone stopped what they were doing and gathered at the edge of the lake.

"I'm going in," said Lire.

"Okay, knowing those two, they are probably just playing, but be careful anyway, son. We don't know this lake. Report back in five minutes," said Abdi.

"Yes, sir."

The water was clear below, and Matt and Patience could see a good distance all around them. He pointed to an odd-looking object about 20 feet below them.

Matt, what is that?

I don't know, but it appears to be moving quickly towards us. I don't like the looks of it.

Me either. Let's go.

As they began to surface, the object increased its approach. To their unpleasant surprise, there was more than one. At least four creatures were coming after them, and Matt knew from the shape that it was bostis—an underwater breed but still bostis.

Suddenly, Patience heard Matt yelling in her mind, *Patience, get out of here. Right now! I'll hold them back.*

What?

Get out of here!

Reluctantly, she headed for the surface. When she almost reached the top, she glanced back and saw four bostis approaching her. Fear overtaking her heart for Matt, she paused *I'm not leaving you.*

Yes, you are. I can't fight them thinking about your safety. Now go! He had never yelled at her before. She didn't like it, even if it was his desire to safeguard her. She obeyed, and came to the surface, she screamed. She swam toward the camp, just as Lire was going into the lake.

"There's something down there. It was coming after Matt and me."

Lire didn't wait for an explanation he went under for Matt. Patience yelled and waved her hand, signaling that Matt was in trouble. Abdi gave the order to plunge in after Matt and Lire.

"Wait, Uncle Abdi. Matt said to keep everyone out of the lake. There are water bostis in the lake."

"My Lord, how many?"

"I saw about four of them, but there could be more."

"Lord Almighty, we have to go in. He can't handle that many by himself."

"I'm going too!" Patience gasped, trying to catch her breath.

"No, you are not!" Abdi said.

"Uncle, yes, I am. The only reason I came up was to alert you. Matt is my husband, and my place is always by his side. Now I'm going, with or without you, but I'm going."

He threw his hands up, muttering something about her being just like her mother. In seconds, the whole team was underwater. What they saw amazed them. There in front of them was Matt, battling the creatures as if he was on dry ground.

It wasn't long before the beasts spotted and charged the warriors. There were enough for each warrior to battle. Lire had already engaged a beast, and handled it well, despite the limited amount of air left in his lungs. Abdi gave orders with his hands to attack. Patience held out her empty hand and called out the name of her bow. The bow appeared in her hand with an arrow set ready to be expelled. With one shot, the arrow pierced the head of the beast, sending it down to the floor of the lake.

One water bosti gripped Layla tightly at her waist, despite the many dagger wounds she had put into its chest. It was squeezing the air from her lungs, attempting to sever her in half. Caleb took one swing, and the head of the bosti went drifting to the floor of the lake, releasing its grip on Layla. Caleb took Layla to surface. He could tell that she would be hard-pressed to make it alone. He got her to the shore and gently sat her down.

"I'm fine, Caleb. It's just a little scratch. Hurry, and help the others," Layla said, annoyed that she couldn't be of further help.

Bruk and Abdi struck down two more beasts, sending them to their doom. Suddenly, Lire pointed towards Matt. To everyone's horror, more bostis were racing towards him. Matt was the closet target. Matt engaged with an abnormally large bosti in front of him, while another approached him from the back. Just before it plunged its fangs into Matt's back, an arrow entered its eye, penetrating its brain. Patience saw several more beast heading towards Matt, but she had no air left. The thought of leaving him terrified her. Nevertheless, she had to surface. On her way up to the surface, she took one last shot from her bow, killing two bostis, before bolting upward.

"God, help him. Protect my husband," she said as she broke the surface.

The other warriors were airless as well and had to surface before continuing. Abdi counted at least five more heading towards Matt before he surfaced. Matt saw them leaving and knew that none of them could last for long fighting these beasts underwater. In his mind, he called on the Lord for help.

Where is your faith, Matt? came the voice to his mind.

Matt saw the beasts coming. He could not summon his companions aloud, and he was running out of air. In desperation, he used his mind and said the words, *Trueball and Lightening, don't you hear your master calling you?* It was his faith that summoned them. Suddenly a gigantic burst of energy hit Matt and filled his lungs with air. Then his two faithful friends appeared before him. *I'm glad to see you guys! Thank you, God,* Matt thought.

"Let's get back down there, now!" Abdi ordered. As soon as each of them took a deep breath, they returned. Patience was already on her way back down to Matt. In midstroke, she stopped, watching in amazement the sight before her. Abdi and the warriors joined her just in time to see the spectacle. Right before their eyes, Matt battled the last five bostis. However, most peculiarly, he was not alone. Two large animals fought by his side. In a matter of a few minutes, the whole ordeal was over.

Everyone surfaced, waiting for Matt to appear. The water splashed wildly as Matt surfaced. He came out of the water, accompanied by Trueball and Lightening. After seeing him safely to shore, they disappeared back into the water. Matt walked towards everyone, exhausted. Patience was the first to reach him.

"Are you all right, my darling?"

"Yes, love. I'm fine," he replied.

"Well, I'm not," complained Lire. "What was that all about?"

"What are you referring to?" asked Matt, completely drained.

"Oh, so you're going to act as if you are oblivious to what I'm saying? You know what I'm talking about—more of those people-eating beasts, the ones that live underwater," said Lire.

"I'm as surprised as you are, Lire. I don't know where they came from and certainly didn't expect them to be underwater. I would have never entered that lake if I had known. No way would I have put Patience in that kind of danger."

"I'm relieved to hear it. By the way, I'm glad your friends showed up, and they're on our side. Where did they come from anyway?"

"It's a long story that I will have to share some other time. I think it's best if we be on our way. We still have about five days until we reach my home. And I'm anxious to see my folks."

"So be it," Abdi said, putting an end to the interrogation and curiosity. While the others continued to talk about the battle, Patience went to see how her cousin was doing after her ordeal with the bostis.

"I'm okay, sis. I have a few bruises, but nothing life-threatening. A little rest, and I'll be as good as new," said Layla. Patience embraced her and prayed over her, despite Layla's feeling towards God.

After drying off and resting, the team was ready to move out. Matt and Patience took the lead while Abdi gave instructions to his sons and Layla.

"We are under attack by an evil presence. I can feel it, so keep your eyes open."

"And I thought that this was going to be a boring journey," said Bruk sarcastically.

"So far, there has not been one boring moment being with Matt," said Caleb.

"Yes, the boy continuously surrounds himself with life-threating occurrences. It's crazy," said Lire. "Look at what we just came out of. What other person do you know has monsters that follow them around?" he joked, attempting to add levity to the situation.

"You have a point there, little brother," said Caleb.

"I don't know what you two are complaining about. You've always asked for adventure," laughed Layla.

"Who's complaining? I'm glad Matt came into our lives. We haven't had a dull minute since we met him, and what more could a Pia Warrior ask for than adventure?" Lire laughed, watching the expressions on the faces around him.

Abdi, observing Layla, walked over to his daughter with concern. "How is your side, my daughter?"

"I'm fine, Father. It was just a little gash on my side. Patience prayed for me. It will heal in a couple of days."

"Let me see it."

She lifted the garment and displayed the teeth marks in her side. Some were deep, but most were surface skin abrasions. Abdi made sure the wounds were clean then covered them with healing salve. He kissed his baby girl on the head and began preparing for the rest of the journey.

14

Wagon Ho!

After an hour of recouping from their water adventure, they all boarded the wagons and set off towards Columbidae. Layla felt oddly energetic. When she lifted her garment, she discovered that her wounds were completely gone. She was pleased with being healed but refused to acknowledge the Lord's intervention.

"Okay, I'm ready," Matt said with enthusiasm as he and Patience settled on the wagon.

"Ready for what," Patience responded, surprised.

"More of your family journal."

"Really? After all we just went through, you want to hear about that?"

"Yes indeed, kind maiden, and don't leave anything out," he said, tipping his head playfully. All she could do was giggle.

"I'd like to hear more about the founder of the Growers. He sounds like my kind of man." He grinned. There was excitement in his voice, like a kid in a sweet shop.

"Matt, I can't start there, or it will throw me out of order," she said, trying to explain.

"Out of order? I wouldn't want to do that. Please, just continue the way you were going."

"You're not disappointed?" she asked, hoping she hadn't hurt his feelings.

"No way. As long as I get to hear your journal, I'm fine." He smiled and listened with great interest.

"There was more than one founder," she said with a smile. "My great-great-grandmother, Julia, was King Joel's wife. She helped him create a wonderful community. Father Trobus never spoke much about his mother, Julia," Patience said sadly. "I suppose that's because she died when he was a young man. However, my great-grandfather Trobus often sat me on his lap while my brothers sat on the floor in front of him. He told of wild, wonderful stories of adventure about his father Joel, himself, and Poppy. We had no idea that all of those stories were true. I learned many things about Mother Julia from Father Trobus. She was short, no more than five feet." She laughed. "Her eyes were gray like a wolf, and her hair was long and raven black. Her lips were the color of strawberries, and she had fair skin, which was darkened by the sun. I'm told that my great-great-grandmother was very shapely and beautiful to look upon."

"If she was anything like you, I can understand that," Matt said, taking her hand as they traveled along the road.

"She was strong for her size and could pull the string of a bow as easily as any woman twice her size."

"How do you know all of this? You talk as if you were there," Matt inquired, amazed at her ability to describe a woman she had never met.

"I can sometimes read things and become part of the whole historical scenery. I don't know how or why—I just can. Maybe it's just part of the prophetic gift. Kind of strange, huh?"

"I'll say, but I like it," he said, taking an irresistible kiss from her lips.

"Behave yourself, or I'll never finish telling you the story. Besides, we are drawing too much attention." Matt laughed and kissed her again.

"Okay, I'll compose myself for the moment. Only because I want to hear the rest of the story," Matt said.

"I could sense that there was much joy in great-grandfather Trobus' heart when he talked about his mother, but there was a sadness as well. Despite the sadness, he loved to talk about her. All but the death part. I suppose that is why Poppy shared the story of her death with my brothers and me rather than great-grandfather Trobus. I could tell that they were very close, more so than most boys to their mothers. Even great-grandmother Emma, Trobus' wife, talked very little about Julia's death. I suppose that's why they wrote it all down. That way, we could one day read for ourselves just what happened. The way Poppy explained it was beautiful and painful at the same time."

"It happened one day when Father Joel and Mother Julia were taking provisions to one of the City Dweller's towns. A day never passed that she didn't help someone. Poppy told me of the many people she helped. It didn't matter if they were rich, poor, dirty, or clean. She saw only people in need of a Savior, and she was the Lord's means to reach them. Hospitality was in her blood. Given a chance, her loving smile could warm the coldest of hearts, and her kind words could stop almost any conflict between people."

"There was this one story he told of her that captured my heart. A family was struggling with a lack of food and shelter. The father of the family was addicted to drinking.

He often mistreated his young wife and child until Julia confronted him. He threatened to harm his wife, but the woman's four-year-old daughter stepped in between her parents. Julia was surprised, and so was the child's mother. Of course, Julia moved the child aside as she continued to censure the father for his mistreatment of his family. After she finished, somehow, the inebriated man became sober. She prayed for them, and from what Poppy told me, the man never touched another drop of the stuff."

"Julia may have been small, and she looked frail, but her spirit was enormous. She often wore colorful garments that expressed her personality. Visiting families was her passion; she showed such love and kindness to them that they wanted to know all about her life. Edifying, building up, encouraging, and sometimes reproving people was her calling. Those she served never knew that they were in the presence of a queen. And Mother Julia never told them."

"Time passed, and Father Joel and Mother Julia made many trips back and forth throughout the cities. One day, the little four-year-old girl became very ill and would have died, but God used the faith in Mother Julia to heal her. The child grew and became very attached to Julia, who loved her as one of her own children. However, the little girl's mother became ill and grew very weak and frail. Julia treated her with much care and desperately tried to bring her back to health. Unfortunately, the poor care she received over the years had robbed her of life. Her name was Bivi. She was blessed to even see her daughter Lola's fifteenth year. Julia counted Bivi among her dearest friends, and when Bivi died, she secretly provided for the family by making sure Bivi's husband had work. She also had men from the Growers' community periodically visit Lola and her father to make sure all was well with them. Julia thrived on helping others. She, along with Father Joel and Trobus, did great work among the City Dwellers. She was blessed and most precious among kings and paupers."

Matt listened intensely to Patience, the woman to whom his heart belonged. Her words captured his attention and held him spellbound. He smiled as she continued uninterrupted.

"On the last day of Julia's life, Joel was preoccupied with the elders of the City Dwellers. He was trying to convince them to turn away from evil and turn to God. He pulled scriptures from the Holy Book to show them the outcome of those who didn't heed sound doctrine. Father Joel told the City Dwellers about the guilt and punishment of nations and people in the past who failed to listen. The people of the great flood and those of Sodom and Gomorrah were City Dwellers whose wickedness brought about the collapse of their civilization. The same fate awaited those Father Joel sought to help."

"I imagine him saying, 'Listen! The Lord is calling to your city in hopes that you have sense enough to fear Him and turn to wisdom. The Lord will not forget a wicked house and ill-gotten treasures. It says so in the book of Micah.' Despite their failure to heed the warning, he still tried to organize their people to work together in building storage bens before the great famine."

"How often do famines come?" Matt asked, wondering if there was any connection to his own experience with them.

"I don't know. Usually, they come from God because of judgment on disobedience or as a lesson to teach humility to the proud. However, not all catastrophes come from

God. We live in a fallen world, and most of our problems come because of our own sin. Nevertheless, before catastrophes come, Poppy said, a warning from the Lord's watchman always comes. I am amazed at how often prophets are sent among the people to warn them, and I am stunned when no one listens. According to the Book of Proverbs, it's like the man who takes hold of a passing dog's ear; he knows that the dog is going to bite him, and yet he foolishly does it anyway."

"Despite all the evidence of an oncoming catastrophe, no one changed. The City Dwellers were a people accustomed to taking without giving or ever putting anything back into the earth. The land was constantly being stripped of nutrients. According to the journal, Father Joel and great-grandfather Trobus tried to show the City Dwellers methods of crop rotation many times. They even told them what plants to put down to build up the soil, but no one wanted to learn. There was no work ethic. People only sought ways to please themselves. Their minds darkened with demonic activity."

"Bivi's family was the exception. Lola took an interest in Mother Julia and followed her around for years. She learned more about horticulture than anyone in her town. When she turned 15, she had mastered most of the growth techniques needed in providing and maintaining food for her people. Lola loved her way into Julia's heart. Later as I read through Father Joel's writings, I found that even after Lola had grown up and had her own family, most of the City Dwellers remained the same."

"Do you think Father Joel had any hope for the City Dwellers?" Matt questioned.

"Of course, he would never give up on them." Patience said, taking Matt's hand in her own.

"You sound very sure of yourself." Matt smiled.

"Mom said I have a way of just knowing things. She said I got it from the Lord, just like great-grandmother Emma," she said, blushing.

Matt wondered how children survived among the City Dwellers with things so out of balance.

Patience settled herself more comfortably by leaning against Matt while she continued looking through the journal.

"I have a question before you continue," Matt said.

"You were about to explain the last day of Mother Julia's life. Are you going to share what happened?"

"Yes, I was just about to do that. On the day of the terrible tragedy, it was late in the evening, just before the sun went down. As he usually did, Father Joel was busy talking with the elders of the City Dwellers. He became so involved that he hadn't noticed that Mother Julia wandered out of his sight. It wasn't unusual for her to do so. He just didn't want her away from him for too long. She walked towards an area where a cluster of women and children needed food. Julia carried a food basket made from a special almond wood. It is believed that it was made from the same kind of wood from which Aaron's rod was made; the rod is described in the Holy Book. Remember how Aaron's rod budded and produced almonds in the same day? Well, Mother Julia's basket produced abundant food whenever she prayed over it. She intended to share the provisions that God had given her with the women and their children. The children were crying, and one little boy was coughing so badly that he could be heard from a great distance."

"Before she could reach them, four men in hiding jumped her. She had no warning or time to react. All it took was one blow to her head with an iron bar, and she was down. Lola was on her way to meet Julia and was only a short distance from her. She, too, heard the coughing child. Suddenly, there was a loud scream from Lola that got Joel's attention. Julia was out of his sight, and he knew that a terrible thing had happened by Lola's scream and by the Spirit."

"The men who attacked her stood over her, thinking she was dead. As one of them reached down to search her for valuables, the others were keeping watch. None of them expected what happened next. She touched the hand of the man searching her and spoke to him. He tried to snatch back his hand. She had no forceful grip on him, yet he could not break free. Panic not only gripped him but also the men with him."

"She said, 'You are evil men, and you have robbed and even killed innocent people for the love of fading treasure.' She paused to let her words sink in, and then she continued. 'Evil gain will never be enjoyed. You have harmed me in a way that I will not recover, but you have done yourselves greater harm.' The man in her grasp continued to try to escape but could not. The other three were paralyzed, unable to move. They heard every word but could not respond. There was power in her spirit and conviction in her words that made them understand. The man in her grasp was sure of only one thing—he had to be free of her at once."

"'Let me go, you witch!' he called to her." Patience paused, perturbed.

"What is it, my love?" asked Matt.

"I have read this part of the journal a hundred times, and it still bothers me how evil and hypocritical people are. They label, judge, and accuse the innocent of evil when they are doing evil themselves. They refuse to even acknowledge the evil intent of their own hearts. It confuses my mind how the man could ever conclude that Mother Julia was a witch. He and his cohorts hurt an old woman whose only concern was providing for helpless, poor women and children."

Matt could see that Patience was having a harder time dealing with her feelings than she realized. He wanted to help but wasn't sure how to go about it. He decided to listen instead of voicing a solution. He figured that she was not in the mood to be interrupted. Silence permeated the atmosphere surrounding Patience and Matt. Two minutes of silence seemed like a lifetime to him, but he waited until Patience spoke.

"Because this evil man could not escape Julia's grasp, he assumed that she was a necromancer or, as he called her, a witch. If only he had known who had hold of him and the gifts she had, he would have longed for the peace and kindness she offered. His life would have been different. Mother Julia looked him in the eyes, and prophetic words came out of her," Patience stated sorrowfully. "'You have had many warnings and many opportunities to repent, and you have ignored them all. The Lord has great love for you, but you have disregarded the mercy and grace of God and squandered away your only opportunity for life. Because you refuse to obey the Lord, he has allowed your action to bring its deadly consequences upon you.'"

Patience read the journal as if it was her speaking to the man and not Mother Julia. Matt was amazed at how the whole atmosphere changed. He could actually sense the presence of Patience's ancestor.

Patience continued reading. "'I see even now love beckoning your resistant heart, ready to forgive you, but you are unwilling.' The man simply laughed in her face, and the echo of the others' behind him mocked love's invitation to life. Her hand gently slipped from his to the ground as she blacked out. That is when Lola came upon the men standing over Julia. Her screams drove them away."

"Father Joel had left the elders and rushed to find her. By the time he reached her, her life was at its end. Lola held her head in her lap, weeping hysterically. Joel fell to his knees and gathered Julia to himself, only to discover that she was bleeding. He desperately tried to revive her. When she opened her eyes, she smiled. Poppy said Julia's last requests to her husband were, 'Tell Trobus not to fear. Tell him to serve the Lord and love people.' She told Joel to do all he could to save the City Dwellers and care for the children. His tears fell upon her garment. She touched his face and smiled. Her last words to him were, 'My love,' and then she was gone.

"Those men killed the love of his life, yet he still continued to help City Dwellers. It wasn't that he was void of feelings and emotions—it was that he understood the purpose of her life. He had the same purpose, but he was to remain a while longer. Poppy told me that all people will die. However, the Lord walks through death with those who love Him." There was a strong conviction in Patience's voice, a kind Matt had not noticed in her before.

She no longer needed the journal to express what she had virtually memorized. "Great-grandfather Trobus did not feel the same as his father. The death of his mother put the cry of war in his heart. He wanted to destroy them all, but his father would not allow it. Father Joel said that revenge was not the way of the Lord for mankind. Love was stronger than death, forgiveness more powerful than hatred. Father Joel agreed that the men who did this terrible deed to Mother Julia must be brought to justice. He assured Trobus that they would be, but he reminded his son that justice had to be done according to their law and the Lord's righteousness. Then Father Joel placed his hand on his son's head and wept as he prayed for them both to overcome the pain of their loss and against the evil spirit that pressed them both to take revenge."

"The loss of Mother Julia turned part of her son's heart to stone. Against the king's command, Trobus hunted down the four men who took his mother's life. When they saw him, the fierce look on his face told them that they had to fight, run, or die. Since there was no place to run, they joined forces to fight. After all, they were thieves and cutthroats with experience; he was still a youth, just getting facial hairs. It was Father Trobus against four men. Unfortunately, they found out too late that they were no match for Trobus' strength, and the rage in him was too much for anyone to withstand. He would have killed them all if it had not been for his mother's face appearing before his eyes. When he had finished, the men were too broken to move, but at least they lived. In the heat of his most bitter moment, his mother's love for life, through the God she served, took the desire to kill out of his heart."

"The provision basket was found in their possession. As I alluded to, Mother Julia had the gift of provision. The basket she made had the ability to multiply. When food was placed into the basket and prayed over, the basket multiplied whatever food was in it. The men who took her life only had to ask, and she would have freely given them provisions. In their conceited, demon-driven hearts, they never considered there were people like Mother Julia, who would have freely shared provisions with them," Patience said sadly.

"People cannot embrace what they do not know or refuse to understand," Matt said, holding her hand.

"I know, my love. The concept of giving out of love evades them. Their savage need to survive throws love and mercy to the wind. It is as if all City Dwellers are infected with a dark bitter disease. It even goes on to this day. Everyone seems to be doing what they think is right in their own eyes. Those men who murdered her only knew how to take whatever they wanted and kill whoever got in their way. To their dismay, the basket didn't even work, and to their despair, the wrath of Trobus left them broken. They were not aware that prayer was the key to the basket's prosperity."

"It was several years before Trobus found the heart to completely forgive them. Still, the pain did not fully dissipate. It took many talks and great patience with his father Joel before he released his anger. Joel wrote of Julia and her good deeds and, of course, her great love for people. It's all in the journal he kept. Poppy used to let me read it often. I learned more about her from the journal. I only wish that I could have met her. I think we would have been great friends," she said with eyes full of tears.

"I think so too," Matt said, saddened by her response to sharing the story. "We can stop if you want, my darling. I didn't mean to bring you sadness."

"Oh, I'm fine. I always cry when I'm moved by emotions." She reached out and brushed strands of hair covering Matt's face. She paused a moment to regain her composure.

"Now, where was I? Oh yes, Joel took the basket with him. The journal later revealed that Julia made four such baskets and placed them in secret locations; they were to be discovered by women of the royal family on or around their twenty-fifth celebratory year from their birth. When Trobus took Poppy and the others to the land of Truevine, Father Joel gave one of Mother Julia's baskets to Emma. The other three baskets were distributed in unknown parts of Truevine. When the right time comes, the locations will be revealed. The baskets have been in our family for as long as I can remember. My mother says one such basket will belong to me whenever I finish my training. I'm not sure what that means, but I can hardly wait for the day to come."

"That means you have four years to wait, my love, right?" Matt asked, still messing with her about her age. Patience just smiled and continued.

"I found out later that Father Joel kept another journal of our family that reaches back 28 generations. You can imagine the time I had as a child reading about our people."

The way Patience responded to issues and situations caused Matt to smile. "Your family is fascinating. I am blessed to be a part of it." Matt whispered words into her ear that brought a blush and then a kiss.

****

Another full day passed. The time for setting up camp was upon them. Abdi gave orders for the warriors to set up while he spoke with Matt and Patience.

"How much longer before we get to Columbidae?" inquired Abdi.

"We should be home in a few days," Matt said.

Abdi called everyone together for instructions. "We have been traveling for several days. If the Lord wills, I would like to spend the rest of our journey without incident. So, no swimming, fishing, hunting, or taking nature walks. Keep your eyes open and stay alert. We have enough provisions to last us until Jesus comes, so relax for tonight. Caleb and Lire will take first watch. Matt and Bruk will relieve them in four hours. The rest of us will get some rest, and first thing in the morning, we will start out fresh."

Abdi gathered wood for a fire and pointed to the warriors to do the same. There was snickering all around the camp. Every time Abdi passed by, he heard light laughter. Finally, he stopped and turned around to face everyone. "What's going on?" he asked.

Bruk answered immediately. "Father, asking us not to do the things you mentioned is like asking a bird not to fly."

"Yeah, or a horse not to run or chicken not to cluck…" chimed in Lire.

"Okay, I get the picture, son," Abdi said, laughing with them. "I suppose you're right. Just do me a favor and pray before any of you venture out." After getting affirmation from them, he decided to turn in early. To his surprise, everyone else did the same. Abdi was pleased.

Sleeping in a tent had been a challenge; Matt knew that Patience was exhausted even if she didn't say so. He thought spending the rest of the time in the wagon would be cozier. Morning came early, and everybody rose with the sun. Camp broke up, and Matt gave the word to follow him. It had been a silent night, and the day looked promising.

"Matt, I'm really excited about reaching your village," Patience said, scooting closer to him. "I am a little curious to know about the people of Columbidae. What are they like?"

Matt beamed with joy. "Most of our villagers are quite welcoming. You'll see once we get there. We should arrive before nightfall."

Nodding, Patience snuggled close to Matt while watching God's beautiful landscape. The wagons moved steadily across the terrain without incident. The road led them into woodlands with tall trees and rolling hills. The scenery was breathtaking, and Patience enjoyed every minute of it. About midday, without warning, a large oak tree fell across the road.

"Whoa," Matt said to the four horses pulling his wagon. He pulled them to a stop with one hand and kept Patience from falling out of the wagon with the other. The wagons behind them also came to an abrupt stop. Abdi and his sons jumped down from their wagons, Layla close behind. They came forward to see what was going on.

"What is it?" asked Abdi.

"I'm not sure, but I don't like it," said Matt.

Patience was uneasy, as well. "Matt, do you feel that?" she asked.

"Feel what?" asked Abdi, looking around for signs of danger.

"Yes, Patience, I can feel it."

"Feel what?" Abdi asked again, but this time, he pulled out his sword, as did the others when they saw Abdi's reaction.

"There is a strong evil presence in this place, stronger than I've felt before," explained Patience.

"What does that mean?" asked Caleb.

"It means trouble. That's what it means—trouble," Lire bellowed.

"What do you make of it, Matt?" asked Layla, taking her bow into her hands.

"I don't' know, but it has no business in the realm of the Growers," he replied.

"This land is blessed of the Lord," Patience said, perturbed at the thought of evil invaders.

"Even though this land is part of Truevine, could it be possible that parts of it have been taken over by City Dwellers?" asked Matt.

"City Dwellers? What makes you think that, Matt?" she asked.

"Don't you remember Poppy telling us to be careful because of the rumors regarding City Dwellers? There are some badlands not far from here," said Matt.

"Yes, I remember, but I didn't expect to feel a force like this. How far are we from the badlands?" asked Patience.

"It's several miles west of us, but we won't travel that way," replied Matt.

"What should we do?" asked Layla.

"We will continue our journey and handle threats when they come," said Bruk.

"Sounds good to me. Let's keep moving," Layla replied.

"Don't you think that we should move that tree first?" chuckled Lire.

Suddenly, the sound of horses and voices were heard a few yards away. Matt jumped down from the wagon and held up his hand. "Patience, Layla, stay hidden in the back of the wagon. Be ready with your bows in case the unexpected happens." Nodding, Layla entered the back of the wagon. The two women felt Matt was being overprotective, but they followed his orders.

"Where are you going, Matt?" asked Patience.

"I'm going to see if trouble is afoot."

"Uncle Abdi, be alert," Patience called out as Bruk signaled the other warriors to fan out in different directions.

Turning, Matt saw that Patience and Layla were still visible. "I know you two want to know what is going on; nevertheless, I would appreciate it if you stay where you are and out of sight."

"Why should we? We are Pia Warriors, just as you are," said Layla, annoyed.

"Because he said so, warrior! Follow orders," said Abdi, disappointed with her behavior.

Matt stepped closer to the wagon. "I know that you are very capable, Layla. It's not to demean your honor. It's to give us an advantage in case you have to use your bows," he explained. "Now, get down in those wagons, both of you!" They did so, just before a band of men came from the woods and stood behind the fallen tree. Matt looked slowly in every direction to count how many there were. Finally, a brawny man, larger than all his companions, stepped forward. Matt assumed that he was the leader.

With his hand on his weapon, the brawny man addressed Matt and the Pia Warriors. "I see that you are carrying supplies, and the horses look good too," he said, grinning and revealing multiple teeth missing from his mouth.

"We are on our way to Columbidae with provisions. You are welcome to share in a part of what we have," Matt said politely.

The band of men laughed loudly at Matt's suggestion, thinking he was jesting with them. "He's going to share with us!" yelled one of the men.

"Yeah, share his little supper," said another. Then, the intruders became angry, and several swore under their breath at Matt. Matt was not shaken or moved by the insults or crude gestures made by the band.

"If you don't want or need any provisions, please step aside," Matt said with authoritative calmness.

"And if we choose to stay where we are?" retorted the leader.

"Then you will remain empty-handed," Matt responded.

When the band of men heard Matt's last remark, which they interpreted as a threat, some pulled their swords, and others readied their bows. The leader slanted his eyes at Matt, and his voice took on a deadly serious tone.

"My men don't agree with your offer, friend," he retorted.

"Why? I think my offer was very generous. Don't you, Uncle Abdi?"

Abdi nodded at Matt, eyes never leaving the intruders. "Most kind of you, if I must say so myself," said Abdi, still looking over the band of men who were blocking their way.

Observing Matt and the Pia Warriors, the leader of the band concluded that these were men of war. He didn't see fear in any of their eyes. That had to change if he was going to carry out his plan of robbery. Intimidation had always worked before, and he saw no reason not to use it this time as well.

"Do you know who we are?" asked the leader, taking a step closer.

"I suppose they call you Toothless. Other than that, I have no idea," said Matt sarcastically. Lire and his brothers broke into laughter at Matt's comical statement.

"So, we have a funny man in our midst," exclaimed Toothless. "We'll see how funny it is when I stick your head on the end of my spear."

"You have been asked twice to clear the way. Could it be that you lack the ability to understand my words?" Matt said, taking two steps forward. Bruk and Lire tried to maintain their composure at how Matt's comments left the poor fellow confused and rattled. "We must reach our destination before nightfall," Matt said, growing impatient.

Enraged by Matt's words, the bandits drew in closer. "I'm afraid that you are going to be late to your destination," said Toothless. Without warning, he jumped over the tree and charged Matt. Within seconds, he grabbed hold of Matt's clothes. His assault was futile; instead, he found himself being lifted off the ground, dangling in midair. Gripping Toothless' leather garment, along with a fist full of chest hairs, Matt looked the man in the eyes without blinking.

Matt's powerful strength shocked the haughty man and caused his subordinates to back up. Nervous at seeing their leader lifted off the ground, two of the thieves shot arrows at Matt, hoping to kill him on the spot. Pulling Toothless around, Matt used him as a shield. One arrow pierced Toothless' shoulder and another his buttocks, bringing a painful yell.

"Stop it, you idiots! Are you trying to kill me?" said Toothless.

"You don't hear or see that every day," snorted Lire.

"What's that, little brother?" asked Caleb.

"A man with an arrow sticking out of his butt, claiming he's going to die from it," laughed Lire.

"Tell your men to put down their arrows and get back, unless they want to see how many arrows your body can hold," yelled Abdi.

"Get back, you fools, and put down those stupid weapons." Toothless was convinced that the mysterious man holding him was capable of anything. It worked, and the bandits backed off.

Patience and Layla wanted to see what was going on outside. The curiosity was killing them. They were thankful that they could at least hear everything. It tickled Patience to hear her husband speak with authority. Abdi and his sons stood ready with their own swords but made no move to aid Matt without his consent.

"Why are you hiding and robbing people? Don't you know that people are doing their best to make an honest living to provide for their families?" Matt said angrily. Toothless, still in pain from the arrows, only groaned, unable to answer. "If you spent half the time it takes to rob people, doing honest work, you would have all the provision you need and then some. Instead, you and your band of thieves come out of the woods to harm and take what others have labored for. It is not right."

Hearing Matt's speech, Lire laughed and felt sorry for the bandits. Bruk and Caleb chuckled as Matt dragged the big man across the ground to where the large tree laid across the road. In the process, the arrow in his bottom dislodged itself. The bandits were dumbfounded at the sight of seeing a man half Toothless' size manhandle their leader with such force.

Matt looked with contempt at the lot of them. "If I ever come back this way and find you harming or robbing our people, I will have you all thrown into prison," Matt said with authority.

"You don't look like Growers anyway," commented Caleb. "Where did you come from, and what are you doing here?"

No one answered as Toothless' men were waiting for him to do something. Embarrassed by the ordeal, Toothless tried his best to regain control. Taking hold of the protruding arrow, Toothless pulled it out of his shoulder and tried to gouge out Matt's eye. He was not quick enough, and when he raised his hand to try a second time, he found another arrow protruding from his hand. He let out an excruciating scream. The arrow had pierced his hand dead center.

"I told you all to stop shooting those arrows, you fools. Who did that? What part of 'don't shoot' don't you understand? I'll have the head of whoever shot me," Toothless screamed angrily. All of his archers denied shooting. "I know one of you did it, and when I find out, you're going to wish you had never been born." Toothless quieted and watched as Matt once again stood in front of him.

"I suggest that you take your men and leave this land while you still can," Matt said.

Ignoring Matt's warning, Toothless yelled for his men to attack. Matt picked Toothless up and threw him towards the oncoming men. They paused long enough to catch their leader, and then, they intended to cut Matt down. However, right before their eyes, Matt stooped down and took the fallen tree by one of its large limbs and lifted it over his head and cleared it from the road. Everyone, including the Pia Warriors, was astonished at what they witnessed. Matt turned and looked at the band of men and smiled. Fear was written on their faces. Every man scattered into the woods. Matt caught hold of Toothless before he could run.

"Listen to me. The next time I see you and your lawless band of men, you better be working for the good of others and not robbing them."

Toothless stuttered out a promise that he would obey Matt's words. When Matt let him go, Toothless took off, hobbling after his men without looking back. Abdi and his boys laughed, for they had never seen such a sight.

"That seemed easier than the other problems we've faced. Right, Father?" exclaimed Lire.

Abdi, watching the bandits run away in the distance, said, "You are right. Real thieves don't give up so easily. You and your brothers keep a sharp eye out in case our visitors return. We should be on our way shortly."

"Yes, sir," Lire replied.

Finally, after Matt gave them the all-clear, Patience and Layla came up out of the wagon. They laughed at how Matt terrified those men, particularly by lifting and throwing the huge tree from the roadway.

"You were magnificent, Matt," Patience said, kissing him as he climbed back into the wagon. "I am grateful to the Lord for protecting my eyes by piercing Toothless' hand with an arrow. That was an amazing shot. Of course, I know it wasn't you or Layla because you two had orders to stay low," Matt teased.

"I couldn't let that crazy heathen hurt you," Patience protested, then smiled.

"I'm glad you were there," he said, as she kissed him again.

Interrupting the newlyweds, Abdi remarked, "Matt! Every day that we spend with you, I am constantly surprised." Abdi smiled and shook his head as he and his boys got back into their own wagons.

On the road again, Patience began to think about Matt's childhood and became curious. "Matt, I've been talking about my family a lot, but I would love to hear a little more about yours. Tell me about your childhood and your parents," she asked.

Layla perked up with curiosity. "Yes, I'd like to know more about that myself."

Patience was startled by Layla's voice. "What are you doing in our wagon? I thought that you were riding with Uncle Abdi?"

"I was, but it seemed more exciting in your wagon than mine, so here I am. Besides, I want to keep you company."

"I bet you do," said Patience, smiling.

"Are there any more like you at your home, Matt?" Layla asked, giggling.

"Now, Layla!" laughed Patience.

"What? Anyone with eyes can see that you got a nice catch. If there are more available, you wouldn't want to deprive your only sister, now would you?" Layla teased back.

Matt, amused at their verbal jousting, played along. "You won't find any at home, but in the village, you may find a few prospects." As the wagon continued to move towards its destination, Matt turned the conversation back to Patience's question about his family. "What do you want to know?"

"Everything," Patience said, hooking her arm through his. "Tell me about your family," she insisted.

"As I remember, you did not tell me everything about yours," grumbled Matt.

"I told you enough, and you are not getting out of this by escaping back into my history," she said, giving his arm a firm jerk.

"Come on, you two. I'm waiting," Layla jokingly whined.

Matt laughed. "Let's see ... I'm an only child."

"I can see this is going to be boring," said Layla, giggling and crawling into the back of the wagon. "I'm going to get some sleep. Call me when you get to the good stuff. Like male cousins or something," she said, sighing.

"I'll wake you up when we get there," said Patience as she kissed Matt. "Go ahead. I'm listening, my darling."

"Oh brother," mumbled Layla. Patience ignored the remark and urged Matt to continue.

"I grew up in Columbidae with my mother and father. My father has three brothers and two sisters, and my mother has two brothers, but they all live in the village of Deer Run. I was told that it was named that because of the abundance of deer, moose, and elk. I had a normal childhood with dozens of cousins to play with. I grew up working hard by my father's side and learned many lessons from Dad and Mom. Boring, huh?" remarked Matt.

"I'll say," mumbled Layla.

"I thought that you were going to sleep," replied Patience. "Please continue, Matt. Nothing you say is boring. I love it. Tell me more."

For the next three hours, Matt talked in detail about his family, and at the end, Patience just smiled, thinking what an amazing husband she had. She leaned her head against Matt's shoulder, then started singing again as they proceeded towards Columbidae. By evening, just before the sunset, they arrived safely. Matt asked Uncle Abdi and the men to put the provisions away. Abdi and his family made their way towards the Village Inn while Matt and Patience approached his birthplace.

"There it is, my love—the place I was born." Patience looked up the winding road and saw tall trees all around and colorful flowers everywhere. The mountains in the background completed the whole scene. And there sat a magnificent log house with a small replica of the log house sitting off to the side.

"Matt, it's beautiful," she exclaimed, holding on to his arm.

When they arrived at his parent's house, Matt climbed down from the wagon and held out his arms. Without hesitation, Patience dove into them. He caught her and placed her gently by his side and walked towards the front door.

15

The Arrival

Matt knocked on the door of the cabin, and immediately, there was the sound of movement inside. The door opened, and there stood a wide-eyed woman in her early forties, her husband looking over her shoulder. Surprised and overjoyed, their eyes filled with tears as they stood, staring at the young couple in their doorway. At last, their son was home. At least, he looked like their son. The young man in front of them was twice the size of the young man who had left years ago. Where had the time gone? One year away for Matt had turned into three years for Frances and Jeremy. Jedidiah had a way of altering elements, and time was one of them.

Frances looked in his eyes and knew without a doubt that it was Matt. And with him was a woman of uncommon, exquisite beauty. Matt stood with the biggest grin on his face, and it was clear to Frances and Jeremy that the young woman belonged to him.

"Son, I've missed you so much, even to the point of having dreams and visitations about you in the Spirit. For the last few months, I've done nothing but think about you and pray for you. Today the Lord has answered my prayers, and I'm so thankful," Frances said tearfully. Without further hesitation, she leaped into her son's arms and wept like a baby. The emotion was too much for her to hold inside. Jeremy could hardly hold his composure as well but decided to let Frances have her moment with their son. He was so pleased to see them that way.

Patience watched the interaction between mother and son and felt tears of joy stream down her face. She was so happy for Matt, and seeing his mother in his arms was absolutely delightful. Patience moved passed them and embraced Jeremy.

"I'm Patience, your new daughter," she said teary-eyed.

"I suspected as much," said Jeremy, opening his arms to receive her. "I am so happy that Matt found you. Just by looking at the two of you standing here, I can tell that you belong together." Patience blushed, smiling with satisfaction at Jeremy's words.

After a moment, Jeremy and Frances switched, and the greetings started all over again. Frances hugged Patience tightly. "Welcome to our home, my daughter," she said, holding her with delight. Patience embraced her back and kissed her on the cheek.

"It is my joy to be your daughter. I hope that we will grow in love for each other and that your home will be a place of peace and love."

"What a pleasant thing to say, dear, and I hope the same for you and Matt. Now come in, and let us hear all about how you two found each other and how my son was able to capture a treasure like you."

Matt was surprised that his mother was able to capture perfectly what Patience was to him after having just met her. Patience was his treasure and one he would forever cherish. "Mom, I couldn't agree with you more, and Patience is not only my treasure—she's also my heart."

Jeremy smiled at hearing such passion coming from his son. Frances laughed and took her children by their hands and led them to the front room. "Tell me all the details of how you met and how you came to be married," she said. Longing to hear how this young woman won the heart of her son, Frances signaled for her husband to get seats. Jeremy pulled up two comfortable chairs for Frances and himself to sit in while Matt and Patience sat in a worn-out love seat that obviously was a favorite spot for his parents.

"Wow, you two must really love Patience if you are willing to let us have your love seat," Matt said, teasing his parents. They laughed, and Frances gestured for them to sit.

"I'll be right back with refreshments, and then you can tell us your story."

"Would you like me to help you?" asked Patience.

"Oh, no dear, it will only take a moment. I always have a pitcher of tea and a plate of cookies or cake on hand for such occasions."

"That's a fact," said Jeremy. "Ask any kid in the village, and they'll attest to that." They all laughed as Frances made her way to the kitchen where she paused a moment to catch her breath. A moment later, she returned with refreshments, ready to hear all that Matt and Patience had to say. Matt started while Patience listened, eager to hear again what she remembered in detail.

"It was a crazy day," Matt began. "I had just finished with the fields when she walked up. I was talking to Master Jedidiah when she captured my gaze. She was about fifty yards away from us, but even at that distance, I could tell that she was beautiful. Poppy, that's what Patience calls her grandfather, told me to close my mouth. He was laughing because I was gawking at his granddaughter. I couldn't help it, and I couldn't believe that, as dirty and grimy as I was, he wanted to introduce me to her right then and there. I was too embarrassed to meet such a beautiful woman, and I told him so. I told him I was not going to meet her dressed in dirt from head to foot. I was glad that she stayed where she was. After I washed up and felt presentable, Poppy introduced us. It was love at first sight."

Frances clasped her hands over her mouth as sounds of laughter seeped through her fingers. Jeremy watched her, knowing that she was thoroughly enjoying listening to Matt's first encounter with Patience. He was also moved by what he heard. This young woman had made an indelible impression on his son, which made his heart glad.

"You want to tell them how you grabbed me from my parents and practically knocked them over, twirling me around?"

"Matt, you didn't," said Frances. Patience sat there, giggling as if she hadn't said anything. Matt looked at her and knew that she was in the mood for teasing him.

"Are you trying to get me in trouble?" he said, laughing.

"Well, I would like to hear about it," said Jeremy.

"Dad, it wasn't like that at all."

"Oh, so you didn't swing me around in front of my parents?" Patience said, eyeing Matt for a response.

"Of course, I did, but not the way you're saying it." Matt laughed as Patience went to great lengths to get him in trouble." "You're enjoying this, aren't you?" he said, taking hold of her and tickling her.

"Stop, Matt, stop," she said, laughing.

"Not until you tell the truth."

"I am telling the truth," she exclaimed.

"You know what I mean. Tell them what really happened, or I'll tickle you forever."

"Okay, just stop tickling me." Matt paused to see what his little bride had up her sleeves. "Ok, what really happened," she said, snickering, "was that when Matt twirled me around, my feet hit my mother, and she fell onto my father, and they both fell into the fountain behind them."

"Oh, Matt, you didn't," exclaimed Frances.

"No, I didn't." Matt started tickling Patience again. "Are you going to tell the truth?"

Patience laughed until tears came out.

Jeremy and Frances had never seen this side of Matt before. They both knew by now that Patience was teasing him, but to see him play with her in such a fashion made them love her all the more.

"Okay, okay. I'll tell the truth. I promise I'll tell." Matt stopped and allowed Patience to catch her breath and regain her composure. She told them the wonderful truth about how Matt stole the rest of her heart by unashamedly kneeling on one knee and asking for her hand in front of her family. Her big brown eyes lit up as she relived the story.

Jeremy and Frances were deeply moved by what they heard. It was like a fairytale come true. It was evident that Matt was deeply in love with Patience and that she was a delightful addition to their family.

16

Revenge

FRANCES WAS DELIGHTED BY SEEING THE LOVE BETWEEN MATT and Patience. She did not want to interrupt the intimate moment, but the question of why he was away so long burned inside her.

"Matt, your father and I have missed you so much. Why has it taken three years for you to come home?"

Smiling at his mother's serious expression, Matt said, "It's a long story, Mom. I'm sorry it took so long, but there were circumstances beyond my control. I would be delighted to share with you and Dad in full detail; however, I can't tell you everything. What I can say is that the Lord was with me the whole time. And because of it, Patience is my treasure." Frances and Jeremy smiled as the love birds took each other's hand. Unexpectedly, the expression on Patience's face changed.

"What is it, dear?" asked Frances.

"Oh, I'm not sure. I guess I'm just a little famished."

"Of course, you are. Here we are, chatting away, while the two of you must be starving."

Hearing those words, Junia entered from the kitchen. "I guess we need to set extra places for Matt and his young lady," Junia said with a cordial smile.

"Mrs. Jackson, what are you doing here?" Matt asked, caught off guard. Junia looked hurt by his words. "Oh, I'm sorry, Mrs. Jackson. I didn't mean to imply—"

"That's all right, Matt. No offense taken. I should have announced myself," she said, looking at Frances for support.

"I am so embarrassed by my lack of manners. Please forgive me, Junia," Frances said, feeling obligated to explain. "Junia and her son are staying in our guesthouse until a new house is built for her."

"Oh … Frances, you don't have to go into detail this very moment about all that. Give the young people a chance to refresh themselves with a pleasant meal," said Junia with a smile.

"Of course, you're right. Let's all move to the dining room where we can enjoy a good meal and continue our conversation," replied Frances.

In the adjacent room, Junia listened intently to the conversation between Frances and her family. The love and interaction between them displeased her.

As the family moved into the dining room, Frances felt faint and caught hold of the chair in front of her. "Are you all right, dear?" asked Jeremy, taking her by the arm.

"I feel a little dizzy. It's probably nothing but the excitement of my children being home," she said, not wanting to worry them.

"I don't' know, honey. This isn't the first time you've felt this way. Perhaps you should see the doctor again," said Jeremy, concerned.

"Again? How many times has Mom been to the doctor?" asked Matt.

"Twice before."

Frances gently squeezed her husband's hand. "Oh Jeremy, don't worry Matt and our new daughter with that right now. Let's just sit and enjoy each other while we have dinner."

Junia stood close by, waiting to serve them. "I'm sure she will be fine, Jeremy. I'll make her my special tea. It will settle her nerves, especially with a spoon of honey," said Junia with a smile.

"Thank you, Junia. That's just what I need." Junia excused herself and went for the tea.

Frances was pleased with the thought of having extra help. "Junia has been so kind and helpful. Even before their home burned down, she regularly visited just to talk. She can come across as being overly attentive, but I think it's due to missing her husband." Frances paused for a moment to catch her breath. "When her home burned down, I felt the least we could do was to allow her and her son to stay in the guesthouse until things got better," continued Frances.

"When did their home burn down?" Matt asked with a sympathetic tone.

"Oh, about three months ago," Frances responded.

"What happened?" Patience inquired.

Frances pondered for a moment. "I don't really know. We heard that it was a candle fire. It doesn't take much for that kind of fire to spread. She almost lost her life but managed to escape with only minor burns," Frances explained.

"I'm sorry to hear she was injured," Patience said compassionately.

"Are her injuries healed?" Matt asked.

"Yes, her wounds have healed," Frances commented with a reassuring smile.

Looking around, Matt wondered where his old friend was. "Was Jackson injured in the fire? By the way, where is Jackson?"

"Paul is perfectly healthy, son, and he is away on business in Peak Valley," said Jeremy.

"What kind of business would he have in Peak valley?" Matt asked curiously.

"I'm not sure, son. We can ask Junia when she returns."

"I'm sorry, Dad, I didn't mean to pry. It is very kind of you and Mom to help them. I'm sure they appreciate it," acknowledged Matt.

Jeremy nodded. "Yes, son, they do. They have been a tremendous help around here since they arrived."

"With these sudden dizzy spells, I would be in a pinch without Junia's help," Frances said, sitting down by Jeremy.

"Speaking of that, how long did you say you've had these dizzy spells?" Matt asked.

"I think it's been about two months," said Jeremy.

"Two months, and you haven't found out what's wrong with her?" Matt asked, obviously disturbed.

"Son, I have spoken with Doctor Ben several times, and he can't seem to put his finger on the cause," said Jeremy.

"I don't mean to sound harsh, Dad, but did I hear you say Doc Ben can't find anything?"

"Nothing, son. He's run tests and poked and prodded her entire body and still comes up clueless."

"Can we discuss this after dinner?" requested Frances.

"Of course, Mother," said Matt, watching his father nod his head.

"Tell us about your trip. How was it?" Frances asked with a wide smile.

"It was exciting," blurted out Patience.

"How so? I would love to hear." As Patience began to tell of their adventure, Junia returned with Frances' hot cup of tea and placed it to the side where she could easily reach it.

"Dinner is prepared, Frances, for whenever your family is ready."

"Thank you, Junia. I think we are ready now. Of course, you know that you and Paul are always welcome at our table." The family casually moved to the dining area, where Junia served a delightful dinner. The room filled with laughter and small talk as everyone enjoyed themselves. After dinner, Junia brought out dessert.

"Junia, dinner was wonderful. Everything was so perfect."

"Thank you, Frances. It was my pleasure. It's so good to see Matt again, as well as his beautiful young bride. You two make the evening complete," Junia said, smiling.

"Paul will be thrilled to see you, Matt. It's been quite a long time since you've been home. Everyone really thought you were dead, except Paul, of course. He never gave up on you like so many others did. As a matter of fact, the village named the new inn after you in your honor. Paul told them how you helped bring our village out of the famine."

As Matt listened to Junia, he quietly observed every move in the house. The Pia Warrior training was imbedded within his very core. Glancing at Patience, he decided to give his mind link a try.

You look confused, my darling. What's going on in that beautiful head of yours? he asked.

Who is Paul? Patience questioned.

Paul is Jackson. Paul is his first name, smiled Matt.

I wasn't aware of that. Thank you, my husband. By the way, your mind linking is wonderful.

Not bad yourself, he returned the compliment.

"Again, we are so glad you returned safely, Matt," said Junia.

"Thank you, Mrs. Jackson. I'm glad to be back home."

Frances and Jeremy had been silent while Patience observed the interaction between everyone.

"Why don't we move to the sitting room to allow our dinner to settle?" suggested Frances.

"Sounds like a good idea," said Jeremy, pulling her chair out and taking her arm. He led her to the sitting room, and they all sat by the fireplace. "I can tell that there are many questions on your mind, son. Your mother and I will try to explain whatever it is that you wish to know, but first, let me give you a little background on the past three years," said Jeremy.

Frances and Jeremy told Matt how Jackson had cared for them in his absence. "Due to the extreme famine, food was rationed. You remember how your father had been hurt by a rampaging crowd because he was trying to distribute food rations? Matters got worse when Jeremy strained his back, tore his shoulder muscle, and damaged his right leg trying to keep Jack from falling out of a tree. Unfortunately, Jack lost his life from the fall that day, and Junia became a widow. It was a time of suffering for the entire village. It was awful. Junia lost her husband, Jeremy ended up in poor health, and you and Paul went off to see the old seer for help. As time passed, I must say that I was very thankful that Jeremy received a miraculous healing from the Lord that cleared up his pain."

Frances noticed Jeremy watching her. Suddenly, an overwhelming old burden tugged at Frances' heart. Eyes locked on her beloved, she couldn't help but express escalating concerns for her husband. "In the past couple of months, other forms of sickness have caused your father difficulty. Jeremy, I know you don't want to bother our children with this being that they have just arrived, but I think it's necessary," Frances said, hoping she hadn't embarrassed him for sharing his condition.

Matt was surprised by his mother's comments. "I thought you said Dad was fully recovered. I had no idea that he still had problems," Matt said, concerned.

"Your father was completely well until a couple of months ago. It's not his shoulder and leg that bothers him. Since he started putting up that new fence, he's been complaining about numbness in his hands and arms. He's also had stomach cramps, skin rashes, and headaches," said Frances.

Jeremy, not wanting to cause concern or panic, attempted to put his family's minds at ease, "I'm fine, son. It was just a little spider bite. I'm still trying to figure out how it got into my glove, but my body is growing stronger every day. The Lord takes his time getting some things done," Jeremy commented with a smile.

"Dad, has Doctor Ben had a chance to look you over?"

"No, he hasn't," replied Jeremy.

"I'm afraid your father has been too preoccupied with me to think about himself," responded Frances.

"I think it would be wise to have Doc Ben examine you immediately," urged Matt.

"You are right, and we should be praying fervently for his healing," stated Frances.

"Yes, I agree, Mother," chimed in Patience. "Why don't we pray for Dad now." Without hesitation, Patience placed her hand on Jeremy's shoulder. "Father God, we pray for Dad's healing right now in the name of Jesus. We know that whatever we pray in your name, according to your will, you hear us. And since you hear us, we know that our petition is answered. Amen."

"How do you feel, Dad?" asked Matt.

"Wow, I really feel relief, thank God. That is amazing. Thank you, Patience. That's some gift the Lord has given you," remarked Jeremy.

"The gift belongs to the Holy Spirit. I'm just a willing vessel," she smiled. Matt grinned, watching his parents enjoy their new daughter.

"Let's start some fervent prayer meetings. What time should they start?" inquired Matt.

"How about first thing tomorrow morning around six?" suggested Frances.

"Sounds good. And right after breakfast, I'll take a look at the fences while Dad takes a break."

Jeremy smiled to himself at all the attention he was getting from his family.

"Mom, before the prayer, you were talking about Jackson. Please continue."

Frances nodded and picked up the conversation where she had left off. "Well, when Paul returned, he was nice enough to offer us his help. It was a lot of work taking care of Jeremy and the property. He must have also talked with Junia because she became more amenable, for which we were thankful," Frances said with gratitude.

It pleased Matt that Jackson had done this wonderful deed and that his mother Junia seemed to have had a change of heart. But was his motive of a pure heart? Matt couldn't help wondering, remembering that the old seer had said that "not all is as it appears" when it came to Jackson. It was true that Jackson had provided for Matt's family, but was it kindness, or was it all pretense?

Pushing aside feelings of uncertainty, Matt continued enjoying the fellowship with his family. The rest of the evening was spent talking about the trip, encounters, strange beings, narrow escapes, as well as family matters and village conditions.

The time passed quickly, and before anyone realized how late it was, the clock on the wall chimed 10 times. "Oh, my goodness, it's way past my bedtime," voiced Frances.

"I have had the best time. I'm so glad to be home," exclaimed Matt.

"Me too, but I think we ought to be getting rest ourselves. It's been a long day for us." Patience smiled, pulling on Matt's arm.

Junia entered the room quietly. "Frances, Matt's room is prepared for him and his new bride. By the way, does anyone care for a nightcap or anything else before I leave for the guesthouse?"

"I don't think so, Junia. Everything was wonderful, and you have been very helpful. Thank you," said Frances.

"You are very welcome," said Junia, slightly smiling before turning to exit.

Frances and Jeremy stood to retire to their bedroom, bidding Matt and Patience good-night. Matt and Patience kissed their parents and departed in the opposite direction to the bedroom upstairs at the end of the hall. Abruptly stopping, Matt turned.

"By the way, Abdi and his family will be here in the morning for breakfast."

"Abdi?"

"Yes, ma'am. Patience's uncle and cousins. There will be four of them."

"I see. It shouldn't be a problem. We have plenty, son."

"Sweet dreams you two," came a call from Jeremy.

"You too, Dad," Matt replied.

Matt swept Patience off her feet and stepped into the open room. "It's beautiful. The woodwork has such detail, and the décor is breathtaking," said Patience.

"Dad is an excellent woodsman, and Mom is a great decorator. She can make anything look good. They have always worked well together."

"They are wonderful. I never expected a log cabin to be so luxurious and enjoyable. One can't help but love it all."

"I know what you mean, but woodwork is not on my mind right now, my love," he said with a playful grin. Patience smiled and kissed him, then quickly pulled back. Matt was alarmed by Patience's reaction, "What's wrong, my love?"

"I am concerned about your mother."

"Me too. She has always been healthy and vibrant. I don't know what's going on, but I am going to talk with Doc Ben myself tomorrow and find out what is really going on with her."

"I agree. I watched her throughout the night. She didn't eat enough to sustain a bird. I would like to check the kind of food she's eating and also find out what her daily diet consists of. Do you think she'll mind?"

"I think she will be delighted to have her daughter fussing over her." Patience smiled. Matt pulled her close and kissed her.

Throughout the night, Matt and Patience slept peacefully until suddenly Patience awoke and sat up. Usually, it happened when the Spirit moved her. Matt stayed asleep as Patience quietly watched him. She started to wake him but began to reminisce about her grandfather.

When she was no more than three years old, Poppy took a piece of the Sun Stone and ground it into dust particles. Then he mixed the particles into a glass of milk and gave it to Patience to drink.

"Why did he do that to me?" she whispered to herself. "It had to be orchestrated by the Spirit. Poppy would never do anything without God's permission." It was always clear to Patience that Jedidiah's primary duty was to protect his family. Letting her drink the stone particles had to be of the Lord. When he gave her the stone in the milk, she drank it, smiled, and hugged his neck.

"That's my girl," he had said. "Nothing will keep you from your destiny, for it is written that you will serve the Lord well."

"Lord … I remember the prophecy over me. I remember Poppy's joy and laughter. I remember you pouring love into my heart. And now here I am, years later full of wonder and delight. Thank you, Lord, for loving me, for guiding me, and for giving me my family."

She sat, smiling, watching her husband. She and Matt were starting their journey, and it had brought joy to her entire family. Gratitude was the word her soul embraced. She and Matt had embarked on the prophetic journey God ordained for them. Embracing the fruit of the Spirit had taught them the meaning of serving. Jedidiah's little granddaughter had grown up to become the young woman he had always known she would be and was now married to a most wonderful, humble man with a family who loved and adored them both. What more could one ask for?

Yet she felt in her spirit that all was not as it should be in Matt's home. The Spirit had not given her clear insight on the matter, but she knew in her heart that Matt's mother was troubled and that evil was seeking an opportunity to do harm. It wasn't the first time she sensed such a presence. She could have easily searched everyone's mind for answers but knew she had no right to invade the private thoughts of others without permission. Tomorrow she would simply ask questions to find answers to what she wanted to know. She laid her head down next to Matt.

****

First light of the sun came shining through the slit in the drapes. It was dawn, and a sweet sound awakened Patience. She heard singing coming from the kitchen. *It must be Mother Frances preparing breakfast.* Patience grinned at the thought of eating Frances' food. Turning to Matt, she gently pushed him. "Matt, wake up. Mom is making noise in the kitchen, and I'm going to help," she said, crawling out of bed.

A loud knock at the front door told Frances that guests had arrived. "Get the door, honey. It's probably Matt's friends," called Frances.

"I'll get the door," yelled Jeremy as if he hadn't heard Frances ask him. Opening the door, Jeremy wasted no time in introducing himself. "By the size of you, you must be

Abdi, and these must be your sons, and of course, your beautiful daughter."

Abdi smiled. "Yes, sir, you are correct. We are happy to make your acquaintance," said Abdi, revealing a heavy accent.

"Matt told me that you were big, but I thought that he was exaggerating. I see that he wasn't. I'm Jeremy, Matt's dad." Jeremy stuck out his hand and received a hardy handshake from Abdi. "Come on in and make yourselves at home. My wife, Frances, is in the kitchen." Jeremy suddenly looked toward the stairs, "I'll see if Matt and Patience are up."

As Jeremy went to check on the newlyweds, Frances came in to greet her new guests. "My, my," Frances said, looking up at them. "I am delighted to meet you. Matt and Patience have told us all about you."

"Not too much, I hope," said Lire with a cheerful smile on his face.

Layla pushed her way through her brothers and embraced Frances as if she had known her forever. "I'm Layla, and we have heard a lot about you as well. At least, I have," she giggled, looking back at her brothers.

By the time Jeremy got to the newlyweds, Patience had awakened Matt, and the two were dressed and almost ready to present themselves. Opening the door, Matt found his father inches away from knocking on their door.

"Patience's family is here, and your mother is probably entertaining them downstairs," Jeremy said. With a nod, Matt grabbed Patience's hand, and they walked down the stairs to welcome the new arrivals as Jeremy followed.

Frances made everyone comfortable by seating them next to the hearth while offering them beverages. "This should keep you until I finished setting the table."

Hearing those words, Patience followed her new mother into the kitchen, prompting Layla to follow. The three women talked comfortably while preparing the food. Within the hour, breakfast was prepared and displayed on the table.

"Looks like everything is ready. Come and get it!" Layla yelled. It was a stampede to the breakfast table; however, no one was trampled. Frances was delighted to see the rush of men seating themselves at her table, Jeremy and Matt among them. "Dear, will you offer thanks to the Lord?"

Jeremy smiled and reached for her hand and placed his other hand on Abdi's shoulder as he prayed. All eyes closed and every hand joined, including Layla's, for a time of thanksgiving.

After the prayer, Frances said, "I hope you enjoy the food."

"I'm sure we will, Mrs. Loman," said Abdi.

"Matt didn't tell us how good your cooking was," said Caleb.

"If he had, we would have been here a lot sooner," responded Bruk.

"You got that right," chimed in Lire with a mouth full of food.

"I hope you're enjoying it," Frances said, smiling at Lire.

The room filled with laughter and good conversation. The young warriors joked about Matt and told of his adventures with them, while Abdi and Jeremy listened with delight. Frances felt true peace in the presence of Matt's and Patience's friends and family. While observing her guest, she thought to herself, *Thank you, Lord, for bringing my boy home."*

"You all are so delightful. I'm so glad the Lord brought you all together, and I am thrilled that Matt found Patience," she said aloud, teary-eyed. Pausing a moment, she composed herself. "Tell us where you come from? What is your homeland?"

Everyone looked at Abdi, expecting him to answer Frances' inquiry. Abdi was amused at the stares he received from his children. Giving a nod, he decided to provide a little history to Matt's parents regarding their homeland and how his family had settled in Ethiopia. Before the group realized it, an hour had passed.

"I'm amazed at your history and culture," said Jeremy.

"Yes, and you all have such beautiful features," interjected Frances.

"I better warn you, Mom, before you go a step further. The first day I saw Patience, I couldn't turn my eyes from her. Her grandfather asked me if it was because of her dark complexion. He was teasing, of course, but I didn't know it. Patience is the daughter of King Steven and Queen Heather Marwari. Abdi is King Steven's brother, and these warriors sitting here devouring your food are her cousins. As you can see, they are from the motherland and have become my family," said Matt with pride.

After breakfast, Frances started to clear the table, but her guests stopped her, insisting that the least they could do was to clean up. "Thank you so much. I hope that you enjoyed the meal as much as I enjoyed the conversation," she said with hopes of hearing more stories.

"I assure you that everything was perfect, Mrs. Loman," said Abdi. "Okay, boys, let's do this."

Frances headed for the sitting room but stumbled as she crossed the threshold. Thankfully, Jeremy was there to catch her.

"Are you all right, my dear?"

"I don't know. This dizzy spell is worse than before. I feel extremely weak and drowsy. Maybe I overdid it in the kitchen. Let me sit by the fire a little while."

Matt and Patience came immediately to her side. "Mom, what's wrong?" Matt asked.

"I'm not sure, son. One moment I'm fine, and the next I'm falling to the floor."

"That's not good. I'm going to get Doctor Ben."

"There's no need for that, son. I'll be all right in just a few minutes."

"You rest, Mom, I'll be back in a little while. Patience will stay with you until I return with Doc Ben."

"Hey Matt, hold on, and I'll go with you," said Lire.

"Me too," said Caleb. As they headed out the door, Patience talked with Frances while Jeremy simultaneously hosted his guests and kept an eye on Frances.

"Good morning. Did I miss something?" asked Junia, coming through the side door from the guesthouse. Observing the atmosphere, Junia was astounded at the sight of the people in the house. Walking by Abdi and Layla and seeing Frances lying on the couch, she felt something was off. "I saw Matt leaving in a hurry with two large men. Is everything alright?" she asked, concerned.

"They're making a fuss over me, that's all. I stumbled a little, and now everyone thinks I need a doctor," said Frances.

"Are you all right?"

"Yes, of course, no need to worry, I'm in good hands with Patience."

"I'll just slip into the kitchen and make you a cup of nice hot honey mint tea."

"Thank you, Junia. That would be nice," said Frances. Patience knelt down next to Frances and took hold of her wrist. "What are you doing, dear?"

"I'm counting the beats of your heart, Mother Frances."

"I didn't know that we had a doctor in the house."

"I'm not, but I have learned many things from my mother and grandmother."

"How delightful. What are your findings?"

"I can't tell from just your heartbeat. I'll have to check you all over."

"Oh, dear, you don't have to go through all that trouble. Matt will be back with Doc Ben soon."

"It's no problem, Mom. We can talk as I check you over," Patience smiled.

"How can I resist such a beautiful smile?" Frances said, observing Patience's attentiveness.

Junia returned with the tea and sat it on a small Cherrywood table to the right of Frances' chair. "Can I get you anything else, Frances?" Junia asked, watching Patience closely.

"No, dear, Patience is mothering me very well, thank you."

"I'll see if anything needs cleaning, and I will return in a while," Junia said with a smile.

"Thank you, Junia."

As Patience examined Frances with a thorough hand, she said, "Mom, tell me again when you started feeling faint or weak."

"It was about two and a half months ago."

"Before that, how did you feel?"

"I felt fine."

"So, it's only been within the past couple of months that you've been experiencing this?"

"Yes, dear," sighed Frances.

Abdi could tell that Jeremy's mind was not with them. His attention was across the room with Frances and Patience.

"Why don't we go over and see what's going on," said Abdi.

Jeremy didn't waste another second. He stood up abruptly and walked over to Frances. "What is it? Patience, can you tell us what's going on with her?" asked Jeremy.

"I can't now, but I will pray about the matter," she said.

"Why don't you just pray for her now?" said Jeremy.

"I would love to, Father Jeremy, but I sense that there is something else going on, and I must consult the Lord. When Matt gets back, I would like to hear what the doctor has to say." She smiled. It wasn't long before the door opened and in walked Matt, Lire, Caleb, and Doctor Ben.

"Hello, everyone. I hear that my patient is still experiencing dizziness," Ben said with a smile.

"Hello, Ben. Please come in," said Jeremy.

"And who is this beautiful young woman sitting next to you, Frances?" Ben asked.

With a smile, she said, "My new daughter, Matt's wife."

"Wonderful. Nice to meet you. I'm Ben. Who might this other young lady be?" he asked curiously.

"That's my cousin, Layla, and right beside her is my Uncle Abdi and my cousin Bruk. We are delighted to meet you, Doctor Ben," said Patience, holding out her hand to greet him.

"Patience has been taking care of me since Matt went to fetch you," said Frances with beaming pride.

"I see. What have you found, my dear?" asked Doc Ben.

Patience took a breath and said, "Just that her heartbeat is a little elevated, and she has been experiencing nausea and trouble breathing. Her pupils are enlarged, and lastly, before you entered the room, Mother Frances was complaining of having muscle pain. Beyond that, I have to wait on the Lord."

"Oh, my word," said Doc Ben.

"I'll say," said Frances.

"Where did you learn all of that?"

"She learned it from her mother and grandmother," said Frances.

"I see. Do you mind if I take a look?" he asked politely.

"Please do, Doctor Ben. I hope I haven't overstepped my—"

Doc Ben raised his hand. "Don't be concerned. I appreciate those who use their skills to help others. Now, if everyone will excuse us for a moment, I'll take a look at you, Frances," he said, looking into his medical bag.

Everyone left the room. Ben gave Frances an extensive examination, and when he finished, he came to Patience, surprised. "My dear, it looks like you are exactly right. The last two times I was here, she had very little signs of illness, but today her symptoms are more defined. What do you think is going on with our patient?" he asked.

Patience smiled, pleased that Doctor Ben included her in his diagnosis. "Please, excuse me for a moment. I shall return shortly." Before anyone could object, Patience took Matt by the hand and left the room. When she reached the bedroom, she closed the door behind them. "Matt, I feel that something terrible is happening to Mom."

"What is it?"

She knelt and pulled Matt down by her. "Lord Jesus, I don't know how to proceed. Tell me what is wrong with Mom. Show me, Holy Spirit. Reveal to my mind the cause and cure for Mom's illness. Show us, Lord, show us," she prayed.

Matt remained silent. He knew that Patience was a woman of faith with many gifts. As she rose from her knees, Matt could see that she was deeply concerned. "What is it? Matt asked, trying not to panic.

"It's poison, Matt. Mom is being poisoned."

"She's what! How?" Confusion was written on Matt's face.

"She ingested it somehow. Try to stay calm, my darling. We don't want to upset her," said Patience.

Being calm was not a reasonable request for Matt. Without delay, he took Patience by the hand and rushed to the room.

"What's wrong, son?" asked Jeremy.

"Patience has something to tell us. Go ahead, Patience. Tell them what the Lord revealed to you," Matt said.

Observing everyone's reaction, Patience reluctantly followed her husband's request. "Mom has been poisoned, though I'm not sure what kind yet," stated Patience, eyeing Frances.

"I believe you're right," Doc Ben said with wide eyes. "You are very astute, young lady. From all indications of your symptoms, Frances, it looks like Patience is correct."

"But how? How could this be?" asked Jeremy.

"Have you changed any of your eating or drinking habits lately, Frances?" asked Ben.

"No, not that I know of."

"Are you sure? Have you ingested anything new over the past two months that you haven't had before?" asked Patience.

Pausing, Frances thought for a moment, "The only thing that comes to mind is the tea Junia makes. Junia fixes a special honey mint tea for me daily, but I'm sure it couldn't be that," exclaimed Frances.

"May I examine it?" asked Ben.

"Of course. Here is a cup next to me."

Ben took the cup and smelled it, then dipped his finger in and placed it on his tongue.

"Find anything?" asked Jeremy.

"I can't really tell with this slight head cold of mine," Ben answered.

"May I see it?" requested Patience. Ben passed the cup to Patience. She took a sip and immediately spit it out.

"What is it?" inquired Ben.

"It is as the Spirit said—it is poison. Mint and honey are the main ingredients in the tea, and the strong scent of them covers the pinch of hemlock and nightshade."

"What the devil!" shouted Ben.

"Are you sure?" said Frances.

"I am. It is not enough to kill immediately, but over a period of time, it is fatal," voiced Patience, taking Frances' hand.

"Who could have done such a thing?" asked Abdi.

"Junia is the only one who makes that tea for her," said Jeremy suspiciously.

"You don't think Mrs. Jackson is behind this, do you?" probed Matt.

"Did I hear my name called?" asked Junia, coming into the room with refreshments. She placed the tray down next to Lire and Caleb, who looked at each other and abruptly pushed the tray away.

"You did," said Jeremy firmly. "It has been discovered that Frances' sudden illness is due to the tea she has been drinking. It has been laced with poison. You wouldn't happen to know anything about that, would you?" Jeremy moved closer to her.

Junia remained calm as Jeremy and Matt approached. "I can assure you that I know nothing about poison. And the last thing I'd do is cause harm to the family that has taken in my son and me and given us shelter. I can't believe that you would think such a thing," said Junia, placing her hands over her face as she broke into tears.

"I'm sure that there must be some other explanation, Jeremy. I just can't believe that Junia did this, at least not deliberately," said Frances.

"If that is so, maybe she can share the explanation with us," said Matt sternly.

Junia lifted her head, drying her tears with the shawl around her shoulders. "The only way it could have possibly happened is when I purchased the mint from the mercantile. I purchased a large bag of mint. Somehow the poisons must have fallen into the bag."

"I can understand the probability of one poison getting into the bag, but the probability of two poisons? I don't think so," said Matt, doubting her explanation.

"Bring the bag, and let me see it," said Ben.

Junia turned to fetch the bag. "Matt will accompany you," said Jeremy.

Upon their return, Ben examined the bag and found traces of the poison hemlock and nightshade in it. "Junia, tell me again— where did you get the bag?" queried Doc Ben.

"I got it from the market. There were several, I picked up one, and the merchant filled it with mint. I had no idea that it had a poisonous residue in it."

Patience watched and observed Junia's demeanor but said nothing.

"I think this has all been a terrible mistake," said Frances.

"Yes, but one that could have cost you your life. You have been drinking that stuff for over two months. I'm not sure how much of that poison is in you. Both hemlock and nightshade are toxic and have no cure," said Doc Ben.

"Yes, and it has to come out of your system over time," said Patience.

"Patience is right. I don't know what else to do except direct your family to keep a close eye on you," said Ben.

"I suggest that we pray," said Patience.

"Please do," requested Frances.

"And while you are at it, I just remembered that I was going to ask Doc Ben to take a look at Dad. He was having some problems with numbness in his hands and legs," said Matt.

"When did this occur, Jeremy?" asked Ben.

"About a month or so ago. I was fooling around my tool shed, getting ready to mend some fences, and was bitten by a spider that was in one of my gloves. The numbness comes and goes."

"How do you feel right now?"

"I feel fine."

"Sit down for a moment, and let me take a look."

"I'm telling you that I feel fine. Let's take care of Frances."

"With lots of rest and no tea, she will be fine. It's you that I need to examine right now, so sit down and stop fussing." Jeremy sat down, and Doc Ben took the next half hour examining him. "Well, whatever it was seems to have worked itself out of your system. You say it started a couple of months ago?"

"Yes," Jeremy said.

"Do you think you got into something in your tool shed?"

"I don't know. It's possible."

"Doctor Ben, why don't we pray for Mom and Dad, and then we can check out the shed to see if there's any connection," said Patience.

"Good idea. Please proceed," said Ben. Everyone knelt before Frances and laid their hands on her and Jeremy.

Even though Junia seemed more anxious than before, she too bowed her head. However, when she started to place her hand on Frances, her eyes met with Patience's. Junia immediately dropped her hand. Something in the young woman's eyes prevented Junia from joining in the prayer. Layla stood to the side, watching.

"Abba, we love you and beseech you on Mom's and Dad's behalf to heal their bodies, from the crown of their heads to the soles of their feet. We have no earthly cure. Only you, Abba. It is in the name of Jesus, your son, our Lord, that we pray and thank you," Patience prayed.

When the prayer was done, they all rose as did Frances, who felt strength enter her body. "I am healed," Frances said. Everyone was silent, in awe. "I'm really healed."

Doc Ben looked in her eyes, checked her heartbeat, and told her to walk around. Frances started running around the room, laughing and clapping her hands. "My Lord, she is healed," said Doc Ben.

"I told you that I was. No more dizzy spells," said Frances.

"Praise Jesus," said Jeremy. "I feel refreshed myself." Smiling, Jeremy took Frances' hand and wrapped his arm around hers.

"I'm glad that you are all right, Frances," said Junia, smiling.

"I am too, Junia. Thank you."

"I have other things to take care of, so I will see you later," said Junia.

"That's fine. Thank you, Junia," replied Frances. Jeremy's eyes followed Junia as she departed. "What is it, dear?" Frances asked.

"This isn't over. I'm going to check this whole thing out. You could have died! What if someone else gets a contaminated bag?"

"I would pray that they have a daughter like ours to help them. However, it might be a good idea to send Matt and Ben to the mercantile to make sure that no one else is harmed," Frances said, still in Jeremy's arms.

Patience reached for them, happy to see Matt's parents embracing each other. Frances loosened her hold on Jeremy and reached out to Patience. Feeling assured that Frances would be safe with Patience, Jeremy decided to leave with Matt and Ben to investigate the tea incident.

"Once we check out the bags at the Mercantile, we'll go by Jeremy's shed. If you have an infestation of poisonous spiders, I want to see. We don't want a repeat of what happened to you, nor do we want it to happen to someone else," said Ben.

"Good idea," agreed Matt.

Frances pulled Patience aside. "Tell me, my dear. How did you learn to pray so effectively?"

Patience blushed slightly and said humbly but confidently, "From my family. They taught me how to pray in faith, according to God's will. Since God wants to answer our prayers, it's only reasonable to believe that He will."

How can such wisdom come out of such a young woman? Frances asked herself.

After a long conversation about the miraculous recovery, Patience's mind suddenly became engulfed with thoughts of Junia. "Mother Frances, how long have you known Mrs. Jackson?"

Pondering the question, Frances said, "I've known Junia since we were very young. We weren't really close until we became adults. Junia has always been a loner but a very nice person." Frances smiled, reminiscing on her childhood. Nodding, Patience remained silent. Frances noticed Patience's solemn expression. "My dear, what's wrong?" asked Frances, concerned.

"It seems that Ms. Junia is in a dark place of hatred and bitterness. Unfortunately, she is unwilling to leave it," Patience said sadly, staring out of the window in the direction of the little cabin Junia and her son were occupying.

"Hatred and bitterness? Are you sure, dear?" Frances asked, deeply concerned.

"Yes, Mother Frances, but there is still time for her to change if she wants to and if she embraces the Lord's help."

Frances was speechless. "How is it that I never noticed that about Junia?" Frances quietly asked herself. Frances let Patience's words sink into her heart.

Layla entered, abruptly interrupting Frances' conversation with Patience. "Please forgive my intrusion. Patience, I caught up with Matt, Doc Ben, and Mr. Loman. I asked if you should join them since you discovered the poison. Don't you think it would be a good idea to go with them and find out about the tea incident since you have more knowledge about the poison?" asked Layla. Patience looked concerned about leaving Frances. Observing Patience hesitation, Layla said, "Oh, don't worry about Mother Frances. My brothers and I will keep her safe." Then, feeling bold and playful, Layla whispered, "Tell me, Patience—is Ms. Junia a threat? Do you want us to get rid of her?"

"Seriously, Layla, what am I going to do with you?" Patience said in shock, shushing her. She turned to Frances. "Mother Frances, I'm sure Layla can't whisper. She was only teasing. They wouldn't do such a thing," said Patience, in case Frances overheard Layla's comment.

Frances smiled. "I have enjoyed our talk, dear. Run and catch up with your husband. He's waiting for you."

Patience hugged Frances. "Thank you, Mom. I will." Immediately, Patience took off after Matt. Frances silently prayed for Junia in hopes that what Patience said about her still having time to change was true.

After checking into the details of the poisons at the local mercantile, everyone walked with Doctor Ben to his home.

"Thank you for coming over to take care of Mom," said Matt, holding Patience's hand.

"It was my pleasure, Matt. Your parents and I have been friends long before I delivered you and your ... ah..." Ben stopped before the next word came out of his mouth.

"My what?" Matt asked curiously.

"Oh ... that old dog of yours. You know I'm the local animal doctor around here as well." Ben chuckled nervously, eyeing Jeremy, hoping to change the subject. "Patience, you'll have to share your knowledge of poisons with me. You sure surprised old Dan when you told him about poison being in his storehouse."

"Yes, and even more so when we found them. Old Dan is still mystified as to how such a mix up could have happened," said Matt.

"Patience, I am amazed at how God works through you," Ben said, smiling.

"We can get together sometime this week. I'll write down a few poisons, and you can select which poison you would like to discuss first."

"That sounds wonderful, Patience."

"Did you know that it was poison hemlock that killed Socrates?" she asked.

"No, I didn't. How interesting. We will certainly talk about this another day," he said as he waved goodbye and turned down the road to his house.

"Didn't Doc Ben seem nervous to you, Matt? And why was he in such a rush?" asked Patience.

"I don't know, but when Mom feels better, I'll catch up with Doc Ben and ask."

"I'm sure he has other patients," chimed in Jeremy.

"Yes, you're probably right, Dad. Maybe it's nothing."

"Matt, how about taking a walk with me? Show me the sites." Patience giggled, locking her arms through his.

"While we are walking, you can recite the different kinds of poisons," he said playfully.

Smiling, Jeremy knew it was his time to exit. "I'll see you lovebirds back at the house. I'll tell your mother that old Dan found the same kind of poison in several empty bags lying against the back wall of his storehouse. How they got mixed in with the tea bags was a mystery to him. Thank God he burned them to prevent other possible incidents. Have a wonderful walk, and be back by supper time," Jeremy said.

Watching his dad leave, Matt could tell that he was more relaxed. Getting back to his mother was definitely on his father's mind. Matt wrapped his arm around Patience and kissed her on the head. As his hand slid down to her hand, she smiled and began to recite poisons. "Jimson weed, water hemlock, poison hemlock, nightshade, white snakeroot, castor bean, jequirity beans, and the oleander. There are hundreds more. Do you want to hear them?" Patience beamed.

"Never mind, my love. I was only teasing," Matt said, surprised at how much she did know.

"I know," she said, laughing.

****

Matt and Patience took daily walks throughout Columbidae. He showed her his places of solitude, work, and recreation. God's handiwork stood out through the beauty of nature, so Patience found the walks in the woods were most exciting. On one of those occasions, Matt took hold of Patience and swung her over a hot spring, teasing that he was going to drop her in. As she squealed, he caught her up in his arms, bringing her in for a kiss.

"You could have dropped me," she said, both arms around his neck.

"Not on your life, and not with the grip you have around my neck," he laughed.

They had been together now for only four normal weeks as husband and wife, not counting Jedidiah's time continuum, but Matt felt like he had loved her for a lifetime. Patience watched him closely while he held her hand and talked about everything in his heart regarding her. At times, his open heart and passion made her blush and giggle. During other times, there were tears. The sound of his voice made her feel safe and comfortable. Matt was her soulmate.

She was thankful that her father and grandfather had been extremely careful guarding her against would-be suitors who only had their own interest at heart. She remembered one occasion when she, at fifteen-years-old, had protested their interference with her life. Her mother had stepped in to correct her, saying, "Patience! A wise man once said that 'a beautiful woman who lacks discretion is like a gold ring in a pig's snout.' You cannot dishonor your elders or ignore sound instruction from those who guard your heart. If you do, you invite spirits of rebellion and destruction, which will cause you more harm than you can imagine. To obey now is far better than the sorrows you will experience later."

Those were days Patience wanted to forget, and over time, she did. Thank God that she accepted the merit of their wisdom, which was far greater than her own. She was the happiest woman in the world now, married to a man she deeply loved, and she knew that his love was returned a thousand times more. Walking with him was her heart's delight. It was evident that everything else held very little interest. They were in a world of "just them," two hearts melting together as one in love and friendship. Matt never laughed, loved, and played so hard in his life than with Patience. Patience found herself submerged in Matt's enthusiasm, having more pleasure and fun than anyone could imagine. It was a love made in heaven, and complaint was nowhere to be found.

17

Jackson Returns Home

At dusk, Junia sat on the small porch, waiting for her son's return, while a breeze cooled her face. *Paul Jackson should be here by now,* she thought to herself. As soon as the thought crossed her mind, she heard a familiar voice.

"Mom..."

Turning to see her son, she immediately felt relief, and the subtle lines in her face subsided. "My son," Junia said, springing from her chair and into the waiting arms of her son.

Smiling, Jackson gave his mom a warm hug. He told her that the business trip was prosperous, and he had interesting news to share. Before Jackson could impart his news, Junia interrupted.

"I'm so glad you're back. You would not believe the ordeal I've been through. It's not enough that we have to go through the humiliation of living in the servant's quarters, but we also have to put up with Frances' pity towards us. It is a bit much. It would be tolerable if she didn't mean it, but the poor woman can't help feeling sorry for everyone in trouble," said Junia, finally taking a breath.

"I'm happy to see you too, Mother. I don't see why you're complaining. It allows her an opportunity to serve us," Jackson said smugly, giving Junia a kiss on the head before taking a seat.

Ignoring Jackson's remarks, she continued her rampaging comments. "Matt Loman has returned and brought back with him, what he calls, his family. That wife that he brought back with him has become a fly in my eye," Junia said, biting her lip. Jackson was silent, so Junia rolled her eyes and continued. "Did you hear anything I just said? Why aren't you listening?" Junia said, almost in tears.

"Mom ... I'm sorry…" Scratching his head in puzzlement, Jackson allowed his mom to continue her ranting.

"I hate the Loman family for what they did to us. I set out to take my revenge by poisoning Frances slowly, and then I later strategically placed a few black-widow spiders in Jeremy's shed. He always puts his gloves on without checking them. I had already extracted venom from several poisonous spiders and placed some on several of his tools. He has a nasty habit of putting his finger in his mouth to test the weather, a good way to ingest poison if you don't wash your hands," she mused. "The plan was working perfectly until that wife of Matt's stuck her nose into the pot," Junia said, slamming her hand on the table. Startled by her reaction, Jackson jumped.

"What did she do to upset you like this?" inquired Jackson. Ignoring her son's question, Junia continued.

"I don't know how she detected the poisons, but she did and then told the others," she said, pouting.

"You mean she figured out that you were poisoning Matt's mom? How could she do that?" questioned Jackson.

"I don't know, and they almost caught me in my efforts. I had given her a fresh cup of tea only an hour before the girl examined her. I barely got away to go to the mercantile and slip poisonous residue into the bags to cover myself," Junia said, letting out a sigh.

In the past, Jackson felt hurting the Loman family, especially to the extent of poisoning Frances, was wrong, but appeasing his mother took precedence over his conscience. Now he felt Junia was justified in her revenge against the Loman family.

"Don't worry, Mother. The men I'm meeting are shrewd and cunning. They'll know how to take care of our problem and make a profit from it too," smirked Jackson.

"Who are these men? Do I know them?"

Chuckling, Jackson shook his head and said, "No, Mother, you haven't met them. On my way home, I met a well-dressed man on the outskirts of Peak Valley. He said his name was Marcus and he knew who I was. I was confused by his statement. Suddenly, he told me everything about my life leading up to my disappearance. It was like Marcus was a seer. It was creepy at first, but I became more fascinated as he spoke about my past. The conversation caused me to visually remember my time in the Great Tree," he smiled.

"Great Tree? What is the Great Tree?" Junia asked curiously.

"The Great Tree, as I remember, was a magnificent place with all kinds of treasure. I hope to take you there one day." Jackson smiled, happy about the restored memories of his past.

"So, are you going to go back?" Junia asked, intrigued by what she heard.

"He told me if I desired to go back to the Great Tree, I must first accomplish several tasks. I asked him what type of tasks. Suddenly, I felt an eerie presence, which raised the hairs on the back of my neck. It gave me the willies," Jackson responded, shifting in his chair. He watched Junia's solemn expression as he continued talking.

Marcus said, "You must acquire for me the Sun Stone that is in the Great Tree. No one has seen it for generations. It was taken from the land of Nod, the place of City Dwellers many years ago by what my people call Growers. They stole it to benefit themselves. Ancient writings have told us that the Growers sailed away to the east in ships that fly. Many have gone out from us, trying to locate the stone, but each time failed. That is until a few years ago. We came into this land and landed at the shores of what many call the Great Falls. From there, we searched for our precious stone that fell from the sky. We discovered that it rests in the land of Truevine. Only Growers and their allies can enter Truevine's territory, the land in which you currently live. I believe you call your quaint little village Columbidae. We know that you once entered the Great Tree. If you help us retrieve the stone, we will reward you. Remember, my homeland needs the Sun Stone to survive. If you help my comrades and me, then you can have all the treasure in the Great Tree you can carry.'"

"I was excited at his words but then remembered that he mentioned comrades. I wondered who he was talking about. Suddenly, two men appeared out of nowhere. As they approached, they looked very intimidating. I stood my ground as Marcus introduced us. Observing the men, I could tell they needed me more than I needed them. It seemed like hours went by as they explained their homeland. Oh, what was it that they called themselves? Oh yes, City Dwellers. They said they came a long way looking for me. It was puzzling how they knew me. I asked Marcus, and he told me that his god revealed me to him. Sounds creepy, doesn't it?" said Jackson.

"No more than what I've heard others say about their connections with spirits," replied Junia. "Son, I must tell you that this Marcus is not telling you the whole truth. We are Growers, and what I was told by my parents doesn't agree with what this Marcus has told you."

"What do you mean, Mother?"

"The legend of Growers says that the fiery stone fell from the sky and that King Joel retrieved the stone from the great crater before the City Dwellers even arrived. The stone belongs to the Growers. However, if it will profit us, I see no reason not to help your friend," she said with a cunning smile. "What did you decide?"

"I finally agreed to help them. To tell you the truth, I don't even know if I can get back into the Great Tree. From my memories, it was the old seer that got us into it the last time. But I thought of you, Mom. We can use the treasure to build a new life," Jackson said proudly.

Junia touched her son's cheeks with motherly affection. "You are such a good son, Paul."

"I know, Mom," Jackson said jokingly. "There's something else, Mother. As I was departing, Marcus told me my longtime friend Matt had returned with his new wife, Patience. I knew that Matt had favor with the old man. These mysterious men told me that Matt was home and that he had married the old man's granddaughter."

"Why didn't you tell me that you knew Matt was back?" Junia asked angrily.

"Mom, when you get in one of your rants, no one can stop you," Jackson said timidly. Clearing his throat, he continued. "Marcus told me that Matt was the cause of me not getting what was rightfully mine. He also warned me to be careful, or they could hinder us from getting the treasure. I assured Marcus there would be no problem. I have not seen the plans yet, but Marcus told me he had a sound strategy and that he and his comrades would be here in a few days," said Jackson, taking a sip from the cup his mother placed in front of him.

"Yes, Paul, I do believe you're right. Marcus seems to be some kind of seer. Now I completely understand why you weren't shocked when I told you Matt came home with a wife," Junia said, watching the smile on Jackson's face.

Jackson's thoughts trailed for a moment on Marcus' hints that Matt was his opposition. *If not for Matt, I would have wed the old man's granddaughter.* Shaking off the thought, Jackson continued. "All we have to do is be persistent and wait for the appropriate time. Then we will enjoy a pleasurable and prosperous life for the rest of our days," boasted Jackson.

"When will you meet them again?" Junia asked.

"Marcus said he would contact me in a few days with his men."

"Good. When they arrive, I would like to meet them," Junia said with a confident smile.

"They are not the kind of people I want you to meet," he insisted.

"Nevertheless, you will introduce me to them. I'll decide for myself what kind of people they are," she bellowed.

"Very well. If you insist, I'll make the arrangements," Jackson said reluctantly. "In the meantime, I think it would be a good idea to slip over to see the Lomans."

"It's not too late to intrude but late enough not to stay long," said Junia, giving Jackson another hug and kiss.

Within an hour, Jackson and Junia had made their way to the Lomans' home, allowing the Lomans an opportunity to welcome Jackson home and introduce him to Patience and her family.

****

"Matt, it's good to see you, my friend. I'm glad you're back, and I can see by the looks of things you're doing well for yourself," Jackson said, hiding his envy.

"It's good to see you too, Jackson. I hope that we get to see a lot of each other over the next few weeks."

"I promise to make a real effort, my friend," said Jackson, taking a long look at Patience. *Man, what a beautiful woman. Just think—Patience could have been mine,* he thought resentfully.

"I'm sorry to leave, Frances, but Paul returned this night, and he needs to rest. Please excuse us," implored Junia.

"That's fine, Junia. We're glad you came over. Get some rest, Paul. We will see you both tomorrow," said Jeremy, walking them to the door.

"Thanks, Mr. Loman, and thank you all for your love and hospitality," Jackson said, smiling as he walked out the door, his mother holding onto his arm.

"Oh, Jackson, just a minute. I have something for you." Matt rushed to his room and returned with a gift from Jedidiah.

"What is it?" asked Jackson, unwrapping the gift.

"I don't know. The old seer just told me to give it to you with his blessing."

Jackson hurriedly opened the gift, sure that it had to be priceless coming from a king. To Jackson's unpleasant surprise, he unwrapped a leather-bound book with the inscription *"Wisdom."* Jackson opened the pages and thumbed through it, hoping to find some tangible form of wealth.

"What is this?" Jackson asked as he tossed the book back to Matt.

"Just what it says—a book of wisdom."

"Gold would have been a better gift coming from a king who has everything," Jackson said with an ungrateful smirk.

"Jackson, the way to wealth is in the book," Matt proclaimed, trying to calm the atmosphere.

"You keep it, and when you find the wealth, let me know. I'll see you around," Jackson turned and walked out with Junia attached to his arm. Matt and the others stood dumbfounded.

"That's the same kind of attitude he had when we worked in the fields of plenty. He fails to see that in Proverbs, it is written that the reward for humility and fear of the Lord are riches, honor, and life. Jackson has no sense of honor," Matt voiced with disappointment.

Patience slipped her arm through Matt's and hugged him. "Don't worry, Matt. You can't give him something that he doesn't want."

"Yes, son, you tried your best," acknowledged Frances as she and Jeremy retired for the evening.

Matt remembered that Jedidiah had said, "If he doesn't take the gift, then you will know that his heart hasn't changed."

"Matt?"

"Yes, Patience?"

"May I have the book that Jackson rejected?"

"Of course, you may, my darling, and with Poppy's blessing."

Patience took the precious gift, then called forth her bow and placed the book inside a pocket that appeared on the side of the quiver. The book shifted its shape to fit into the bow, which turned back into the beautiful leather belt that wrapped itself around Patience's waist.

18

DECEPTION

THE FOLLOWING DAYS BROUGHT WITH IT WHAT SEEMED LIKE A heartfelt reunion between Jackson and Matt. Jackson informed Matt of all the intricate details over the past three years.

"It's great to hear that you and your mother are doing well. I know my parents are thankful that you've been a great help around the house," Matt said, feeling him out.

"I didn't know if you would even be coming home. Strangely, I couldn't remember where I was when I left to come back home from the trip, until..." Jackson's conversation abruptly trailed off as he thought about the ramifications if Matt found out about the seer who brought his memories back.

"Until what?" Matt asked, waiting for Jackson's response.

"It's really nothing. Only that Mother and I are glad you're home and bringing with you a new family no less," Jackson said, evading Matt's eyes.

"I can see that you are uncomfortable talking about our past venture, so tell me what kind of business did you have in Peak Valley?"

"I'm trying my hand at selling goods in Peak Valley."

"Really? What kind of goods?" asked Matt.

"All kinds—herbs, spices, and grains, and I'm also taking timber, fish, and fowl to the markets. We currently have plenty and can sell to neighboring lands," voiced Jackson.

"That sounds interesting, but isn't that a good distance away? Is it profitable?" asked Matt, noticing a shift in Jackson's demeanor at his questioning.

"What's with all the inquiries, Matt? I feel like I'm being interrogated," retorted Jackson.

"I apologize. It wasn't my intention to be intrusive."

"Forget it. I seem to overreact a little these days. To answer your questions, it's very lucrative, and I've been traveling to Peak Valley for over a year. As soon as I acquire enough money, I'll build my mother a new house," Jackson stated proudly.

Matt nodded, agreeing that Jackson's decision was great and showed his growth as a man. The conversation became less intense and soon came to an end.

"Well, Matt, I'd better be on my way. I'll come by tomorrow, hopefully, if work doesn't consume me," remarked Jackson.

"Hang on for just a minute. I'm sorry, I don't know where my manners are. Let me introduce you to my new family." Before Jackson could protest, Matt called in the Pia Warriors. Jackson stood by while Matt proudly introduced his family. Lastly, he introduced Layla. Jackson was taken aback by their presence and seemed more delighted to meet Layla than the others.

"Wow, wherever you come from, they sure grow them big. It's nice to meet all of you. Hopefully, we will see each other later. Matt, I really have to be on my way. Thank you for the introductions."

"You are welcome," Matt said, slapping Jackson on the back. Then he stood in the doorway watching his friend depart. Suddenly Matt felt lovely slender hands slip around his waist.

"Have a great time with Jackson?" Patience asked with a luminous grin.

Grabbing her hands gently, he pulled her around and kissed her. "As a matter of fact, I did. Thank you for giving me time to talk with him," Matt said, feeling his wife's warm embrace.

"This is the most wonderful part of the day. Just look at that sunset. It's breathtaking," she said, clapping her hands in amazement as they continued to stand in the doorway.

"God is the greatest artist ever known, isn't He?" responded Matt.

"He is, my love, and there is no other," she agreed. They stood holding each other, watching as one of God's greatest masterpieces sat peacefully behind a high peaked mountain and reflected an array of breathtaking colors.

****

Jackson walked through the door, slamming it behind him. Junia turned at the noisy entrance. "Is everything all right, son?" inquired Junia.

"The man infuriates me. I don't know why. He just does. Every time I'm around him, I feel small, as though I'm being interrogated." Jackson rolled his eyes.

"Are we talking about Matt?" Junia asked, knowing very well he was.

"He thinks he's better than me, and he thinks he's so perfect in everything he does. He shows off that wife of his like she's the rarest possession on earth," complained Jackson, wishing that Patience was his. The more Jackson thought about Matt's possessions, the angrier he got.

"You're obviously angry about Matt. However, I can tell that something else is bothering you. What is it?"

"It's Marcus. He should have been here days ago. Serves me right, thinking that what he said was true. We need to think of our own ways to get rich," insisted Jackson. As he spoke the last few words, Jackson and Junia suddenly heard a light knock on the door. Puzzled, they eyed each other. "Are you expecting company, Mom?" Jackson asked, watching the door.

"At this hour? No, I'm not expecting anyone."

The knock intensified. Finally, Jackson walked to the door. "Who is it?" Silence followed Jackson's inquiry. The knock came again, more forcefully.

Finally, Junia said, "Jackson, just open the door. That knocking is giving me a frightful headache."

Sighing, Jackson obeyed. As he opened the door, he saw a slightly smiling, familiar man. "It's you!" Jackson exclaimed, relieved that his savior had come.

"May I come in?" Marcus asked.

"Yes, yes, come in."

As Marcus entered, his two comrades followed closely behind. With wide eyes, Junia observed the close proximity of the three strange men. It was a little too close for her comfort.

"Which one of you is Marcus?" Junia asked.

Amused, Marcus stepped forward. "I am. It's a pleasure to meet such a charming and beautiful woman. You most certainly couldn't be Jackson's mother," Marcus smiled and reached for Junia's hand.

As he kissed her hand, Junia's heart suddenly began to race. *This man is cunning and attractive. I have to watch myself around him,* Junia thought. She took in his tall, slender, muscular build, as well as his piercing hazel eyes and soothing, deep voice. Junia cleared her throat. "And who are these other men with you?"

Moving slightly to the side, Marcus pointed towards each man. "This is Cavis and Barren. These men are trustworthy and will be on board with our mission," Marcus said, eyeing Jackson. "I assume you told your mother everything, correct?" Marcus asked.

Jackson nodded, clearing his throat. "She has only been informed of what I know," he responded.

"Good," said Marcus, looking Junia's way. "My dear lady, I wonder if it would be too much of an inconvenience to have some refreshments, something to wet our throats," asked Marcus. Junia, studying the men, only nodded and went to the kitchen to prepare refreshments.

Jackson turned to Marcus and said, "What took you so long? I thought you would have been here a week ago."

Marcus coughed to clear his throat. "We had some difficulty getting further into Truevine. Evidently, I misplaced the clearance tag I acquired from you."

"You acquired it from me? How?"

"You invited us to help you, so we were able to create clearance tags to enter."

"Clearance tags? You can't get those unless you have connections. I'm not connected at all," retorted Jackson.

"Not to worry," Marcus said, smiling at Jackson. "All I needed was your consent. The tags took a while to process through the different gates of entry, but now we're here."

"Yes, and I would like to know the real reason you're here," Junia said impatiently, entering the room with refreshments.

"My good lady, whatever do you mean?" asked Marcus, looking at his comrades.

"I am not a stupid woman, as you may presume. Men of your kind do not venture into a place like Truevine unless it's for something more than riches."

Marcus reached for a cup of tea and sat down in front of Junia. "I know that you and Jackson are here in pretense. You are not here for shelter but for revenge. And I can help you get that revenge if you and your son are willing to partner with us in our venture," uttered Marcus.

"And what might that venture be?" asked Junia.

"If I tell you, you must swear to secrecy. And never disclose anything about us to anyone. If you do, you will both lose your lives," announced Marcus.

Junia was frightened by Marcus' comments but felt pressed to comply in order to carry out her quest for revenge. Jackson silently listened. Marcus waited for their reply. Contemplating her choices, Junia glanced around the room and eyed Barren and Cavis. The room was still silent, causing Junia to become more nervous. But her hatred was too deep to turn back. *This may be the only chance to destroy the Lomans,* Junia thought to herself. Nodding, Junia pulled Jackson toward her and said, "Let's do it. I've already tried on my own. Maybe they could help us get rid of them once and for all," Junia remarked.

Jackson let out a deep breath. "I understand your bitterness towards Mr. and Mrs. Loman, but I'm not so sure we should get rid of Matt and his wife. They had nothing to do with Dad's death."

Squeezing Jackson's arm in frustration, Junia whispered, "I know that, but I want Frances and Jeremy to feel the same kind of pain they caused me. What better way for them to experience my pain than to watch their own child die?" Junia said without remorse. Jackson was silent. Noticing Marcus' posture, Junia fell silent and waited for him to continue talking.

"You're right in that we are here for more than riches. We are here for the Sun Stone, which will enable us to restore the glory and power of our homeland. Locating and entering the Great Tree will afford us the opportunity to take back our lost stone." Marcus turned to Jackson. "We know you once entered the Great Tree. We want you to help us gain access, and then we will do the rest."

With downcast eyes, Jackson wavered. "I am afraid that you have the wrong guy for this job. Don't get me wrong. I love riches, but getting into the Treasure Tree can't be done without an invitation. And that comes from the old seer."

"We are aware of this, too, my friend. That is why, with your help, we are going to abduct the seer's granddaughter," Marcus said emphatically.

"Abduct Patience? Have you lost your minds? You are talking suicide. She's the granddaughter of the seer, who happens to be in charge of the Growers. To get to Patience, you have to get rid of Matt and his Pia Warriors. It simply can't be done," Jackson said frustrated, rising from his seat. The two men sitting behind Marcus also rose.

"Come, Jackson. Let's not be hasty. I assure you that it can be done. All we have to do is brainstorm a bit, and I'm sure we will come up with a mutual plan. You'll have all the riches you could ever have, and we will have the means to restore Nod," laughed Marcus, trying to rid the room of tension.

Junia was listening intensely to the entire discourse. "Why don't you give us a few days to ponder these things over? I'm sure that in a few days, we will give you an answer," Junia remarked.

"That sounds reasonable, but let me say this—if anyone finds out about this night, it will be your last night. Are we clear, my good lady?" said Marcus with a cunning tone in his voice.

"Very clear, sir," said Jackson.

"By the way, do your men ever speak, or are they deaf?" Junia asked.

Marcus laughed. "They speak when they need too." The three men turned towards the door, bidding Junia and Jackson a good night.

Junia watched the men as they walked away from the house. Astonishingly, Marcus and the men suddenly seemed to disappear in the night. As the darkness engulfed them, Junia's eyes widened in disbelief. "What? Who are those men? They just disappeared."

****

"Marcus, what do you think about Jackson and his mother? Can they be trusted?" Cavis questioned.

Pondering, Marcus answered, "They are not naturally deceptive creatures, but their lust for riches and revenge will cause them to side with us. However, we do need to be mindful of the woman. She can be most intrusive, even to the point of challenging us." Cavis nodded his head in agreement. Marcus held up his hand in a slight protest. "Not to worry though, as she is very predictable. All we have to do is give them what they want, and we will gain what our people have been searching for," Marcus mused. "Once we acquire the Sun Stone, we can implement our true plan without interference."

"I look forward to the day we rid ourselves of these menacing Growers," said Barren, keeping pace with Cavis.

"I have one other question, my lord," interrupted Cavis. "How is it that Jackson doesn't remember the horror he experienced in the Great Tree? You told us that he encountered a beast that sought to devour him. Why would he go back to such a place?" asked Cavis curiously.

Marcus gazed at the moon, pondering how gullible Jackson and his mother turned out to be. "I never revealed that incident to his mind. He has no memory. It is safely locked away deep in his subconscious," Marcus explained. "They eventually will be destroyed right along with every resident of Truevine. Junia and her son are so taken with their own desires that they have allowed riches and revenge to cloud their judgment, causing them to be easily deceived." Turning, Marcus eyed each of his comrades and said, "We will not only be restoring Nod but will also be taking over this land by using the Sun Stone."

In his silence, both men nodded in agreement, eagerly waiting for Marcus to continue. "We learned from our ancestors and prophets of long ago that the Sun Stone will provide us with control over almost anything. That includes the lands, food, famines, rains, and winds. We will have the ability to control portions of the elements. We can even control human life in these lands to do our bidding. Our prophets told me the Sun Stone was given to Trobus, a menacing king and seer of the Growers from the past. His god gave him power over the people of Nod, both City Dwellers and Growers. He did keep order, but he also opposed our way of life. When we acquire the Sun Stone, we will have the power to defeat our enemy," Marcus said with amusement.

"We will be able to create our own home for our people, and we will flourish," Cavis said, rubbing his hands together. "Marcus, you have truly become one of our greatest seers; you had all this figured out. I just have one question. How will you control all the beasts in the Great Falls?"

Barren, shaking his head, addressed his comrade. "Cavis, jewels from the Great Falls and the badlands will help control the beasts. Powerful demons from the spirit world have shown our prophets where to locate the kind of jewels we need. Our own Marcus has the power to control demons to complete our task. I am surprised that you are not aware of this knowledge. How can you not know that?" Barren snorted.

"I just thought that since the Sun Stone was the most powerful stone, it could control everything, including the beasts," Cavis said.

"Unfortunately, the Sun Stone is only used for good. It brings life to everything. There is, however, a possibility that it can be altered to bring about destruction if placed in the right hands. The day is coming when we will take over everything—the badlands, the Great Falls, and Truevine. It's been a long time coming, but we are about to realize our destiny," Marcus smirked as the three of them continued walking into the darkness.

****

Jackson rubbed the back of his neck, staring over his mother's shoulder as she looked out the window. "What do you think about our guests tonight?" Jackson asked Junia, now watching her facial expression.

With a sigh, Junia said, "I'm not sure they can be trusted. There's an ulterior motive behind all that facade, but we can use them for this short period of time," Junia said, stretching out her arms in an attempt to force herself to relax.

"I'll need to contact friends of mine near the outskirts of Peak Valley," said Jackson.

"The outskirts of Peak Valley are extremely far from here and near the badlands. Isn't that dangerous?" asked Junia, deeply concerned.

"Somewhat, but no more than other large villages," he said, not ready to give a full explanation.

"Who do you know from Peak Valley?" she inquired.

"Don't sound so disturbed. A lot of people meet up in Peak Valley. They are reliable men," Jackson assured his mother.

"Why are you meeting with them?"

"I want to use them for backup," Jackson said, exhaling in annoyance. "I just feel more secure having my own men than being completely at the mercy of Marcus."

"I don't like it, but I guess it won't hurt to meet them," said Junia.

"Meet them? Mother, you're not coming with me to Peak Valley. It's too dangerous, and I'm going by horseback. If I take you, we will have to use the wagon. Horseback alone is a three-day trip. The wagon will take at least five days. You will meet them when we meet with Marcus," said Jackson sternly.

Junia rolled her eyes, dissatisfied with Jackson's objections. "I am not comfortable being left here alone with the possibility of Marcus and his so-called comrades returning. There has to be another way to contact your men without making another trip," protested Junia.

Jackson scratched his head, thinking of a way to pacify his mother. "I could send one of our homing birds with a message; however, it's not always the best way to ensure that the message is delivered. Then again, it would only take a day to reach them," replied Jackson.

Junia's face filled with relief as she looked up at Jackson and smiled. "How will Marcus react to your men being in the meeting with us?"

"I don't know, but I'm going to have them here anyway."

"My concern is that he threatened us with death if we told anyone about our plan," Junia stressed.

"I am aware of that, Mother. However, we are not divulging the plan. If Marcus has any objections, we will simply tell my men to step outside." At Jackson's words, relief crossed his mother's face.

****

Matt and Patience sat quietly in his parent's love seat pondering the last few days. "I know that you're glad to see

Jackson, but something seems a little off with him," Patience said.

"What do you mean?" asked Matt with intense eyes.

"He seems to be disturbed about something the past few days, and he keeps staring at me, which makes me uneasy."

Matt pulled her closer and kissed her forehead. "My love, that's how Jackson has always been. As for staring at you, every man in the village has been doing that." Matt chuckled, pulling her even closer to himself. Smiling, Patience relaxed. "What do you think about Mom? Is she going to be all right?"

"Yes, Mom will be fine, provided she doesn't ingest any more poison. I can see a real positive change in her health. She is very strong to have regained her strength so quickly. However, I really don't know what to say about where the poison came from. That is still a mystery," she said, looking into his emerald eyes. "I'm still suspicious of Ms. Junia. Even though reasonable explanations were given, my gut tells me that something is not right."

Matt was silent, processing what Patience was saying. Trying to reassure himself and Patience, he said, "Don't worry, my love. The Lord will reveal the truth in His own good time. Let's just keep our eyes open."

****

A hard knock came at the door, alarming Junia with the force of it. Looking through the peephole, she was startled by the hazel eye staring back at her. Jumping back, she took a deep breath.

"What is it, Mother?" Jackson asked.

"Marcus is staring at me through the peephole. I declare, he can read our minds," Junia hissed. Opening the door, Junia forced a smile while eyeing Marcus and his comrades.

"Greetings, my dear lady, and you as well, Jackson," Marcus said with a mischievous smile.

Junia cleared her throat. "Please, take a seat. I'll make some tea before we get started," Junia said, rushing to the kitchen.

Marcus and his comrades walked closer to Jackson and stood by the open fireplace. Silence engulfed the room as Marcus studied Jackson's movement intensely. "I take it that you are ready to discuss arrangements regarding the abduction," said Marcus.

Once the words left Marcus' mouth, Junia entered the room with a beautifully decorated tea tray with biscuits for everyone.

"Actually, my mother has suggested a few ideas, right, Mom?" Jackson said with a crack in his voice and pleading eyes.

Junia stepped between Cavis and Marcus to take a seat next to Jackson. "Excuse my interruption, Marcus. Please continue." She motioned for everyone to sit. Jackson was surprised to see Marcus and the others obey her.

Marcus caught Jackson's eyes and decided to stand in order to establish his authority. Marcus tugged at the greed in them all as he laid out for them the wealth and prestige that would be lavished upon them at the close of their venture. "Let me say this to all of you—the girl must not be harmed until we gain access to the Great Tree. After that, she's yours to do whatever your little minds desire. Now, what do you have to say to us, my dear lady?" asked Marcus.

"I think I have a way of getting what we want without raising suspicion." They all listened as Junia presented her idea. "I will convince Frances and Jeremy to throw a homecoming celebration for the young couple to celebrate the return of their son and his lovely bride. The entire community will be obliged to come. The Village Inn has a large upper room that will accommodate the crowd."

"Brilliant, Mother. I think that will work." Jackson leaned over and kissed his mother on the head while the other three men looked on.

Marcus commended her for her innovative thinking. "It's refreshing to know that I have at least one among us who thinks like me," proclaimed Marcus as he placed his cold hand on her shoulder, assuring her that this was the beginning of a long friendship between them.

"Although, what if she doesn't come to the celebration?" asked Junia, more than aware of his icy hand.

"Oh, she will come. It is extremely hard for her to be rude and unaccommodating, especially since you and her new mother are so cozy. And wasn't it you who suggested the celebration in the first place? You are clever, my dear. Just appeal to the natural inclination of parents. They all love to celebrate their children," chuckled Marcus.

"Doesn't it cost a lot to throw that kind of celebration?" asked Jackson, biting into a biscuit.

"Of course, it does!" answered Junia. "But with the wealth they have, no one will quibble about a few gold pieces. I will handle it. You boys just make plans to abduct the girl when she is alone."

"And just how are you going to get her alone, especially since Jackson says that her husband sticks to her like quills on a porcupine's back?" asked Cavis.

"Not to mention she has a whole army surrounding her with those warriors," complained Barren.

Junia raised her brow in annoyance. "I always have more than one way to get a job done. One thing about women that you must understand, my uninformed allies, is that all women want to look their best. And if food or a beverage just happens to spill onto Patience's dress, well ... that will give her reason enough to leave the room. When she does, you just make sure that the three of you are ready. We will also need a distraction to pull her guardians' attention away. Maybe an explosion somewhere in the back of the building or simply falling on the food tables will do," said Junia.

Nervously, Jackson cleared his throat while turning his attention to Marcus. "I had intended to talk with you earlier but didn't have the opportunity. I have enlisted the help of reliable men I know from the outskirts of Peak Valley. I know you said not to tell anyone, and I didn't. I just told them there is an opportunity to make money. If they received the message, they should be here in three days," said Jackson.

"Isn't that close to the badlands? Can anyone reliable come out of that place?" asked Cavis.

"I can vouch for these men. We have worked together before," retorted Jackson.

"Fine. We cannot gain access to the Great Tree without the girl, and we need competent men to execute this mission," said Barren, watching Marcus approach Jackson.

With a deadly stare, Marcus looked at Jackson, revealing in his eyes a demonic presence. "Just make sure that your men can do the job because it will cost you your life if they fail," said Marcus.

In the tension, Junia interrupted by offering more biscuits and tea. "How about another cup of tea?" Junia asked with a smile. The atmosphere calmed, allowing Junia to continue dialoguing with Marcus. "Paul and I will attend the party to deter suspicion. And like Marcus said, Paul will see to it that the girl is not hurt; she'll be of no use to us incapacitated," said Junia, smiling at Marcus as she fixed an out of place piece of hair hanging down over Jackson's brow. "I will talk with Frances, telling her how pleased the Columbidae community will be to see Matt and Patience. I will remind her how grateful I am to her for letting Jackson and me live in the guesthouse. And for giving me the opportunity to plan a village celebration for the happy couple. I will spend every day for the next two weeks helping her arrange it. She will be so excited that she'll never suspect foul play." Jackson was surprised at how his mother could put together such an elaborate plan, acceptable even to Marcus, who liked it and saw no reason why it wouldn't work.

"We will meet again in three days to confirm everything. Bring your men. I want to make sure they meet my standards," said Marcus. "There are to be no glitches and no talk of the matter outside this room. Remember—"

"Our lives depend on it, right?" remarked Junia. Marcus scowled at Junia for finishing his sentence, and his eyes flashed an amber that frightened Junia and Jackson.

"Farewell until we meet again," he said, signaling for Barren and Cavis to follow.

The door closed, and Jackson wiped the sweat from his brow. "Did you see his eyes, Mother? What kind of man are we dealing with?"

"I don't know, son, but if he is willing to fulfill his part of the deal, I don't care if he's the devil himself," Junia said, bitterness spilling from her lips. "The thought of taking revenge on Frances and Jeremy is enough for me. I will meet with her tomorrow and suggest the celebration. Knowing Frances, she will not be able to resist the chance of displaying her children. No mother can," she said cynically.

****

The next day, Junia entered the side door of the Loman home and met Frances standing in the kitchen. "Hello, Frances. I was just in the village and happened to overhear people talking about Matt and his new bride. Many were wondering if they would ever get a chance to see Matt and meet Patience, so I thought that it would be wonderful to throw a welcome celebration for the newlyweds. Then the whole village could honor Matt for what he did in saving our village." Junia smiled, waiting for Frances' response.

A big smile came across Frances' face as she burst into laughter. "I think that is a wonderful idea. It would take some planning, but I'm sure with your help and the support of the village ladies, we could do a good job," Frances said elatedly.

"I think it will take about three weeks to plan the celebration," said Junia.

"Yes, you are right, and maybe Abdi can get word to Patience's parents to join us. Wouldn't it be grand if we could get them to come?" Frances said, beside herself with joy.

"I don't know if it would be a good idea to invite people outside of Columbidae. It may be too much," said Junia, unprepared for Frances' suggestion.

"Oh, no, it will be quite all right. I'm sure that Abdi, Layla, and the boys can arrange that part," insisted Frances, smiling to herself.

Junia faked a smile, agreeing with Frances' suggestion only to avoid raising suspicion.

"Do me a favor and gather the village ladies and ask them to meet me at my house tomorrow. It will be good seeing them, and I know that they will be delighted to help," requested Frances.

"Yes, I will see to it at once," Junia said reluctantly.

"Is there anything wrong, Junia?" asked Frances noticing a change in her demeanor.

"No, not at all. I just don't want you to be overwhelmed with all of this," Junia said, lightly patting Frances on the hand.

"It is my delight. Oh, I want to give you a list of the ladies who will work with us. Make sure you invite them all because each of them has special talents that will be useful in preparing the celebration." Frances wrote out the list and gave it to Junia. "Thank you so much, Junia. I don't know why I didn't come up with the idea myself, but that's why the Good Lord gave us friends to help," she said, giggling. "I have to tell Jeremy and the others about this. I really appreciate your help, Junia. God bless you."

Frances headed towards the sitting room to inform Jeremy of her good news. As she left, Junia grimaced. *I didn't expect her to invite all of Truevine. This could pose a problem in getting the girl alone if her parents and relatives are there. This calls for extra planning.*

****

Looking up at the sky, Abdi inhaled the sweet smells of the land around them. "Are you all ready to leave?" Abdi asked, watching the young warriors interact. Their smiling nods told him that they were. They stepped outside of the inn, enthusiastically preparing to visit the Loman's home for dinner.

"Man, I sure hope that Mrs. Loman makes some more of that apple pie. I never had anything so good," said Lire, smiling.

"We never had anything so good either because you ate it all," complained Bruk.

"Hey, I didn't tell you guys to keep feeding your faces with dinner when dessert was waiting on the table," laughed Lire.

"No need to quibble, boys. I'm sure Mrs. Loman will be expecting hardy appetites, and you'll all be satisfied with whatever is provided," interjected Abdi, stepping down from the porch.

As the warriors walked into town, they noticed a familiar face. "Say, isn't that Ms. Junia?" asked Layla, holding onto Abdi.

"Yes, it is. I wonder what brings her to the village market," pondered Caleb.

"She's probably picking up more apples for the pies," teased Layla.

"Let's not stand here all day talking when there is a feast waiting at Matt's house," insisted Lire.

Back at the house, Frances told her husband, "You wouldn't believe the wonderful conversation I just had with Junia." As Frances walked closer to Jeremy, she suddenly noticed Matt and Patience sitting in the love seat. "Hi, my darlings. I didn't see you. I was so focused on sharing some good news with your father."

"You seem excited about something," said Matt, cuddling next to Patience.

"What are you up to, and can we help?" offered Patience.

"You better tell us what's going on before we all explode from curiosity," Jeremy said, laughing at Frances' excitement. Frances couldn't help smiling.

"We are going to plan a homecoming celebration for you both. Junia came up with the idea. I don't know why I didn't think of it myself, but I'm glad that Junia suggested it. In about three weeks, we will have a celebration for the whole village to welcome Matt and meet Patience. What do you think?"

"I think it's a fabulous idea, honey. How much planning will that take?" queried Jeremy.

"Not to worry, dear. I sent Junia to recruit several of the village ladies who will help us put on the most wonderful celebration. The only concern I have is getting Patience's parents here on time. Do you think that Abdi could arrange that for us?" she suggested, looking to Patience for confirmation.

"Of course, he can, Mother Frances. We will discuss the matter at dinner tonight."

"Wonderful! This is so exciting," Frances said, wrapping her arms around Jeremy.

"Mother, I know that you and Dad like to take care of things yourselves, but I know that much of your wealth is tied up in the land and livestock. Will you allow Patience and me to take care of the cost?"

"No, dear. It would be unthinkable to allow you to pay for your own celebration. Jeremy and I have been very frugal with the Lord's provision. He has blessed us more than you can imagine. And having you and Patience here caused our cups to overflow. Thank you for asking, but we will manage."

There was a sudden knock at the door. "Hey in there! Is dinner ready yet?" came the loud voice of Lire, followed by laughter outside.

"Come on in, and no, dinner isn't quite ready yet. But there is food to nibble on that will hold you over until dinner is prepared." Laughter filled Frances' voice as they each embraced her. Lire picked her up and swung her around.

"I'm expecting an extra piece of pie," he winked. The others simply pushed him aside as Frances enjoyed a heart full of attention from her new family.

Patience, Matt, and Jeremy joined in the greetings as Layla pushed her way through to embrace Patience. "How's the inn? Are you all comfortable?" asked Patience.

"More than you can ever imagine. Everyone made us feel welcomed. However, no one can match Mother Frances' home cooking, except Moa," Layla said, smiling.

"I agree with that only because Moa has been cooking before my mother was even born," Matt chuckled, enjoying the commotion surrounding them all.

"We have a little time before dinner is ready, so let's move into the sitting room," suggested Frances.

As they moved towards the sitting room, Patience pulled Matt to the side, excited. "Don't you think that it is sweet of Mom and the people of Columbidae to give us a homecoming reception?" asked Patience.

"Yes, but I never expected for Mrs. Jackson to suggest anything like this. I'm really surprised," said Matt. Patience bit her lip. "What is it, Patience?" asked Matt.

"I'm really happy that Mom is doing this for us, but I can't help being suspicious. Ms. Junia seems sincere, but I can't bring myself to completely trust her or her son."

"What do you mean?" asked Matt, pulling her more into the hallway for privacy.

"Only a little while ago, she was a prime suspect in poisoning Mother Frances. There are still questions and unexplained feelings in my spirit that bother me about them both." Matt was silent, pondering Patience's assessment. "I just don't know Jackson that well. From what Poppy told me, he wasn't the most gracious of people," exclaimed Patience.

"I can understand your concerns. I have some of the same thoughts running through my mind. However, I think that working for your grandfather taught Jackson a valuable lesson in serving others," Matt responded.

"You think so?" Patience asked.

"His mother did suggest giving us a celebration, and anyone who does that is obviously trying to show a sign of goodwill."

"I hope you're right, my love," she responded. Patience took Matt by the arm and headed toward the sitting room.

Frances watched the newlyweds as they entered. Her heart was full of joy to see her son and new daughter so in love, still so innocent. *Lord, please keep them safe and give them long life in serving You,* she prayed. With outstretched arms, she stood and waited for an embrace from Patience. Patience let go of Matt's arm and stepped towards Frances. When Patience reached her, she threw her arms around Frances.

"How are you feeling, Mom?"

Frances happily received the affection of her daughter. "I'm feeling fine, dear."

Patience whispered in her ear, "Thank you so much for Matt. You have done a wonderful thing for me by putting such love in his heart. I will be forever grateful."

From the time they first met, Frances knew that she loved this young woman. Now she knew why. Patience deeply believed in honor. It was evident that the grace of the Lord flowed through her. Frances realized that it was the influence of Patience's family and their love that made her so humble. They never allowed her to think of herself better than others. Of course, Patience hadn't known that this was the reason she spent summers assisting her grandfather in serving the villagers, but now Frances, Matt, and those who surrounded Patience were benefiting from what others had poured into her life.

Soon the delicious aroma from the kitchen filled the entire home. It was time for dinner, and everyone eagerly anticipated the meal Frances prepared. "Time to eat..." Frances said as she directed the hungry bunch toward the dining room.

Matt and Patience took their time following the others. Suddenly a thought popped into Matt's mind. "Excuse me, my darling, but I have a question that's been on my mind since we met."

"What is it, love?"

"Why didn't I ever see you during the time Jackson and I were sowing the fields?"

She laughed, saying, "It wasn't summer when you came, and it wasn't Poppy's desire that I be seen by men."

Matt laughed and told her that it was a good thing; otherwise, he would have never gotten any work done. The two of them laughed as she leaned against him.

"I'm glad we met, my love," Patience whispered.

"Me too," he said, punctuating it with an affectionate kiss.

19

Celebration

A few days later, Patience met with Abdi to discuss making arrangements for her parents to attend the celebration.

"Patience, you know that your father and grandfather are deep in planning war strategies for the upcoming war. Every leader from the lands of our allies will be meeting with the kings to discuss their part in the mission."

"I know, Uncle Abdi, but this kind of celebration will not take much time away from the mission. Mother Frances and the village ladies are doing all the planning. Poppy and my parents only have to attend," she pleaded.

"If I closed my eyes, I could imagine it was your mother standing in front of me," he said with a chuckle.

Patience smiled and threw her arms around Abdi's neck, then ran off to locate Matt, assuming Uncle Abdi would make arrangements for her family to attend the celebration.

"Where are you going?" came a voice behind Patience.

"Oh, Layla, I'm looking for Matt. Have you seen him?"

"He's with my brothers. Matt was going to show them his horses."

"Horses?"

"Yes. Evidently, they have stables and everything," said Layla.

"Matt hadn't told me about his family having horses. Which way are the stables?" asked Patience.

"Come on. I can show you better than I can explain it." She looped her arm through Patience's and headed for the stables. "They are just over that hill. Matt said there were a couple of large barns over the hill to the left."

"Yes, I see them. Come on, I'll race you," said Patience.

"Go!" said Layla, getting a head start.

"I'll get you for that," yelled Patience, running after her. By the time Layla reached the barns, Patience had caught up with her. Both women laughed, falling on the ground and breathing hard. Matt, Caleb, Bruk, and Lire came out of the barn to see what the ruckus was about. Both women were still taking in deep breaths.

"Who won?" asked Caleb smilingly.

"It was a tie," exclaimed Patience.

"Only because I took off before you," chimed in Layla.

Matt extended his hands for them both and pulled them to their feet. "What brings you out here?" asked Matt.

"Well, I just found out that you had horses," responded Patience.

"I'm sorry, love. It completely slipped my mind. We use them to haul logs after we cut the trees down. It's part of our business. Come on in, and I'll show you around."

As Patience entered the barn, she saw the most beautiful breed of workhorses she had ever seen. "Wow, these are your horses?" Patience asked in awe.

"Yes, they are, and they have remarkable abilities. They are larger than Clydesdales, stronger than elephants, and faster than cheetahs," explained Matt.

"I've never seen anything like them. Where did you get such animals?" asked Patience.

"We had the same reaction," said Bruk, still amazed.

"You'll have to ask my father that question, "chimed in Matt. "We have been in the lumber and farming business for as long as I can remember. We were really struggling for a while, but Dad never gave up. He inspired many of the growers to join him in caring for the land. He made sure that for every tree that was cut down, three more were planted. As we prospered, so did the villagers around us. That is until the famine hit us. The trees were fine, but the food supply died out. We had to ration food for a while until the Lord sent me to Old Seer Jedediah." Matt looked at Patience, and his eyes filled with water. "I am the most blessed man, for not only did the Lord provide for our land, but He gave me a most precious gift."

Patience blushed, noticing her grinning cousins but thankful for a strong man with a gentle heart. Matt regained his composure and cleared his throat and continued speaking. "When I was born, Dad was five years into the business. One day, he took a walk in the woods to pray. There's a secluded place where he goes to be by himself and falls on his face before God if the Spirit leads him to do so. He told me on one of those occasions, the Lord told him to build barns large enough to hold many horses," Matt said, pausing.

"Sounds like Noa—" Lire started.

"Don't say it. I know it sounds like the Ark story," Matt said, laughing. "Dad obeyed, and he built those barns with many stalls. Three days after he finished, thirteen mares and two grand stallions mysteriously appeared in the barns. That was over 24 years ago. Since then, those original

15 have grown to almost 400 horses. I've always played with them and know each of them by name. It just never occurred to me to discuss them." Matt glanced at Patience, who smiled and took his hand.

"But do you have any idea where they came from?" Caleb asked.

"To this day, we don't know. We believe the Lord gave the horses to us," Matt said with confidence.

Matt decided to open the barns and let the horses enjoy the grasslands. As they all stood watching the horses roam the pastures, Patience noticed Matt had a faraway look on his face.

"Matt, what are you thinking about?" Patience asked, nudging him.

"I used to spend most of my time in a secret hideout when I was a boy. I would like to show you. It's one of my favorite places."

"That sounds like fun. Where is it?" she asked enthusiastically.

Pointing, Matt said, "About 10 miles down that wooded trail. We can take a couple of horses and be there in no time."

"Are you sure?" Patience asked in disbelief.

"Yes, the horses are very fast. We'll take Cloud and Cactus. They will get us there and back before sunset," Matt said, taking her up and swinging her around once before slipping away without being noticed by the family, who were still deeply intrigued by the horses.

"Matt, you have to stop spinning me around like that."

"Why? Don't you like it?"

"Of course, I like it, but you have this habit of spinning me wherever we are. One day you're going to knock some little old lady down, and then what will you say?" she said teasingly.

"No problem, honey. I'd catch her before she falls," Matt said, kissing her on the forehead.

Patience laughed. "I'm curious about something."

"What would that be?"

"Who named your horses?"

Matt played with long strands of her hair as he answered. "I did. Why do you ask?"

"I was just wondering why you named one of your horses Cactus."

He laughed. "I call him Cactus because he has a prickly personality. In fact, he only lets me ride him. You can take Cloud. She is very friendly."

Patience looked at both horses and calmly walked towards Cactus. She looked him in the eyes and put her hand on his head and laid her head against his. The animal immediately put his face against hers.

"He's never done that before!" exclaimed Matt.

"I think I want to ride Cactus if that's ok with you."

"Of course, it's okay. Just be careful. I know that you are a Pia Warrior now, but Cactus is a powerful animal, and sometimes he has a mind of his own. He'll run over every hill and down every valley if you let him. He loves to run."

"That's okay. He can run as much as he wants, can't you, boy?" Patience said, rubbing Cactus' head.

"Okay, let's do it," said Matt, lifting Patience and placing her on Cactus. Grabbing the reigns, Matt eyed the horse and said, "You listen to me, Cactus. Patience is mine, and you make sure that you protect her at all costs." Cactus reared his head as if he knew exactly what Matt was saying.

Matt easily mounted Cloud, and off they went towards Matt's favorite place.

"Where do you suppose they are headed this time?" asked Lire.

"Not my business," exclaimed Caleb.

"Wonderful animals, don't you think?" said Layla, changing the subject as they headed back into the barn.

While riding, Matt and Patience talked about the upcoming celebration. Soon they came to a road covered by a canopy of large oak limbs stretching across to each other as if they were shaking hands.

"It's breathtaking," Patience said with smiling eyes. Straight ahead of them, she could see a running river with a waterfall. The smell of roses and wildflowers was in the air as they passed open fields on both sides of the trail. Matt filled with delight as he heard the sweet sound of unveiled passion flow through Patience's voice as she viewed the sea of spectacular flowers. "No wonder you call this your favorite place. It's breathtaking. I've never seen such an array of vibrant roses and wildflowers grow together. How did it all get here?" A blush came over Matt's face. "What is it?"

"If you must know, my love, I was inspired by the Lord to plant the flowers for my future bride. I found a bag of seeds near one of the barns. I planted them, and each year, they bloom just as you see now. I never guessed that I would have a bride as beautiful as the flowers I planted. But here you are," he stated proudly.

Her eyes filled with tears of joy. "Who else knows about this place?" she asked, wiping away happy tears.

"Only Mom and Dad. I used to come here to think and pray. When Dad was injured, I spent a lot of time here praying. When my parents suggested that I find the Great Seer to help our village out of the famine, I knew that my time here with the Lord prepared me for the task." Matt took Patience down from Cactus and held her close. "I had no idea that you would be part of the result of that prayer."

Patience hugged him. "I think this has become one of my favorite places too."

"I'm glad," Matt said, still holding her.

"We should probably get back before night catches us," Patience suggested, watching the sun disappear behind the waterfall.

"It's okay, Patience. Cactus and Cloud see very well in the dark. There's no cause for alarm."

"Still, I like to see where I'm going," she said, laughing. Matt allowed her to mount Cactus on her own as he leaped onto Cloud. They headed back with great speed and reached the barns before the sun completely hid behind the mountains. "I had a wonderful time, Matt. Maybe we can do it again soon," she said excitedly.

"Anytime, my love."

During their walk back to the house, Patience felt overwhelming joy and started skipping to the house. Matt shook his head at Patience's childlike behavior. "You are one of a kind, Patience."

"I know," she said, continuing to skip up the porch stairs. Before entering the house, she said, "I'm going to freshen up a little bit before we join everyone."

Nodding, Matt opened the door, and Patience walked past him. While watching his love exit, he overheard his parents softly talking in the kitchen. Curiosity overtook him. As he slightly pushed open the kitchen door, he overheard his parents talking.

"Frances, I often think about my old friend Jack Jackson. His death was so sudden. I still feel guilty that he died on my watch. Junia seems better now that she finally understands that I wasn't responsible, yet I sometimes feel a coldness coming from her eyes as if she still blames me for Jack's death."

"You tried your best to save him. You have to give the guilt over to the Lord. If you keep dwelling on those negative thoughts, it could destroy you." Frances grabbed her husband's hands and kissed them. "I will pray that the Lord delivers this burden from your heart."

Matt felt a twinge of pain tug at his heart. As his parents' conversation came to an end, he backed away until he heard a familiar voice.

"What are doing, Matt?" asked Patience, tugging on his arm.

"I was just remembering some things I overheard my dad say to my mom."

"What things?" she asked.

"I'll ... uh, tell you later. Let's go into the other room."

Patience could tell by the expression on his face that he was concentrating on something. "Is there anything else running through that mind of yours?" she asked, hoping to pull him back into the present.

He chuckled, thinking how his lovely wife had impacted the lives of everyone around her. His dad made no secret about how much he adored Patience and her family because of what he had learned from them. Matt could tell that his father had great respect for Patience. Her kindness couldn't help but be seen. Her deep devotion to God and him was wonderful.

20

Frances' and Junia's Interaction

Every day, Junia visited Frances to plan and make arrangements for the celebration. She laughed, talked, and embraced Frances as if the rift in their relationship had never occurred.

"It was the Lord who laid it on my heart to forgive and love even in my loss. Thank you again. You and Jeremy have helped Paul and me through our hard time," Junia said with tearful eyes.

"We were glad to do whatever we could. We are so grateful for all that Jackson did for us while Matt was away," Frances said, taking Junia's hand.

Junia smiled. "You'll never know how grateful I am to you for allowing me to help you with this celebration. It means the world to Paul and me."

"That is so nice of you, Junia, and even nicer for suggesting the whole thing. I truly appreciate your help," said Frances. Junia smiled and placed her hand over Frances' hand, expressing her affection and gratitude.

21

The Abduction

Three days swiftly passed, and as predicted, Marcus and his men stood in front of Jackson's door, eagerly awaiting to hear the final plans of the abduction. As Marcus lifted his hand to knock on the door, it suddenly swung open. Standing in the doorway was Junia with a faint smile, ready to greet her expected guests.

"Marcus, glad you're here," she said, watching to see the reaction of the men who stood in front of her. "Everyone, please come in and take a seat."

As Marcus entered, his men followed, observing Junia's newfound confidence. Junia closed the door behind them.

Marcus scanned the room. "I see Jackson isn't here. Where might he be?" asked Marcus, perturbed at his absence.

Marcus' intense stare caused Junia to take a deep breath. She exhaled slowly to calm herself. "Paul went to meet his friends at the village entrance. He should be back soon. In the meantime, let me get you and your men some refreshments. I'm sure it will help relax you from your journey." Not waiting for a response, Junia swiftly went to the kitchen to fetch refreshments.

"What do you think?" Barren asked, eyeing Marcus.

"I think their plan better be solid, or they will disappear without a trace," Marcus said, grimacing at the thought of being inconvenienced.

****

Jackson waited nervously beside a large tree just outside the village entrance, eyeballing the road leading out of Columbidae. *Where are they? They should be here by now,* he thought. It felt like an eternity. He pondered on the possibility of losing his life if his comrades failed to show, and worry began to engulf his mind. Suddenly he felt a strong arm choking him from behind. In an attempt to free himself, Jackson wrestled out of the chokehold to face what he thought was a foe—until he got a good look at the man facing him.

"Fray? What are you trying to do? Kill me?" Jackson said, rubbing his neck in pain. The other two men laughed as they watched the spectacle from a few yards away. Fray, a broad, muscular man with a receding hairline which made him look older than his comrades, hit Jackson's back in friendship. Jackson eyed Fray in frustration, while Landon, a tall, lanky man with a large nose and beady eyes, and Gabb, a shorter stout man of tremendous strength, walked up to join them.

"It's about time you two joined us," Fray said, sarcastically.

"Landon. Gabb. Glad you are here," Jackson said with relief.

"We would have been here earlier if Fray hadn't given us the wrong directions," Landon said, annoyed.

"Yes, if we hadn't turned around at the crossway, we wouldn't be here until tomorrow," Gabb said, making a face at Fray.

Jackson smiled at Landon and Gabb, thankful that these men would be his backbone if he needed to stand up to Marcus. Clearing his throat, Jackson proceeded. "Okay, we have to reach my house by sunset. Marcus and his men are probably already waiting for us."

"Marcus? Who is Marcus?" Gabb asked curiously.

"Listen to me—Marcus is a serious, no-nonsense man. If you value your lives, you'll keep silent and listen to what he has to say," Jackson explained.

"So … what is he? The devil?" Fray said with laughter. All that followed was silence.

Jackson, shaking his head, said, "I brought you in on this deal because I need backup. And you need the wealth. We can all get what we want if we cooperate and do what we're told. Fray, this man is probably the devil's favorite servant. Now let's go. I don't want to be late," Jackson said, reminding himself how dangerous Marcus was.

****

"Okay, I have your refreshments," Junia said in a pleasant voice. As soon as the words left her mouth, Jackson walked confidently through the door, followed by his men. Marcus gave Jackson and his crew an intense look and pointed for them to stand against the far wall.

"Nice of you to join us," he said to Jackson. "You are late. My time is valuable, and I don't like waiting," grimaced Marcus.

"My apologies, sir," Jackson quickly responded. "I briefed my men on protocol in hopes of saving you the time in going over menial details."

"I appreciate your efforts, Jackson; however, allow me the privilege of deciding what's best for the group," retorted Marcus, eyeing them all. "Now, without further delay, let us turn to your mother for her report."

Junia assured Marcus and the others that everything was in place. "Just make sure that you are all on time and at your stations. One mistake will be our last mistake. I was informed that the girl's family will be attending, so we must be extra careful," Junia said hesitantly.

"Wait a minute. Does that mean more of those warriors will be showing up?" Jackson asked, concerned.

"It makes no difference to me if God himself is attending. We are still going through with this plan," Marcus stated malevolently.

Junia continued to divulge her plans in detail while they listened intently. "As you can see, my plan is flawless," Junia spoke with pride.

Marcus nodded with approval as he rose from his seat. "If there are any glitches, contact me immediately. We will not meet again until the day before the celebration. Everyone should know their tasks. Cavis will be your contact in case I want to inform you of any changes. In the meantime, make sure you all adhere to the plan." On his way out, in his usual form, Marcus took hold of Junia's hand and kissed it, turned, and signaled for Barren and Cavis to follow him.

22

Family Reunion

"It's the day before the celebration. Are you excited?" Layla asked Patience.

"Yes, I can't wait. Everyone has been working so hard to welcome Matt and me. I'm thankful to the Lord for this celebratory honor," Patience exclaimed, standing on the front porch with Layla, watching Lire as he ran towards them.

"Are you two coming? Matt's mom is preparing a big meal in the backyard. If you don't hurry, you're going to miss out on some good food, and I'm not sharing my meal with anyone," Lire said, laughing as he ran past them towards the back of the house.

Both women shook their heads as Lire sprinted ahead of them. Patience and Layla laughed at the sight of Lire bumping into Caleb and Bruk when he turned the corner. Both men picked themselves up and continued towards the feast. Patience and Layla were laughing so hard that they hardly heard the soft call of Patience's name. The voice was very familiar to them. Simultaneously, they turned with wide eyes and overwhelming joy at the sight of their beloved family.

"Are you just going to stand there gawking, or are you going to come over here and give us a hug?" said Jedidiah with open arms.

"Poppy, Moa, Mom, Dad! You are all here!" Patience said with tears in her eyes and laughter in her voice. She ran, Layla close behind, and they hugged them all.

"We couldn't miss your celebration, darling," Heather said, running her slender fingers through Patience's dark brown tresses.

"Let's go meet your in-laws," Steven said.

"Yes, let's! From the smell of things, I know Mrs. Loman has made her special apple pie. And if we don't hurry, Lire will be done with it before anyone else gets a slice," Abdi said with a large grin.

"Let's go then, meet our new kin, and have some of that pie before it's too late," chuckled Steven.

Patience hooked arms with her parents, and Layla did the same to Jedidiah and Moa. They happily walked toward the back of the house, where they saw the wonderful interactions of a lovely family. Food and drink were plentiful along with loud and numerous conversations.

Layla gave a loud whistle, getting everyone's attention. "Our family is here!"

Matt turned, almost choking on the chicken leg his mother had put on his plate. When he saw the newcomers, he jumped up from the table and rushed towards them, but not before he told Lire not to touch his slice of pie. With open arms and great admiration, Matt embraced his family.

"I'm so glad you could come to the celebration. Let me introduce you to my parents," Matt said, leading them through the small crowd of Pia Warriors who stood in honor of the royal family.

"Uncle Steven, wait until you taste some of this apple pie," said Lire with his mouth full.

"That boy will never change," said Jedidiah, chuckling at the fun-filled atmosphere.

"Dad, Mom, allow me to introduce you to King Jedidiah and King Steven. And of course, their queens, Pricilla and Heather. They are my mentors and my family. They love the Lord, and they love me," Matt said with pride.

"It's so nice to meet you all. Matt has told us so much about you, and we are truly blessed to have you all in our son's life," voiced Frances as Jeremy agreed in silence, stunned at the fact that they were in the presence of the royal family.

"The privilege is ours," said Pricilla, extending her arms to embrace Frances.

"Yes, we love Matt, and he is so good for our daughter. We couldn't have picked a better man. We feel that he was sent to us from God," said Heather, smiling at the blushing couple.

Matt proudly held Patience close. "I also wanted to introduce you to Mrs. Junia Jackson. She's the one who suggested the celebration. I don't see her. Dad, where is Mrs. Jackson? She was here a moment ago."

"I'm not sure, son. Maybe she went to get additional plates and food," Jeremy said, taking hold of Jedidiah's hand in greeting.

"I guess you're right," responded Matt, a little confused at how quickly she left.

Abdi signaled Bruk and Caleb to bring comfortable seats for Patience's family while Matt, Patience, and Layla sat down on the soft grass. Hours that seemed like minutes passed as Matt gave details of some of the adventures, training, and mental exercises Jedidiah gave him. It amused everyone as Matt teased his old mentor. Jedidiah tapped Matt on the head with his staff.

"Son, when we get back, you'll have additional training for those remarks you just made," Jedidiah said, causing everyone to laugh except Matt.

"It seems that it's getting late, and I believe our guests should rest before tomorrow's celebration," suggested Jeremy.

"We have reserved rooms in the inn, and I believe that you will be very comfortable," replied Frances.

"We will escort you to the inn, Your Majesties," Abdi said, signaling his sons to take action.

"We will be here tomorrow morning to help you, Frances," Pricilla said, squeezing her hand in delight.

"That would be wonderful. I look forward to tomorrow." After everyone gave affectionate farewells, Frances walked her royal guests to their awaiting coach. Patience and Matt watched her family leave, amazed at how wonderful their whole day had been.

"It's going to be a glorious day tomorrow," Matt said, kissing the back of Patience's neck.

"Yes, and I can't wait," she said, resting against him.

"I didn't see Mrs. Jackson. I wanted to introduce her to Poppy," Patience said, disappointed.

"I'm sure she will meet them tomorrow. She's probably busy with the preparations," Matt said.

"Yes, of course, you're right," she smiled.

"It's time for us to get some rest too," Matt said, picking Patience up to carry her to their bedroom.

"Oh, Matt, I pray that all goes well tomorrow. I'm so happy that my family is here, and I'm glad that we belong to each other," she said, wrapping her arms around him as he took her upstairs.

****

Looking out the kitchen window of the Lomans' home, Junia discreetly monitored Patience's family's arrival for the picnic. "This is bad. Her entire family is here. What a mess. I can't believe this is happening. Who would have ever expected that her family would be the kings of True-vine and Ethiopia? Why didn't Paul tell me? Marcus is not going to like this," Junia said to herself. "I'd better get word to everyone so that adjustments can be made. It's probably impossible to keep secrets from that old seer."

Junia inconspicuously rushed to the guesthouse, hoping to catch up with Jackson. The door flew open, and Jackson was standing in the middle of the room, talking with Landon, Gabb, and Fray. They looked at the distorted face of Jackson's mother as she stepped into the room.

"What's wrong? What happened?" asked Jackson, concerned.

She threw her bag across the room, still agitated at the thought of having to deal with unexpected opposition. They all stared, stunned at her reaction. Junia took a deep breath. "I just found out that ... that ... that girl is related to the kings of this land. Why didn't you tell me? This could make things more difficult. We need to contact Marcus immediately and adjust our plans," Junia said in a high-pitched voice.

"Calm down, Mother. It just slipped my mind. Marcus is aware, and I'm sure that he has considered all possibilities. He has a special insight about these things."

"I hope he does," responded Fray sarcastically, elbowing Landon in the side.

"Before we all jump to conclusions, let's contact Marcus, and find out his instructions," said Jackson in a calmer demeanor than usual. Junia agreed. Jackson and Landon started toward the door immediately to find and inform Marcus of the situation while Gabb and Fray stayed to help Junia with any unfinished business regarding the abduction. Jackson opened the door to leave and was startled to see Marcus and his comrades standing in front of him.

"Whoa! You scared the gibbers out of me," said Jackson before he could catch his words.

"Gibbers," mocked Marcus, laughing sardonically at Jackson's reaction. He then pushed Jackson and Landon aside. Walking in, he observed Junia biting her nails while pondering her next move to solve the unforeseen problem. Marcus slowly approached Junia, not making a sound. Observing her features, he grinned slightly.

Junia, looking down, suddenly saw an unfamiliar pair of shoes approaching. She quickly lifted her head and saw Marcus studying her. "Marcus … how … when did you get here?" Junia asked, stunned to see him standing in front of her.

"I hope I didn't interrupt you, my dear. I sensed you needed me," he said with a grin.

"How did you know that? I just informed Jackson and the others only a few minutes ago."

"I have my ways, and you have nothing to worry about. I am aware that Patience is a princess and that the kings will be attending. This is a good thing. If we strategize correctly, we will have the girl before they notice she's gone. While they are here, we will already be on our way to the Great Tree. You will remain here to entertain and occupy their time with your charming flattery." Junia smiled at how Marcus relieved her worry. "Do you think that my comrades and I could have something to refresh ourselves?" Marcus asked, knowing he had given Junia back her confidence.

"Yes, indeed. I shall be back in a few minutes," she stated, rushing towards the kitchen.

As Marcus' eyes trailed after Junia, Cavis approached and whispered, "Just how do you plan to handle the kings, not to mention those Pia Warriors who seem to be attached to Matt and his family?"

"You know as well as Barren who has called us here. Our spirit guides have already warned us of the oncoming events. The Great War that is coming will determine many things. Our outcome depends on us getting into that tree to obtain the Sun Stone. Our war strategies depend on it. It is the will of the spirit guides. You and Barren will do what you are told and let the spirit guides handle the details. Are we clear?" threatened Marcus. Cavis shook his head as he studied Marcus' eyes change color from hazel to a fiery yellow, warning him not to ask any more questions.

"This is weird," whispered Fray to Jackson and his cohorts. Jackson felt it too. The eerie presence seemed to take over the room. Jackson felt unsure but decided to interrupt Marcus' conversation with Cavis, hoping Marcus wouldn't take offense at his inquiry.

"Excuse me, sir," Jackson said, hoping to avoid hostility. "I have some questions. How are we going to solve the problem of the kings?"

Marcus swallowed hard, trying not to explode at what he considered an excessive, foolish question. "Didn't you hear my answer to Cavis? He just asked me the same question," Marcus bellowed.

"I'm sorry, sir. I did not hear Cavis ask, nor did I hear your answer."

Breathing deeply, Marcus said maliciously, "It's not for you or your mother to worry about Jackson. Things are going on in the unseen world that most people never pay attention too."

"What things?" asked Gabb.

Marcus ignored Gabb's question and continued his venting. "Listen to me, all of you. If I want you to know my next steps, I'll tell you. Don't waste my time with superfluous questions. I am a seer of the highest order. Just as I knew that your mother had need of me, I also know how to keep Matt and his entire family occupied while we carry out my plan."

****

The kings, Jedidiah, and Steven, along with members of the Royal family, settled into the village inn.

"This is absolutely wonderful," exclaimed Heather.

"What is?" asked Pricilla, beaming with anticipation.

"That we are here celebrating with our children. Meeting Matt's wonderful family and friends. The surrounding scenery of Columbidae is so beautiful. The valley and mountains, the river that runs through the meadows and the blooming flowers filling the air with their lovely fragrances. It's as grand as some of the places in the Great Tree."

Heather turned to her father. "I am amazed at the number of horses the Lomans have now accumulated. When you took them out of the Great Tree, I had no idea where you were taking them. Now look at them—beautiful, all grown up, and producing many offspring of their own," Heather laughed happily.

It made Jedidiah happy to see his daughter filled with sweet contentment. "I am delighted at how well Jeremy has kept the land and stock, especially after that terrible famine," said Jedidiah.

"It just goes to show you that people of faith and good work habits will accomplish what's in their hearts," said Steven, putting his arm around Heather. As they started toward their rooms, they heard a voice call out.

"Your Majesty," called Abdi. Jedidiah and Steven looked quickly towards the voice.

"Abdi, are things for the celebration ready?" asked Steven.

"Yes, little brother," he teased. "We met with Junia and her helpers. All the food and gifts are ready and will be delivered first thing in the morning," Abdi answered reassuringly.

"Well done, Abdi! I guess the next best thing we can do is get a good night's sleep," exclaimed Pricilla.

"Sounds good to me," grinned Jedidiah, lifting Pricilla up in his arms. "We'll see you in the morning." He laughed, climbing the stairs with ease as Pricilla blushed and waved goodnight to their astonished family.

"That's something you don't see every day," giggled Layla.

"I don't want to see that every day, and maybe not ever again," laughed Lire.

"I think it's great to see the old man still has it," said Steven. Heather elbowed him in the side. "What? You want me to carry you up too?" Before she could protest, Steven gathered Heather into his arms and followed Jedidiah's lead up the stairs. Abdi slapped Caleb on the back, laughing hard as the others stood with their mouths opened. Layla headed for her room before she blushed herself to death.

"That is remarkable! I hope I have that kind of energy when I'm that old," said Lire, still laughing.

"Come on, boys. Good comfortable beds are awaiting us," chuckled Abdi.

****

Now was the time. The Elders, Village Council, and other important members of Columbidae had readied themselves for the celebration. The celebration began mid-evening in the assembly room of the inn. It was crowded with villagers and dignitaries that traveled from afar. No one was sure how the surrounding villagers were aware of the celebration, but they seemed to be enjoying the festivities just as much as the Columbidaeans. The entire Royal Family had arrived and was overjoyed to see such a large group of Growers gathered in one place. No one came empty-handed; all were thrilled to meet and offer gifts to the beloved couple.

Suddenly a familiar voice called out to Matt. "Hey, Matt?"

Matt turned and waved to Jackson. Jackson approached, extending his hand in greeting. Matt smiled and wrapped his arms around his old friend. "It's good to see you, Jackson. Glad you could come to the celebration."

Jackson nodded and smiled. "Wouldn't have missed it for the world."

While Patience was conversing with Poppy and her parents, she saw Matt talking to Jackson and excused herself to join them. As Patience walked towards them, Jackson was taken aback and couldn't help staring at her. *And to think, she could have been yours*. The words of Marcus came into his mind.

"Matt, your wife looks beautiful," Jackson said with a crooked smile.

Matt chuckled. "My mother gave her one of the dresses she wore as a young woman. It actually fits her perfectly."

"I'll say," said Jackson, unable to keep his eyes off of her until Matt elbowed him.

"Like it says in the wisdom book, he who finds a wife finds a good thing," Matt said. Startled, Jackson forcibly shifted his eyes back to Matt.

"It is nice to see you again, Jackson. Thank you for coming." Patience extended her hand as a courtesy.

Jackson studied her for a moment, then nervously took her hand. "It's nice to see you again, as well, Princess. My mother thinks the world of you. She told me how knowledgeable you are with plants and poisons."

Patience felt a little awkward at Jackson's comment but disregarded it. Sensing her discomfort, Matt said, "If you'll excuse us, we are going to make our rounds to greet our guests. We'll catch up later. Please enjoy yourself."

"Thanks, Matt. I will." As the couple walked away, Jackson stared after them as the rage of not having Patience grew in him. Patience was truly beautiful, and Matt had her as his wife. If he had stayed a little longer at the Great Tree, he would be the one married to Patience. *Control yourself, man. There may still be a time when both she and the treasure are yours if everything works according to plan,* Jackson thought to himself.

"Isn't this the most wonderful thing in the world?" said Patience, hanging onto Matt as they moved around the crowd of people interacting with each other. Most people knew Matt and appreciated what he had done in giving his heart to the people by providing the food and provision through the work in Jedidiah's fields.

Eventually, Abdi had Caleb sound his horn to get the attention of the guests. "Honored guests, may I have your attention? Our King Jedidiah has something to say," bellowed Abdi, extending his hand towards the old seer. Jedidiah took the opportunity to thank everyone for coming and for their generosity. He also praised Matt in front of the people of Columbidae for staying the course in the fields of plenty.

"Matt did well, and I'm glad that you are all proud of him. This wonderful celebration proves how much you think of him."

The king did not mention Paul Jackson. It wasn't in his heart to reveal the poor conduct he displayed during his time in the field. He did, however, mention Jackson's part in helping Matt's family while he was away. The people loved him for it, but Junia and Jackson allowed bitterness to overshadow all the good that had been done. Jackson could not get over his jealousy that Matt got everything, even a beautiful wife, the daughter of kings. Junia clung to her hatred even though the entire village benefited from Matt's diligence.

In the distance, Marcus studied the royal family's every move. It was evident that Jedidiah and his family were enjoying themselves as they watched the villagers' interactions with the newlyweds. Without bringing attention to himself, he whispered commands under his breath.

Jedidiah and Steven sharply turned as if they heard something in the distance. "Do you feel that?" asked Jedidiah, Steven nodded affirmatively. "We should take a look just in case something's out there. No need to alert the others. Let them enjoy the festivities," said Jedidiah.

However, Heather noticed their movement. "Steven, where are you two going? The celebration is just getting started."

Turning his head, Steven smiled slightly. "Poppy and I sensed something strange just outside of Truevine. It may be headed towards Columbidae. We're going to investigate. We will be back soon."

"Okay, dear, just be careful." Heather turned back to give her attention to Patience and Matt enjoying themselves.

Marcus observed with glee. He was satisfied that the distraction had worked. Now all that was needed was for Junia to carry out her part of the plan. With Jedidiah and Steven's absence, he signaled for Jackson and his men to engage.

As Junia watched Heather and the rest of the family interact with everyone, she took the opportunity to pull Patience aside. "Matt, may I borrow your beautiful bride for a moment? We'll be right back."

Matt's eyebrow raised. Something was going on in his spirit. He had an uneasy feeling but was at a loss for words at Junia's request. However, Junia's smile disarmed him.

"My dear, I brought you a cup of punch," offered Junia, handing it to her. Patience grabbed the drink while Junia pointed out a flaw in her dress. "I couldn't help but notice that you have a stain on the side of your dress. Some careless fool probably bumped into you."

Pulling her dress around, Patience saw a small stain that seemed to just appear. "No damage is done as long as everyone is enjoying themselves" was her unexpected response.

Pressing her lips together to conceal her annoyance, Junia continued to insist, "Come with me, and we can take care of it, so it won't leave a stain. After all, it is your mother-in-law's dress."

"Okay, if you insist." Patience looked to Matt for an option, but his nod told her he had no options.

"We'll be right back, Matt," Junia stated. Her words relaxed his mind.

"Yes, ma'am, as long as I get her back," he said half-jokingly. Patience assured Matt that she would return right away. Junia guided Patience to a washroom near the balcony.

"Isn't this the most wonderful punch?" said Junia, taking a deep swallow of the drink. Patience smiled and took a sip as well.

"My, this does taste good, but it seems to have an aftertaste to it," said Patience, now standing in front of the washroom. Junia opened the door for her to enter. Patience nodded and proceeded to enter the washroom. The taste in her mouth reminded her of something she couldn't quite figure out. As she entered the washroom, she smelled a light and unfamiliar but pleasant scent. As she breathed it in, she felt lightheaded. When she attempted to wash out the stain, she was surprised to find that it was gone. "What in the world?" Patience said, leaving the washroom confused.

"Is there something wrong, my dear?" asked Junia.

"I was just surprised that the stain in my dress was gone when I entered the washroom."

"That is bizarre. Come over here near the balcony. I want you to see something."

As Patience walked towards the opened doors of the balcony, the same uneasiness Matt felt suddenly came over Patience. However, despite the feeling, she kept walking toward the balcony at Junia's request. After all, wasn't it Junia and Jackson who thought of this great celebration, and weren't she and Matt enjoying themselves to the fullest? Why should there be any suspicion? Then without warning, she felt the room swirling. Barren stood with Jackson's men behind the balcony door, out of sight, ready to abduct Patience. Marcus, Jackson, and Cavis waited at the bottom of the dimly lit balcony.

"What's going on?" Patience said softly, unable to speak loudly. The drug was working rapidly. "Matt ... Matt..." she called softly. *Girma ... Girma,* she called in her mind.

The rug in the Great Hall of The Treasure Tree stirred as Girma emerged. In a matter of seconds, Girma's presence could be felt by both Jedidiah and Patience. *Return to your place, my friend,* came the voice of Jedidiah to the mind of the beast. And just as quickly as he had arrived, he disappeared. Jedidiah gave Steven a serious glance, then closed his eyes.

"What is it, sir?" asked Steven, puzzled.

"Do you still sense an evil presence beyond Columbidae or Truevine?" asked Jedidiah.

Steven, shaking his head, said, "Surprisingly, no. Once we left the inn, it seemed to dissipate."

"It's a diversion. We should return to the inn immediately," said Jedidiah. Steven wasted no time in following the old seer back to the celebration.

****

Patience was slightly confused. It was not like Girma to vanish without a word or at least a greeting. Her thoughts were interrupted by a hand on her arm as Junia led her through the dimly lit balcony towards the stairs. Once there, Junia, with exaggerated motherly affection, put her arm around the princess' shoulder and began to tell her how proud she was of Matt for helping the villagers and how she was so pleased that they were married. Patience was groggy but still tried to understand Junia's vague words.

"Thank you, Ms. Junia. I appreciate you for helping with the celebration arrangements," Patience said, slurring her words. She leaned over to give Junia a hug but felt herself falling. She looked into Junia's eyes, catching a glimpse of shadows moving towards her. Just before Patience's limp body fell to the floor, strong hands caught and held her tightly around the waist.

"Barren! Hurry up. We got to go," Cavis whispered in a commanding tone.

Barren rolled his eyes in annoyance. "Here, gag the woman, and tie her up quickly," Barren said, shoving her into the arms of Fray and Landon. The two men obeyed without delay. Barren kept watch to ensure no one saw the abduction. Once the task had been accomplished, Barren hurled her down to the bottom of the steps where Gabb and Cavis caught her.

"You must be crazy, throwing her down the steps," Jackson murmured to himself while placing a hood over her head.

Marcus was pleased with the outcome and ordered his men to depart. "Let's go. We don't have much time before everyone starts looking for the girl."

As the abductors hurried off, Junia quickly made her way back into the room and mingled among other guests as if she had been there the entire time. Jedidiah and Steven had returned and noticed Junia returning from the balcony. The old seer was well aware of the attack against his granddaughter. He had foreseen the kidnapping but knew that it was not the time for him to intervene.

Matt became alarmed when he spotted Junia but did not see Patience. His stomach knotted with concern as he quickly crossed the room. "Excuse me, Mrs. Jackson, I thought that Patience was with you."

"She was, but I left her at the punch bowl just a moment ago."

Matt looked towards the bowl. "I don't see her." It was not like Patience to wander off without Matt. Though he was worried, he was mostly missing her. Since the day they met, he hadn't been able to keep his eyes off her, and now that they were married, it was natural for him to search her out. He looked throughout the room but could not find her. The old man's hand suddenly rested on Matt's shoulder. Matt quickly turned, expecting to see Patience. The strange look on Jedidiah's face told Matt that something was wrong.

"Matt, she has been abducted," he said with his hand still on Matt's shoulder.

Somehow the words didn't register in Matt's brain. "Who has been abducted?" he asked, hoping that Jedidiah wasn't referring to Patience.

"It is Patience, my son, but you are not to worry."

"Not to worry?" Matt thought that the old man had lost his mind. How could he not worry about the kidnapping of his wife? The whole matter was maddening. "How can you stand there telling me not to worry about Patience? How do you know that she has been taken?"

"I saw the abduction, son."

"You saw it, and you did nothing to stop it? You didn't even call to me?" Matt was so distraught that he tore through the crowd. He went on the balcony to see if he could spot any activity among the shadows, but there were none. He didn't want to make a scene in front of everyone, but many could sense that something was wrong. Matt rushed back to Jedidiah, who was now standing next to Patience's parents. "What are we to do, Master?" Matt anxiously asked the old man.

"Presently, we will pray but take no action."

"I believe in prayer, but I also believe in doing whatever I can to get her back," exclaimed Matt.

Patience's parents laid their hands on Matt's shoulders to confirm Jedidiah's words to pray. "Matt, it is beyond your understanding right now to comprehend what is transpiring at this very moment, but let us assure you that Patience is safe," said Steven. He diligently prayed that his daughter would be safe. "Lord, help us and guide us in making the right decision. Please protect my little girl," he whispered as a slight tear streamed down his cheek.

Heather knew that her husband was as shaken as she was over their daughter's kidnapping. She also knew that Jesus was always faithful.

"Listen to me, Matt. Even though Patience is in the hands of evil men, no harm will come to her," Jedidiah reassured him.

"How do you know that for sure?" snapped Matt, momentarily forgetting it was the king he was addressing. Heather placed her hand on Matt's shoulder and urged him to follow her husband. Matt looked into the eyes of the three who stood before him. They were full of tears as they looked back into his eyes. Their consoling expressions gave him courage to hope. "I believe you, but what happened to her? How could this happen with all these people around us? And … wait? Where are Abdi, Lire, and the others who are supposed to be protecting us?" he questioned in frustration. Looking for the warriors, Matt saw Lire happily eating a piece of pie while conversing with Frances. The other warriors were engulfed in the crowd of people who were treating them like royalty since their features and stature stood out amongst the Growers.

Matt's tension grew with every passing moment. He ran his fingers through his hair, revealing blood-filled veins protruding from his temples. Furious eyes perused the room again as Matt grew angrier. Jedidiah moved closer to Matt, laid his hand on his head, and prayed. Immediately, the tension subsided, and Matt's anger dissipated. The old man smiled to reassure him again.

"Come, gather your parents, and we will go to their home. There I will tell you all that you need to know," said Jedidiah.

Steven called the innkeeper and instructed him to dismiss the guests. "Please tell them that the happy couple extends their thanks and appreciates all who came." The innkeeper acknowledged Steven's instruction and proceeded to carry them out. People wondered why the couple had not bid them farewell, according to custom. Nevertheless, what the innkeeper said seemed to pacify the crowd, and before long, the inn was empty.

****

As they carried Patience a good distance from the inn, Jackson's irritation grew toward Barren. Finally, he decided to voice his objections to him over the handling of the princess. "It was a stupid thing you did back there. You could have killed the girl and ruined our whole plan," hissed Jackson.

In a full rage, Barren backhanded Jackson across the mouth, sending him backward. If not for his three companions, Jackson would have fallen into the nearby pond. "How dare you speak to me in that tone. I can smell the attraction you have for the princess. I will break your spine if you ever talk to me like that again," yelled Barren.

"I ... I wasn't talking to you, Barren. I was actually talking to Landon and Fray. They should know how vital the princess' safety is to our futures." He eyed his friends, his facial expression pleading for them to play along until the tense atmosphere subsided. Barren ignored Jackson's excuses, and his demeanor told them all to be cautious as to how they addressed him.

If Barren had been a mere man, Jackson would not have taken such an insult. He knew that these strange fellows had a connection with something very evil. He felt himself being pulled towards it every minute he spent with them. The creepy darkness in Marcus' team made them unpredictable.

"We know what we are doing, my friend," Marcus said with a sinister tone. "This is not, as you would say, my first venture. If left to you and your three clumsy buffoons, everyone in the inn would have heard you trampling down the steps with the girl. As it is, we have made our escape without anyone interfering with our plans."

Landon, Gabb, and Fray were insulted by Marcus' comment, but Jackson knew that he was right. Jackson decided to keep Landon and the others in check while trying to find out the next move. "Now what?" Jackson asked Cavis, still a little stunned from the blow he received from Barren.

"Bring the wagon around. It's a good thing we hid it away from the inn. Those horses would have alerted the whole village. By the time those fools figure things out, we will be long gone," said Cavis.

"We should arrive at the Great Tree before sunrise," voiced Marcus.

Jackson and Landon climbed aboard the wagon, and Gabb and Fray lifted Patience up to them. While the men secured her in the wagon, Marcus climbed into the front seat. "Cavis, you stay back with Junia to cover loose ends and keep others from following us. Barren, you take the reins," commanded Marcus.

Nodding, Barren obeyed. "You sluggards back there, hurry up," shouted Barren, spitting to the side of the wagon. As everyone climbed aboard, Barren snapped the reins, and the horses took off into the dark distance.

Jackson and his three cronies were terrified by the speed at which they traveled. Never had they seen horses or a wagon move so fast. If Jackson had doubted before, he didn't any longer. He knew now that there were more than human hands at work. As they drove in the eerie darkness, Jackson and the others couldn't see their hands in front of their faces. How in the world were Marcus and Barren driving the wagon without crashing into something? He also wondered how horses and a wagon could ride so smooth on a road he knew was filled with bumps and holes. It was evident that the two men sitting in front were filled with evil spirits.

"This whole thing smells of black magic," said Landon, eyes wide.

"The devil must be driving this thing," complained Fray.

Their suspicions were confirmed when they saw the wagon being pulled by glowing beastly creatures instead of horses. The wind under the creatures' feet allowed them to move swiftly towards their destination. With all that was occurring, it was still hard for Jackson and his friends to believe what was happening right in front of their eyes. Still, Jackson reasoned with himself, things were not that bad. After all, no one had died, and he and his crew would soon be rich and satisfied. Smiling to himself, Jackson felt they would be able to do anything they desired. Just thinking about the treasure that laid ahead soothed his conscience.

23

PATIENCE'S AWAKENING

SUDDENLY, PATIENCE FELT A LARGE THUMP ON THE BACK OF her head. As she awakened, she could hear men's voices in the background. Squinting her eyes, Patience could barely make out the figures of the men talking, but she could tell they were traveling extremely fast. The destination she didn't know. Her acute sense of smell alerted her to her surroundings. It was obvious they were passing forests and lakes that she, Matt, and the Pia Warriors passed weeks ago.

What is going on? What happened to me? she thought. The effects of the drug were slowly wearing off. Suddenly, her body went cold with fright. She vaguely remembered the reflection in Junia's eyes of intruders coming towards her. She remembered just before she lost consciousness seeing the smug look on Junia's face.

Feeling less groggy, Patience moved slightly without alerting the men. She was finally fully awake. She remained silent, thoughts running through her mind as to what to do. Surely, Matt, grandfather, and her parents knew that she was missing. But Patience was still somewhat confused by Girma not appearing when she called. Patience closed her eyes and attempted to call Girma again but to no avail.

What is going on, Lord? Why can't I call Girma? What is my family waiting for, and why haven't they taken steps to rescue me? She had never been under this kind of stress, and she never thought that she would be in the hands of abductors. She felt tears stream down her face, and for the first time in her life, she felt alone as true fear overtook her.

Breathing in slowly, Patience tried to focus. *Okay, Patience, what about all that training you've had? Calm down and concentrate,* she reminded herself. Deciding she needed to confront her captors head-on, she started moving noticeably.

Hearing Patience's heavy breathing, Jackson leaned over and took the hood off. At first, she couldn't make out any of the figures, but as her eyes adjusted, she couldn't believe who knelt in front of her.

"No … no," In utter shock, Patience saw the familiar but emotionless face of Jackson over her. Patience was alarmed to see he was one of her captures.

"What do you think you're doing?" yelled Marcus. Immediately, Jackson backed away. The piercing evil eyes of Marcus and Barren burned through him.

"She can't breathe. We do want her alive when we get there, don't we?" he said.

"Yes, of course, we do, but the hood could have been left on her head. However, since you took it off, you will do the honor of killing her," said Marcus.

"Killing her? Who said anything about killing her? I'm in this for the money, not for murder," shouted Jackson, eyeing Patience.

"You let her see our faces," exclaimed Barren.

"She hasn't seen anything. How could she in all this darkness? I can hardly see my hand in front of my own face."

"What you don't understand, you stupid fool, is that this girl can see in the dark. We do not know how she sees in the dark, but we have good information that she can," hissed Marcus.

"I didn't know," said Jackson.

"Of course, you didn't. That's why you will not do another thing without checking with me first. Is that clear?" barked Marcus. Jackson shook his head affirmatively and remained quiet.

How do they know that I can see in the dark? It just started happening a few days ago. I haven't even told Matt, so how do they know? In her pondering, Patience realized that there were spies in the spirit world, just like in the physical. *Lord Jesus, tell me what to do,* she prayed and waited.

Remember to use your gifts and training, beloved. You are never alone, and the spirit of fear has no power over you, came the calming voice to her mind.

24

Matt's Outcry

Matt was frantic and could not understand why Jedidiah and Steven still weren't doing anything. "Are we just going to sit here while Patience is in the hands of kidnappers, murderers, or heaven knows what else?" Matt questioned, unable to control his rising anger. "I just can't wait around here while Patience is in the hands of some mad man."

"You mean, mad men and a woman," said Jedidiah.

"What ... what did you say?" Matt asked again, not believing his ears.

"I said men and a woman, eight in all. Four of them are deeply controlled by the spirit world, and four of them are your common roughneck thieves, Jackson among them."

Matt was puzzled. "And you know this, how?"

"You know that we share mind communication with each other. The Spirit has given us discernment. You and Patience also share the same gift. She has unknowingly informed Heather and me of her condition."

"What does that mean?" inquired Matt, more frustrated than ever. Jedidiah briefly explained to Matt the gifts and the functions of the Spirit, just enough to assure him that Patience was aware that they knew where she was and the type of danger she was in. Relief filled Matt's heart. "So, is there a plan to retrieve Patience? Tell me that you or Father Steven have a plan."

"I have a plan," said Jedidiah, squeezing Heather's hand to reassure her. Matt's ears immediately perked up, anticipating Jedidiah's plan. To his dismay, only silence followed and seemed like an eternity.

Matt bit his lip to hold himself from blurting out irrational words. Taking a deep breath, he said, "Master, I know Patience is aware, but I'm sure she is frightened. What is your plan? Are we leaving right now to get her?"

The old man looked into Matt's vulnerable eyes and said, "No, we are not. If we interfere now, the three men controlled by those spirits will get away, and we cannot allow that to happen."

"Patience is aware of our strategy, and she is capable of handling things quite well. After all, she too is a Pia Warrior," Steven reminded him.

Frustrated, Matt found himself unable to hold his temper any longer. "It's not like either of you to do nothing." He turned to Steven. "I thought at least you would go after your own daughter with me."

Steven remained silent; he understood Matt's anxious concern and frustration. The moisture in Steven's eyes showed Matt that his perception of Steven was incorrect. Matt felt a tinge of regret for lashing out at Steven. Deep in his heart, Matt knew Steven would gladly trade his own life for Patience.

Much turmoil was in Steven's heart. He knew that it was not wise to proceed to rescue Patience without Jedidiah's approval. "Excuse me, Father. I need a moment,"

Steven said, receiving a nod from Jedidiah as he walked away.

Still filled with emotion, Matt turned to Jedidiah for more answers but decided to hold his tongue. The seer looked at Matt intensely and corrected him. "Matt, I know that you are apprehensive, but you have misjudged Steven. He is far from being unconcerned, and you know that! There is a strength in him that he must keep under control. The more you pressure Steven, the harder it becomes for him to restrain himself from going after his daughter."

"What do you mean? What's wrong with him?" Matt asked.

Jedidiah said, "The warrior in him will not stand by much longer."

"What do you mean by that? I don't understand."

"You see, son, when Steven was a boy, about nine, I met him and his parents, Peter and Mary, who used to be Terrus and Phenia. They were from Treabouti and moved to Ethiopia. They had met Micah, an old missionary. Micah lived among pagan people, some who threatened to kill him for teaching the truth. The pagans also heard that miracles often happened among the people when he prayed for them. I knew Micah, the missionary prophet, very well. He had the gift of healing from the Lord and used it as much as he could. He was told by the authorities that if he continued to preach his lies among their people, he would die. They made good on their threat, but the day before his death, Mary and Peter took their son Steven, who was named Addisu, to see him."

"Steven had a clubfoot and a deformed hand. There wasn't a cure to be found among their people. Taking a chance by faith, Peter and Mary took Steven to Micah and asked if he would heal him. Of course, he said no, and then explained that only Jesus could heal the boy. I happened to be there that day. Peter and Mary believed, and God sent power from the Holy Spirit that day to heal both Steven's foot and hand. Micah also spoke of Steven's future as king. His older brother, Abdi, was also present, and to their parents' joy, both received Christ as Savior."

"Terrus and Phenia took on the new names of Peter and Mary to honor their newfound faith. Micah baptized and blessed them all and commissioned them for the work of Christ. They also gave their son Addisu the name Steven after the first martyr of the first church. How ironic, since Micah died the following day for the same reason as the first Christian martyr."

"From that time forward, Mary and Peter have served the Lord. When they heard that Micah had been beheaded by the authorities on account of serving the Lord, they too decided to serve, even if it meant their death. The Lord gained two more servants to build his church that day, and the message of truth continued."

"Since then, thousands have given their lives to Jesus. Peter and Mary are still serving somewhere in the motherland among the pagan people. I suppose that they will do this until the Lord returns or until they end up like Micah. They have meetings three nights a week. Wherever they preached, crowds of people would gather," Jedidiah said excitedly. "It is amazing what the Lord has done through them. Steven becoming king was the Lord's way of providing protection for Peter and Mary. No one would dare put their hands on the royal family without forfeiting their life. This, of course, allows his parents to move freely among most of the villages; however, it does not stop the attempts made against them. But I digress," Jedidiah said, forcing himself back to the point.

"Before the sun went down, on a fine day just like this, my daughter Heather and I arrived at Peter and Mary's gathering. There must have been a hundred people there. Heather was fifteen, and Steven was eighteen. Instantly, I could tell they had a fancy for each other. They asked to go for a walk around the camp, and I had no objections, as long as they stayed inside the camp. It wasn't that I didn't trust the young people, but evil people were looking to destroy Peter and his family as they had done to Micah. I was also cautious because lions were in the area, and they often hunted around the edge of the campsite, snatching whoever and whatever came within their grasp."

"Can you believe that not even five minutes had gone by before I heard a terrifying scream come from the direction where Heather and Steven had gone? I got there just in time to see the most extraordinary act of valor I had ever witnessed. Keep in mind that Steven was 18 years old, six feet, six inches tall, and weighed 265 pounds. To the human eye, that was no match for two full-grown male lions. The boy stood his ground, and as they approached, he told them to stop. To my surprise, they did, at least for a moment. I suppose they were taken by surprise to see a human stand up to them. I heard Steven say, 'If you keep coming, you're going to end up like a bear and a lion I once read about in the Holy Book.' The beasts did not grasp or sense the emotion in his voice. They continued forward, readying themselves for the kill. 'I need help, Lord!' Steven said out loud. There was neither fear nor doubt in the boy's words. Heather stood behind him, staring at the beasts as they charged Steven. It was over in a matter of minutes."

Matt stood listening as Jedidiah continued with the story. "You'll never guess what happened next." He paused to see if Matt was still with him.

"Please continue, sir," Matt stated, still pushing down the desire to run after Patience.

"He pushed my daughter back from him as the lions charged. With one foot, he kicked the blue stars out of the first one and sent it about 15 feet in the air, broken jaw and all. It landed on the ground motionless, blood seeping from its mouth. The second lion leaped at him, and he caught it in midair and slammed it down so hard on the ground that it left the beast breathless. Then he lifted his foot and crushed its head right into the ground. Everyone, I mean everyone, stood watching, unable to say anything. All this took place before he worked in the fields of plenty in Truevine. Steven's strength was part of the result of the Lord healing his body. When I finally got him alone after everyone had congratulated him for his valor, I asked what went through his mind while facing those lions."

"What did he say?" asked Matt.

"Steven said that he feared for Heather's safety and asked God to give him the strength to protect her. Three years later, they were married."

Matt stood before the old man, thinking about all that had been said. This was a wild tale, but he had experienced similar situations and knew the power of God. No one in Matt's home village would ever believe the wild stories he had. What he needed now was faith and strength like Steven's to get him through the tough ordeal Patience was experiencing.

Jedidiah placed his hand on Matt's shoulder. "Being led by the Spirit is not always easy, but obedience is always better than opposing the Lord's will. Steven could easily go after those men and defeat them, but he is under the authority of the Spirit, the same as you and me."

25

CONFRONTATION

"WHY ARE YOU DOING THIS? I HAVE DONE YOU NO WRONG," Patience said with conviction.

"We know that," said Jackson.

"So, why would you harm me?" she asked, hoping that one of them would feel some sense of remorse, but no one did. The only thing these men felt was the urge to get rich and find an opportunity to harm her.

Their opportunity was before them as the Treasure Tree was just over the next hill. Soon its contents would belong to them. Marcus knew this because he had seen others go into the tree poor and come out wealthy. Most people who entered the tree also came out with a changed heart, but Marcus was only interested in obtaining the Sun Stone and power. He made up his mind that if he had to sacrifice everyone, even his own men, he would.

In a matter of minutes, they were in front of the tree, but there was no entry point. The tree was large and full, its branches strong, and its roots could barely be seen above the ground. It appeared to be different than what Jackson remembered. This time the limbs did not move, and a door did not appear; only a large tree stood before them.

Cavis was just catching up to them and explained that no one had left the inn. Junia was still with the crowd, playing the part of the hostess. "I made sure that I wasn't followed. I told Junia to stall the family by consoling them as long as she could. I see I have arrived just in time to enter the Great Tree," he said gleefully.

"Bring the girl," ordered Marcus.

Barren grabbed the girl and brought her to the front of the wagon to face Marcus. The other men, including Jackson, followed behind.

"Cavis, when is my mother joining us?" asked Jackson.

"I already told you," Cavis said, rolling his eyes. "Oh, she also said she was staying back to see the looks on the faces of her husband's murderers or something like that. You should have seen her; she was gloating with pride over what she had done to the Lomans. She was swearing, cursing, invoking the power of hell to crush the Lomans and avenge her husband's death," Cavis said, snickering.

Hearing such a wild report worried Jackson. "Maybe I should go back and see if she is alright," Jackson said with a concerned look.

"You are not going anywhere. Get over here and bring that girl with you," ordered Marcus. Reluctantly, Jackson took Patience by the arm, and Barren propelled them both forward. "Okay, little lady, open the entry. I know that it is here and that you have the power to open it," commanded Marcus.

"And if I don't?" she retorted.

"Then I will kill you and simply wait for another opportunity. I know the other members of your family can get us in. If we have to kill your entire family to get what we desire, then so be it," quipped Marcus.

She looked into the eyes of the evil man before her and scanned the faces of the others around her and knew that talking to these men would not gain her an ounce of consideration. The urge to stop them was overwhelming. With all her training as a Pia Warrior, she could take out at least half of them. In her spirit, though, she knew it was not the Lord's will. She had to remain still and let the Lord's word to Jedidiah be fulfilled. There was only evil in these men, and her interference may delay God's justice. Even Jackson, whom she thought would have a little compassion, had none. Only contempt filled their faces. She closed her eyes and listened.

"What are you doing?" asked Barren.

"I am closing my eyes to alleviate distractions so that I may concentrate on opening the pathway."

"Very well," smirked Marcus. "You may continue."

Patience closed her eyes again, and this time she called out in her mind to her mother and grandfather.

Father, do you hear her? asked Heather.

Yes, my dear, I hear her, said Jedidiah to the frantic mother. *Listen to me, my granddaughter. Open the pathway, and let them in. Do not be afraid because, once inside, they will not be able to harm you or carry out their evil plan. The Lord is your protection and will not allow you to be harmed. Girma, Tah, and Epsilon are ready. After you get in, proceed to the sunroom. When you get there, run into it, and no one will be able to follow you.*

Yes, Poppy.

Be careful, my child. These men are controlled by a very strong demonic spirit. He resides inside the man called Marcus. He is without mercy and will stop at nothing to achieve his will.

The two men with Marcus are just like him but not as strong. They have an unquenchable thirst to do evil, said Heather.

Yes, Mother. I will be careful.

"Who are you communicating with? I sense a strong presence around here," said Barren, breaking Patience's concentration.

"What else would you expect? I belong to the Lord King," retorted Patience, looking him in the eyes.

"All right, you have had enough time to do whatever it is that you are trying to do," said Cavis, as he took hold of her arm. "It's time to give us what we came for."

They could all see the concern in her eyes, and they thought that it was for herself. They had no idea that her concern was for their souls. She decided to give them one more chance to change their minds, to give up their evil ambition, and let her go.

"It is useless for you to persist on this course of destruction. You will all be lost if you do not turn back now," she said.

The intruders, including Jackson, could not let go of the thought of having great wealth and power.

You cannot reason with these men, Patience, came another voice.

Let those who desire to do wickedness continue to do it. The Lord has set His face against them, voiced Jedidiah.

Patience turned towards the Great Tree, lifted her hands, and spoke in her heart words that compelled the pathway to open. Right before their eyes, the grand mansion appeared with large double doors made of solid gold—a change from what Jackson last remembered and an irresistible enticement to a greedy heart.

"I knew that it was here, but I never knew that it was so grand," remarked Barren. The others stood in awe as the doors opened to grant them entry.

"Wait!" bellowed Marcus. "I am as anxious to enter as you are, but we must let the girl go first. I know that an unrighteous heart cannot enter this place without someone pure going before them. So, let the girl go first, and then we will follow."

Marcus was right—if one of them had gone before Patience, they all would have immediately perished. As they stepped into the mansion, their eyes were dazzled by what they saw. Jackson was even more stunned than the others. The last time he was here, the place was filled with a multitude of riches, but looking at it now, he could not believe the elaborate increase of gold and jewels. Fray, Landon, and Gabb were beside themselves with greedy excitement.

"I never dreamed that there was this much gold and silver and diamonds. And look! Look at all that other stuff!" said Landon, pointing toward a large golden vase.

Patience kept walking, and the men kept following her until they reached the east wing. From it came a glowing light, and Jackson remembered the Sun Stone was there. He also remembered that no one was to enter without the old man's permission. As they all approached, Patience started to enter, but Jackson stopped her. Memories of the past suddenly flooded his mind.

"Wait, don't let her enter that room," he said frantically.

"What is the meaning of this? Why did you stop her?" demanded Marcus.

"Because no one can enter the sunroom without the old man's consent. There is a Sun Stone in there that has great power. I was once in there, and I heard creepy things. You don't want to go in there." Jackson looked at Patience and grinned. "You thought that I forgot, didn't you?" Patience did not speak. She only looked at them. "I don't know what she's trying to pull. Maybe she wishes to end her own life by bringing us here, but I know that if anyone goes in there without consent from the old man, they will die or suffer worse."

"Thank you, Jackson, for your insightful information, but I think that we can safely enter since we have, as you say, the old man's granddaughter. Besides, the Sun Stone is the reason I'm here," snapped Marcus.

"I am not going in there!" Jackson contended. "Listen to me—there are things in this place that are not of this world. I remember now, and I don't know what possessed me to come back here." The three demon-filled men chuckled at the absurdity of Jackson's remark. "We have to get out. We have to get out of this tree now!" exclaimed Jackson.

"No, we are not going anywhere. We came to get wealth, and we are not leaving without it," shouted Gabb.

"Look around you, man. Are you willing to leave all this for some nightmare in your mind?" asked Fray.

"Yes!" shouted Jackson. "And it's not a nightmare. It's real, and if we don't leave now, it will be too late." But the evil spirits in Marcus, Barren, and Cavis would not allow them to leave, and the three thieves were so mesmerized by what they saw that it was impossible to talk them out of it.

Patience stood in front of the sunroom and told the men that unless she entered first, they would die. "Just as I had to enter the pathway first, so I must enter the sunroom."

Jackson was now screaming and shouting for them not to go in. "It's a trap! It's a trap, I tell you! You are fools, fools, if you don't leave now!" No one listened; their minds were now so consumed with insatiability that nothing could persuade them to turn back.

"Go on, princess, and we will see if you survive the light from the room. If you do, then we will follow," sneered Marcus with great expectations to receive the Sun Stone.

****

Matt fought with his emotions. His mind was racing, trying to figure out a way to get Patience back. *I have to do something, rather than standing around here doing nothing.*

Jedidiah knew what Matt was experiencing, and he knew that he needed to calm and reassure him that Patience was their priority, "Rushing into the situation without proper assessment could lead to catastrophe, son. A foolish man believes anything his eyes tell him, but a man of wisdom makes sure of things before he acts," said the old man.

Matt understood what his mentor was saying, but it did not diminish his concern for his bride. To ease his mind, Jedidiah assigned him the task of fetching horses so that they could ride to the Great Tree. Matt was eager to rescue Patience and wasted no time carrying out Jedidiah's request. The natural glow stones that Jeremy and Matt lined the pathways with made it easy to follow the roads and layout of structures on the property. By the time everyone came out of Frances' house, Matt was sitting on his horse waiting for the others. Abdi and the Pia Warriors mounted their horses and were about to leave until Jeremy insisted that he and Frances go along.

"That will be fine, Jeremy. Layla will help you, while Steven and the others head out," instructed Jedidiah.

Jeremy ran toward the stables. Matt and the warriors wasted no time in following Steven to the Great Tree.

"Layla, make sure you take precautions in guiding Matt's parents to the Great Tree," said Abdi. Nodding her head, Layla ran to the stables to help Jeremy ready the horses.

Jedidiah, Heather, and Pricilla were mounted and about to leave when Jedidiah paused a moment and gazed upon Junia. She had her arm around Frances' shoulder, still playing the part of a friend. Sitting astride his horse, Jedidiah's piercing eyes saw into Junia's heart. It was the look of an uncompromising seer. "I know what you and your son have done, Junia, and I am saddened by it. However, if you want to live, now is the time for you to amend your ways."

She quickly removed her arms from around Frances' shoulder and tried to stare the old seer down. "I do not know what you are talking about, sir," she said rebelliously.

"Yes, you do! Because of your hatred and bitterness towards Jeremy and Frances, you have doomed yourself and your son to a fate you can't comprehend. Out of love and concern, they have only tried to befriend you. You have deceived them and contrived in your heart to harm not only the Loman family but also mine. And for your treachery, you and your son will lose your lives."

Frances looked at Junia in disbelief. "Junia, what is he talking about? What have you done?"

Junia stiffened her neck and stared at Frances with a look of satisfaction and contempt. "I have done no more to you than what you have done to me," she shrieked.

"I don't know what you are talking about. What have I done to you?" asked Frances, deeply concerned about what Jedidiah had said.

A darkness came into Junia's eyes as the spirit of bitterness plunged its way deeper into her soul. Like a volcano ready to erupt, poisonous words of condemnation and cursing spewed from her mouth. So foul were the accusations that Frances backed away from her, falling back over a stool into the wicker chair that happened to be there.

"If you will not repent," said Jedidiah, "then you have made your choice against life." Jedidiah swung his horse around and chased after Matt and the others who had already started homeward towards the Great Tree.

Jeremy was occupied in the stables with Layla, trying to hurry with transportation for Frances and himself. He was glad for Layla's assistance. It kept his mind busy while thinking about his new daughter.

Frances watched Jedidiah ride off then turned back to Junia. "What is it that you think that I have done to you, Junia?" asked Frances.

"You know very well that you and Jeremy caused my husband's death," she screamed, spewing words of venom.

"And just how did we do that?" queried Frances.

"Jeremy let that heavy limb crush my Jack's head. He knew that Jack couldn't hold that limb, but he let him hold it anyway, while he cut it from the tree," sobbed Junia.

"You have it all wrong, Junia. Jeremy held that limb as long as he could. He was yelling for Jack to move out of the way, but Jack had been drinking and was too confused to avoid the limb. The limb grew too heavy for Jeremy to hold, and it slipped from his hands. Jack was warned many times before not to come to work drunk. You know this for yourself."

"He was not drunk," retorted Junia. "He may have had a drink or two, but he was not drunk."

"It doesn't matter how many drinks he had, Junia. He was not supposed to drink on the job. It impaired his judgment and caused his death. If Jeremy had known he was intoxicated, he wouldn't have let him work at all. It was because of Jack's drunkenness that Jeremy got hurt."

"You're a liar, and now you're trying to blame your own bad luck on my Jack. No matter what you say, you'll never justify what you did to Jack," she wailed. "I wish that the poison had done its job on you! I even burned my own house down to gain your trust and sympathy, and you did exactly what I knew you would do. Your sense of love and Christian compassion compelled you to take us into your home. I loathe your self-righteous piety."

Her toxic words sunk deep into Frances' heart. All she could do was look at Junia in disbelief.

"If it hadn't been for that wretched daughter-in-law of yours, you would be dead by now!" screeched Junia. Frances was shocked, unable to even move. Suddenly as if another person was speaking, Junia calmly voiced murderous words at Frances. "No matter," Junia said with a sinister smile. "When your new daughter dies by the hand of my son and his men, you will know the pain I suffered."

Without warning, Frances slapped Junia across the face and threw her to the ground. Immediately, regret filled her heart, but anger gripped her soul. "How dare you harm my family. Get out. Get out of here, Junia, before I do something I'll regret!"

Junia laughed loudly, knowing she had succeeded in delivering her bitter seed into the heart of her enemy. "A curse on you, Frances, and all those you love," she ranted. Her eyes enlarged with rage like someone gone mad, and there was nothing Frances could do to calm herself or the woman she once called a friend.

Without warning, Junia picked up a stone with the intent to kill Frances but suddenly heard a rustle in the bushes from behind her, accentuated by a low growl. Both women heard the growl but saw nothing. The growl became louder, and something slowly emerged from the bushes only enough for its large glowing green eyes to be seen. Junia's ranting and raving had ceased, and terror had taken over her and Frances. Both women started backing up towards the front door, hoping to reach it before what stirred in the bushes caught them. As Junia started backing up, Frances found herself incapacitated, unable to move an inch.

The huge figure jumped out, bypassing Frances, and caught Junia before she took another step. Frances had never seen anything so swift and terrifying in all her life. The beast was huge, ten times the size of a normal lion, with a head large enough to devour a full-grown horse. Frances closed her eyes, thinking that if she was going to be eaten, she didn't want to know about it. She heard Junia scream, and she opened her eyes just in time to see the gigantic beast take to the air, its huge wings propelling it upward. Junia hung from its mouth, screaming hysterically as the beast flew away.

Jeremy and Layla came riding from the stables when they first heard the screams. By the time Jeremy and Layla dismounted and entered the backdoor of the house, he heard the second screams from Frances. When he pushed through the front door, he was too late to help. By the light of the moon, he saw the beast flying away and could hear Junia's terrifying screams in the distance. There was nothing he could do.

"It all happened so fast!" Frances said, collapsing. Jeremy caught her in his arms and took her immediately into their home. After he placed her on the couch, he quickly went back outside, hoping to see where the beast was carrying Junia.

"It's too late. We can't help Mrs. Jackson now," Layla said.

Reentering the house, Jeremy brought a cup of well water to Frances. After reviving Frances, Jeremy wrapped his arms around her as she explained all that had happened between Junia and herself.

"Unbelievable. Who would have ever believed that Junia could have planned such atrocities? And then try and kill you with a stone? That's so diabolical that it's still hard to comprehend," said Jeremy.

Frances was still shaken. Sitting up, she tried to calm herself. "I don't know why that ... that beast didn't take us both. I was right there, and it went past me and took Junia. It was horrible. I'll never forget that huge lion-like face with glowing green eyes coming after..." sobbed Frances, unable to get the words out.

"I know that you are shaken, Mrs. Loman, but we need to get to the Great Tree. Are you able to travel?" asked Layla.

"Yes, dear. I'll be all right. Just help me up." Jeremy took hold of Frances' arm as he and Layla helped her stand.

****

In the meantime, Jedidiah had caught up with the others. What took five days by wagon took only an hour with the old seer along. Jedidiah needed to give Patience a chance to carry out the Lord's plan. He encouraged the others to stay calm and wait on the Lord's timing. As they traveled swiftly towards the mansion, evil spirits came in from every side to deter Jedidiah from interfering with their diabolical plan.

"Keep your focus, and move with me," he said to the warriors. "The devil's workers are doing all they can to prevent us from carrying out the Lord's command." Arriving in front of the Treasure Tree, they dismounted and waited for further instructions from the old seer.

****

Patience walked into the sunroom and was immediately hit with the brightness of the Sun Stone. The Sun Stone had no harmful effect on Patience, but the men behind her were blinded. They could no longer clearly see her. Only an outline of her image stood out. Reaching out, they tried to recapture her. The light from the Sun Stone turned fiery hot and prevented further access to the room. Gabb made one last attempt to recapture her, only to receive burns from the heat of the stone. His agonizing cry deterred the others from trying.

Patience stood safely inside without any injury, and the door closed. Suddenly the men realized that they were standing outside of the sunroom with their only hope of escape inside. They tried desperately to reopen the door. Every man started banging on it to no avail, and not even a scratch or dent appeared on the door.

I am safely in the sunroom, Poppy, Patience reported to Jedidiah.

Good. Stay there until we arrive, he said.

Matt also heard her for the first time and was relieved. It seems that his mind linking practice with her paid off. The smile on Matt's face told everyone something had changed.

"She is in the sunroom and unharmed," said Jedidiah. Everyone could breathe easy again. Matt hugged the nearest person to him, who happened to be Steven, and thanked God with gratitude in his heart. Steven smiled and slapped Matt on the back.

"I am thankful too, son," he said. "Let's go get our girl."

****

"We are wasting time trying to get in there. Why even bother? Gabb already burned his hand messing with that girl; to try it again isn't smart. Besides, there's enough treasure out here to last us ten lifetimes," spouted Landon.

Perturbed, Jackson ignored Landon's statement and attempted again to persuade his comrades. "Look, I know that you may think it's a good idea to stay and gather as many jewels and as much gold as you can, but I'm telling you if you value your lives, we better get out of this place now!"

No one listened to Jackson; they were too driven by greed. The chance for wealth and power was too much to pass up.

"What are we going to carry our stuff in?" asked Fray. No sooner had the thought came into Fray's mind than a bag appeared before each of them. Jackson screamed in terror, and it scared his comrades.

"Man! What the devil is wrong with you, Jackson? You don't scream in a man's ear like that," yelled Gabb.

"Yeah, get hold of yourself. You're the one who convinced us to come here in the first place," added Fray.

"So stop trying to keep us from taking what's ours," protested Landon.

Jackson began ripping his hair out, trying to persuade everyone to leave. "Don't you understand that the bags are only a ploy to keep you occupied until that beast comes?" he screamed. The horrible thoughts of being trapped in the rug for eternity came rushing back into his mind.

"What's wrong with you? We are here to get a job done. Now get with it or get out of the way," Marcus said, pushing him aside.

No one seemed to understand the danger nor the horror that awaited them. Jackson clearly understood how he had allowed greed to blind him but failed to convey it to the men with him. With mounting excitement, every man began to fill his bag with treasure, while Jackson stood idly by, fearfully watching. Cavis' eyes enlarged as he broke into laughter, watching his bag enlarge with every new item he placed into it.

"Look!" Cavis said with amazement. They all turned to watch as Cavis placed another item into his bag. "Did you see that? Did you see? My bag grows with every treasure I put in it." He laughed again.

"That's incredible ... I hadn't noticed until now. That means we can literally carry everything out of here that can fit into our bags, and it must be okay. Otherwise, why would we be given such incredible bags," said Gabb.

"It's to keep you busy, you fool. Can't you see that this is all a trap? I'm going to get out of here right now. Stay if you want, but I'm telling you it's a trap," Jackson said, walking away and shaking his head in frustration. Everyone laughed and continued their quest to fill up their bags with treasure.

"This is what I've been looking for all my life," said Fray.

"Me too," chimed in Landon.

As Jackson's friends continued to fill their bags, Fray suddenly noticed Marcus', Barren's, and Cavis' bags were twice the size of theirs. Envy started to creep into his heart as he said, "Barren, why is your bag larger than ours? We've been filling our bags as long as you and Cavis."

"What did you say?" Barren expressed eyes full of annoyance.

Just before another word was spoken, Marcus stepped forward. "What business is it of yours, Fray? You have your way of collecting, and we have ours. If I were you, I'd be content with what you have."

Realizing the absurdity of his inquiry, Fray returned to the business of stuffing his bag with more.

"Have you ever seen so much in all your life?" chuckled Gabb.

"We can sit back and eat, drink, and enjoy life to the fullest without a care for tomorrow," said Landon.

"What a glorious day this has turned out to be," said Cavis, dragging his loot.

"But what about the girl?" inquired Barren.

"What about her?" retorted Marcus.

"Didn't you say that you were going to have Jackson kill her? Remember, she saw us."

"And how do you propose I make him kill her since she is behind an impenetrable wall of gold and fire? What I suggest is that you grab your bags and follow me." Speechless Barren nodded, and they all did as Marcus suggested. As he hurried toward the front door, they all followed. Marcus spotted Jackson curled up in a corner, wringing his hands and murmuring like a mad man, something about them coming.

Landon pushed his way through the others, oblivious to Jackson's fear. "You told us that there was treasure up here and, man, were you right. Any ideas as to how to get out of here besides the obvious?" he asked, waiting for an answer.

Marcus pushed Landon aside, making his way towards the entry point. Jackson was almost catatonic as fear continued to wrap around him. He managed to get a few tangible words out, telling them about his last visit to the Great Tree with the old seer and a ferocious beast. None of it made any sense to them.

"Who is coming, Jackson?" asked Gabb.

"Is the old man on his way?" inquired Fray. Jackson shook his head affirmatively.

Suddenly, Marcus turned and approached Jackson. "Of course, the old seer is coming. Once he discovered that his granddaughter was missing, did you think that he was just going to sit around and do nothing? We will vacate this place after we get the Sun Stone."

For the next few minutes, the entire room was full of nervous tension. Marcus kicked Jackson on the leg to bring some sense of rationality back to his mind. "I swear that I'm not leaving until I get that stone."

Jackson looked up at them all with fear so heavy that Landon's knees started to knock together, and Gabb broke out into a cold sweat. Fray just stood watching, but they all felt a mysterious presence. Marcus suddenly turned, feeling a holy presence approach. The unclean spirits inside Marcus and his cohorts felt the presence of the old seer drawing closer. In an attempt to rally them all together, Barren changed the focus.

"Marcus, what is the plan?" Barren asked, looking desperate.

Eyeing everyone, Marcus shouted with rage, "Shut up. I will tell you when I'm ready." As Marcus snapped at his men, Fray, Gabb, and Landon slowly backed away from the scene.

"I think it's time for us to leave. Let's grab Jackson and get the heck out of here," Fray said intently. His cronies picked Jackson up by the arms and started toward the exit.

Gabb was so irritated at Jackson's comatose state that he pushed and screamed at Jackson. "Jackson, you are a fool! You had ample time to collect your riches, and what did you do? Sit in a corner whimpering like a scared dog. Pull yourself together, and let's get out of here," shouted Gabb. He waited to see if his words had any effect on the petrified Jackson. Nothing seemed to pull Jackson out of his stupor.

Fray had one last trick up his sleeve to bring the man back to his senses. He raised his hand and whacked Jackson hard enough to break a man's jaw. Jackson, however, was fit enough to take several blows, but it only took one to bring him to his senses long enough to tell them that there was no escape without the girl.

"It took a pure heart to get in, and it takes a pure heart to get out!" trembled Jackson. Jackson's comrades felt sudden hopelessness overwhelm them.

When they reached the door, they concluded what Jackson had said was true. Eyeing the large door that seemed impossible to open, Gabb said, "What do you think, Fray? Do you see a way out of here?"

Fray leaned against the front door, exhausted from trying to find a way out. Jackson had told him that it was no use, but Fray, if nothing else, was persistent. "Come on, let's give it one more try!" Fray screamed. Setting their bags aside, they banged on the large front door with all their strength, but nothing happened.

Finally, Landon said, "This isn't working! We are running out of time. Let's go back to Marcus and see if they have made any progress with getting into the room." Everyone started toward the sunroom, and Landon picked up Jackson.

"You'll never get out of here. Never!" Jackson whispered for only Landon to hear. Swallowing hard, Landon glanced at Jackson and decided to hasten his pace toward Marcus.

As they approached the sunroom, Gabb turned to his comrades and said under his breath, "We just need to find another way to get out of here before the old man comes."

Jackson started laughing uncontrollably, causing everyone, including Marcus and his associates, to stop and look strangely at him. Had he truly gone mad?

"I think he's lost his mind. Look at him. That kind of laughter is not normal!" stated Fray.

"What's so funny, Jackson? You want to share the joke with us?" queried Marcus, more irritated than he wanted to admit.

"He is coming with Pia Warriors," said Jackson.

"What are you talking about? How do you know this?" asked Gabb. Marcus and the others stared at Jackson, waiting for an explanation, but none was given.

"If he's coming with Pia Warriors, we better move quickly to exit this place. I suggest that we find something to help us get into that sunroom. That door is smaller than the door we just left. It shouldn't be that hard to enter," said Landon.

Marcus became irate. "Go find something to pry open the door to the sunroom," demanded Marcus.

Running up and down the halls, they finally found a large bronze table. "We can use this table to ram that door. Surely, it will give way," insisted Landon. Each man took hold of the large table and walked towards the sunroom. As they stood in front of the impenetrable door, Marcus looked on, unamused at their crude attempt. "On my count, we will ram the door with all our might," Landon instructed. Just before the order to ram the door was given, Jackson joined them, to everyone's surprise.

"I'm glad you joined us. Maybe we can get this door opened with all of us working together," said Fray with relief. "On my count, let's ram this door with all our strength."

As they began ramming the door, a sudden dent seemed to appear. To Marcus' surprise, he could see a possible way into the sunroom. As they began to lift the heavy table again, Marcus encouraged them by speaking words of incantations against the door. "One, two, three … everyone, now," Marcus screamed.

After about ten minutes of ramming the door, it began to slowly open. "Look, it's opening," said Cavis as the rest looked on, amazed.

"Strange … the dent seems to have disappeared," Marcus said with suspicion.

The men stood, ready to pounce on Patience as soon as the door opened. However, Gabb refused to go near the door. He'd had enough of the sunroom and made sure everyone knew how he felt. When it was fully opened, they did not see Patience, nor was the room illuminated.

"Go and check it out," Gabb said to Landon.

"I'm sorry, but I got more sense than that. Get Fray to go in."

"Not me. I'm not going in there. It's too dark."

"Don't be a coward," said Landon, leaning close to his face.

"I don't see you going in," Fray replied angrily.

Then Marcus said with contempt in his voice, "Move aside, you imbeciles. It's a girl we have to defeat, not some Pia Warrior. Cavis, you and Barren move in on her while I retrieve the Sun Stone." Marcus became perturbed at the cowardly response of Jackson's men. "Fray, you are coming with us whether you like it or not. Jackson is no good to me in his state of mind."

"Why me? Gabb can go. His mind is okay," grumbled Fray.

Marcus became so irate that he grabbed Fray by his neck and lifted him off the floor and propelled him past Cavis and Barren towards the sunroom. "You are nothing but a coward. You can go with us or die here." For a second, Fray looked for an escape but saw the look in Marcus' eyes. Everyone seemed surprised by Marcus' power. Annoyed by Cavis and Barren's lack of motivation, Marcus raised his voice, "Don't just stand there. Go get her, and make sure that before you kill her, she tells you how to open the blasted front door so we can get out of here."

As the men stealthily tried to creep into the sunroom, they felt a cold chill run through their bones.

"I feel uneasy about this. I can't even see my hand in front of my face," Fray remarked. They could feel the darkness in the room, and each man tried to push down the fear that seemed to suffocate them.

"Do you see anything, Marcus?" yelled Gabb from outside the room.

"Can you be any louder? If you want to know what's going on in here, you should have joined us," commented Marcus, annoyed by Gabb's outburst. Gabb grew quiet since he had decided to stay back with Landon and Jackson.

Fray grumbled that Gabb's lack of courage had forced him to take Gabb's place. *If I ever get out of this, Gabb will pay for getting me involved. I'll make sure of it,* he thought to himself.

Jackson's gasp startled Gabb. He turned and saw the intense look on Jackson's face as Jackson stared at the sunroom. He attempted to follow Jackson's gaze. However, nothing was revealed. "What are you looking at, Jackson?"

asked the concerned Gabb. There was no answer from Jackson. He just continued to stare. "Don't worry. We will get out of here," Gabb said, assuring an unresponsive Jackson.

No one understood the terror that was going through Jackson's mind. He was aware that the world inside the mansion worked differently. They were in the seer's domain, and there was no telling what they were up against. Jackson remained silent, staring into what seemed like nothingness.

As the others moved forward into the doorway, the room became brighter. There in the room, about 20 feet away, stood Patience. Horrified, Jackson saw the familiar light that once blinded him. Screaming, he rushed to the door, calling out to the men and begging them to go no further. He knew that there was something terribly wrong.

The Sun Stone was now shining, and the heat from it was too hot for Marcus to approach. The evil spirits within him would not allow him to relinquish his objective. Ignoring Jackson's frantic warnings, the next steps they took froze them in their tracks. Even the evil spirit guides inside of Marcus could not move. Although Jackson did not enter the room, he too was unable to move.

"What is this? What have you gotten us into, Marcus?" yelled Barren.

Marcus was deeply concerned but concealed it as best he could. As the sweat ran down his face, he called on his spirit guide for help. Soon it became apparent that his spirit guide was as incapacitated as he. Marcus could hear the others struggling to free themselves. Without warning, the brightness of the Sun Stone suddenly started to diminish.

Deep fear once again crept into Jackson's mind when he saw Patience walking towards them. As she stood before them, regal in appearance and firm in her demeanor, she looked directly at them and said, "You have violated this holy place with your unclean hearts. It wasn't enough to kidnap me from my husband and family; you also ruined our celebration of love and honor. You went further in your diabolical scheme by planning to rob, steal, and even kill to satisfy your lust. You intended to murder me and anyone else who got in your way."

They all stood, frozen, scared out of their minds, and unable to speak. She stared at Jackson in the doorway, not with the smile she once gave him but with a face of severity. "You were once welcomed here with my husband at a time of great opportunity. The world of wealth and prosperity were offered to you; instead, you chose to squander it all away through deception and contempt. You were still given a chance to redeem yourself, and at first, we thought that there was hope for you. However, in your heart, you sought only to please yourself. Your actions revealed an evil, unrepentant heart. Even now, while you are cowering in your soul, you agreed to take my life and escape with what you have stolen."

She turned from Jackson and addressed the others. "The same is true of you all. You thought that by taking me, you would have access to great treasure. You were right. There is great treasure here." The men glanced at each other, not knowing what to say or do. Patience pointed her hand towards the surrounding walls. "You see all of those indentations in the great wall where precious stones protrude? Behind each of those stones is a box filled with precious treasure. Look all you want, but know this—they are not for you. My heart breaks over the loss of your souls. They are for those whose hearts belong to the Lord. Because there was no pity found in your hearts towards others, you yourselves will not receive pity. Have you not heard the saying from the Holy Book, 'The measure you give will be the measure you receive'? You were allowed to see what you will never possess."

Suddenly, the power of the Lord moved them all outside the sunroom. Patience raised her hand and motioned for the door to close. They found themselves immediately transported to the golden entrance that Jackson and his comrades attempted to exit earlier. Panic ripped through them all.

"How did we get here? What is going on, Marcus?" demanded Cavis.

"I don't know, but stand back and let me try to get us out of here." Everyone stood back to watch the evil seer work his magic. Marcus instructed Cavis and Barren to join him as he cut himself. They watched as Marcus allowed his blood to drip into a special challis taken from a secret pouch inside his garment. Cavis and Barren knew that they were expected to join their blood with his to give more power to the spirit guide. Spells and incantations from his spirit guide caused objects in the Great Hall to move and smash against the door. All efforts failed.

"What do we do now? How are we going to get out of here?" asked Cavis. Growing fear filled the room as Cavis' last words fell from his lips. Every eye focused on the enormous golden door as eerie sounding screams came from the other side of the door.

"What in the blue blazes is that?" asked Jackson, unable to control his rising panic. "Do you hear that shriek? You have to hear that," cried Jackson, taking hold of Gabb's arm as sweat poured from his face.

"Let me go, Jackson. Get a hold of yourself," said Gabb, feeling the same panic as Jackson. Seconds later, terror seized the entire group.

Suddenly, the large golden doors opened as if they had a will of their own. The screams became louder as the doors opened wider. Marcus winced at the sight. The group of men with him couldn't take their eyes off the doorway as the creature came into full view. All the men promptly backed up, staring at the huge beast. Junia's pale terrorized face could be plainly seen in its mouth.

"Mother!" shrieked Jackson, letting go of Gabb, stunned by the sight of his mother in the mouth of the beast.

"Help me, help me, Paul," came her cries as the beast moved forward.

Marcus called on his spirit guide to aid him but to no avail. The creature was larger in stature than any land animal they had ever seen, including the bosti. Its wings spread out in front of the door, preventing anything from coming in or going out. The men backed further away from it, except Jackson. The sight of seeing his mother in the mouth of the beast, and hearing her screams, put insane courage in his heart. He took hold of a golden candelabrum that was near the door and flung it at the beast, hitting it squarely in the face.

"Jackson! Have you lost your mind? You want that thing coming after us?" yelled Fray.

"It has my mother, you dullard. I'm not just going to stand here and let it take her into that rug," cried Jackson, picking up another object, ready to throw it. Suddenly, Jackson's face became pale as the creature turned its head towards Jackson and the others.

"Mother ... Moth—" he stuttered.

In an attempt to keep the beast from coming after them, Fray, Landon, and Gabb grabbed Jackson. Fray put his hand over Jackson's mouth as Landon and Gabb held him down. The beast stared at the men with intense fury.

"You trying to get us all killed? Stop provoking that monster," hissed Fray.

Jackson could feel his mouth going dry as his heart pounded faster with anguish. The beast clamped down tighter on Junia's body. The sounds of Junia's screams echoed in his ears. Hearing her screeches drove him to hysteria. "Mother … I'm sorry … I'm so sorry, Mother!" he cried aloud.

Suddenly, a creepy voice came from the creature. "You have trespassed. Your evil has caught up with you, and there is no escape. I shall return for you shortly," said Tah, and he resumed his course towards the rug.

When the creature spoke, he struck ultimate fear in their hearts, which caused the men to frantically look for a way out. Cavis and Barren were disturbed to the point of directly confronting Marcus. "How do you plan to get us out of this chaos? Your incantations are futile against such a beast," retorted Barren.

Fray, Landon, and Gabb decided to leave Jackson mumbling to himself and fled for their lives, hoping to somehow escape destiny. However, the door had closed behind the creature, and from all appearances, there was no other way out of the Great Tree.

Barren and Cavis realized that with all Marcus' boasting of being a great seer, he didn't have the power to get them out of this deathtrap. The thought of dying terrified them as they watched in horror how the beast handled Jackson's mother. The previous warnings of Jackson flooded their minds. Now they understood. What Jackson said finally made sense. Everyone who didn't belong in the Great Tree was doomed. They cringed as they heard shrieks and screams from Junia as Tah took her down into the rug. Greater panic gripped them as they heard more screams coming out of the rug. Cavis and Barren thought it more prudent to join Fray, Landon, and Gabb as they ran down the Great Hall, hoping to find a way out.

Jackson also ran back down the Great Hall, screaming. Only he took the direction that led to the sunroom. The others briefly paused to take note of Jackson's actions. "Jackson has lost his mind," said Gabb.

"Better to be crazy and not know what's going to happen to you than to be in your right mind and face that beast," said Fray.

"What's he doing?" asked Landon.

"Looks like he's heading back towards the sunroom," responded Gabb.

"You think he knows another way out of here?" asked Landon.

"I don't know. Let's follow and see," replied Fray.

They were not the only ones watching Jackson. Marcus had not been successful with his spirit guide. He thought it best to join the others who were quickly following Jackson to the sunroom.

Jackson somehow had it in his mind that Patience would be merciful and let him live. After all, her name was Patience. Arriving at the sunroom, Jackson fell on his face, loudly pleading for his life. The other men observed Jackson's action. Fray, Gabb, and Landon decided to join Jackson by falling on their faces as well. They were pleading and begging for their lives from the one whom they had planned to harm. However, Marcus refused to bow and prevented Barren and Cavis from joining Jackson and his spineless cohorts in groveling at the feet of a girl. Patience could hear their pleas but was not allowed to answer them nor open the sunroom door.

There was a loud noise at the front entrance. "Is the door reopening?" Landon asked.

"It sounds like it. Let's get out of here," Fray said, delighted at the possibility of escaping.

To their amazement, the enormous golden doors started to open. Jackson, Fray, Gabb, and Landon immediately ran back towards the door, overjoyed. Marcus and the others followed them. Their bags were still where they had left them. As the door opened, they thought that they would at last escape with all their loot, despite what Patience had said, but as they reached the opened door, they realized it was not a passageway to freedom. Through the large golden doors came Jedidiah, Steven, Matt, and the Pia Warriors. Jackson at once ran towards them, falling on his face along with his three cohorts, pleading for their lives.

Angered by Jackson's display of cowardice, Marcus moved next to Barren and Cavis to ensure that they remained loyal to him. "Unbelievable. Look at how those weak-minded fools grovel as if these men were gods," Marcus said under his breath, disgusted by the scene. "Barren, Cavis, do you see them? Without spirit guides, it's laughable to see how low men will bow." As Marcus looked on, the spirit guide within him fueled his hatred of Jedidiah and the Pia Warriors. "We will not be destroyed by this so-called prophet of God," boasted Marcus.

Barren and Cavis found themselves out of control. It seemed as though they were being taken over by other forces. The spirit guides in Marcus, Cavis, and Barren had enough and refused to let their human host humiliate them any longer.

Jedidiah stood with his staff in his hand just in front of Marcus and his men. The wickedness inside the possessed men gave them the backbone to defy the old seer. "The Lord has anointed me to be seer and king over the land of Truevine. You have no business in this land, nor do you have the right to abduct my granddaughter. You were all given many opportunities to repent of your evil intent, but you chose to ignore them. Your actions have brought you grave consequences. I see some of you lying face down to appease me, but it is the Lord that you have offended. And you who remain standing defiantly only prove that there is no change in any of your hearts."

A loud, defiant laugh echoed throughout the halls. "We've heard this superfluous clatter already from your granddaughter. So, what's the point?" voiced Marcus boldly.

"The catlian that took Junia into the abyss will soon be back for you," stated Jedidiah sorrowfully. His words of pity infuriated them.

"You call yourself a king and seer of the realm, yet you threaten to kill us? We have not killed anyone or committed a crime that deserves death. We have only trespassed into this great mansion that should belong to the people you claim to serve. We have done no wrong," claimed Marcus.

"Why should we be punished for what belongs to us?" chimed in Gabb.

Matt could no longer hold his tongue. "I should end all of your miserable lives right now for putting your hands on my bride. Your tongue is as twisted as your minds. Everyone in the realm knows that if you put forth your hand towards a member of the royal family, it is a death sentence. You not only put forth your hand to harm the princess, but you intended to kill her. If there is one bruise on her, you will have no need to consider tomorrow. I will tear your heads from your bodies with my own hands," Matt said with fire in his eyes and ferocity in his voice. Jedidiah held up his hand to Matt for silence. Matt took no offense. He simply waited for his mentor's next move.

Marcus was quietly watching the reaction of the old prophet and his warriors. He was scheming to take advantage of words and emotions that filled the atmosphere around them. Finally, he decided to put accusing thoughts into Jackson's mind. It was one of his controlling specialties.

"Shouldn't you, as a man of God, have mercy and give grace to poor sinners like us?" Jackson said, using guilt and shame to convince the old seer to let them go.

Jedidiah was well aware of their treachery. Jedidiah looked at Jackson with sorrow in his heart. "Jackson, you were once given a chance out of compassion to leave here. You failed to learn your lesson. You instigated this whole plot against the very people who were gracious to you. You and your mother even tried to kill Frances and Jeremy to satisfy your revenge and greedy appetite. Now you are here again, but this time without the Lord's compassion. Jackson, you will suffer the same punishment that Junia received."

In disbelief, Jackson began to shake and tried to run past the old seer toward the front door but to no avail. Tah rose from the rug and moved toward Jackson and his cohorts.

"Whoa, what is that?" stammered Lire, drawing his bow. "Put your bow away, Lire. It is one of the three catlians, a guardian of Truevine. He is not here for us," said Steven.

Terrified of the oncoming monster, Jackson and his men took off running. Gabb deliberately tripped Landon and Fray down in a wild attempt to get away. Jackson was already far ahead of them; he hoped that the beast would be too busy with his friends to come after him. Fray quickly got to his feet and caught up with Gabb.

As the men attempted to escape with their lives, another catlian emerged from the rug. Its presence filled the room. Its face was like a white tiger, and it was covered in what looked like dragon scales. Streaks of gold accented his long black mane that reached the floor. The claws on his feet resembled eagle's claws, large and curved for catching prey. His roar caused the chandeliers to shake.

"I take it that … that is also one of the catlians," said Bruk, watching with interest as the new edition joined the hunt.

"His name is Epsilon, and yes, he is one of the three catlians," explained Jedidiah.

At the sound of the beast behind them, Fray looked back and stumbled over his own feet.

"You fool, look where you're going," yelled Gabb as he passed him.

"Here it comes. Run for your lives!" exclaimed Landon, running past Gabb, but it was no use. Epsilon took to the air and swooped down on top of Fray. Fray desperately tried to escape, but in a matter of seconds, the majestic catlian caught the shrieking man and wrapped his talons around him. Fray stabbed Epsilon with his short blade, which had no effect. As Epsilon started to ascend, Fray struggled with all his strength and managed to wiggle an arm loose enough to grab Gabb by his garment. Fray was hoping the weight of them both would cause the creature to drop them.

"Let go of me, you fool!" Gabb screamed and cursed at Fray.

Fray's foolish plan had no luck. The creature simply took them both, Gabb kicking, screaming, cursing, and trying to get loose from Fray. Gabb finally managed to break loose from his friend by biting him on the arm. To his horror, Gabb didn't fall. He was held up by some unseen force and taken right along with Fray toward the awaiting rug.

Tah had now returned for Jackson and Landon. The catlian approached the souls with one intent—to deliver them to the place of torment and despair. He snatched them up with fangs that pierced and burned their bodies as they were dragged into the rug. Terrifying screams erupted from the captured men.

"Help me, Matt! Help me," Jackson begged while tears of anguish filled his eyes, but Matt remained still and silent. Jackson's life flickered before him as he headed into eternity. His heart ruptured with the evil deeds he had committed. The darkness in him surfaced like a volcano. The horror he dreaded became a reality as Tah reached the rug. With rage in his eyes, Paul Jackson cursed God, Jedidiah, and those who stood by watching as he took his last breath of freedom. Seconds later, Jackson and his cohorts were taken into the abyss.

Matt felt sadness towards his lost friend, but he knew he could not help him this time. What bothered Matt even more was his own reluctance to help Jackson. He knew that he should have made an attempt, but the thought of Patience's abduction held him back.

"I know how you feel, Matt, but you couldn't help them even if you wanted too. This whole matter is out of our hands," exclaimed Jedidiah.

Barren and Cavis looked on in horror, seeing Jackson and the others dragged down into the rug screaming for help.

"That is not going to happen to us! I swear it. Do you hear me?" Marcus said loud enough for all to hear. He stood contemptuously, staring at Jedidiah, waiting for the old seer's next move.

****

Back at Columbidae, Layla stood ready with the horses but held her peace.

"It was all a nightmare right out of a horror story. Nothing so bizarre has ever happened in Columbidae. There is no such thing as flying beasts. At least not like the one that took Junia away," Frances sobbed. "I know that there are spirits and demons, but, but … what I saw is … is impossible," said Frances, trying to calm herself.

Jeremy reassured Frances that she was not hallucinating. "I saw it too, as it flew away, and it was as real as we are." Jeremy gave her a comforting kiss and stood her on her feet. "We need to go, my darling. Our daughter has been abducted, and we need to be with Matt and the others to give them our support," he said, trying to take her mind off of the terrifying experience. Jeremy knew that if he had not seen it with his own eyes, he would have never believed it either.

Holding his shaking wife in his arms, he guided her towards Layla. Taking a deep breath, Frances moved slowly, knees still a little shaky but ready to mount her horse. "Remember, my love, this is our family we are going after, and we need to be there for support." Jeremy's words seem to rouse her motherly concerns, which moved her beyond her fear.

Suddenly they heard a rider coming through the brush. Layla drew her bow, expecting perhaps another beast. However, she was pleased to see Caleb, and relief filled her eyes.

"King Jedidiah sent me back to check on the Lomans. Do you need some help?" asked Caleb.

"Yes, we do," said Jeremy.

"The king thought as much," said Caleb, who took out a small vial of oil, honey, lemon, and a touch of one of Pricilla's herbs and passed it to Frances. She took a little of the tonic.

"How do you feel now?" inquired Layla.

Immediately Frances' fears subsided, and she smiled.

"What is that?" asked Layla.

"It's a tonic made from one of the trees in the king's garden. The queen gave it to me to use for Mrs. Loman." Caleb then took Layla with one arm and swung her upon her horse, something she hadn't expected.

"Thank you, Caleb."

"You are most welcome," he said, smiling.

Jeremy took Frances by the waist and lifted her onto her horse. Frances took a deep breath. The tonic had done its work. She was ready to follow the two young warriors wherever they were leading her and Jeremy. "Lord, please help us…" was the plea of a desperate mother as the four riders headed out.

As soon as the Lomans and the two warriors arrived at the Great Tree, a mansion appeared before their eyes. Suddenly, the large golden doors opened as if expecting the visitors. The Lomans were surprised by all they saw. Layla and Caleb walked in, Jeremy and Frances tagging a few steps behind.

"Have we missed the battle, my lord?" asked Caleb. Steven placed a hand on Caleb's shoulder, signaling for everyone to hold their peace. The impenetrable golden doors were once again closed at the wave of Jedidiah's hand. King Jedidiah was pleased to see Frances and Jeremy.

"Old man, do you think by closing the doors, we won't be able to escape? My power has increased by the deep magic of my spirit guide. And it is so much greater than yours. We will not bend or submit to the likes of you," Marcus said with a sinister voice and contorted face. His rebellious words rekindled his men's lost confidence. They drew closer to Marcus, who continued to spew out venomous accusations at the old seer. Barren and Cavis believed the strong stand that Marcus took against Jedidiah had placed them in the position of power. Their arrogance surged to new heights, to the point that they even dismissed the possibility of suffering the same fate as Jackson.

Cavis, looking back and forth at members of the royal family, walked a few feet closer to Marcus and whispered, "Would you like for me to cut off the heads of those Pia Warriors and bring them back to you?"

"Be still, Cavis. I'm more than prepared to handle those Pia Warriors and the old seer," boasted Marcus.

"As you wish," responded Cavis.

Jedidiah looked at them grimly. "Do you think that I am unaware of the demons who control your minds?

A surprised look crossed Marcus' face. Nevertheless, he rigidly stood against Jedidiah, all the time thinking about how to defeat him.

"We know who you are, prophet, and to whom you belong. Do not be mistaken and think you can dismiss us as easily as Jackson and his lot. The prince of this world is our master, and we have the power and the right to destroy you," hissed the evil spirit dwelling inside Marcus.

Barren and Cavis saw the dramatic change in Marcus and backed away to give room to his continued violent rampaging. As Matt and the Pia Warriors looked on, it became alarmingly apparent that a battle was about to emerge.

"We came here by the invitation of Jackson and your granddaughter," Marcus retorted, gloating over the fact that he was in the right.

"Look at his eyes. He gives me the creeps," said Lire, pointing in Marcus' direction. Jedidiah was silent as the demon spirits rallied their defense against every accusation the old seer had against them.

"You have insulted us long enough, and we will not tolerate another word from you, you empty shell of a prophet," uttered Cavis, trying to impress Marcus and the others with his intellectual aptitude, only to have Marcus push him aside.

"I am the spirit guide's host, and it is my right and mine alone to rebuke the old prophet," retorted Marcus. Cavis resented Marcus' words of reproach but remained silent as Marcus continued. "You know the rules, seer. If we are invited in by humans, you know for yourself that we have the right to leave with all that we have collected, and there is nothing that you can do about it. It is the law," he bragged, while Barren and Cavis laughed. "Stand aside, prophet, or do you intend to go against the law of free will?" spewed Marcus contemptuously.

Jedidiah stood his ground, Steven and the Pia Warriors behind him. Barren proudly stood by watching Marcus as he took a stand against Jedidiah. No demon had ever challenged Jedidiah directly. However, the ones in Marcus were desperate.

"You dare challenge me concerning the law and rights? You have no rights in here," said Jedidiah, raising his staff and sending Marcus and his comrades tumbling backward.

Surprised at the intense reaction of the old seer, Cavis nervously mumbled to himself, "Marcus said that he can handle that old seer, but how is it that we were pushed back so easily by a mere wooden staff?" Cavis scorned the thought of being defeated by an old man and a handful of ridiculous warriors.

****

"Why doesn't Poppy just expel the lot of them out of here or, better yet, send them into the rug with Jackson and the others?" remarked Bruk angered by the old prophet's delay.

"He has to follow protocol," responded Steven.

"What protocol?" asked Matt.

"The ones that explain the interactions between demons and humans. If anybody invites a spirit into their domain, that person forfeits their right of control, just as Marcus and these men have given permission to spirit guides. The spirit guides are well aware that they have rightful access to Marcus and the others. Jedidiah knows that if that spirit is foolish enough to allow his human host to take him into a holy place or into the presence of a believer, it becomes subject to holy expulsion."

"I still don't understand," exclaimed Matt.

"Evidently, things are going on that you and I don't have knowledge of," voiced Steven.

As Cavis listened to the dialog between Jedidiah and Marcus, he realized that there was more danger building in the atmosphere, and he had no idea who was going to win. More uncertainty and fear grew in Cavis as he pondered the outcome. In an attempt to distance himself, he took a slight step back behind Marcus.

"Where do you think you're going?" asked Barren, taking hold of Cavis' shoulder.

Cavis retorted, "Let me go. I'm trying to position myself to give us more of an advantage."

"It doesn't look that way to me. Just hold your ground until Marcus tells us what he wants us to do," insisted Barren with raised eyebrows, knowing Cavis was lying through his teeth.

Jedidiah took another step closer to Marcus. Marcus could feel fiery heat emanating from the staff. Jedidiah pointed his staff at Marcus' face, causing him to choke on the putrid smell of sulfur.

"The demons you house have deceived you into believing that you can actually win a war against God. You will spend eternity in a place that you cannot escape."

The old seer's words shook Marcus' confidence. He struggled hard to push the old man's words out of his mind. Marcus needed the Sun Stone to complete his mission. The only way to acquire the stone was to defeat Jedidiah. Realizing he needed help, he motioned for Cavis and Barren to move into a better position. He gave Barren a nod to move with him in a more direct frontal position to attack.

Confident, Marcus spoke incantations and conjured up a two-ended double-edge jetting spear. Suddenly, like a crouching bosti, Marcus sprung towards Jedidiah. With lightning speed, he brought the spear straight down over Jedidiah's head. Jedidiah anticipated his attack and swiftly moved to the side, evading the weapon by blocking it with his staff.

"No one has ever evaded my attacks. You are more agile than I thought, old man. No matter. I will eventually destroy you and everyone you cherish," barked Marcus, grinning as he began to speak more incantations, willing the spirits to give him supernatural strength. To his own astonishment, it worked. The spell had actually provided him with greater strength. With his newfound strength came an intense obsession with killing.

"Cavis, Barren, look at me, and receive," shouted Marcus. With the wave of the spear in his hand, Cavis and Barren received supernatural strength. Their newfound power displayed in them a malevolent physical transformation. Screams could be heard from both Barren and Cavis as their human forms took on hideous elongated faces and protruding yellow eyes.

"What's going on now?" asked Lire, pulling out his weapon.

"They have opened themselves to be consumed by legions of demons," said Steven.

"Legions…? Can you see the demons?" Lire asked, surprised.

"Yes, and once you have more experience, you will be able to see them as well," explained Steven.

"I thought only Trianthropos could call on demons," Bruk stated.

"Trianthropos controls the deathmus, but they can also call out demons," said Abdi, cautiously walking forward, the warriors following closely.

"Then is Marcus a trianthropos?" asked Caleb.

"Who knows what that man is?" replied Bruk.

Abdi sternly commanded, "Stop asking questions and prepare yourselves for battle."

"That suits me. I was getting bored standing around," responded Lire.

As Matt and the others cautiously observed the actions of their opponents, Cavis let out a blood-curdling scream and rushed towards Matt. Immediately, the Pia Warriors raised their weapons to engage Cavis but were interrupted as Barren unexpectedly charged towards Steven. The warriors had little time to act to protect the king.

The grotesque hands on Cavis doubled in size as he conjured up an enlarged sword. One swipe of his sword could easily take Matt's head off. Cavis lunged at Matt, hoping to end the ordeal, but Matt side-stepped to the left and came upward with a left punch to Cavis' jaw. Cavis' body staggered back. Before Cavis could recover, Matt's right knee crushed into his ribs, sending him flying through the air and landing him on his head.

Meanwhile, Steven met Barren with a powerful right fist in the solar plexus, sending him back and landing him at the feet of Caleb and Lire.

"Look out, Lire," yelled Caleb, bringing his sword down swiftly to behead Barren, but Barren was too fast for either of the warriors to finish him. The increased strength from the demons promptly aided Barren in defending himself. Barren regained his footing then turned to face them, swinging his sword left and right, trying to take off their heads. If not for Bruk's bolas wrapping around the blade, his brothers would have met their doom.

Bruk, Lire, and Caleb fought Barren, while Steven and Abdi went to aid Matt. Swiftly, Matt moved toward Cavis to make sure that he wouldn't cause any more trouble. When he reached him, he found Cavis' body limp and his neck broken. Landing on his head had been fatal. At least that's what Matt concluded until he saw the demon spirits in Cavis raise him up. Cavis' neck snapped back in place as his body seemed to grow to another size.

"Watch out, Matt!" yelled Layla, too late. Cavis backhanded Matt, sending him flying across the room. Matt caught himself on an immobile bronze lamp stand and swung himself back around towards Cavis. Before Matt could reach him, Steven grabbed Cavis with one hand and threw him into Marcus. It was the first time Matt and the others ever saw Steven filled with rage.

"What's the matter with you, Cavis? Get out of my way. It's enough fighting this wild prophet without you on my back," yelled Marcus.

"Don't yell at me. I got my own problems with two of them," exclaimed Cavis, rising back on his feet.

"You just make sure that you and Barren get that Sun Stone," snapped Marcus. Ignoring Marcus' command, Cavis raced back toward Matt and Steven, while the other Pia Warriors occupied Barren.

The battle ensued for what seemed like hours, both opponents growing weary. "These men have uncommon strength. Even with our enhanced powers, we are still no match for them. We can't beat them this way. We have to join forces!" yelled Cavis.

"I have a plan," Barren yelled back.

"What kind of plan?" retorted Cavis.

Barren explained the plan in their native language, assuming none of the warriors would understand. "We will hit them from both sides using the power of the spirit guides. When they fall, cut them to pieces with your blade. Before they realize what happened, they will be dead."

****

Layla was rapidly shooting arrows in every direction. To her annoyance, every arrow somehow missed its mark.

Cavis drew out a dagger from behind his back and threw it at Steven's throat, attempting to carry out Barren's command. Unfortunately for Cavis, Steven saw him reach behind his back and knew that he was up to no good. Steven turned sideways and let the dagger fly by him, then rushed towards Cavis and Barren.

"He's coming fast," shouted Cavis.

"Then use your brain and stop him," retorted Barren.

"I have a good idea. You keep them busy while I go for help," yelled Cavis.

"You'll stay where you are, or I'll run you through with this blade myself and feed your stinking carcass to the bostis."

More afraid of Barren's threat than he was of the Pia Warriors, Cavis reluctantly rejoined Barren in the attack.

As they both charged like ragging bulls, one from the left and the other on the right, Abdi already had foreseen the outcome in his mind. Lire jumped upward, while Caleb and Bruk stepped back seconds before the impact and allowed the two charging bulls to collide. The collision of flesh and bone resulted in an explosion. When it was over, Barren lay dead with Cavis' blade sticking in his chest. Regaining his senses and seeing Barren lying motionless on the floor, Cavis threw his weapon at the warriors and fled the scene. Steven and Matt looked at Barren lying before them, sorry that his life had ended in greed and selfishness.

Marcus was too busy fighting Jedidiah to notice that he lost his comrades. The demons in him wanted one thing, and that was to kill the man who kept them from getting what they wanted, the Sun Stone. Marcus thrust the spear at Jedidiah, but each time it was deflected by the seer's staff.

"You cannot win this battle, Marcus. You are out of your domain. All that is left for you is judgment from God."

Suddenly, Marcus' eyes followed Jedidiah's pointing finger to where Barren laid dead. Looking around, he noticed that Cavis was not to be found. He thought to himself in rage, *The coward. I will deal with him when I finish with this seer.*

As he turned back towards Jedidiah, bloodcurdling screams came out of Marcus as the demons inside gained complete control of his mind. His body grew larger and stronger. Hair fell from his head as he grew more repulsive, and infectious lesions covered his entire body. His teeth lengthened like that of the bosti and oozed venom. The spear in his hand split in two, displaying the power of the ominous spirits that controlled him. Double edge blades appeared on both ends of the spear. In deep fury, he hurled it at Jedidiah. The weapon moved at its own will against the old seer.

"Look out, Poppy!" bellowed Matt. The spear smoothly glided towards Jedidiah's heart, inches away from its target. The power of the spear seemed to grow with every inch it gained. Suddenly, a force propelled Jedidiah back, causing him to drop his staff. Everyone looked on in disbelief that Jedidiah's life could possibly be threatened. Gasps could be heard from Jedidiah as he held tightly onto the spear, now only centimeters away from his chest.

Marcus stood back, grinning and mocking. "Where are your courageous words now, prophet? Where is your pitiful faith, the God you trust in so much? Now you will see that I am not alone in this so-called holy place. We are more than you and your little family can handle. It will not be me that dies here today but you." Marcus raised his hands as if to give more power to the weapon.

Matt attempted to move towards Jedidiah, but Steven grabbed his shoulder, forbidding him from interfering.

"You will not interfere. This is not your fight. Your attempt to help will only break Father's concentration. He will be thinking more about you than the task at hand," Matt acknowledged the command, but the desire to help burned in his heart.

Marcus cursed and commanded the weapon forward, hoping to cut the old man down. With gritted teeth, Jedidiah started to push the spear back. Pain could be felt through Jedidiah's body, but he was called by God to fight this intruder. Jedidiah suddenly whispered under his breath, "Lord, keep me." With those silent words, a magnificent strength moved through the old seer.

"What is happening?" Marcus said in disbelief. The hands of the old seer were covered in blood.

"I rebuke you in Jesus' name," Jedidiah said as he started to crush the spear. In awe, everyone saw the evil spear drop to the floor. Jedidiah, carefully eyeing Marcus, called his staff back to his hands.

He is too fast, and his faith is ever increasing. Marcus thought to himself.

Marcus knew he was running out of time and suspected that he only had one last attempt to succeed. "I command my spear to revive," shouted Marcus.

Leaping high in the air, he came down with the full force of his weapon on top of Jedidiah's waiting staff. It was all the seer could do to keep Marcus off of him.

"I call upon sickness, disease, and plagues to aid me in destroying this menacing prophet." *Now is the time to destroy my enemies and seize the opportunity to take the Sun Stone,* Marcus reminded himself. Crouching into a fighting position, Marcus spewed fire from his weapon, intending to incinerate Jedidiah. The staff of faith left Jedidiah's hand and began to spin like a fan in front of him, deflecting the fire back upon Marcus.

As Matt watched, he began to understand why his father-in-law forbade him to help. The fire caught Marcus' garment, but before it could consume him, he tightened his grip on his weapon and tapped once on the floor. The flame was sucked into the spear, while Marcus, full of pride, brushed off the smoldering remains from his garment.

Steven and his warriors stood dumbfounded as they watched their master battle against a legion of demons. Observing closely, Matt saw blood drip from Jedidiah's nose. He could sense that Jedidiah was becoming exhausted.

"I'm sorry, but I can no longer stand here and do nothing, while Poppy is struggling against that legion." Before Steven could stop him, Matt took a golden table against the south wall and hurled it at Marcus. If not for Marcus' double-edged weapon in his hand, the table would have taken him out. Marcus used the weapon to repel the table back towards Matt. Steven pushed Matt to the side with one hand and deflected the oncoming table with his right foot, sending it skirting across the floor into the east wall.

Marcus was furious at Matt's interference and conjured up another spear and threw it at Matt with such force that he barely had time to evade. Marcus raised his hand to command the spear to pursue Matt until it killed him. The spear turned and came back at Matt, who then took off running in order to escape. Steven took off behind Matt while Jedidiah battled the other weapon with his staff of faith. The spear was gaining on Matt, and in a matter of seconds, it would be in a position to kill him. Steven had never seen anyone run as fast as Matt.

Lord, I could really use your help about now.

Use your faith, Matt. Call your companions, said the voice in Matt's head.

Matt did not waste time and did exactly what the voice told him to do. He opened his mouth and called out with a loud voice, "Trueball and Lightning. Your master needs you!"

There was a sudden rumble in the air as two large dog-like animals joined Matt. Steven couldn't believe his eyes. In an instant, Matt turned and faced the oncoming weapon. To Steven's surprise, Lightening jumped and seized the weapon, snapping it in half while Trueball consumed its fire until it crumbled into dust.

"Praise God! Am I glad to see you guys!" Matt said. They jumped on Matt, licking and rubbing against him like they hadn't seen their master in ages. Relieved, Steven finally reached Matt.

"I am glad that your companions joined you. You are a blessed man. Hard-headed but blessed," said Steven. As quickly as Matt's companions appeared, they disappeared. "You're going to have to tell me about them later, but for now, we need to get back to Father." Matt nodded, and they hurried back to the battle.

As Matt and Steven approached the others, they found Marcus and Jedidiah still fighting. Jedidiah stood firm in his position, while Marcus was wearing himself out. Abdi and the warriors were watching every move made by the fighters.

It was evident that the old seer could not be destroyed by physical weapons. Marcus pondered hard regarding his next decision. He couldn't help thinking about Jackson and those fools of his and how they had allowed themselves to be dragged down into the abyss. *How stupid they were. That will not happen to me,* he boasted to himself.

As he approached Jedidiah, the spirit guide inside of him suddenly began to manifest itself in a way that shook the Great Halls. Diabolical forces spoke to Marcus, encouraging him to move against Jedidiah with confidence, assuring him that he would prevail. Marcus became calm as the demons within took over the last part of his humanity.

Marcus, we have given you all the power you need to end this battle. Your only mission is to terminate Jedidiah, said the voice in his head.

"But I thought that I was to get the Sun Stone," uttered Marcus, confused.

That was the initial plan; however, since you have encountered so much opposition, achieving that goal seems unlikely. The master desires that you kill the prophet and as many of his family members as you can. Concentrate on Matthew. He is the old seer's focus.

"And what of me? How will I escape this place?" Marcus asked incredulously.

There is no need for you to be concerned about that. We will extract you when the time comes, voiced his spirit guide.

Even with the assurance of the spirits, Marcus knew that a fiery hell would be his fate if he lost the battle. His thoughts were interrupted by a surge of energy, which gave him the incantations of sickness and disease. With a loud voice, he bellowed out the words of the demons within him for all to hear.

"Beelzebub, prince of demons, we call on you to help us for we are your legion from times passed. Come and aid us, for we are trapped in this wretched holy place. Our only escape is that you aid us, prince of darkness. Do not delay. Show these fools that you are more powerful than their puny god. Destroy this prophet and his obtuse, disruptive family that they may never stand in the way of your malevolent will again," Marcus said with renewed energy. His eyes became blood red, black excretion oozing from the corners. His hands grew twice the size of bear paws with six protruding fingerlike spikes on each hand. Yellow venom seeped from each spike.

"He's no longer a man. Prepare yourselves, warriors," shouted Abdi.

Marcus had now become the diabolical beast that lurked in his heart. When the transformation completed, Marcus had become the expression of all the unclean spirits residing in him. He boasted and bellowed obscenities and curses on his enemies.

"Attack me now, prophet, and you will see your own loved ones die." He laughed hideously as mucus dripped from the sides of his mouth. "I will give your guts to the birds and your blood to the bosti," guffawed Marcus, watching the reaction of his enemy.

The warriors were astounded at what they saw. "I think we should do something," said Lire.

"I'm open for suggestions," said Caleb as he moved next to Matt and Steven.

"We will do nothing. Do you hear me? Nothing," said Steven, his eyes focused on Jedidiah and the evil manifestation of Marcus.

Marcus felt more powerful than ever before, and when he placed his hand on the spear, it also grew in size to fit his hands. The weapon weighed more than Matt and Lire's weight combined.

"Poppy, let me take him," Matt cried out.

As Matt moved to intercept, Jedidiah sternly shook his head and said, "No."

Steven put out his arm "I'm sorry, son. You cannot interfere. Things are going on in the spirit world that you are not aware of. Hold your peace for now," Steven said with forceful authority.

Frances, Jeremy, Heather, and Pricilla had been watching and praying the entire time from a distance. They prayed loudly as the battle between Jedidiah and the transformed Marcus continued. Jedidiah grew deeply concerned for Pricilla and spoke to her in his mind to take the others into one of the rooms where they would be more protected while they prayed.

"Come with me," said Pricilla, turning to the wall behind her.

"Mother, what are you doing? Shouldn't we stay and pray?" asked Heather.

"Didn't you hear your father tell us to move into a safe room?" responded Pricilla.

"I'm sorry. I was deep in prayer and didn't hear him."

"Let us go so that we will not be a distraction to Jedidiah." Pricilla placed her hand on the wall of the Great Hall, and a door appeared.

"Mother, you go ahead with Frances and Jeremy. I must join Steven. I need to touch him and agree with him in prayer. I'll be careful—I promise," she said, kissing Pricilla before walking away.

Even as they entered the safe room, Marcus increased his assault on Jedidiah. "I will kill you with my own hands," ranted Marcus. His massive body did not hinder him from rushing at the old prophet. Heather saw the deadly blow coming down on her father and screamed. Marcus' doubled edge spear came down hard on King Jedidiah, but his staff of faith prevented the spear from taking his life. Nevertheless, the force behind Marcus' brutal assault hurled Jedidiah against the wall of the Great Hall. For a moment, the old man was down and shaken.

It was impossible for Steven or anyone else to hold Matt back. With great speed, Matt was in front of his master, awaiting the next blow from the demon-possessed man. When the blow was seconds away from Matt's face, Matt took hold of Marcus' arm and, with great strength, hurled him against the opposite wall of the Great Hall.

"How dare you put your hands on the Lord's anointed," shouted Matt with rage. The other warriors had never seen Matt's face so livid. Jedidiah grabbed Matt by the arm and swung him around.

"Matt, go stand by Steven and Heather. You are not allowed to fight in this battle. There is something afoot that I am not aware of, but it concerns you. Now stand back, and do not interfere again."

Matt, shocked by Jedidiah's protest, didn't know what to say. He simply obeyed.

Enraged by Matt's interference, Marcus slowly raised himself from the floor, laughing. "You have great strength, little man, but you are not immortal. You can die as easily as any human." Marcus felt his power continue to increase with every desire to do evil. His thoughts to kill Matt and the others propelled him forward.

Matt was amazed at how swiftly Marcus could move. To give Jedidiah a chance to regain his footing, Steven gave orders for the warriors to intervene. Caleb and Lire shot piercing arrows, while Abdi sent his spear at the demonic with lightning speed. To their dismay, the weapons proved ineffective against the armor that covered his body. Just as Marcus reached for Jedidiah, he was met with a powerful kick from Matt that sent him flying across the room, slamming him again into the wall. Steven immediately snatched Matt and ushered him away from the fight, strongly reprimanding him for his constant interference.

"Matt, you must learn to listen. I told you that you were not to interfere."

"But you gave orders to engage just a minute ago," said Matt, still torn inside.

"That was only to give Father a chance to gain his footing," explained Steven.

Heather put her hand on Matt's shoulder. "I know that you are concerned about Poppy, but you don't have to be. The Lord protects him," she said, trying to alleviate his worries.

"Listen to me," said Steven, addressing everyone. "This battle cannot be won by power and might alone. It can only be won by the Spirit of the Lord."

Abdi and the others held their positions and waited for Steven's next command. Steven understood their concern but held the young warriors back.

Matt tried to contain himself, but how could he let the man who loved him like a son and taught him so much wisdom stand alone to face such an ominous creature? Every part of his being told him to protect Jedidiah at all costs. Even if it cost him his life.

"Let me help Poppy. Let me help him," Matt pleaded tearfully.

"The Lord has his way of doing things, which is something I suggest you quickly learn," uttered Steven with a firm grip on Matt's shoulder.

The demon-filled man was confident that this would be the old man's last stand. Through the years, Marcus had enjoyed power and worldly pleasures. Everything the demons promised had come true for him. However, what he felt now as he prepared to kill one of the great nemesis of the demon world was nothing short of pure ecstasy. At last, one of the great prophets would be destroyed, ushering in diabolical evil into the realm of Truevine—an evil that would be felt as far as the Great Falls.

"I am ready for you, old man," he taunted as he rushed towards Jedidiah. "All of Truevine and the Great Falls will know that it was I, Marcus, who killed their great king," he laughed cynically. "In a moment, I will wrap my hands around your meddlesome throat and crush the life out of you for all your followers to see. The world of demons and men will know who rules over this principality," Marcus bragged.

Jedidiah simply stood straight and strong, unmoved by Marcus' threats, as the faith in his heart dispelled his fatigue.

"That's right. Stand there, and it will all be over in a second," gloated Marcus. As he raised his hand, his remaining spear came to him. He pointed it at Jedidiah and opened his mouth to speak incantations of curses; however, to his horror, he could not speak. With all his might, he tried to curse the old prophet, but his mouth was forced closed. The Lord would not allow his prophet to be cursed.

The next words spoken by Jedidiah were loud and clear and shook the foundation of every unclean spirit. "In the name of Jesus of Nazareth, the Lord rebukes you!"

Marcus placed his hands over his ears and screamed as if someone had thrown fiery coals on him. Jedidiah held out his staff, commanding the unclean spirits to leave. Marcus fell to the floor, foaming at the mouth, his hands exuding a clear substance. The forces inside Marcus urged him to keep fighting.

"We will not leave. We will fight, we will stay, and you have no authority over us ... prophet," spewed the voices in Marcus.

Whatever the prophet was going to do, Marcus readied himself to resist. Jedidiah's words kept invading Marcus' mind. The rebuke was too much to resist, too hard to bear, too overwhelming to fight. The unclean spirits in the man knew that in a moment, they would be expelled.

Marcus cried out in desperation, "Don't abandon me! Where is the power you promised?" To his dismay, as his life began to end, all seemed unreal and empty. Here he was, getting ready to face the reality of his bad choices. What else could he do? It was too late to change the course of his life, and if he wanted that life to continue, he had to find a way to quickly defeat the seer and the warriors. Barren had thought the same as Marcus until death had propelled him into the awaiting horrors of the abyss.

Marcus' life flashed before his eyes. He saw in his mind the bodies of Jackson and his band of thieves taken by the catlians hours earlier. Even as those thoughts plagued him, a catlian instantly appeared and dragged Barren's body and soul into the abyss. His confidence turned to silence and knocking knees; defiance turned to begging. Marcus saw the Great Hall turn red in color, and the rugs on the floor gave off a suffocating atmosphere as did the portraits on the walls.

Only the disembodied spirits could detect the horrors before them, and there was no place to run. All the pleading and begging had gained them nothing. Within seconds, a great host of the demons from Marcus' body felt Epsilon and Tah seize them. Their screams and cries were drowned out as they were taken into the rug.

****

Only Cavis and Marcus remained. While Marcus battled the old seer for his life, Cavis continued to run from door to door, yelling as loud as he could, pleading with whatever power that could hear him.

"Let me out of this place. I promise I will never come back. I won't tell a soul about this place—you have my word," Cavis bellowed in desperation. All the opportunities he had to turn from evil came rushing into his mind. How could he have been so blind and stupid? Patience had warned them the entire time they held her captive. She had pleaded with them to let her go and leave while they could. Now it was too late. He knew that he could not evade the inevitable doom for long. He couldn't get Barren's dead image out of his mind. He saw Jackson and the others meet their doom and knew in his soul that he and Marcus would be next.

While Marcus fought hard and long against all hope to stay free, the remaining evil spirits within him tried to look for another host. The one they occupied would soon be destroyed.

Without further delay, the catlians approached the two remaining men. Their time had arrived. Tah watched Cavis as he continued running wildly down the Great Hall. Epsilon, in one quick motion, opened his large mouth and began to pull the demons from Marcus' body into the abyss. Marcus could feel his strength evaporate as the demons screamed and protested, but their resistance yielded no results.

"You can't do this. You have no authority, prophet. Let us go our way," demanded the demons. Everyone could hear the ear-piercing screams of the evil spirits in Marcus.

"The Lord has rebuked you, and you have been found guilty of deception, murder, and blasphemy. You are sentenced to the abyss where you may do no more harm until the appointed time," said Jedidiah to the departing demons.

Marcus still stood his ground, determined to destroy Jedidiah with what strength he had left. The poisonous spikes on his hands were his last defense. He swiftly raised his hand and threw all he had at Jedidiah with precision, keeping only one in tack. The spikes never reached their target. Jedidiah had not moved, but somehow, they were deflected away from the king.

A smile came over the old prophet's face. "So, you are here, my friend," said the king.

"Yes, I am here," replied Girma, ready to protect the royal family at all cost.

"Are you here to end this battle?" asked Jedidiah.

"I cannot. You must stand your ground. Your charge is to trust the Lord, my friend. All will work out in the end," said Girma.

Jedidiah heard him but did not respond. His attention was focused on the battle. He knew that the legion would soon be dispelled completely from Marcus and vanquished into the nether world. He prayed silently for strength.

Steven and Matt watched intently as the seer continued to engage the possessed man. They were taken aback watching the catlians in action. They had never seen such creatures. They had a full view of Girma and were amazed as the beast stood by while Jedidiah fought.

"Does it talk?" asked Matt.

"They don't usually show themselves," said Steven.

Matt looked to Heather for an answer. "Mom, do you know them well?" asked Matt.

"Yes, of course, they are the Lord's guardians and protectors. They do whatever He wills. It is rare to see them except on these kinds of occasions, which I'm thankful are also rare," explained Heather.

"Why aren't they helping Poppy now?" asked Matt, disturbed by the relaxed mood.

She just smiled at him and said, "In God's time, son. The battle isn't over yet."

"What do you mean? Please explain."

"All believers are tested regardless of age or position. The Lord has His purpose for allowing us to go through this trial," Heather responded.

Matt was doing everything in his power to restrain himself from jumping in to help. Heather rested her hand on Matt's arm, while Frances and Jeremy held on to each other as they watched the spectacle in horror. The remaining unclean spirits in Marcus prompted him to jumped with outstretched arms to overcome Jedidiah. Reluctantly, the Pia Warriors, especially Matt, found it difficult to stay out of the fight.

"All of you, hold your peace," Steven commanded.

A devious smile crossed Marcus' face. Suddenly, he laughed hysterically, abruptly moving toward Matt. He knew that the bond between the old seer and the boy was special. The whole royal family was drawn to the young Grower. Marcus realized killing Matt would give him great satisfaction. It would end the dreams of the old seer and ruin the future of the Growers. Raising his hand that held the last spike, he aimed not at Matt but at the old prophet's daughter, Heather. He knew that Matt would certainly make an attempt to save Heather. In doing so, he would forfeit his own life. Marcus swiftly shot the poisonous spike towards Heather.

"Watch out..." Matt yelled, stepping in front of her and simultaneously pushing her aside. The poisonous spike pierced Matt in the side, immediately causing him to double over. Frances screamed as she watched from the safe room. Heather caught Matt in her arms and, with Steven's help, laid him on the floor.

"We can't stay in this safe room! We must go to our son..." Jeremy said, tears streaming down his face. Pricilla nodded, opening the doors to enter the Great Hall. Jeremy guided Frances towards Matt, Pricilla closely behind. Jeremy and Frances dropped down next to Matt, and their hysteria filled the hall.

The entire scene played out in slow motion in front of the old seer's eyes. Fear quickly engulfed Jedidiah's heart, causing him to lose his focus. Marcus stood, watching the whole scene, smirking with satisfaction.

What are you waiting for? This is your time to take action. Kill the old seer now! screamed the remaining demons in his mind. With all his might, Marcus swung the spear around towards Jedidiah, hoping to end the conflict.

Inches away from Marcus reaching his goal, Jedidiah was jolted back to reality by a sudden call to his mind, *Jedidiah!* Startled, he avoided Marcus' deadly spear by dodging it and throwing up his staff.

"I command you to protect in the name of the Lord," uttered the old prophet. Immediately, the staff took over and hurled Marcus to the other side of the room. Jedidiah sighed in relief. "Thank you, Lord. If not for you, I'd be headless."

Marcus, unscathed by the staff's assault, charged toward Jedidiah. The old seer glanced towards his family. Deeply concerned for Matt's survival, he decided the best course was to get him to the sunroom.

"Get Matt and yourselves to safety. Go to the sunroom now!" yelled Jedidiah. Nodding, Steven lifted Matt into his arms as Heather led the others.

Patience had been in a state of deep prayer for her family since the ordeal began. She had fought hard in the Spirit. Pricilla spoke to the sunroom's door, and it immediately opened to them.

"Patience, Matt is hurt," Layla said in despair. Patience could not believe her ears regarding her most beloved. She instantly ran toward them as the family rushed in, Matt in Steven's arms.

"Where do we place him? Will this room be enough to tend to Matt?" Frances asked Steven frantically. Suddenly the thought of a bed came to Steven's mind, and it instantly appeared before their eyes. "Oh my, thank you, Lord," said Frances, eyeing the bed. Steven placed Matt on the bed in the back of the sunroom.

With tearful eyes, Patience knelt down by her beloved and began to weep uncontrollably. Layla knelt down by her side, feeling what she had felt years ago when her mother died. She placed her arm around her sister and wept with her.

"What happened to him? Why is he so pale?" Patience asked between sobs. Steven placed his hand on his daughter's head, hoping to bring her comfort.

"He took a poisonous spike that was aimed at Aunt Heather," said Lire, holding back his rising anger. As Matt laid motionless on the quilted bed, Patience, feeling helpless, continued sobbing.

****

No more words came from the Prophet, only action. The staff of power came back to his hand as he approached the remaining demons housed in Marcus.

"I see you are not as protected as you thought old man," spewed Marcus. Still, no words came from Jedidiah. "I see everyone has abandoned you, just as I have been abandoned by that fool Cavis," he screamed, purposely causing an echo throughout the tree for Cavis to hear. Seconds passed without a response from Cavis. "You coward! Come and help me now, and I may spare your life. If you don't, I will surely kill you! Don't think that you will escape this fate, you coward. Drag your sorry carcass out of your hole, and do what the spirit guides have commanded us to do. Together we will be able to defeat him and gain the Sun Stone.

As Marcus continued his ranting, Cavis continued his escape. *I'm not going back. To return is too much of a risk. If Marcus wants to continue with his pathetic charade against the old seer, that is his choice. As for me, I am going to do everything in my power to escape,* he said to himself. Cavis continued running and putting a good distance between him and the battle. He ran as fast as he could, constantly looking back to see if he was being followed.

Feeling he could rest a little, he stopped and bent over, placing his hands on his knees for support. On the wall to the left of him was a painting of mysterious trees. When he raised his head up from resting, Tah was in front of him, staring with large eyes and sharp fangs. Cavis backed up against the painting on the wall. Unexpectedly, large tree-like hands emerged from the painting, grabbing Cavis tightly. Cavis tried with all his might to free himself from the hands but could not. Screaming and on the verge of hysteria, Cavis hopelessly stretched out his arms to keep from being dragged into the painting. His pleads to be free went unheeded. Tah watched Cavis as darkness engulfed him into the gloom of the nether world of the abyss.

Marcus heard Cavis' screams and laughed to himself. "Serves the coward right," he said with elation. Marcus raised his weapon to the seer, expecting the fight to continue.

"I no longer am required to fight you. My testing is over. The Lord has given you over to the catlians. You are doomed to the abyss without mercy or grace." When Jedidiah raised his hand, the catlians were given the command to take Marcus. Swiftly, Epsilon took hold of Marcus. The evil seer brought down the sharp spear on Epsilon's head. There was no effect. The catlian tore the spear from Marcus' hands and crushed it between his enormous teeth. Epsilon reached down and grabbed Marcus around his torso, sinking his fangs into the demoniac's body.

With his last breath, Marcus cursed and swore, vomiting out sickness and disease at the old seer, but the staff of faith in Jedidiah's hand drew every vile curse and disease into its purging fire. Tah joined Epsilon by clamping down on Marcus' shoulder with powerful teeth. The scream and groans died out as Marcus' life left him. All that remained of Marcus was his terrified soul that hung from the mouth of the enormous beast that held him. His life as he knew it was over, and now the same fate that awaited Jackson now awaited him. The evil spirits within him fled like sheep from a roaring lion, but none escaped. The catlians collected every unclean spirit and delivered them to the abyss.

From all signs, Jedidiah believed the battle to be over until he heard loud sobbing coming from the sunroom. Cautiously, he entered and saw Frances, Patience, and Heather kneeling over Matt.

"What's going on? What's happened to Matt?" asked the old prophet.

"There was poison in the spike that struck Matt. I removed it from his body just moments ago," said Pricilla.

"It seems to have contained some deadly disease. His face is pale, and his eyes are cloudy," stated Heather.

"He also has a high temperature, and he's shivering," added Layla.

Jedidiah stood silent, observing everyone's countenance. Marcus, though now gone, had accomplished his objective. The plan of the enemy unfolded before Jedidiah's eyes. *I see, Lord. The enemy against us knew that Matt was destined to become a leader among Growers and Warriors. The enemy could not allow that to happen. In a last effort, the spirit guide caused Marcus to spew out sickness and disease. What better way to pour out vengeance than through killing our most beloved prince? Lord, I pray that you would not allow this to happen,* sighed Jedidiah.

Jedidiah placed his hand on Patience's head. Steven and the Pia Warriors slipped to the other side of the bed and knelt, except Layla, who had positioned herself into the background, unnoticed—or so she thought.

Patience anointed Matt's head and, placing her hand on his brow, prayed, "Abba, you know that I love you very much, and I have no words to express how grateful I am to you that you gave Matt to me. We have only been married for a short time, yet our hearts are tied to each other in a way that only you know. We are both so grateful."

Layla listened tearfully as her cousin prayed, remembering how her father had also prayed for her mother seconds before she died.

"Please heal him and spare his life and give us a chance at love." As Patience pleaded with the Lord, she grabbed one of Matt's limp hands and raised it to her lips, crying uncontrollably. Matt felt her and brought his other arm up to embrace her. It was hard for him to breathe or speak. There was so much he wanted to say to her, but the words wouldn't come. "You don't have to speak my love," she said, kissing his hand. "I hear you in my mind," she wept.

Jedidiah wiped tears from his own eyes, tapping Steven on the shoulder. "I need to inquire of the Lord. Keep an eye on things in my absence." Steven did not ask questions. He nodded, intending to do Jedidiah's bidding.

Heather caught Jedidiah's eye as he moved towards her. In a mind link, he instructed her. *I need you to comfort Matt's parents in my absence, my dear. I will return as soon as I can."* Nodding, Heather obeyed her father.

Pricilla was aware of all the emotional feelings that weighed on everyone. She especially noticed Layla and knew she needed to be consoled. Walking over to Layla, she placed her arms around her waist just as she had when she was a small child. "My dear, the Lord sees everything, and He is aware of what you are going through. Do not rely on your own understandings. If you do, it will cause your heart much distress. This is a matter of prayer and supplication, in which I urge you to engage," Pricilla explained. Layla listened with eyes full of tears yet remained silent.

Abdi glanced at his daughter and saw tears streaming down her face. He could tell that she was torn by more than Matt's condition and took comfort in knowing that Pricilla reached out to his daughter. The whole family was in turmoil. Abdi prayed that peace would soon come to them all.

Frances and Jeremy knelt down next to Patience as she prayed over Matt. Frances placed her hand on Patience's arm, praying for her as she prayed for Matt.

Jedidiah took one last glimpse at Matt as his granddaughter poured out her heart to God on Matt's behalf. He had never seen a sickness act so fast. There had to be something else to this, and he knew it. *What is this, Lord? Demons have no power over us, so why is this particular disease hard to combat?* There was a deep silence in his spirit, and then a word pierced his mind.

To get rid of this kind of sickness, you must fast and pray.

Jedidiah immediately left the room, saying nothing to the family. He gave no indication as to where he was going. There was only a look of determination and focus on his face. Heather followed him to the door.

"Has his condition worsened, Father?" she asked. When he did not answer, she knew that Matt's condition was dire. Jedidiah took his staff of faith from behind the door of the sunroom and walked towards the rug.

Pricilla moved towards Heather. "We need to join our faith in prayer, my dear. We are faith walkers, and we must war in prayer. Do not be concerned about Jedidiah. Your father walks by the Holy Spirit and will follow the Lord's will, whatever the cost," she said.

Heather grabbed Pricilla's hand tightly, knowing she would gain strength. She knew that prayer worked according to the will of the Lord, and it was what she and Pricilla had spent all of their lives doing.

"I still feel great anguish in my heart, not only for Matt but for our Patience as well," said Pricilla. Heather became alarmed over her mother's words. Pricilla was not only a prayer warrior but a prophetess as well. Her words were to be taken seriously. She took hold of Frances and Heather's hands and surrounded their children. "We are here to pray and console our children until Jedidiah returns," said Pricilla.

Heather was grateful and knew that Patience's heart would gain encouragement as her grandmother prayed. Pricilla knelt closer to her weeping granddaughter and placed her arms around her. At Pricilla's touch, peace came over Patience. She didn't have to look up to know who it was.

Turning, she said, "Oh Moa, I think he's going to die."

"Nonsense, child. We leave those kinds of results in God's hand. Our part is to pray and stand firm in faith." Everyone in the room, except Layla, knelt around Matt's bed and laid their hands on him, hoping for an intervention from God.

As they prayed, Heather couldn't help visualizing Jedidiah's face. She had only seen her father in that state of mind three times in her life.

26

In the Presence of God

Battling flesh and bone was one thing, but spiritual warfare was another matter. Fighting sickness caused by evil forces was tough. Matt was barely breathing and trying his best to survive. Frances, Jeremy, and the others continued to kneel by his bed in prayer. Two days passed, and Matt wasn't any better. Patience, Pricilla, and Heather had tried every herb, spice, root, and other healing remedies known to them. Even Pricilla, who was extremely proficient in locating healing plants and earth remedies, failed at finding a cure. On the third day at noon, Matt was so weak that everyone in the room knew that death was imminent.

Patience couldn't help herself—she laid her head on his chest and pleaded with him. "Matt, don't leave me, my darling. Don't leave me. Please, my love. I can't live in this world without you! I love you. Please don't die," she sobbed.

Through her tears and anguish, she heard his voice say, "I'll try, my love. I'll try." A stillness filled the room, and Matt's hand slipped from Patience's bowed head. Patience lifted her head, placed her hands on Matt's lifeless body, and then burst into loud sobs.

Her tears soaked his garment. No one could pull her away from him. She looked at him lying there. His demeanor and strong body spoke life to her, yet he lay there, not moving, not breathing, not reaching for her. She turned to her family with pleading eyes.

"I don't understand. We were just married, we had our whole lives ahead of us, and now he's gone. What am I going to do, Moa? How can I go on without Matt? Mommy, I don't want to go on without him," she sobbed, sinking deeper into depression with broken dreams.

Heather looked at her daughter with eyes full of tears. "Lord, help us," she cried. Layla wept by her cousin's side, trying to console her, trying to understand and believe with everyone else that this was not so.

By evening, all hope was gone. Patience turned to the four women kneeling beside her and fell into their arms. A somber hush fell over the room. Pricilla said nothing, and neither did Heather or Frances. They simply allowed their child to weep until she could weep no more. With every passing moment, the anger in Layla grew. Seeing her cousin and the family she loved hurting was too much for her to bear.

To make things worse, Patience's life started to wane. Heather looked into her own mother's eyes in despair. "Mother, what is going on? I feel life going out of her," Heather said with great alarm. Pricilla held her granddaughter in her arms and prayed. Patience's life was going out of her, and no one in the room could stop it.

Heather finally understood that her daughter was tied to Matt in unexplainable ways. Matt's death was pulling Patience into the realm of death with him. How could it be? How could two people be so entangled that one could not live without the other? Her love for Steven was deep, but what Patience felt for Matt was wrapped in deep mystery.

Layla screamed at God, "You let my mother die, then Matt, and now you are taking my sister? Why? If you are God, then please don't let my family die. Please don't let Patience die. I'm begging you, God. Please, please, please." She wept profusely.

At midnight, they all felt the end coming. Matt and Patience would be together, if not in this life, then with the Lord. With her last breath, Patience looked into her father's tearful eyes. "Daddy, I'm sorry. I can't stay without Matt." Tears fell from her eyes as she closed them and followed Matt, leaving unbearable heartbreak and emptiness for those left behind.

The parents wept together over their children, pondering over the many thoughts of what they could have done to keep this from happening. In their search, they found no answers, only loss. Pricilla placed her hands on the two lovers and prayed. She knew the power of prayer. In her mind, she heard the call of Jedidiah telling her to continue praying. The others joined her. Steven placed his hand on Jeremy's shoulder. The two men wept over their children as they joined the women in prayer in hopes of reaching heaven.

A messenger was sent to Peter and Mary, Steven's parents, informing them of the tragic situation. They immediately sent out messages to all the kingdoms of the motherland and surrounding villages to pray for the princess and her husband, who lay dying. The whole realm of Truevine and Steven's kingdom prayed until the heavens were shaken. Layla slipped out from the room—away from her family, and even further away from God.

****

In the land of the Great Falls, Jedidiah emerged from the rug. He stood at the edge of the waters and dove deep into the lake and down to the depth beyond the coral wall. The staff in his hand glowed with power as he continued down to where no human had ever been. Listening to the Spirit, he moved toward a small blue light behind a great stone. When he reached it, the stone opened, and the light flooded the area. An invisible force pulled Jedidiah in, and the stone closed behind him. Jedidiah didn't know if he was in a vision or reality. He did, however, know that he was in the presence of God. In his mind, he had many questions, and somehow, he knew that the Lord heard them all. The one simple answer as always was God.

Most beloved, my ways are my ways, and my plans are my plans. There is no place that I am not. In the by and by, you will understand. For now, trust me and do not faint in this hour. Place your staff into the blue light, and then go and place it into the Sun Stone. Finally, place it on Patience. Seek out my servant, your father. He will travel back with you.

Jedidiah was astonished. As he turned to leave, he realized that he could breathe underwater. Staff in hand, he pointed it towards the surface, and it propelled him upward. In the distance, he could see monstrous water bostis coming towards him from all sides. It was a sign that the Trianthropos were working to stop him. Jedidiah kept his eyes ahead of him, ignoring the oncoming bostis. The beasts reached him but were unable to attack. The water became a gigantic hand that lifted Jedidiah out of the water and sat him down on the shore of the lake. There in front of him was Trobus, waiting with open arms.

"Father, I was told to seek you out," said Jedidiah, surprised.

With open arms, Trobus approached Jedidiah. "It's been a while, son. The Lord told me to meet you here." Jedidiah started to explain all that had taken place. "There is no need for explanation, son. The Spirit has revealed all that is necessary for me to know. Let us go without delay."

In a moment, Jedidiah found himself inside a cave behind a waterfall. To his surprise, his sister Beverly was standing there with Heather and Steven's other children—Daniel, Thomas, and Ross. He rushed to embrace her. She met him with open arms and kisses.

"It's been a while, big brother. I'm sorry it's on an occasion like this. Nevertheless, I'm thankful to see you," she said with a big smile on her face.

"It's so good seeing you, Bev, and the boys have grown considerably," he said, wrapping his arms around them.

"Is Patience's husband going to die, Poppy?" asked Thomas, clinging to him.

Jedidiah looked at Beverly, wondering how the boys knew about Matt's condition. "Father told us, Jedidiah," she informed him. He looked at his father, questioning why his father told them.

"Everyone in the family is involved, son. Everyone should be praying regarding this matter, including the boys."

Jedidiah looked at his grandsons with compassion. "Right now, your great-grandfather and I must return immediately with the cure."

"We are going with you, Jedidiah," insisted Beverly. Jedidiah knew it was useless debating with her. Even as a child, he had always given her what she wanted. Smiling, she pushed him toward their father as she and the boys followed.

Trobus led them towards the wall behind the falls. He placed his hand on the wall, and moments later, they emerged from the rug into the Great Hall. Jedidiah immediately went straight to the sunroom. There he found his family standing over his children, both lying in the same bed, side-by-side and lifeless.

Heather went to her father and wept loudly as she laid her head on his chest. "They are gone, Poppy; our babies are gone." Tears filled Jedidiah's eyes. He gently pushed Heather aside into Steven's arms. Her sons joined her, not fully understanding what had happened.

"What's wrong with Patience?" asked Ross, the youngest of the three sons.

"Later, son," replied Steven.

Jeremy and Frances observed closely as Jedidiah moved toward his granddaughter; the others made room for the king. Jedidiah was overcome with emotion seeing Matt's and Patience's lifeless bodies lying before his eyes. He took hold of Pricilla's hand along with his Staff of Faith and walked over to the Sun Stone. He placed the staff in the heart of the stone and came back to where Matt and Patience were lying. He then placed the end of his staff on Patience's heart. The family stood watching, unsure of what to think. No one said anything out loud, but neither did they stop praying in their hearts.

When the staff touched Patience, there was still no sign of life. Jedidiah was silent. Everyone was watching and waiting, mystified that nothing happened. "Father, I do not know what else to do," said Jedidiah. They all thought that he was speaking to the Lord until Trobus moved in next to Jedidiah.

With all that was transpiring, no one noticed Father Trobus. He took Jedidiah's hand and spoke to the others to join them. As each person connected hands, Patience began to glow. When the last hand connected, each of them prayed to the Lord with one heart. Then her eyes opened, and she sat up in the bed. Joy and awe gripped the family, but all still remained silent.

Jedidiah spoke to her in his mind. *Patience, my dear, long ago in a vision, the Lord told me to grind up a piece of the Sun Stone and give it to you in a glass of milk. Do you remember?*

Yes, Poppy.

He did not tell me why, nor did I inquire. I have been in the presence of the Lord these past three days, praying for Matt. I was told to come back quickly; otherwise, you would die as well. I came back as quickly as I could, but when I arrived, you were already gone. Your death was too much for me, for my life is tied up in yours, and I feared that I would not have the strength to do what had to be done. I suppose that is why the Lord sent my father to me. I needed assurance and encouragement; the Lord knows that all of us need support. That is why we are called the body of Christ. The whole family is here, even your brothers and Aunt Beverly. The Lord has blessed us more than words can explain. Your great-grandfather has a word for you.

Patience could not express the joy that came over her seeing Trobus in front of her. She stood and wrapped her arms around him and wept.

"There, there, my child. Things are going to be all right."

"But Father Trobus, he's dead. Matt is gone."

"Try to understand, my child, that God is sovereign. Nothing escapes Him. He brought us all together for a reason. Let's allow Him the opportunity to show us." Trobus held her close as he explained. "The Lord honored our request. As Jedidiah and I walked into the room, I knew that we had arrived too late, but the Lord was gracious and told me that He had put healing power in the Sun Stone, just as He had put water in a rock long ago."

Patience rested her head on Trobus' shoulder, letting his words rest in her heart. "So, what is my part in this? I feel so different, so strange. It's not an unpleasant feeling, just unfamiliar," said Patience.

"No need to worry, my dear. In this case, God is using you as his instrument to bind everyone together. Out of sorrow will come joy, and out of death will come life. The Lord is the resurrection and the life. Let him do what he does best. Turn to your husband and kiss him with affection," said Trobus.

Patience gave him a curious look thinking, *Will a kiss bring him back? This isn't some sweet little fairytale. My husband is dead, and there's nothing to be done*. Then it dawned on Patience that her great-grandfather could hear her thoughts. *No use denying my doubts now. I'm sure my facial expression has also revealed everything.*

"I know that you think this only happens in fairytales, but I can assure you that this is no fairytale. These are the instructions I received, and I'm giving them to you," said Father Trobus.

Jedidiah looked straight into his granddaughter's eyes and asked, "What does the Holy Book mean when it says, 'Have faith in God. You can tell the mountain to throw itself into the sea, and if you do not doubt in your heart, it will happen'?"

She smiled. "It means just what it says, Poppy, and there's no doubt in my heart that the Lord will intervene," Patience declared with confidence.

The family was anxiously waiting, hoping that, like Patience, Matt would be given life as well. Jeremy wrapped his arm around Frances as they watched Patience turn to Matt. Patience put one hand on Matt's head and the other on his chin and leaned forward and kissed him. As her lips softly touched his, she felt the coldness of his mouth. Doubt immediately rushed in.

Is this a goodbye kiss?

Tears started to form at the corners of her eyes. It seemed like a goodbye kiss to their wonderful, short time together. She heard a whisper ring in her ears.

Take captive every thought and bring it under obedience to your Lord.

Concentrating on obeying the voice, Patience shut her eyes. As she held the kiss, she felt heat go from her mouth to Matt's heart. The family could see that something was happening. Signs of life flooded Matt's face, and before long, Matt too was sitting up, staring at his bride and looking around at his family. Patience was a little startled and unsure of what to do next.

"Man! I've got to find me a wife who can kiss like that," said Lire, elbowing Bruk.

When Matt smiled at her, her face lit up, and she jumped into his arms. Everyone rushed to the bed, and no kisses and hugs were held back. There was no end to their thanksgiving and celebration towards God. It was a day of real celebration because two hearts that were dead were now alive again. It was the day that Matt and Patience truly became one.

Peaking around Matt, Patience couldn't help but see teary-eyed, mischief-making brothers standing by Trobus and Beverly. She smiled as they ran to her.

"Are you all right?" asked Daniel. Thomas and Ross waited to hear as well.

"I'm fine, boys. The Lord is good." She could tell that they had been crying. When she reached for them, they wasted no time in wrapping their arms around her. Even in their joy, they cried, and she knew that in spite of the heart-breaking event they had just gone through, they would be strengthened by it. She kissed and hugged them affectionately then attempted to move away, but they wouldn't let go of her. Steven and Heather stood behind the boys watching with teary eyes.

"I think Patience and Matt need rest for now. You can visit later," said Heather. The boys reluctantly took several steps back but refused to move any further. Big sister was alive and well. They were there to make sure she stayed that way.

Steven placed his hands on his sons and squeezed through them. He needed to get a kiss and hug from his firstborn and from his new son. Jeremy and Frances anxiously awaited their turn to embrace.

"What a scare you two gave us," said Frances, wrapping her arms around them.

With bowed heads, Jedidiah said a prayer of thanksgiving. This was one day that would be remembered forever. God had proven himself a Savior and Father to those who believed and trusted him.

The next morning, Matt and Patience were sitting together, unwilling to let each other out of sight. "I heard you calling me," Matt said, holding Patience's hands in his own.

"You mean while you were down and under?" she teased.

"I guess you can say that."

She smiled and kissed him. "I don't ever want you down and under again," she said with a serious tone in her voice. "I didn't want to survive without you." Tears filled Patience's eyes. Matt lightly smiled and kissed her tears away.

"We are one now, and no one except the Lord will pull you away from me," Matt said.

"Nor I from you." Patience smiled with joy in her heart.

Matt wondered to himself, H*ow did a woman like this ever notice me*? How he loved her and how he loved to hear the sound of her voice. "I thought I had lost you, my love," Matt said.

"I did too," she said with solemnity.

"I am thankful to the Lord for you," he said, holding her closely.

"You know what?" asked Matt.

"What?" Patience grinned.

"All the time I laid ill in bed, I was thinking about Columbidae and seeing my folks and reminiscing about all the things I used to do in my hometown. I arrived at an unusual conclusion."

She smiled and took his hand. "And what conclusion is that?"

Matt smiled, then kissed her. "I have concluded that my home is where the Lord is and where you are. I love you, Patience."

"Me too."

Family Devotional Lessons

Build a house of prayer by reading through the Bible verses below; write them all down and share with others.

> ...everyone who keeps the sabbath, and does not
> profane it, and holds fast my covenant—
> these I will bring to my holy mountain, and
> make them joyful in my house of prayer;
> their burnt offerings and their sacrifices will be
> accepted on my altar;
> for my house shall be called a house of prayer
> for all peoples. (Isaiah 56:6-7)

Building a physical house is not an easy task, nor is building a spiritual one. Both take hard work and much time. A physical house is built on sand, a spiritual house is built on the everlasting Rock (Matthew 7:24-27).

The physical house is limited in that it will one day pass away. John 3:6 explains the spiritual house in Christ will last forever. Things born of the flesh will pass away; things born of the Spirit will last forever.

BUILDING A GODLY HOME FROM GOD'S WORD

1. Tools: 2 Timothy 2:15 and 3:16
2. Fervent prayer: James 5:16
3. Fellowship with other believers: 1 Corinthians 12:12-14

The first step to building an everlasting home is to accept our Lord Jesus as your Savior; by confessing your sin, asking forgiveness of your sins, and then inviting Him of your own free will into your heart.

The act of accepting Christ makes you a child of God (John 1:12) and transforms you into a temple of God (1 Corinthians 6:19).

Secondly, you will want to develop a regular time to talk with Jesus. It's called prayer. Read your Bible and discover what Philippians 4:6-7 has to offer you (you will find at least 8 things). Then share it with family and friends.

Remember, whatever you allow into your mind and heart will go into your house (Proverb 23:7).

Your house is your mind and heart. You must keep them clean by not allowing unwholesome things to come in (Philippians 4:8-9).

Guard your eyes and ears against evil things. Be careful what you look at and what you hear. Think on good things.

God's word is full of light; read it, and your light will shine like the sun. Your heart and mind will want to follow Jesus.

The way to make your home into a house of prayer is by becoming a disciple of Jesus. To be a disciple, you must (Matthew 16:24):

1. Deny yourself (means putting God and others first).
2. Take up your cross (means obeying the Lord with a joyful heart).
3. Follow Jesus (means relying on the Holy Spirit to help you in all things).

Find seven verses in your Bible that will help you complete the building of your house of Prayer (example: Galatians 5:22).

Good hunting. Blessings on you!

Pastor Bruce

CHARACTERS

Trobus Devoble: King of the Growers, seer, watchman, husband of Emma, father of Jedidiah and Beverly

Jedidiah Devoble: King of the Growers; seer; watchman; husband of Pricilla; father of Heather grandfather of Patience, Daniel, Thomas, and Ross

Pricilla Devoble (Moa): Queen of the Growers; prophetess; wife of Jedidiah; mother of Heather; grandmother of Patience, Daniel, Thomas and Ross

Heather Marwari: Daughter of Jedidiah and Pricilla; wife of Steven; Queen of Ethiopia and Treabouti; mother of Patience, Daniel, Thomas, and Ross

Steven Marwari: Son of Peter and Mary; King of Ethiopia and Treabouti; husband of Heather father of Patience, Daniel, Thomas, and Ross

Patience Loman: Wife of Matt; princess; daughter of Steven and Heather Marwari; sister of Daniel, Thomas, and Ross

Daniel, Thomas, and Ross: Sons of Steven and Heather, brothers of Patience

Matthew Loman: Husband of Patience, son of Jeremy and Frances Loman, a Prince of Truevine

Peter and Mary Marwari: Father and mother of Steven and Abdi

Abdi Marwari: Brother of Steven; father of Bruk, Lire, Layla, and his adoptive son, Caleb

Susanna: Abdi's deceased wife; mother of Bruk, Lire (pronounced *Leer*), and Layla

Layla: Daughter of Abdi, niece of Steven and Heather, cousin of Patience

Bruk (Brook) and Lire: Sons of Abdi, brothers of Layla, cousins of Patience, Pia Warriors

Caleb: Adopted son of Abdi, Pia Warrior

Elias, Ezera, and Gedeyon: Pia Warriors

Bree: The happy little mocking bird

Barren, Cavis (Cav-is), and Marcus: Demon-possessed men who want access to the Treasure Tree

Paul Jackson: Son of Junia and Jack Jackson

Junia Jackson: Mother of Paul Jackson

Landon, Fray, and Gabb: Cohorts to Paul Jackson

Girma, Tah, and Epsilon: Catlians, protectors of the innocent, fierce and ferocious, eternal in nature, immortal

Trueball and Lightening: Faith protectors to Matt

Bosti: Wild, ruthless beast who craves human blood and will devour anything it kills

Trianthropos: Human-like beings with three eyes that have the power to control bostis and deathmus

Deathmus: Large, monstrous beast with three horns—two sticking out the side of its head and one larger horn at the tip of its nose. Large, crooked mouth filled with sharp jagged teeth. The Trianthropos ride and controlled these beasts.

Excerpt from Book Three:

The Reign of War

BREE, THE LITTLE MOCKING BIRD, WAS PERCHED HIGH IN A TREE singing loudly while Patience and Matt listened. Patience clapped her hands when she finished. Bree immediately flew down and sat on a branch directly in front of Matt and Patience.

"That was wonderful, Bree. I've never heard that song before. What a delightful tune. Where did you get it?" Bree chirped a few notes and waited. "You did. I should have known. It sounds like something my mom would sing," said Patience, talking to the little mocking bird.

"Don't tell me that you are actually having a conversation with that bird," laughed Matt.

"Why, yes, I am. I told you that Bree and I have been friends forever."

"Friends, yes, but you didn't say that you actually had conversations with her. What did she say?"

"She said that she heard Mom singing it this morning while she sat in the window watching her prepare breakfast."

Matt shook his head in disbelief. "How do you like that; I have a wife who understands a bird's brain." He chuckled. Bree chirped out a few notes and took off right over Matt, leaving a trail of poop behind. Patience burst out laughing as Matt stood there with bird poop on his head. "Why you little ... what did she do that for?" asked Matt, wiping his head.

Patience could hardly stop laughing to explain. "You insulted her by calling me a birdbrain."

"I didn't call you a birdbrain, honey. I said that you understood a bird's brain."

"Well, she didn't understand the difference," snorted Patience, unable to contain her laughter.

"It's not funny. I suggest that you explain to your little friend that she can't go around pooping on people just because she gets her little feelings hurt," said Matt, sticking his head under a fountain.

Jedidiah and Pricilla, followed by Steven and Heather, walked up on Matt and Patience as Matt washed his head off.

"Forget to wash behind your ears, Matt?" Jedidiah asked, smiling and wondering why he had his head under the fountain.

"No, sir ... I..."

"He was washing the poop out of his hair that Bree dropped on him for insulting her," said Patience, teasing Matt.

"What?" chuckled Steven.

"I did no such thing. I didn't even know that she could understand me. Then she misinterpreted what I said."

Patience took the scarf from around her neck and wiped Matt's face and kissed him. "It will be all right, love. Just don't insult her again," she teased. Matt laughed and decided that trying to explain would only give Patience more cause to keep teasing him.

Her grandparents knew exactly what she was doing and chuckled at how Matt struggled to get out of the conversation. Heather laughed while watching Patience tease Matt; she remembered doing similar things to Steven when they were younger.

"Come over here, young lady, and let me have a kiss from my favorite granddaughter," said Jedidiah, holding out his arms.

"You mean your only granddaughter," Patience said, immediately withdrawing herself from Matt's arms.

"That's true, but you are still my favorite," he said, smiling and hugging her.

"Don't let the boys hear you say that," she said, smiling.

"They already know it." He pinched her face.

"Speaking of my brothers, where are they? I haven't seen them for a while," said Patience.

"The boys will see you sometime today before they leave," said Heather.

"Leave? Where are they going? And why are they leaving?" Patience asked, still concerned about how they were adjusting to the trauma of her death.

"The boys are okay. They wanted to be with your great-grandfather and Beverly. Your mother and I are allowing them to return to the Great Falls with them," Steven said, giving her a kiss on the head.

Clearing his throat, Jedidiah was still amused with the newlywed's interaction. "What are you two love birds doing out here anyway," he teased. Pricilla just smiled, admiring the interaction between her husband and granddaughter.

"We were just admiring Bree's song that she learned from Mom. That is until Matt insulted her."

"Let's not go into that again," Matt said, running his fingers through his wet hair.

It seemed like hours went by as the family enjoyed their interactions with one another.

****

In the evening, Johan and his two brothers spotted an unusual, large tree that could be seen several miles away. The tree looked as if it was beckoning for them to come.

"Did you see that, Johan?" asked Hasher.

"I did, and I think it best that we not go any further until we pray," said Johan.

"But we have to complete our mission," said Riaha.

"We will wait and see what the tree will do," said Johan.

****

Pricilla called for Jedidiah and the family to gather for the evening dinner. They all took their seats, and Jedidiah prayed over the meal. While they were eating and enjoying conversation, Jedidiah's demeanor changed.

"Steven, there are three men coming to us from Treabouti, your father's birthplace. The Lord has guided them here for reasons that have not been disclosed to me as of yet," said Jedidiah.

"Who are they, and what do they want?" asked Patience, passing Matt a piece of fresh-baked bread.

"You will find out, my dear, when they arrive within the hour. In the meantime, I have important arrangements to make, and I will be taking the boys with me right after dinner," said Trobus.

"Father Trobus, what is going on?" asked Patience, now extremely curious. "What important arrangements?"

Frances nudged Jeremy and whispered, "It seems our new daughter has been taken aback by this new mystery." Jeremy simply smiled.

Heather patted Patience on the arm to get her attention. "Be patient, dear. I think Father Trobus is going to start training your brothers sooner than he planned. It's good that your father is leaving them in his care. They will learn much faster under Father Trobus' tutelage than anyone else. All your questions will be answered in due time." Heather smiled.

Patience was still concerned but knew that her elders trusted God to reveal things in His own time. She and Matt would have the opportunity to periodically check on the boys if the need ever arose.

"As I was saying, after we converse with the visitors from Peter's birthplace and discover the reason for their visit, I believe the Lord will direct us on the strategies of this coming war," said Jedidiah.

"Poppy, will you pass me that pitcher of sun tea?" interrupted Matt. As Matt waited for Jedidiah to pass the tea, he suddenly noticed a change in the atmosphere. Jedidiah became solemn in his mood as if something interrupted his thoughts. "What is it, Poppy?" asked Matt. The old seer remained silent and still.

****

The Treasure Tree stretched out its branches towards the three travelers once again, beckoning them to come forward.

"Johan, have you gotten a word from the Lord concerning this matter? The tree is giving us a sign to come," said Riaha.

"It is the confirmation I asked for, my brothers. Let us go," said Johan, leading the way. In minutes, the men found themselves in front of the Great Tree. When it held up its limbs a third time, the men fell with their faces to the ground.

Jedidiah smiled and motioned to Steven. "They are here, open the doors and let them in, Patience," said Jedidiah.

Patience nodded and walked to the entrance and stood before the door as it opened. There in front of her bowing were the three men Jedidiah had mentioned to Steven. "Rise and come in, friends. King Jedidiah is expecting you."

In awe, the men rose and walked forward. "Greetings, my lady. I am Johan from Treabouti, and these are my brothers, Hasher and Riaha. We are looking for Steven Marwari, son of Peter and Mary Marwari of Ethiopia. We have traveled far, and it is most urgent that we speak with him."

As soon as the travelers asked for Steven, he immediately stepped forward. "I am Steven Marwari. What can I do for you?"

Relief filled their eyes at the sight of Steven. "Sir, it is most urgent that you come with us to Treabouti. Our king, your father's brother, was killed by a beast that entered our country four weeks ago. The king, queen, and their two sons were brutally attacked and killed while walking by the

Blue River. Several of our warriors were also killed defending our king. We had never seen such beasts in Treabouti. We killed five of them before journeying to find you," said Johan.

"How can I be of service to you?" asked Steven, stunned by the warrior's words.

"I apologize, my lord. Let me explain, if I may," said Johan, frustrated at himself for his ambiguous bungling. "Your father left our land many years ago because of a great conflict between him, his brother, and their father. Your father, Prince Peter, had heard of a great prophet and healer called Micah. Your father sought him out to see if there was any chance of getting his younger son healed. You were that son, my lord."

"The king was up in age and did not want your father to leave. He felt that his death was coming soon. Prince Peter left without the king's consent, thereby removing himself from the opportunity of becoming king. His brother assumed the role of leadership with your grandfather's approval. Now both your grandfather, uncle, and his entire family are deceased. The council instructed us to search for Prince Peter and his family to bring them back to assume leadership of our people. The elders from the council are interim until your family returns. We have already contacted your father, and he sent us to you. This letter from him explains everything."

Steven took the letter from Johan's hand and read it silently.

Son, your mother and I have given our lives to winning nations to Christ. We will not give up this great work to rule over one nation. However, you and

Heather are suited for just a task. You have been serving Ethiopia long enough; it is time to care for our people in Treabouti. Ethiopia chose you as their king because of your great valor. Treabouti needs you as their king. It is your birthright. Please pray about this matter. I'm sure the Lord will lead you to do the right thing. Love Dad.

Silence filled the room when Steven finished reading his father's letter. The travelers stood in wonder at such beauty and grandeur within the great tree.

"We will speak of this later after you have had time to rest," said Steven.

"Yes, you must be famished. Come with us. We'll prepare you a meal, and you can tell us a little about my husband's homeland," said Heather, followed by Steven and Pricilla.

****

Patience smiled with a familiar look on her face that told her grandfather that she knew that he had more to tell her.

"Yes, there is more," he said with a hint of sorrow in his voice.

"What is it, Poppy?" she asked.

"Layla is missing."

"What do you mean missing?" she inquired with deep concern, feeling somewhat ashamed that she hadn't noticed her cousin's disappearance.

"Your grandmother told me that before I returned from the lake, Layla was praying desperately for God to intervene on your behalf. Matt dying was hard enough, but when you died right there in front of her, she felt that God had abandoned her again. Your mother said that she walked out when you died and hasn't returned. Abdi and his sons looked for her but could not find her. She has left the Treasure Tree and has not left a sign of any kind as to where she has gone. Nevertheless, your cousin Caleb has gone after her and will not return until he finds her. Abdi said to pass on his love to you and Matt. He and the Pia Warriors have been tasked with training responsibilities throughout the kingdoms and must attend to it immediately. He will see you when he returns."

Patience sighed, praying that the Lord would protect and provide for her family and bring Layla home safely.